Enoch's Muse

Sergio Monteiro

Proverse Hong Kong

2018

A woman, running from her past, is led by a mysterious locket to The White City. A father trying to save his dying daughter is preparing to make the greatest sacrifice. A young inventor, on the verge of discovering a new energy source, battles dark forces that he cannot see. What these three strangers don't know is that they have been guided by a man who has walked the earth for five thousand years, **Enoch**. From the days of Babylon to the French Revolution, Enoch has been in the shadows working for a higher power and guided by a love he knows can never be. His enemies have changed but their goal remains the same, control over all humanity. And now, all his battles have led him to three special strangers and one special moment in history, the Chicago World's Fair of 1893.

SERGIO MONTEIRO grew up in Washington DC, moving to Hong Kong when his family relocated there in the early 90s. An alumnus of the English Schools Foundation (ESF) and the University of New Brunswick, Canada, he now works in Hong Kong as a teacher. He started writing short stories in his early twenties but soon after sought out the challenges of writing larger and larger pieces. He views writing as the art of, *"Making someone see in their mind, what you do in yours, but with as few words as possible."* His debut novel, *Other American Dreams*, was praised for offering an unflinching look at the migrant crisis of Western and North Africa. He has since been featured on the Macanese arts program, *Montra Do Lilau*, RTHK's Morning Brew with Peter King, Radio Television Macau with Jorge Vale and the ESF Alumni News quarterly.

ENOCH'S MUSE

Sergio Monteiro

A Proverse Prize Finalist 2017

Proverse Hong Kong

Enoch's Muse
by Sergio Monteiro.
First edition published in paperback in Hong Kong
by Proverse Hong Kong, under sole and exclusive licence,
November 2018.
Alternate Edition: ISBN: 978-988-8491-46-9
Copyright © Sergio Monteiro November 2018.

Distribution (Hong Kong and worldwide):
The Chinese University Press of Hong Kong,
The Chinese University of Hong Kong,
Shatin, New Territories, Hong Kong SAR.
Email: cup-bus@cuhk.edu.hk; Web: https://www.chineseupress.com
Distribution (United Kingdom): Email: chrisp@proversepublishing.com

Enquiries to:
Proverse Hong Kong, P.O. Box 259, Tung Chung Post Office,
Tung Chung, Lantau Island, NT, Hong Kong SAR, China.
Email: proverse@netvigator.com; Web: www.proversepublishing.com

The right of Sergio Monteiro to be identified as the author
of this work has been asserted by him
in accordance with the Copyright, Designs and Patents Act 1988.

Printed in Hong Kong by Artist Hong Kong Company,
Unit D3, G/F, Phase 3, Kwun Tong Industrial Center,
448-458 Kwun Tong Road, Kowloon, Hong Kong SAR, China.

Cover design by Artist Hong Kong

British Library Cataloguing in Publication Data.
A catalogue record for this book is available
from the British Library.

Illustrations acknowledgements and permissions

ADVANCE COMMENTS ON ENOCH'S MUSE

"Monteiro brilliantly blends mythology, history, fantasy, science and theology into an epic adventure that leaves the reader wondering what of this is real, even after the last page turns."
– **Rena Hamstra Dam**, from 'Epic adventure into the unexpected', 5-star review posted on Amazon, 24 October 2018.

Exploring the dynamic between science and religion, the nature of time and other dimensions, Sergio Monteiro's *Enoch's Muse* takes us on a rollercoaster journey from past to present and from ancient Hebrew mythology to modern cosmology.
– **Peter Mann, author of *Sheriff of Wanchai***

ENOCH'S MUSE

Sergio Monteiro

Table of Contents

INTRODUCTION
On Science and Religion
The Battle of the Bands

"It is one thing to worship the Gods but it would be another thing to have them come into your home and start re-arranging your furniture," – Terry Pratchett, "Pyramids"

You're holding this book now. You've bought it hoping to be entertained by the thought streams contained within. And as the author, if I have done my job, then you will: but before that entertainment, consider this – how did this book come to be?

Its pages were arranged for your reading ease and much thought was given to the binding, size and presentation. The ink and font were chosen to be pleasing to your eyes. The content was edited for mistakes and style. There is no denying that intelligent thought went into creating it.

I want you to give the same consideration to your hands holding this book. Your arms, your torso, the orchestra of systems that make up your organs. The super-computer behind your eyes allowing you to decode these alpha-numeric symbols into words. If a book is created with intelligent thought, how could you then have come from nothing? Modern evolutionary theory says we evolved from lower primates into the complex beings we are today. Guided by an instruction manual called deoxyribonucleic acid. However, some questions persist.

Like... which evolved first, the cardio-vascular system or the blood that pumps through it? Did our pulmonary system evolve according to the specifications of our atmosphere or because the heart required it to function? And if so, how was such perfect synergy between the three systems achieved and more importantly, when?

Some will say the answer is in the language of DNA itself. DNA that is similar to this book you are holding. Both, complex groupings of intentions, themes and instructions compiled for a specific purpose, though one is believed by secular science to have developed all on its own. Which is odd because other instances of that don't share the same traits. For example, before humans learned to program computers, the language to do so had first to be created. Which for some leads to the biggest question of all regarding DNA – Could it have really happened on its own as is claimed? A sudden 1000-page instruction manual when before there was nothing? And what are we to make of the millions of other life-forms on Earth and their DNA? Life-forms that appear to be made for the express purpose of sustaining our comfort and balance at the top of the food chain here.

If you agree this book could not have come from nothing, then the natural questions are, did DNA also have an intelligent designer? If so, who or what? And what if the answer means the human experience has more meaning than modern science would like us to believe?

If you think this is where I assert, "God did it", you would be mistaken. Instead, I contend that the interpretation has more to do with perception than a specific divine source. DNA, and all that comes from it, is either formed from a series of cause and effect operations, starting sometime after the Big Bang, or is nothing less than the divine instructions from an extra-dimensional source. And it's our perception of this that informs how spiritual our individual realities are.

As you're reading this now, an innate sense of spirituality exists in you or it doesn't. But whether you came from a spiritual source or from a complex set of mathematical operations, is all your complexity merely an accident?

Consider the observation that expressing any spirituality outwardly these days is often met with eye-rolls. This is largely due to scientific advancement having conditioned us in the modern age to demand evidence. And having seen none to support a divine being creating us from dust, many have concluded that such an event has no basis in reality. Fair enough. After all, if evidence is required to imprison someone, why should not evidence be needed also for faith in a creator? The problem is that this notion has also left many now firmly in the realm of atheism without ever remembering having chosen to be there.

But here again we bump into perception. Perhaps we have an abundance of evidence pointing to an intelligent designer, but we have perceived it as something else. Or perhaps – more willfully – we have all chosen to ignore it. After all, who really wants to entertain the strict moral requirements to enter heaven when there is no evidence that a heaven or a hell really awaits us at the end of our lives? The natural sciences have told us that upon death our bodies break down and are reabsorbed into the Earth; that over time we revert to dust. The difference is that this is something we can actually observe and verify to be true. Intelligent design however, first requires a bit of faith, but it's not alone in that any more.

What the sciences have not told us, however, is what happens to that ethereal part within us. That unquantifiable grouping of senses we feel reacting to music, art and love. That part we have come to call a 'soul' and which modern science, in all its love of nomenclature and definition, has simply not yet explained.

But even so, I still love the sciences. I love the rotundity of scientific explanations and the harmony that exists between diverse biological systems. I love feeling smart knowing how a neutron star is formed, that the nearest one is seven trillion light years away. But some time ago I started hearing religion's classic tune – *"faith"* – playing from some of those scientific explanations. I saw that while the notion of a teaspoon full of neutron star weighing as much as a city block of buildings is awesome to think about, it is also completely unobservable to me or most laymen. I realized I had accepted many of these scientific explanations as true on faith alone. I sat with a friend one night and proposed some questions to him,

"When are we ever going to see a star collapsing to verify the process? The distance alone makes it impossible for us ever to see one for ourselves."

He responded with, "Trust the scientists who study these things, they're smarter than you."

Maybe so but I've never been comfortable with blind deferment. I know that the astrophysicists who study the phenomenon of Neutron stars are actually gathering meta-data and then making the inference that their data represents a star collapsing into an object with immense gravity far away. I told him as much. "No one has ever seen a star collapse with their own eyes. How can the scientists know their data represents what is really happening?"

He again invoked their higher intellect. "Those PHDs don't teach themselves, I think those guys know what they're doing."

"So then, how are they any different from a Cardinal, Rabbi or Imam telling us things happen according to the will of a God, if at the end of the day the scientists just ask us to trust them too?" To that, he offered a valid point.

"The scientists findings are verifiable, the other guys not so much."

And this is where the opening chords of that old tune called *'faith'* would start. This time, however, it was coming from science. Just as religion attempted to dominate over science in a past age, this new tune from modern science sounds like it's posturing for supremacy over anything spiritual. It became clear to me that, at some level, modern science had indeed become similar to organized religion. In spite of one calling the other evil; and the other calling the first, outright fantasy. The end result being stalemate between the two institutions with little chance of ever reconciling their respective assertions on the origins of humankind.

Assertions from the science camp that are backed by science rock stars such as Neil de Grasse Tyson, Lawrence Krauss or Michio Kaku. All three, undoubtedly brilliant men, but who also spend much time promoting a notion that we should have absolute faith in the secular scientific community. They espouse the view that science has now matured past the point of reasonable skepticism on the part of you, me or anyone not as smart as they are. Tyson himself has often said, *"The universe is under no obligation to make sense to us."*

I find that rather unfortunate because I – and many others – are really curious about it. In honesty, I would have no problem deferring to his greater intellect if different interpretations of data, from within his own community, didn't also exist. I've also seen the willingness of Tyson's peers to silence voices which don't agree with the same narrative he promotes. And this begs the more important question of why science even has a narrative now. Shouldn't the observations be speaking for themselves, no matter where they lead?

While the scientific community is not monolithic in this practice, it seems some scientists are willing to use the inherent faith people hold in scientific findings to pass incomplete data off as proof positive. This is dangerous because it allows for unpopular interpretations of specific data to be silenced in some instances. The past is littered with examples of this. Dig a little and you'll find that at key moments in history, the choice was made to conduct science by a form of consensus rather than stated method.

Albert Einstein's theory of relativity had many contradictions and was predicated on the findings from an eclipse in 1919 that was later shown to be inconclusive as proof of the theory. Yet, we never hear of this debate. The exploits of Thomas Edison are taught in schools over those of Nikola Tesla for reasons that I suspect will become clear to humanity in the future when our energy needs – and by extension their costs – increase.

To me, this makes it seem that the truth about the origin of humankind maybe something different than what either of these *bands* has been playing all this time. But to be a layman publicly questioning the intellectual heavyweights opens one up to instant ridicule; followed quickly by allegations of the Dunning-Kruger effect, claiming you simply don't know the breadth of what you don't know.

To that, I shout out "bs" – *blind scientism*, because, knowing there are gaps in your knowledge – if you're motivated enough – will instantly orientate you to filling that specific gap. And it is there, on that path of learning a debatable pre-requisite concept, that you most encounter one of these well-meaning smart men playing a tune one would have never expected from the scientific community. "Faith," they might say. "Look, to explain this to you I would need to get into a complex mathematical equation that I don't have the time to do and you wouldn't understand anyway, so just trust me."

Sounds familiar, right? The lyrics are different but that melody is unmistakable. And here you find yourself perhaps feeling a little *déjà vu*, having just been academically coerced into trusting *Scientism* by the whisper of faith. Curiously, though, it is never called that. I suppose because this tune needs to remain subtle when it comes from science, and calling it outright faith in *Scientism* would make it far too obvious. Nikola Tesla also noticed this a long time ago, when he famously said, "Today's scientists have substituted mathematics for experiments, and they wander off through equation after equation, and eventually build a structure which has no relation to reality."

Perhaps this is why science at large doesn't spend much time expressly debunking religious claims, perhaps having long noticed that humanity as a whole doesn't embrace change that well, but will more easily leave a belief in an old perception if a new one is created and built on an independent system of empirical evidence; that people will then willingly make the leap away from spirituality themselves, despite the steep academic barriers calling them to that new evidence.

I also want to note that my criticisms here are of *scientism* and not science itself. Science, when done correctly, is beautiful. The blind deferral to science called *Scientism*, however, is lazy and seeks to subvert critical thinking. This is too much like the organized religion of a past age, which I also have criticisms for.

For organized religion, "Faith" was their breakout hit but not their most famous, "Morality" holds that title. And while some modern scientists have become smug with their own intellect, organized religion has spent far more time arrogantly looking over its nose at us from this position of unquestionable morality, despite church figure after church figure being caught doing things most of us wouldn't dream of. Still, they too are not monolithic. But does this put Chritianity's claims of Jesus Christ existing into question? I suggest not but perhaps he has been portrayed differently than how he really was.

I'll focus in on Christianity here because, of all the Abrahamic faiths, it has been the most influential to western civilization. And the trigger into atheism I have most encountered is Christianity's assertion that Jesus Christ offered his life as punishment for our sins. It is an assertion often followed by the question, why wouldn't God just punish humans directly? He did it to so many other tribes in the past, so why not at Christ's crucifixion too?

Christian doctrine says that by the time of Christ's cruxifiction many societies had turned away from the morality of the Old Testament and so God offered Christ as a way for us to make atonement. We now know that the concept of a scapegoat came from the ancient Hebrews but I'll admit, I had never fully understood this concept from a god's point of view. That mankind, at one time, had become so degenerate that the only way to save us was to offer a scapegoat to be punished for us. That we, in the modern age, are still culpable for that degeneracy. But that all we have to do now is believe in Jesus Christ and our sins we didn't even know we had committed, from a time none of us had experienced, would be magically forgiven. Logically it made no sense. I had also questioned how degenerate mankind could have become to require such an act. I thought maybe the claims had been exaggerated. Maybe the common folk of that age were not that different from us today and modern faith had overstated the claims of rampant degeneracy. Perhaps the people back then were not even that religious. Perhaps they had previously chosen not to harm others for more trivial reasons than abject morality.

Of course too, there would have been some for whom morality had shifted into a grey area of equivocation. But perhaps they too wondered, "Hold on. Why is the Rabbi so exalted? After all, he gathers the water in the morning the same as I. How can he know all he says he knows?" Maybe the people back then had also seen little tangible evidence of a creator and instead had made the judgment that it was more beneficial to worry about survival than pleasing the said creator; maybe having seen that survival often came down simply to being nice to each other. And maybe it was this that had now been characterized by modern faith as degeneracy.

For the sake of this argument though, imagine the higher being who had created humanity watching all of that back then. Imagine a Hebrew/Christian God or some other alien being, surmising that his guidance was not being heeded; even though, in truth, people were just skeptical about the claims of his existence. Imagine that God-figure knowing that letting such skepticism form and evolve in an earlier age would negatively affect future generations. Might he have seen it as the cost of progress and enlightenment, or would he have known he could not let it continue? If God suddenly had to show humans that he was real, how would he do it? Would he save their souls from whatever it was that awaited an immoral life? Would he love the human experience enough to offer them a way out that doesn't punish them for sins they didn't even know they had committed? And if so, would there still be a cost, for us, involved? Could that cost have been forcing humans to crucify his son?

Fast forward to the modern age and it is not much different. To a lot of people, the evidence for God still isn't there. But what also keeps many modern people comfortable in atheism is the idea that if a God really exists, why does he allow so much suffering in the world? Why didn't God stop that rapist? Why didn't God stop all those children from being murdered? Why doesn't he stop wars? The uncomfortable answer is that it's not his job to, it is ours. What many atheists often forget is that Christianity teaches that God gave humans free will and the choice of whether to be evil or not is ours alone to make. Combine that with political power and you get an idea of the thought-process behind some of humanity's evil decisions. Enter the extra dimension of Satanism.

Perhaps a rapist, murderer or war-monger thinks, "God doesn't stop me so there is no God. No God equals no consequence for my soul. No consequence for my soul means no soul. No soul equals no afterlife. I can do whatever I want." Aleister Crowley, the father of modern Satanism, famously promoted a notion of, "Do what thou wilt shall be the whole of the law." Meaning that you should conduct your life with no thought to moral consequences, and the more immoral your actions, the more pleasing they are to Satan.

But if you spend any time studying the God and Satan dichotomy, you will see that the Satan figure doesn't require an express belief in himself but rather simply, a disbelief in the dichotomy itself. Willingly or unwillingly, secular science has helped achieve this. But even so, fifteen percent of today's mainstream, published scientists still hold the belief in an intelligent designer of our world. And while it may have been easier to convince people of a divine will in the past, today it would take a pretty significant event followed by nothing less than a BBC World headline saying,

"God Proved to be Real and He's a bit Pissed Off"

Could you imagine the water-cooler conversations in the weeks and months afterwards?

> *"So I had to break up with Sarah because, you know, I heard Hell is pretty hot and my eczema really flares up in the heat."*
> *"How hot do you think it will be?"*
> *"Probably too hot to keep any sushi fresh but I suppose that's part of it you know – bad sushi for eternity and all."*

If we suddenly had absolute proof that God and heaven were real, the result might be billions of us suddenly finding the restricting morality of an orthodox doctrine not that hard to bear. Others may still refuse, having grown comfortable with the idea of no moral consequence but the vast majority however, I suspect – like myself –would fall somewhere in between.

And if we take the phenomenon of neutron stars to be unobservable yet fact, what would an unobservable God do in the face of modern, scientifically-conditioned people suddenly turning their faith towards him again if the above happened? What would he do if the entire world suddenly realized the Bible was real and we've been following the wrong direction of the moral compass? According to the Bible, God loved humanity enough to offer a way out of damnation once through Christ's crucifixion. Would he now just shrug and wash his hands of the whole affair?

Judeo-Christian doctrine states that God would, and does, offer a way out under the condition that we accept Jesus Christ as our lord and savior and then honour his teachings. When I learned the historical context of that condition – that was when I finally understood the concept of a Jesus figure as a way for people to atone for past transgressions they didn't even know they had made. I learned that the concept doesn't seek to assert that humans are inherently malevolent because of some distant compounded sin, but that we sometimes collectively forget what true benevolence means. That we sometimes attribute virtue to things undeserving of it; that we often mistakenly embrace iniquity, thinking it is virtue.

As if at the time of Christ's crucifixion God had: 1) Seen us forget what he taught. 2) Knew it would lead to poorer and poorer choices. 3) Showed us he was real to stop that evolution. 4) Saw our faith suddenly return to him. And last, decided he still loved us but said, "Okay people, I'll accept your faith again, but no one gets a free ride, please put my son/me on a cross so you'll always remember."

And while a bit passive-aggressive of the big guy to offer atonement by essentially making humanity complicit in the murder of an innocent man, I suspect most parents can appreciate the value of hard lessons learned the hard way. Warn your child about the danger in touching a space-heater and they may heed your warning, but might soon not remember why. If they accidentally get too close and sense the heat, however, they'll probably not soon forget. Perhaps we in the modern age have also started to forget. Or perhaps the story of the true origin of humans has been misrepresented and we are now too afraid or apathetic to ask what the real one is.

In closing, I hazard that the answers to many of the questions we are not brave enough to ask lie somewhere in the abyss of all that we don't know about the origins of humans; somewhere in those big scientific numbers, locked by a contextual history that has not been shared with us. It is my hope that perhaps an idea of why science borrowed that classic tune from religion is in the story you are about to read.

Enoch's Muse is inspired by the paradigm of science and religion, each seeking to encircle the other for most of recorded history. And if you too have noticed the music, then perhaps you may already know what *Enoch's Muse* is about.

I like to think of it as the tale of an impossible love affair tying together a story that is part historical science-fiction and part journey through a spiritual history. Set at the dawn of recorded time and told through the eyes of a figure whom few outside of ecumenical circles know about – Enoch. A scribe from the days of Jared, who, the scriptures say was taken by God to walk with him in the heavens. If this is the first you've heard of him, I suggest you get a copy of the *Book of Enoch*. It tells an interesting version of creationism.

At the Council of Nicea in 325AD, Enoch's account of the time before Noah's flood was considered for, but ultimately rejected from, inclusion in the modern Bible. It has been difficult to find out exactly why but many think the willful exclusion has something to do with a curious passage from the book of Genesis: "There were giants in the earth in those days; and also after that, when the sons of God had come unto the daughters of men, and bore children to them, who became mighty men which were of old, men of renown." (KJV Genesis 6:4.)

In Hebrew texts the giants are known as the *Nephilim* and the sons of God are called the *Bene Ha Elohim*. The passage stands out because no further context is given about where these giants went or who these men of renown were, though some have posited that the Titans of Greek lore may offer a clue. Nevertheless, the subject is never mentioned again in the Bible. The Book of Enoch however, goes into great detail about where they came from, who the Bene Ha Elohim were and what they did while they were here.

But the most astonishing thing about the Book of Enoch is that, in many ways, it acts as a sort of Rosetta Stone to the Bible and other holy books, making once vague passages and concepts suddenly ring with context. In learning about the *Nephilim* and what their relationship was to God, many of my questions were answered. Like why a supposedly just and kind God would instruct a tribe to commit genocide against another tribe. Or why Jesus is mentioned in the Islamic Quran more times than their own prophet. Why the Quran itself is so accepting of the Torah and the Bible as they existed at the time of their prophet. Why some Islamic scholars feel the Quran was, in fact, the same Christian God's attempt at preserving his true word.

To me, *Enoch's Muse* is a re-imagining of Enoch's lost texts but it didn't come from nothing. I want to thank some people I consulted while researching the historical implications contained in his account. To those people, I say, this book could certainly not have come forth without you.

I want to thank Gillian and Verner Bickley for believing in the work, Matthew Boylan for finding the right words even when he was searching for them, Marty Leeds for showing me the ins and outs of Gematria and Michael Patrick McConnell whose voice on modern faith is like mental floss.

Most importantly, this book would not have been even remotely possible without the support of my wife who came into my life and showed me the meaning of true love. She's grown more used to the back of my head than she would have liked but has never wavered in her support of my effort. Thank you for the time you gave up being there for me, advice when I wasn't listening, care when I needed it most, coffee, silly dances, and most of all, your love. I owe everything to you, Ho Zhu.

In closing, I must warn readers that there is a little violence in the story but one can't expect to set a novel during biblical times and not encounter a little torture between friends.

> "The first gulp from the cup of natural sciences will turn you into an atheist but at the bottom of the glass, God is waiting for you."
> – Werner Heisenberg, the father of modern quantum theory.

Sergio Monteiro
Hong Kong

CHAPTER ONE
Mischa

8:55am, 12 December 1891. River North, Chicago
Yearning for the opposite, all Josef could wish for now was that death would be swift for Mischa. That it wouldn't linger and take her a breath at a time. A child that young wouldn't know how to welcome the final closing of her eyes as the end of suffering. Instead thinking she'd later wake up and find the tattered angel doll resting dutifully on her pillow, having watched over her dreams. More than once Josef had entertained the idea that he might have to do it himself, each time banishing the thought as soon as it was born, but the harder it got for Mischa to breathe, the harder it was for Josef to fight the idea.

The coughing didn't help. Josef, sitting on the bed next to her prone figure, felt like the dull grey light of winter that filled the room. Watching as her coughs came in rapid succession, one after the other, too fast for the little girl to catch her breath in between them. He waited for her head to stop shaking from the jolts so he could wipe her brow, while his other hand stirred the contents of a tin mug placed on the mahogany nightstand next to the bed. Next to the mug, a small wooden box labelled 'Morphine' was also placed. It had sat there for weeks but Josef had stopped counting. It was not time for that he thought. He hoped it would never be.

Mischa stopped when the coughs reached their apex. The moment always gripped Josef's heart but his face showed none. He started counting in his head, *"One...two...three..."* Doctor Jones had explained that this was when Mischa's lungs couldn't retake air fast enough and for a moment the little girl would not be able to breathe. Dr. Jones' instruction was that when the breathless moment lasted more than a minute, it would be time for the morphine. That at that point comfort would become more important than healing.

"...18...19...20..." Her face turned red but still no sound was heard, filling the moment with even more agony. The girl's face was frozen mid-cough but the air finally returned. A raspy noise of air filling her starved lungs dominated the room and her coughing subsided. *"How can you allow this to continue?"* he thought, forcing a smile and wiping his daughter's brow. Her head returned to the sweat-soaked pillow. His hand brought the mug of dark ointment to his lips, blowing the smoke away while stirring the liquid and thinking of a way to make his daughter smile.

"Here Mischa, drink this," he said. She groaned and opened her eyes, watching her father stir the foul smelling liquid. "Now this is very important, little Mischa," his voice was stern and his brow was furrowed. He lifted the spoon and carefully placed it on his nose where it stuck hanging down over his lips. He blew more smoke away. Mischa watched her father try to hold a serious face with a spoon hanging off his nose, she smiled first with her eyes then with the corners of her mouth.

"Have you seen the spoon?" he asked. "I had it here a moment ago."

"It's on your nose, you silly," she responded softly, after taking in another laboured breath. Josef turned quickly to Mischa, as if she'd made the greatest discovery in the history of humanity. "What? I have a nose? Are you sure?" Josef crossed his eyes on the spoon. Mischa smiled at her father with all her heart.

Outside the room, down the long patrician hallway decorated with pictures of the Romanov family of Russia. Past a Persian rug extending to a wooden staircase, ending just before it descended around a crystal chandelier hanging over a marbled foyer – a black housekeeper, Ida, entered an ante-room just beyond the foyer. The round woman wore a black and white maid's uniform and held a silver tray of freshly brewed tea. She set the tea down on a camphor coffee table in front of Dr. Jones who was cleaning his spectacles with a monogrammed cloth from his tweed jacket. The sandy haired but balding doctor didn't look up at her.

Across from him, Irina Goldstein, Mischa's mother, sat on a Chesterfield made across the lake in Ontario. Her tear ducts were red and irritated. It might have been an allergy to the cotton handkerchiefs or it might have been the extended use. In any case, Irina needed a solution but none was coming. The room was in stillness at the notion that no more solutions were coming.

"Thank you, Ida," Irina managed through a sore voice. Ida turned to leave but paused at Irina. The two had spent so many hours consoling each other but in front of Dr. Jones appearances needed to be kept. Still, Ida paused and quietly placed her hand on Irina's shoulder. Tossing appearances aside, Irina's hand instinctively rose to Ida's and her eyes closed, as if Ida's hand was a warm reminder of hope in a room filled with cold reality. Irina was about to cry again but regained her composure just in time to catch a disdainful stare from the doctor. Ida's footsteps continued and faded away, while the sound of Josef's, coming down the stairs, stirred the doctor's attention.

Josef took a seat next to his wife. He poured tea for her and then one for the doctor. Irina broke the silence.

"I have a lunch engagement with the ladies' guild but I'll cancel it," Irina offered.

"No, don't do that. After work I'll come straight home," Josef replied.

"Are you sure you do not want her at Mount Zion, Josef? We can make Mischa comfortable, I assure you," the doctor interjected.

"She's scared of new places," said Josef.

He heard another sob forming in Irina. She got up and left the room.

Josef started to follow but Irina stopped him. "No, you stay here and make the arrangements, Josef, I just need a moment."

Josef remained sitting and turned to the doctor.

The doctor began to speak. "The last check shows that the Tubercle Bacillus has spread to both lungs, Josef. You really have to consider her comfort now."

"Do you have children, doctor?"

"Four boys, all grown."

"Then you know I can not merely think of her *comfort*."

The doctor sipped at his tea. *"This part was never easy,"* he thought. Asking Josef to part with one of his hands would have been easier than asking him to accept Mischa's fate. The doctor was running out of ways to convince Josef to let go.

"Doctor have you heard of a field of study called *antibiotics*?" Josef asked.

"Yes, the Germans swear by them but they're untested here."

"I heard that it was what saved Rockefeller's baby. Have you heard of this?"

The doctor stirred with worry, he knew where Josef was going and he knew the territory was dangerous. "So far, antibiotics have only been shown to work on horses, there's no data to show that they could work against human bacteria." The doctor reached out, he touched Josef's hand and drew in closer. "You must let go. If you wish, I have friends you can talk to."

Josef felt more tears coming, cursing himself with the wish they wouldn't. He looked at the doctor with eyes that asked the question long before his mouth formed the words. "Do you have this treatment?"

"I can get it from the animal clinic but it will be expensive, Josef."

"How much?"

"If it stands a chance of working, Mischa will need it *intravenously*. This method of delivery is new and it would take several doses over a few days. I'd have to acquire the equipment. We're talking maybe 2,000 dollars, Josef," the doctor warned after a pause.

Josef was no pauper but 2,000 dollars would be difficult to come by.

"Bring it tomorrow Doctor!" Josef said as he got up, signaling to the doctor that he needed to leave for work. "Whatever the cost, I'll pay!"

With his resolve set, Josef ushered the doctor out of the ante-room, escorting him to the door, opening it and allowing the cold air to rush in. The soft light of the morning snow suddenly filled the dark foyer. The sound of a horse and buggy crunched against the snow outside. The doctor stepped out into the cold. He stood on the steps of the brownstone walk-up in River North and turned to Josef, offering his last piece of advice.

"Irina is a young women still, you can have other children. Let it go, Josef, it may be for the best."

The doctor turned and entered his buggy. His coachman wore a wide hat and was bundled to the neck for warmth. The man opened the door and the doctor climbed in. As the black coachman closed the door and turned, he narrowly escaped bumping into a woman walking with her head down to avoid the wind.

"Watch it, boy!" she scolded.

"Sorry ma'am! A Merry Christmas to you!" The doctor's coachman tipped his hat and climbed onto the box. "Hiya boy!" he called, shuffling the buggy to life before it trotted off down the road.

Josef closed the door and returned to the foyer to get his coat. He stopped at a mirror and saw his reflection. He needed sleep. The bags under his eyes said as much. Irina came down, dressed for the meeting with the ladies' guild.

"This woman is so much stronger than me," he thought. *"If you asked me to socialize today I will scream."*

She came to him and adjusted his tie.

"Is she sleeping?" Josef asked.

"Yes, the ointment helps, but her breathing still sounds horrid. I don't know how much more I can take."

"I told Dr. Jones to return tomorrow with another type of treatment."

Irina's hands stopped. Her face turned up to his. "Again? And how will you pay this time? We don't have anything left in the accounts and you cannot borrow any more."

"I have a bonus, I'm due it from Harrison!"

"Harrison?...Josef! You're counting money that's not in your hand? Don't be foolish."

Josef knew she was right. It was said that every penny in Chicago was extracted from the tight fingers of Mayor Carter Harrison Senior.

"Do not think this way Irina, I'll find a way for Mischa," he placated her. He hated lying to her but it was best she knew as little as possible. He'd already thought of a way to get the money, and it had nothing to do with the mayor of Chicago. From upstairs Mischa coughed again. Josef heard Ida's footsteps move towards the sound. Irina let go of Josef and walked back upstairs to check for herself.

Josef got his woollen coat and placed his hat on his head. As much as he wanted to stay at home and comfort his wife, comfort his daughter, comfort himself, he still needed to work. Not because the last of the city accounts needed settling before the holiday, but if he missed another day of work, Johnson would surely not let him forget it.

He closed his eyes and thought of his daughter upstairs, fighting to breathe. He knew his wife was right, that Harrison would never pay early but it was never his intention even to ask him to do so. Only two solutions remained for him to end Mischa's suffering; one was a risk and the other a certainty, both relying on what he kept in the drawer in front of him. He glanced upstairs again to listen for any sounds of movement descending toward him. Satisfied that none was coming, he opened the drawer where a cigar box sat alone in the interior.

Josef opened it and took out the Samuel Colt six shot revolver, one of the first of its kind. The firearm felt unnatural in his hand. Fingers more accustomed to jumping quickly between rows of numbers fumbled with the firearm, dropping it to the table with a loud thud. He quickly gathered its cold weight and shoved it into his coat pocket, glancing upstairs to see if anyone heard the sound. It seemed no-one had.

"Mischa suffers and still you're *nervous? You must do this for her!"* he thought to himself, turning toward the staircase. When his foot stepped onto to the first step, it creaked under his weight and made him pause. From the top, Ida suddenly appeared and descended the stairs. Startled by the sight of Josef at the bottom, about to ascend, but dressed as if he was about to leave, she thought perhaps he'd forgotten something.

"Mr. Goldstein, please let me, what do you need from upstairs?" Ida asked.

He wanted to say, a miracle, and if not that then the strength to end his daughter's suffering. Instead he turned and headed to the door. "It's nothing Ida, I was mistaken."

Ida disappeared into the kitchen to prepare lunch for one. Josef walked to the door but didn't walk out. His hand fondled the revolver in his pocket. The cold steel was warmer now, with a comfort in the warmth that was inviting, soothing even. He looked over his shoulder. *"No!"* he thought, *"It is now or never."* He closed the door and chose *now*.

***

3:45pm. Jackson Park, Chicago
Already overshadowed by the industry of New York City and the
history of Philadelphia, Mayor Carter Harrison Sr. thought it was
time for Chicago to shine. As his buggy crunched along the
frozen muddy roads of Jackson Park, the mayor thought Chicago
hadn't had a winter like this since the great storm of 1856. That
storm had seen horses frozen in the streets and the National
Guard called out to quell the food riots. He'd been just twelve
then, not knowing it had nearly been the death of the mid-
western American metropolis he'd one day govern.

Inside the buggy, Mayor Harrison and Steven Johnson,
his number two, gazed over the expansive empty plains of
Jackson Park. Six hundred hectares of land that the city had not
known how to develop. Despite the cold the Mayor only wore a
black three-piece suit and a black bow-tie. His doctor had
warned him about under-dressing for the weather, telling him
that he was not a young man any more. The Mayor's response
had been to fire him, having no use for a man who made
arguments by pointing out the obvious.

"This is going to be expensive Johnson, is there a way
we can raise city taxes?" the Mayor asked through a heavy beard
that had long started the retreat to grey from black.

Johnson, bundled in a black coat with a grey scarf,
agreed. "We can, but it would probably cost you re-election, it
has already been in the papers that Chicago is putting in a bid for
the World's Fair. The unions would see right through it,"
Johnson continued with blue eyes that hid behind a pair of
rimless spectacles.

"What do you propose then?" the mayor asked, hoping
for a creative answer.

"Well, Olmstead's plans are quite spectacular, we could
set up a viewing platform during construction and charge a
quarter to watch it being built."

"Hmmm," the mayor said, looking out of the window.
The little list he kept in the back of his mind grew a new entry.
"We need more young people in the office," it read.

"Conversely Sir, we could just remove ourselves from
the bidding and use the money to fight the firemen's union. Their
case is almost ready for trial."

Harrison turned sharply toward Johnson. Johnson had become somewhat of a pain after moving to City Hall, the mayor thought. It was no secret the man developed his own relationships with every city contractor, no doubt hedging his bets against the day the Mayor lost favour. *"Mild disloyalty,"* the Mayor thought, but tolerable because Harrison had done the same as a younger man. Besides, Johnson's business instinct was sharper than most, even if they did generally bend toward himself first.

"And let New York City get this too? Over my dead body, Johnson! It is about time we showed those Yankee snobs this country has more than one great city."

"But, Sir..."

"We're bidding! No discussion, as for the firemen's union, their budget review is on my desk right now. If I starve them, how can they fight me?" The mayor said, holding firm.

"Of course Sir," relented Johnson, dejected but obedient.

"When can we submit our budget to the Treasury?"

"We should be ready once we decide on which bids to manage the power, I hear Thomas Edison has put in a bid, he has good connections out west for timber and copper. Might be a connection we could use later."

"There's no guarantee in that, and Edison will be expensive, when will the bids come in?"

"Tomorrow, on the 7am bullet from New York."

"Anyone else, besides Edison? He's such a bore lately. My girl in D.C. doesn't need as much reassurance as he. You know, I think the man starts his own rumours," the mayor scoffed.

"George Westinghouse," Johnson added. "He bought up all Nikola Tesla's patents but I hear Edison won't sell them any of their bulbs. Unless Westinghouse makes his own, he's going to have trouble delivering."

"Hmmm," said the Mayor again. It was a sound Johnson had come to know could mean, *"Yes, I agree"* or *"You're a complete twit"*.

"If I may add, Edison already lights up New York City, Sir. Getting him to light the fair may be a little comeuppance to the New York set if you're so inclined," Johnson urged, hoping the sound had been leaning toward the former.

"I am, but it could equally be their comeuppance to me," replied the Mayor. "No matter. Just make sure you have Josef in bright and early tomorrow. I want him to scrutinize the bids with a fine comb. I want a cost analysis against the timber and copper on my desk by five tomorrow afternoon."

"I can do it, Sir. Josef has been distracted lately and I know how important this is to you."

"What's wrong with Josef?" The mayor turned sharply, concerned about the city's financial comptroller.

"Some family issue again. The last few months he's been absent a lot. Are you sure you don't want me to handle it?" Johnson offered.

The mayor's eyes bored into his number two. Johnson, uncomfortable under the gaze, shifted his weight around his seat.

"You don't like Josef, do you?"

"I like him fine," Johnson lied. "I just don't see why you didn't hire someone less..." Johnson searched for the least offensive of offensive comments. He couldn't find one so he changed polarity.

"....or perhaps someone more...uh...Christian. This is a Christian nation after all. Isn't there a Christian as good with numbers as he?"

"There is," the mayor stated. "*Nigger Bill*, the janitor at the observatory, come up from Carolina. I hear the Jesuits go to him when their math isn't right, a scandal if anyone ever found out. Would you be okay with him? He's a Christian," the mayor stared at Johnson, enjoying the man's prejudicial torment.

"You know what I mean, Sir. The Cardinal has reservations about their *tribe*."

"Well, if the Cardinal ever decides to balance our budget then I might give his reservations a thought or two. Right now I seem to be all out," the mayor announced.

"My point is that you don't have to rely on Josef," Johnson retorted. "I didn't spend eight years working for James Pierpont Morgan not to pick up a thing or two about cost analysis myself."

"Hmmm...J.P. Morgan, I've always wondered, is it true about his nose?"

"Sir?"

"Never mind, if Josef isn't in when they come in, then by all means handle it. But honestly man, stop being such a bloody *Edison!*"

"Of course, Sir. One more thing – when should I prepare the bonus cheques? It is nearly Christmas, Sir."

"Handle it in the New Year. I'll need that money to wine and dine the construction union if we win the bid. No-one in the mayor's office is starving; they can wait."

Outside, as the buggy hopped along next to a twenty-five foot drop into a ravine paved with frost-sharpened rocks, the cracking sound of shearing wood suddenly erupted and echoed back into the coach. The entire cab shifted downward a sharp 45 degrees away from the edge. To the mayor and Johnson, it felt as if the bottom had suddenly been swept out from under them.

"Blooming Hell! What now?" the Mayor yelled.
Out of the window, Harrison saw the large back wheel roll to the left in a slow arc, landing by the edge of the swampy marsh. The motion was hypnotic. Reality came crashing in when the coach jolted violently toward the ravine. Out of Johnson's window, the mayor saw the edge now rushing toward them. Terror filled his eyes.

"Jesus help us!" he thought,

"Whoaa!" The frightened sound of the coachman's voice came in from outside. The mayor saw the coachman's shadow leap from his box to the space in between the two horses, each of his arms landing on the neck of a thrusting mare, his gloved hands fighting to grip the reigns or the horse's hair, whichever was closer. The coachman's body was shaking violently. The mayor thought about what would happen when the coach went off the edge, sending the two thousand pound buggy crashing on top of him.

It would be crushed to pieces by the fall, the mayor thought. Even if the mayor and Johnson survived uninjured, there would be no way to make it back to civilization before the cold night air froze them solid. *"Good God man, save yourself!"* the mayor thought as the exposed axle dragged along the rocky path, jostling the mayor and Johnson about the coach like toys in a box thrown down a flight of stairs.

The horses neighed in fright over the coachman's voice that had become frantic with his own fear.

"Whoaa! Now!"

"Lord, help us Johnson," the mayor said softly, closing his eyes and waiting for the impact.

***

Inside the Victorian-era floor of City Hall where the Mayor's office was located, the last two secretaries remained typing up the minutes from the education board meeting the mayor hadn't attended. The others had taken advantage of the Mayor's absence and had left early. The two who remained now battled to see who could finish first. Two rolled cigarettes, each in a separate ashtrays, sat next to each of them. The smoke wafted about the room in slow moving coils that stopped and disappeared at the ceiling, as if conducted by the click-clacking of the dueling typewriters.

Behind them were double wooden doors leading to the mayor's office. Next to them, a staircase ascended from the lobby below. A messenger boy came up the stairs with rosy cheeks stained red from the outside cold. The boy took off his hat and handed a message to one of the secretaries, rubbing his hands together as he waited. The secretary took it dutifully and handed the boy a penny, lighting the boy's eyes with joy.

"Merry Christmas to *ya*, ma'am!" The boy beamed as he turned and walked away flipping the coin in the air. The sight of the happy child only made Josef's heart sink further.

Across the room he sat in his office. He turned from his view of the secretaries and stared blankly out of his window. Below him the winter afternoon droned on as coaches travelled back and forth and the citizens of Chicago walked with the brisk steps of people attempting to avoid the cold. He saw the messenger boy leave the building and run past a constable managing traffic with waves of his hands. The middle-aged constable wore a giant parka that failed to hide a beer belly surely earned over a decorated career of *jook-joint* hopping, Josef thought. The thought that he could probably outrun such a constable, was a comforting one.

Josef reached for the top drawer on his desk where the revolver sat wrapped in a white handkerchief nestled among papers outlining next year's budget. The idea had formed slowly in him. Josef supposed they always did. It had been building a quiet momentum in the back of his mind until he couldn't ignore it any more. An opportunity that had lain invisible until life began killing off his choices.

First he had emptied their savings account for a six-month hospital stay in New York's Knickerbocker hospital. Then he had sold his wife's jewelry to support a full time nurse for a year. The antiques later covered the costs of treatments from the *Orient* but, the only way to cover the costs of an on-call doctor was to remortgage their home. And then, in the cruelest joke of all, life showed Josef that none of it would be enough. They needed more money. That morning he'd learned that they needed it now.

The plan had first taken shape when he walked past the money-wire station at 5:54pm last week. They had been closing and all the desks were emptied out as four cashiers began counting the day's remittances to California, New York and across the pond to England, France and Germany. Easily 5,000 dollars, maybe more. But 2,000 would be enough, Josef had just learned.

The manager, Michael, had walked over to the door, motioning his finger to the same messenger boy, who was then playing with a wooden top outside. The boy had quickly gathered his top and taken off running. Michael had taken a few furtive glances up and down the street and returned to watch over his employees. Josef had started counting.

Counting time was an old game to him. A game born of poverty and growing up on Chicago's Southside as the son of poor Jewish immigrants. As a child, he would roll a ball to his brother down the street and count how long it would take the ball to reach him. Whoever guessed closer would get to roll the ball again, increasing the distance with each throw, until one of them reached the cross street. Remembering the game, Josef had then looked at his watch and started fleshing out the plan.

The police station was three blocks away, he had thought. The evening foot traffic would be heavy as folks left downtown but the nimble messenger boy probably made this journey every day. By now, the young boy had likely deciphered the best path to take, the best moments to turn, the best alley to go down. Josef had estimated it would take the boy seven minutes to get there. Josef visualized that, inside the police station, the boy would run up to the Duty Sergeant's desk towering above him.

The Duty Sergeant would look down, instantly knowing why the little boy was there. An order to the first available constable to report to the money-wire station would be made. Josef had imagined the police would arrive by buggy with the messenger boy hanging off the back, making saluting gestures to his friends watching him from the corner. The buggy, less nimble in the evening vehicle traffic, would arrive at the money-wire station within ten minutes. Josef had been right again. At 6:11 the police buggy had pulled up in front of the money-wire station.

The messenger boy had been crouched on the back of the buggy, poised to let the string fly as soon as the buggy started to slow down, hoping to use the jolting force of the stop to get his best spin of the day. It was a game Josef might have played as a boy but knew now that Mischa never would. Josef had left and continued walking home. His brother would have been proud. Enoch, who had been watching from a roof-top across the road, was not.

In his office a week later, it was just turning 3 o'clock. *"Not long now,"* Josef thought to himself. *"This is the way, it's the only choice left now."* He closed the drawer a little too loudly, getting the attention of the secretaries outside who peered up at the noise. His fingers were shaking. He got up and walked over to his cabinet where a whisky decanter sat with a family of tumblers, but for appearances only. Josef didn't drink. But in working for the Mayor he'd come to realize that men who didn't appear as if they did were seldom ever trusted. He opened the decanter and poured himself a glass. He sat back down and continued his work, hoping that the coachman he'd have waiting around the corner from the money-wire shop, wouldn't make small talk tonight.

***

Back in Jackson Park, the Mayor, Johnson and the coachman were battling to avoid being stranded in the desolate park. The brave coachman was now pinned between the mares and heading fast toward the ravine. He needed to do something quickly. His plan would only work if the mayor returned to City Hall tonight. After tonight there would be no way to get Westinghouse the contract, no other way to help Tesla. The wheel coming off had been exactly what he'd planned, but the sudden turn toward the ravine had come as a surprise.

The coachman reached for the rein closest to his right hand, yanking it down hard toward his chest, fighting the powerful neck muscles of the Clydesdale mare's thrust through the air. The horse's head lowered and slammed into the path of the other horse. It was the coachman's only hope and it worked. The other horse swung his head to the left, trying to avoid the blow, shifting the wooden yoke along with it.

The buggy veered away from the ravine, its massive remaining back wheel loosening a large piece of frozen gravel and hurling it in a tight spin down the ravine.

"Woaah!" screamed the coachman, grabbing the other rein and falling onto the slack with his weight. The horses slowed down and the buggy stopped. Now the horses only wanted their freedom.

Inside the shuttered coach, Johnson gathered his papers, now strewn about inside.

Realizing they weren't pinned to the bottom of the ravine by the mangled coach, the mayor gathered his wits. "Are you alright Johnson?" he asked, his heartbeat softening his tone with knowledge that death might still be upon him.

"I'm alright, but these plans, some of them are torn."

"*Hmmmm,*" muttered the mayor as the horses raged outside.

Johnson stormed out of the coach ready to strangle the coachman. "Good God! You fool! You nearly got the mayor of Chicago killed! What's your name?" Johnson screamed.

The coachman, preoccupied with trying to dodge hooves swinging wildly in the air, didn't answer as the mighty beasts tried to free themselves. The sound of cutting air whipped by his left ear while a descending hoof nearly took off his right. He dodged the blow just in time but not the thought of three more coming after it.

"Easy girl, easy," the coachman said, nestling inbetween the horses, placing his hands on both their necks. The angle meant the powerful hooves couldn't drive their horseshoes into his head anymore, though Johnson might have wished they could.

"Easy, easy now," the coachman's voice softened as the horses settled, their breaths warming his hands now as he stroked their hair.

Mayor Harrison walked around to the wheel and surveyed the damage. The metal ring that had secured the wheel to the axle had come undone. The cold must have expanded it, making it more brittle, he thought. The mayor heard Johnson yell.

"You fool!" Johnson screamed at the coachman.

The mayor went around to join them.

"We're due in the city in an hour. You fix that wheel and get us back to the city immediately and I'll consider only docking your pay over this!"

"Right away, Sir," the coachman replied.

The mayor interjected, "Are you alright man? You could have been killed."

"I'm fine, thank you your Honour, but you know what they say about falling off horses," the coachman said.

"Where is Harvey? He's my usual coachman, who are you?" the mayor asked.

"Harvey is out with the strep. I'm covering for him. My name is Enoch, Sir."

"Which you will be doing no more after today, I assure you," Johnson interjected.

"Please pay him no attention, Enoch. It was lucky you managed to steer us clear of that ravine. Where did you learn to coach so aggressively?"

"Rome, Sir."

"Rome, Maryland? Washington D.C. hasn't been called that in a hundred years."

"Yes, of course," Enoch stammered. "Pardon me, Sir. Sometimes I open my mouth and my grandfather comes out. I was raised on his farm down in Silver Springs." Lying had never come easy to Enoch, but the older he'd become, the more he needed to hide who he actually was.

"Well you have certainly earned a glass of my whiskey! Now come man, let us see what we can do about this wheel," the mayor ordered.

On the plains of Jackson Park, with no buildings to abate the winter gale, the wind had lowered the temperature by 15 degrees. They had to work quickly. The day's defrost was starting to harden again and soon the winter air would make it impossible even to move their fingers. Johnson wore his worry on his face but the Mayor, a former army mountaineer, relaxed into the pressure in the way of men long accustomed to danger.

The mayor rescued the wheel from the bush. Enoch and Johnson leveraged a branch over a rock to raise the coach high enough for the mayor to re-attach the wheel to the axle. Johnson, not used to exertion and clumsy from the cold, strained to hold the lever. His forearms shook under the strain but a mad smile had begun to peek through the mayor's face. It had been a long time since he'd got his hands so dirty, a long time since he'd felt the quiet rush of the wild outdoors. The younger version of himself had grown the reputation of a man used to hardship, embracing each chance to re-earn the title. But as his fingers started freezing now, the older version of himself praised God that he'd survived this long.

Securing the wheel to the axle was going to be problematic. The metal ring cowling had split down the middle. They could ride without one but the second they turned it would come off and the wheel would fly off again. The mayor and Enoch examined the possibilities.

"I think if we put a little mud inside, let it freeze to the wood a bit and take a slow pace home, we may just avoid having to decide which one of us to eat first," the mayor said as they got to work. Johnson was already inside. This had been as much adventure as he was willing to soldier through in the service of Mayor Harrison. He was already contemplating the letter to Edison's timber and copper contacts. A letter that would surely need to wait for tomorrow now, as there was no way to arrive back at city hall in time to catch the 4:40 pony. The ride back was silent. Johnson rambled on about Josef's recent absences but the mayor drowned him out as a vision danced in his mind. A new idea had come to him.

"Rome! Why didn't I think of it before? A modern Rome for the 20th century! It would be a spectacular sight!"

Johnson mentioned something about protocols of office and how long it would take to re-do the plans, but the mayor interrupted him.

"Johnson! When we get back send a boy for Olmstead. I don't care where he is, he's to see me tonight."

"About the plans?"

"Indeed, but we won't need those, I have a new idea and I need his assessment."

"Of course, Sir."

The coach tepidly crawled out of the Jackson Park bush. At least if they crashed again, the fact that the mayor was on board would surely help with flagging down help.

Harrison's thoughts warmed around the idea of a white city on the lake for the Chicago World's Fair of 1892. He decided to nurse the thought with a glass of Tennessee whiskey while he waited for Olmstead, the city architect, to arrive.

The clock tower said 5:47 when the buggy arrived back at the entrance to City Hall on the corner of Washington and Clark Street. The afternoon haze had given way to an evening fog, chilling the night air and helping the shouts of newspaper boys carry from down the street. Johnson and the mayor stepped out of the buggy. Johnson, looking forward to a change of clothes, hurriedly ran up the stairs but the mayor had other ideas.

"Johnson, fetch me an *Evening Tribune*, I want to check New York's steel price."

Johnson stopped in his tracks, his face couldn't hide his annoyance, but his tone was a different matter. "Right away, your honour," he replied and disappeared down the road.

The mayor approached Enoch. The man's hands moved about securing the reins with the ease of a seasoned cable master but this man couldn't have been more than twenty-five years old. "*A man of hardship,*" the Mayor surmised. "*It does have a way of turning the young into masters before their time.*"

"Where are you from? Enoch isn't a common name for these parts. You look a little French?"

"I suspect *Hebrew* would be the word for it, but I've not been home in a long time. My family is originally from the east."

"Well I value a man who thinks fast on his feet. How would you like to come work for me?" the mayor asked. Enoch finished and walked over to the mayor.

"Harvey is a good man your honour, he has four children too."

"Perhaps, but everyone is replaceable and good help is hard to find."

"Maybe so, but a dependable one must be even harder to find, no?"

"Too right...too right indeed. My point is that I reward good work and today you really saved our hides out there. Having the mayor's favour can be a big help in this town. Are you sure you don't want to reconsider?"

"I'll be begging your pardon, Sir. But I couldn't help but overhearing some of your conversation out in Jackson Park. Nature of the beast really...would be unnatural to ferry around powerful people all day and not hear a secret or two, no?" Enoch said.

"Indeed so, speak your mind, young man."

"I heard that your staff were due a bonus, for Christmas like, but you were going to wait for the New Year to give it out, was that correct?"

"Yes," the mayor was surprised, a mental note to ensure his coaches were sound-proofed in the future was also added to his mental list.

"Well, I've never known what it's like to be a rich man, your honour, but I've felt that a nickel at the right moment makes the difference for a thousand moments afterwards. I imagine even a rich man will have moments like that, though I reckon they might be too proud to announce it and such. You get me, Sir? Expectations and that..."

"What can one do, Enoch? People's problems are their problems. If they choose to share, fine. But if they don't, then it can't be helped. You can't do anything if you don't know the moment of need exists."

"I understand that, but when you're the one who could make such a moment, might it not help to pay attention to see who needs it?"

"I suppose you're right." The mayor peered closely at Enoch. "Are you from St. Stephen's parish, on Twelfth?"

"I never knew him, your honour."

"What I mean is, you ask that I help others, yet you take nothing for yourself, a very honourable gesture for you to make. There aren't many honourable men left in Chicago."

"Thank you, your honour, but I feel that title is a little misplaced on me."

"How so?"

"Well, it would not be me making the gesture now would it?" Enoch said, tipping his hat and removing gloves from his pocket. "A Merry Christmas to you, your honour."

Enoch turned and walked down the road toward the sounds of the newspaper touts. Fog was coming in with the early evening and the wind had picked up. Johnson emerged from the fog, flustered and out of breath as Enoch's shadow disappeared, gone with the fog as if he'd never had one.

"What's the matter, Sir?" Johnson asked. "You look startled."

The mayor snapped out of it. He hadn't noticed that he was lost in thought. It seemed the day's adrenaline rush was wearing off and sleep was soon to follow, but first that whiskey and a chat with Olmstead, if only to toast young Enoch, a man wise beyond his years.

"It's nothing, Johnson, let's get inside."

As they climbed the stairs, Josef emerged from the building. His eyes were facing downward and his pace was purposeful. His hands were in his pockets and his collar was turned up. One hand on the gun and the other on the handkerchief ready to cover his face. He bumped into the mayor with a hard thud. His eyes came up, about to tell whoever it was to watch where they were going. When he looked in to the mayor's face, he stopped.

"Your honour, I'm sorry. I should have been more careful."

"Josef! Just the man I needed to see, I need to have a word with you, can you come up to the office?"

The thought to run crossed Josef's mind. It would be easy, run and make an excuse. Was the mayor of Chicago going to chase him in the streets? On further thought, Josef thought Harrison just might.

"Sir, I need to…uh...Can it…?"

The mayor sniffed whisky on Josef's breath. Josef had never been able to fool him with the decanter that year after year, never changed level. *Something must be gravely wrong,* he thought. The mayor's tone softened.

"Are you alright, Josef? I hear you've been having some family trouble."

Josef was boiling below the surface while his hand clenched the firearm in his pocket tighter. Time was running out and the mayor couldn't know what he was impeding with his mindless small talk now. Josef couldn't wait any longer, Mischa couldn't wait any longer. *"Shut up you pompous blowhard!"* Josef thought.

"It will only take a minute, then you can be on your way," the mayor said.

Josef's body trembled with adrenaline. His legs shook with the need to run and get that money now. He didn't have any more minutes. He looked towards the clock-tower and felt his chance slip away. As the hand on the clock tower moved, he felt his chance to save Mischa fall away too. He couldn't stop the tears that now ripped through to the surface and ran down his face. He wouldn't have to let Mischa go, mere circumstance would do that for him.

"Good God man, what is it?" the mayor asked, as Josef broke down on the steps of City Hall. The Mayor grabbed Josef's shoulders and led him inside. They entered while Johnson followed, the trio disappearing into the building.

From across the road Enoch watched. The Mayor would never know that the future of humanity had just rested on him stopping Josef. That it would now ensure Josef was going to be at work tomorrow to assess the power bids. *"He doesn't need to know,"* Enoch thought. Neither does Josef. *"They never did."*

What Enoch knew and Josef hadn't counted on, probably because he was not a criminal, was that an employee of the money-wire station would also be armed. Like Josef, that man also wanted nothing more than to go home and see his daughter's shining face smile at him. But unlike Josef, the man's firearm training had long taught him to react in the space between seconds. This was time Josef had never thought to count.

The gunshot wound to Josef's stomach would have seen him die on the floor of the money-wire station, a mere thirteen minutes from now. Mischa would have died on Monday and it would have taken seven months for Irina; suddenly alone, heartbroken and penniless; to hang herself in the bedroom as bank agents stormed in to foreclose on their home. The mayor would never know it, but in delaying Josef, he'd just saved the man's entire family.

But saving the Goldsteins was not Enoch's mission, which was Tesla. Josef was just another frugal accountant and to Harrison himself, it made even less difference who actually lit the Chicago World's Fair of 1892. The mayor had often bragged. *"One doesn't become mayor of Chicago without learning to sniff out the gain behind any loss."* To him, either industrialist would have suited his needs, but only Westinghouse would do it using Tesla's research. And to allow Johnson a chance to affect that selection process, would mean Nikola Tesla would never become a household name. Enoch's mission was to ensure that it did.

Though Westinghouse's bid would be nearly half of Edison's, Johnson would have fuddled the numbers awarding the contract to Edison, in the process securing a large commission for himself in a future copper deal. Enoch couldn't allow this. There was too much at stake this time. Uriel needed him more than ever. Through no fault of his own, Johnson now stood in the way. Semjaza, the vile trickster, had once again maneuvered another greedy man into a moment his greed would be rewarded. Enoch was left with little choice.

Killing Johnson outright was not to be thought of. Enoch's code wouldn't accept that. Another idea had been to stop Edison's bid from even arriving on the mayor's desk. It would have been easier, nothing more than a swift distraction of the post-handler at the train station. For old hands like Enoch's, it would have been an easy task but it wouldn't have saved Mischa, Josef or Irina. Enoch's code couldn't allow that either, he was left with no choice other than to take the path of greatest resistance.

Enoch looked up to the sky where a shooting star streaked across the evening sky. It was done now, the only thing left was to wait and hope that Holly would show up. He turned up his collar, disappeared down the alley and continued walking into the future, his steps fading into an echo.

CHAPTER TWO
TWO YEARS LATER
Chicago World's Fair of 1893

1 May 1893

Under the Roman archways of a past age, the Chicago World's Fair of 1892 actually opened in 1893. Originally, the fair had been planned to celebrate the 400th anniversary of Columbus discovering the Americas, and set to feature the grandest display of modern technology the world had ever seen. Despite these lofty expectations, only one of those would come to pass.

Luckily for Mayor Harrison, this fact was only noteworthy yesterday. Today, as the fair opened, no-one cared because *The White City* was truly unlike anything the world had ever seen."*And it was right here,*" the mayor had thought. "*On the shores of Lake Michigan. Chicago had finally arrived on the world stage.*"

Two years after Enoch saved Mayor Harrison's life, the swampy plain that used to be Jackson Park had been wrested back from oblivion and converted into a utopian vision for the coming 20th century. It looked like a modern-day version of an ancient Roman citadel. Mayor Harrison dubbed it, "The White City". Johnson had pushed for, "New Rome," instead. But the mayor had refused. "*Rome rose like a phoenix and then it fell, Johnson,*" he had said. "*How wonderful would living in a dream be, if you knew the dream would end, my boy?*" Johnson had given up, he never thought the name would stick. He also never thought that bringing The White City to life would cost the mayor his life.

In D.C. the Treasury department had been furious because the Mayor's new plans over-ran the previous schedule by ten months. It turned out his new vision not only required new building methods but new building materials, creating new enemies for the mayor in the process. Six months from now, the mayor would find himself in front of an assassin's bullet with no-one like Enoch to stop it, but today as he stood on the podium, dressed in a tan linen suit, waving to the thousands of people waiting for the US President to take the stage, the mayor felt that his dream might truly live forever.

President Cleveland was to arrive any minute now and flip the telegraph switch that would see close to a million lights come to life at once all over the fair. The central pavilion he would look out on was now filled with 50,000 waiting people. They mulled about in front of the platform, facing the domed administration building, with the mayor watching over them.

Mayor Harrison looked out and saw a revolving door of well-dressed folks from every corner of America and the travelling class of the world. Industrialists, businessmen, great and small had come to wonder at what the future held. The mayor listened to the rumbling hum of voices, catching a name here and there and hoping to hear his own. But the name he heard most was of the brilliant young inventor sitting next to him, Nikola Tesla.

Despite Edison's efforts, Tesla's boss, George Westinghouse had come through and supplied the fair with 650,000 lights. Lights powered from a machine building that now buzzed with the noise of a thousand electric dynamos running at once. Dynamos built by Tesla himself and ready to power all six hundred acres of the fair. A more ambitious lighting project had never been attempted before, on reflection the mayor didn't mind sharing the recognition with the young man who had illuminated his vision.

Far across the pavilion at the entrance, a well-dressed couple passed under the Roman archway lined with massive columns. The columns extended hundreds of feet on either side around the pavilion. Perched on them were statues of Columbus, the pioneers of the west, President George Washington, and others, all given the Roman treatment and converted to nine foot statues towering over the entrances. The well-dressed man, who in other circles, was known as L. Frank Baum, stepped through them with his wife, Maud Gage. Both strained their necks upward as they gazed up at the modern day titans towering above the fair like cultural sentinels. Baum thought the effect was of history itself watching over humanity as it now marched proudly into a new century. The thought was quickly followed by another, sudden and far more important, epiphany.

Baum, an editor and writer of books, had only married last year and visiting the fair had been a promise to his new wife. He held her gloved hand as they entered but as soon as he caught sight of the Great Basin, surrounded by the seven, massive and Roman-themed buildings he let go to retrieve a pen from the inside pocket of his pinstriped black jacket. His other hand rummaged over the other pockets. Even though the back of his mind knew he'd left his note-diary at home, his hands still searched hoping to avoid confirmation.

"Do you have a handkerchief darling?" he asked, his oiled moustache suddenly twitching with nervous energy. His wife instantly knew what it meant. *"The man could never hide his excitement when an idea formed in his mind,"* she thought.

"Heavens! Frank, can't you just enjoy yourself for once?" She asked as she dug in her leather handbag. Frank saw the diary and was stunned with a smile. He normally carried it everywhere but had thought to leave it at home so he could devote his full attention to his new wife. This was proving to be difficult. The magnificent splendour of the fair had caught him off-guard. He had never seen anything like it. He also hadn't expected that Maud would know him so well. As he watched her gloved hand suddenly produce his diary from her purse, Frank knew in that moment that he'd married the right woman.

"How did you know?" he asked, incredulous as he leaned in and placed a kiss on her forehead. The type of kiss that if asked about later, he'd not remember, betraying a love for his wife that had become far more than just second nature.

"I just hope you're paying attention as much as I am." She said coyly, accepting his kiss with the confidence of a woman who knew she deserved more. She fastened her purse and flicked a dandelion bud that had flown into her long blue summer dress. Baum quickly opened the diary and began making notations as he looked around *The White City*.

The entrance opened out to a wide man-made basin that had been constructed in the middle of the central complex. Crossed by a series of bridges and surrounded by the seven grand buildings, built of wood but covered with a special mix of cement and wax developed just for this purpose, it left the effect that the White City was constructed of the same Pentelic marble as the columns of the Parthenon. Baum and Maud stepped into the shadow of the Statue of the Republic, a six story figure of a woman holding a staff in one hand and an eagle perched on a globe in the other. It stood facing the administration building just across the Great Basin.

As they wound through the pavilion, lined with Cherry Blossom trees in full spring bloom, they followed a gravel path leading out to purposely-built neighborhoods beyond the central construct. One neighborhood contained cultural displays from the 48 states while another housed architectural ones from the countries of the world. France had built a Chateau. Germany – a proud castle, and Japan a flower garden complete with Geishas exuding elegance from even their simplest movements. Baum and Maud watched them sit, reach for cups of tea and pour them – appearing to the couple as one continuous and silent motion.

At a make-shift barn, Baum came upon a group of emissaries from the Ottoman Empire. The dark and turbaned men paraded Arab horses for wealthy white industrialists who watched them with awe but were frustrated when they tried to communicate. Baum watched the face of one industrialist suddenly beam with his own epiphany. The man disappeared only to return ten minutes later with a solution to their language barrier in the form of a case of Tennessee whiskey. Baum overheard the man start a bet to see how many Ottomans they could convince to get drunk.

Maud bought a copy of the *World's Columbian Exposition News*, a special newspaper published just for the fair."Look at this Frank," she said as they came upon the Manufacturing and Liberal Arts Building.

"Apparently there's a serial killer on the loose here!" Maud stated with a gasp. Baum didn't look up from his diary. "Mmm, that's nice dear," he replied automatically, having only listened enough to know his wife had used words.

"Amazing," Maud thought in annoyance. *"Here was the largest building in the world, in a fair where a serial killer was on the loose and Frank couldn't care less."*

"What'll you call this one?" She asked, looking down at his writing. He looked up and gave her a smile, elated at the prospect of talking about his writing.

"I don't know darling, right now I'm having visions of cities made of emeralds, perhaps 'The Emerald City'! What do you think?" he asked proudly, waiting for her to tell him how wonderful it sounded.

"That sounds stupid Frank, a title like that will never sell," she replied.

"Then what would you suggest, darling?" Baum asked, as they dodged a group of actors dressed as wizards. Baum turned and looked at them, smiling himself down another thought thread.

"How about, *'The Man Who Ignored His Wife'*," she offered sarcastically but Baum's hand continued to move furtively over the pages.

"Hmm, that's nice dear," he replied again, writing like a man possessed now. He'd undone his silk tie as his eyes were taking in the wonder of this city within a city. Like a lost land within a land. The ideas were tripping over themselves to fall onto the pages of his diary, he didn't want any detail to escape him as he made his first notes of what would become his greatest novel.

"How about, 'The Wizard in the Emerald City'?" He asked excitedly.

"Utterly dreadful darling," Maud replied, "It sounds utterly dreadful."

***

The long *Manufacturing and Liberal Arts Building* was the centrepiece of the entire fair. No other building on Earth was equal in size at that time and no other building would ever be home to an equal display of what the future held. Inside, the sweet smell of the Indian and African spices called many to sample the flavours from the east, next to the proud German and Swiss exhibits displaying the finest in automatic firearms and watches, and in between, everything else one could ever imagine.

As Frank and Maud entered the building they moved past Josef, Irina and Mischa exiting in a hurry. Josef's arm was extended out in front of him, being pulled by Mischa, whose steps were nearing a full trot with Josef in tow. The little girl needed to get outside now. Josef's gaze landed on Baum's and his eyes widened in recognition of the famous writer. Baum had also noticed and gave Josef a polite smile before entering and disappearing into the mass of people inside. Leaving Josef in mild awe. Mischa, however, brought her father firmly back to reality.

"I want to be at the top when the lights turn on, come on *Aba,* we have to hurry!" Mischa pleaded, pulling harder on her father's sleeve with one hand and the tattered angel doll in her other.

Inside the building, Josef had tried to show her something called an *automobile* but Mischa had called it the *"noisy wheely box"* and dismissed it. The other exhibits of the future were also of little concern to her. What Mischa really wanted to see was the first Ferris wheel ever constructed.

Behind the building, the giant wheel spun giving visitors a panoramic view of the entire fairground every thirteen minutes. Josef's sleeve was threatening to free itself from his jacket under the strain of Mischa pulling him toward the giant wheel, Irina's stern gaze protesting the little girl's anxiety.

"We will get there in time, we still have twenty minutes before the President turns on the lights," Josef said, but Mischa couldn't wait. She suddenly let go and took off running towards the Ferris wheel.

"Mischa!" Irina screamed, lurching forward to grab the little girl but Josef stopped her. His eyes softened at the sight of his daughter's stride, his missed chance to meet L. Frank Baum becoming a distant memory.

"It is okay Irina, let her go," Josef said as he continued to watch his daughter. "I like seeing her run."

Mischa ran through the crowd without a care in the world except the Ferris wheel in front of her. Her lungs working powerfully but she felt no strain, not anymore because the antibiotics had worked. The carnival noises now faded out around her as the screams of joy from the people on the Ferris wheel carried to her ears. A smile was etched into her eyes, blinding her to the woman in her path. Mischa crashed into her, knocking the angel doll to the ground and jolting herself to the right.

The woman also stopped, her eyes suddenly peering downward, she'd also been lost in thought but Mischa had suddenly brought her back to reality too. The girl looked unharmed. The woman crouched down and reached for the doll first. Mischa was already on her feet and dusting off her dress when the woman brought the doll over to her.

"Are you alright? This is yours, right?" asked the woman. Mischa took the doll and said thank you. She looked at the woman curiously wondering why she was dressed like a man. Long grey tweed pants, a white shirt and a woolen vest that couldn't hide the smaller womanly frame and hint of breasts. The flat cap on her head could barely cover the wisps of dark hair that had fallen loose from her head, even as the woman tried quickly now to shove them back into her cap.

"Are you a girl?" Mischa asked, as the woman leaned down. The child's question had been a little too loud for her liking.

"Well, you're a smart girl, how can you tell?"

"Because you're so pretty," Mischa said, smiling. The woman, despite herself smiled back.

"Well, it's a secret, promise you won't tell anyone?"

"Okay," Mischa replied and was off running again. The woman watched her go, watched as her parents chased after her a few seconds later. The smile she'd given the child evaporated and the countenance of the hunted returned to her face. The fair guards were nowhere in sight but she had gathered too much attention sneaking into the fair. She looked around but luckily no-one had noticed her. *"Someone will soon though,"* she thought, considering her disguise couldn't even fool a little girl.

Around the woman, people were ecstatic with the heady excitement of the fair. Young men lined the games hoping to win prizes for the women encouraging them with the whirl of their dresses. Suddenly from her right, she heard the sound of people being ushered by the brusque authority of underpaid guards. Her ears tuned into the noise as it rose above the sound of joy under the Ferris wheel. They were close, she had to move. A man on a box announced the lighting of the White City would take place in ten minutes. *"Oh no!"* the woman thought. She needed cover and she needed it soon. Across the field, a *"Closed"* sign hung on the entrance to an observation tower. She walked briskly over trying to blend in to the crowd.

The tower stood 238 feet and had been rushed to completion in time for opening. The roof still leaked but trappers from Ontario were arriving tomorrow to patch it with maple resin. Tonight though, it would be her refuge. Inside she found a metal door with a placard that read *'Elevator'* across the top and a *call* button placed off to one side. Her curiosity got the better of her and she pressed the *call* button.

The doors opened and she jumped back with a start *"What is this thing?"* She thought, timidly entering the little boxy room adorned with golden patterned plates across the roof and sides. The doors suddenly closed behind her. She tried to turn and stop them but she was too late, she was now trapped inside.

"At least the guards won't find me now," she thought. She noticed a set of buttons numbered from one to six next to the door. It was by chance that she pressed six first. The box suddenly rumbled to life and she felt it lift off the ground. In horror, she extended her arms out to the sides to keep her balance. The rising box ground to a halt at the roof but it seemed the tower was not the only thing that had been rushed to complete. The elevator had stopped early. When the doors opened, she saw that the floor of the roof was now at her waist. Her bad luck hadn't ended. *"Oh no! This too!"* she thought at the realization that the broken elevator had now stranded her on the roof. Finding comfort only with the thought that at least the guards couldn't come up and find her.

She quickly made her way out to the roof to the spectacular view of the entire White City. The roof top of the observation tower was lined with six giant search lights pointed downward over the fair. The noise below had become a distant echo of excitement.

She found a quiet alcove overlooking it all and thought it would be a good place to hide, and later get some sleep. She took off her hat to let her dark brown hair fall to her shoulders. As she sat and wiped the soot mixed with sweat from her face, her stomach suddenly made noises. She wished she'd stolen a hot dog before coming up or at least some popcorn. But it didn't matter, she thought. The hunger would soon pass; it always did; everything always did, even people; especially the people.

She felt the grip of tears start first in her throat then move to her eyes. She fought them off again with a shake of her head. *"Not now, you foolish woman,"* she thought. To calm herself, she reached into her pocket and removed a silver chain. Attached to it was an oval-shaped slice of gold, pressed with the image of an angel. She flipped it to read the inscription again.

"May 1st 1893, the White City"

She returned the chain to her pocket and looked up to the sky where the sun had just started to set behind the horizon. "I'm here now," she whispered, holding back tears, "Show me!"

Below her, a loud speaker boomed to life announcing the official start of the fair. Mayor Carter Harrison Sr. was introducing President Cleveland to the podium. The crowd cheered as the president took the podium.

The President's massive hands waved to the crowd, while a wide smile under a bushy moustache dominated his face. After a few words about the resilience of the American people and his vision for the 20th century, a cloth cover was removed from the telegraph switch in front of him to gasps from the crowd. The moment had come.

The woman in the alcove couldn't see the President actually press the switch. Instead she first heard the low hum of internal motors increasing their revolution. Then the search lights shuttering to attention, sending powerful beams of lights streaking downward to the crowd. The lights below, winding their way along the buildings in the central pavilion, came to life one after the other. She saw the walking paths behind the central complex, hidden previously by the approaching darkness, now suddenly illuminated all over the White City.

Ground lights lit the Statue of the Republic from below, giving it the appearance now of a giant walking across the water toward the administration building.

As incandescent light now radiated from every corner of the White City, people looked at each other as if seeing themselves for the first time in years. Their deafening roar carrying to the now crying woman at the top of the observation tower.

"I came! Show me!" she yelled at the sky through tears she could no longer hold back. She looked towards the sky again as the *John Philip Souza* choir started singing below, the music mocking her tears.

"Show me why, or I'll end it right here!" she screamed, though the crowd could not hear her. She suddenly stood and climbed out to the ledge and looked down at the ground, she felt her feet tingle with vertigo and her head spin from the sight. Her footing slipped but she steadied herself on the railing. The last thing she wanted was to fall because of an accident. If the answer did not come this time, she was going to end it, but she needed to see what she was doing. Even though time had long shown her that an end for her may not even be possible. Still, no answer came to her from the sky, instead it came from behind her.

"Her name is Uriel," Enoch said, using a soft tone to not frighten the woman. *"She must be frightened enough,"* he thought. "And she's beautiful. Just like all those lights, they're beautiful aren't they? It would be a shame to ruin such a beautiful moment."

The woman turned around to the figure dressed in a black suit, a young man, possibly the same age as her, with a gold pocket square the lone piece of colour on his attire. His skin was a dark shade of cream and his eyes were an arresting green, stealing the attention despite the full dark beard covering his face. *"How had he got here?"* she wondered. *"Had he been here the whole time? Had he been waiting for her? Was he one of them?"*

As he stepped forward she took a defensive position. Odd for someone contemplating suicide, Enoch thought, but showing that deep in her heart, she wanted to live. If only to find out why she was still alive, Enoch stopped to show her he meant her no harm.

"How did you get up here?" she asked.

"I was already here. I was waiting for you, Holly."

"How do you know my name? How could you know I'd come here?"

"It's a long story, but I'm sure that isn't your only question," Holly stepped from the edge, she was still fearful but something told her this man was not like *them*. Maybe it was his eyes, they were tired but not dull, as if they knew more than could be explained, with a wisdom that knew when it should be and when it should not.

"Who is Uriel?" she asked.

"The picture on your necklace, she's an *Arch*, her name is Uriel. I'm sure you have always wondered."

"How do you know about that?"

"Because I gave it to Father MacClement and told him to give it to you."

The words hit Holly like a blow to the chest. This stranger was different from the men who had killed Father MacClement. Still, he moved with the same purpose as they. When he mentioned the necklace though, her instincts relaxed. The men who killed Father MacClement had mentioned Mark and every other detail of her life when they trapped her in the abbey six months ago, but they never mentioned the necklace." *"Was this the sign she had sought?"*

"Who are you?" she asked.

"Forgive me, I've had many names, names are just words and words never matter. My first name was Enoch."

"Do you know what is happening to me? Why I'm like *this*?"

"Yes and no, I thought I did once but not anymore. So much has changed, but if it's any comfort, the same happened to me," Enoch said as he produced a flask of soup from inside his jacket.

"Hungry?" he asked. "An annoying occurrence I've come to find but it helps me *remember* sometimes."

Holly approached and took the flask, keeping her eyes on Enoch. She opened it and drank the hot soup, feeling it fill the crevices of her belly.

"Do you know what happened in Scotland too?"

"Yes, with Father MacClement? That must have been trying for you, but worse is yet to come, you have to be ready."

"Ready for what?"

"I know you have a lot of questions, I did too, but drink the soup first, there's time."

"Who were those men that killed Father MacClement?"

"Their names do not matter at all, they change them every few decades or so to hide their intention but their goal is always the same. What is more important is who they serve."

"Who do they serve?"

"Azazel."

"Who is that?"

"An old one, one of the first actually, he's also had many names over the years, no doubt he'll take a new one in the future but today people call him *Lucifer*."

Holly wasn't shocked. She had suspected it could only be one or the other, but that idea had only come to her recently. In the beginning, she hadn't even known to look out for what was happening to her. How could she? How could anyone? It had started with the remarks of her beauty. They had become so commonplace that she hadn't noticed her life changing, by staying exactly the same.

Mark, the young man who inspired her to escape the orphanage, had never told her she was beautiful. He didn't need to. She saw it in the way he looked at her. The way his body language would change in her presence. Mark had been handsome with blond hair and the leonine head of his German ancestors. His muscles rippled through every shirt he wore when they married at seventeen. Her eighteenth to twenty-eighth birthdays had come and passed with all remarking on how youthful she remained, how radiant her skin looked – as if time had created a path for her and her alone to follow. Mark had turned into a strapping man, his shoulders had filled with power as he worked day after day on their farm. The change had come when she was thirty-eight. They had still not had children and Mark had started to acquire a forest of grey hairs on his beard. Over the years lines of age etched their presence onto his face but hers remained as youthful as the day she had married him.

Around her, the polite remarks from neighbours, friends and family about her youthful appearance became a joke, but in the years that followed the polite remarks had turned to grave concern and then fear. The fearful thoughts slowly fuelled what would become a mob that became *mobs*. Forty-eight, fifty-eight had come and gone. The ravages of time had proved unkind to Mark. His hair had faded to grey and his teeth had fallen out one by one. In his face, she'd still seen the man she'd fallen in love with long before; but, when he looked at her, she could see that his face had become tainted with worry which lurked beneath his own love for her. He'd taken to reading the Bible for long stretches of time. The people of Chesterfield, Montana, had begun talking and making plans. The stories had begun reaching to other towns. Tranquility had left their lives but Mark stayed true, loving her till the day he died.

By seventy-eight, Mark was gone. Holly was alone and the dye had been cast. The trial and mob-murder of Mormon leader Joseph Smith was still fresh in everyone's mind. As in the case of Smith, the local ministers got together and declared Holly a witch and spawn of Satan. She had no choice but to uproot her life once again or risk being tried as a witch.

She had escaped to Boston where she convinced a Portuguese sea captain to give her passage to England. She created a new life for herself there while she pondered on her nature. Working as a servant meant that she could pass unnoticed and she did so. She fled to Scotland only when the men in dark suits had first come looking for her.

It was in Scotland that she found Father MacClement. He gave her the necklace and told her that he'd been expecting her. Since 1853, Holly had lived in the cathedral but when the men in dark suits came again, it had been the necklace that told her where to go.

"What am I?" Holly asked, "An angel, a demon?"

"Just words, words never matter, Holly, and as far as I know there has never been a word to describe what we are."

Holly finished the soup and returned the cap to the flask, setting it down beside her. Enoch sat next to her. Down below, no-one thought to look up at the pair dangling their feet over the edge of the observation tower. Even if they had done so, the blinding searchlights hid them in its shadow.

Holly felt comfortable enough to look over at Enoch. She thought he stared out now as if waiting for the air to open up and swallow him, though his eyes said he'd be calm if it did. A question formed in Holly's mind. "How old are *you*?"

"When Babylon was destroyed," Enoch started, "Entire centuries had become but mere seasons, years were like months and the days counted away like minutes. In the beginning, life had been simple, it just didn't stay that way as I remember."

CHAPTER THREE
Taken

Long ago, on the snow-covered flat plateau of Mount Hermon at the centre of the realm, a cave stirred with activity. Deep inside were the bones of two hundred women, abandoned and scattered there in the freezing wind. As girls, the women had disappeared from the land and been taken there to await the coming of age when their bellies had started to grow with children. Their screams, cries and pleas for *Eloah* to deliver them from this unjust imprisonment were swallowed by the height of the mountain. Held there by an invisible barrier at the mouth of the cave that had trapped them inside alone.

The months passed with no-one ever the wiser of what would become of them after their children were born. Their questions never left the cave as they wept with terror day in and day out. They would never know because when their bodies started to purge the fatherless beings, the mothers didn't survive. They were never meant to. They died having only been vessels to deliver Azazel and the other fallen *Archs* into this realm.

The first day the babies had cried next to their dead mothers for the whole night. By the next day they had grown teeth and had eaten the meat of the women who bore them. By the third day, when they could walk and explore their new home, the only remnants of the two hundred women were their bones, surrounded by the pleas for help scratched onto the walls, written in their own blood.

Azazel, then a small boy with blond hair, had emerged from the cave, his face and hands a bloody mess as his tiny feet stepped onto the snow, melting each patch, forming into sprouts of grass that suddenly grew in their place. Three other children, Semjaza, Jamoriel and Balotel stepped out behind him. The other 196 children remained deep inside. Still not used to their new bodies, their new skins, their new vessels, or their new Earthly powers.

"*Now, finally,*" Azazel thought as he took in the mountain air, feeling his skin tingle with cold. He closed his eyes and pushed out a breath. It became a blue formless cloud that expanded across the entire mountain top, melting the rest of the snow, turning it into an oasis of perpetual springtime on a mountain dominated by winter. "*You can have your throne Eloah,*" Azazel thought as he looked towards the sky. "*I will rule here and find out why you treat them so.*"

Had anyone seen them, they would have seen small children who looked like they had only just mastered walking, but this was not who they were. The blood had dried on the cherubic face of the young Azazel who now scanned the area soon to be called the *Village of the Gods*. In his face remained neither anger nor resentment, but only a curiosity for all he surveyed from this mountain top. From the cave, Semjaza joined him, together they walked out to the edge of the mountain top and peered down below to the bottom. Had they been human they would not have been able to see the farm below from this high above, but they weren't human. If they wanted, they could see all of creation through the *Shekinah*.

"We will build here," Azazel said.

"Yes master," answered Semjaza.

Azazel's powerful eyes looked down to the village below. On a farm he saw Madina, a little girl the same size as he, standing next to her mother milking a black cow. The girl's hand rested on her mother's shoulder as if steadying herself from the ground that could shake at any moment. Azazel watched the little girl leave her mother's side and walk over to a black bull behind them. Azazel's head tilted and he felt his pulse quicken. Wonder filling his heart at the sensation itself.

"*No, the beast will harm you,*" Azazel thought. "*He'll throttle your little body to a bloody pulp, why do you not inherently know of this danger?*"

Madina arrived at the bull's head. The animal's coiled strength in front of her was like a wall of muscle and speed. Unaware of the latent danger, the little girl reached out to the bull's face and touched its nose. The bull lowered his head in play with the little girl in front of it. High above, Azazel's eyes softened as he gazed on the interaction, a joyful smile left his face.

Down below, Madina was suddenly taken with the thought to look up to the top of Mount Hermon but all she saw there was a cloud covered peak. She couldn't see Azazel standing at the edge smiling at her. Confident that the bull would not harm her because Azazel would not let it. Semjaza looked on with a new worry.

"Why would *Eloah* create them in this way?" Azazel asked of his oldest ally, not waiting for an answer before he offered his solution. "We must help them, Semjaza. They know not of the danger that is all around them in this realm."

Semjaza though, was not concerned with the humans, he never had been. His thoughts were a whirlwind over the safety of this location and how the humans would take to being led by them. How they would take to being led by Azazel.

Long before, above the firmament, Semjaza had also watched *Eloah* use numbers to set a course for the formation of humans. He too had seen the numbers spiral into a perfect ratio, radiating out from every natural creation along the way. He'd seen how the ratio danced into place like a puzzle chasing a mystery, chasing itself into infinity, getting closer and closer to perfection, yet never reaching it, not like him and not like them. They were the first creations, born perfect and breathed forth from the will of *Eloah* to help with building the realm. Like the other *Archs* – fallen and higher – Semjaza didn't waste time chasing perfection or admiring arrays of numbers. Saving his admiration instead for Azazel, who was the most perfect being he'd ever seen.

Azazel was the first of the firsts, beautiful with a light Semjaza could only mimic as he had listened to Azazel, to describe *Eloah*'s latest evolutions.

"If humans are the painting, then the numbers are the colours and we're the painters," Azazel had observed.

Semjaza had watched as Azazel's perfect spirit became enamoured by the humans, an emotion that turned to worry when he learned that the humans would wander the Earth for eons, never realizing the gift that *Eloah* had given them. The worry formed into questions about why *Eloah* made them exist as if living in a dark cave, watching shadows from outside dance on the walls; shadows which told humans of a perfection beyond what they could conceive. These were questions that only Azazel was brave enough to ask – angry that, while fear would bind humans to safety, it would also bind them to perpetual darkness.

Azazel saw *Eloah* choose to blind humans to their own beauty and power. *"How cruel!"* Azazel had thought. *"Like building a wondrous monument to honour a blind man who would never gaze upon it."*

Azazel had pleaded with *Eloah* to give humans a higher form of consciousness but *Eloah* had refused. The trouble started when Azazel chose not to listen.

Angered by the injustice, Azazel vowed to descend from above the firmament and bring knowledge to the humans, but he'd need help. He gathered nine other powerful *Archs* – only thirteen were created including Semjaza. His fallen *Archs* then gathered 191 *Seraphim* and descended to Earth. He bound them all to an oath that they would follow and help him. Semjaza had been reluctant at first but he couldn't stand the thought of his own existence without Azazel if he didn't follow. In his mind, he told himself that he had followed because he knew Azazel – ever the painter – only thought in broad strokes, wide intentions and grand gestures. He knew Azazel would need someone who thought in detail, strategy and logic. Whatever Azazel wanted to create by coming here, Semjaza knew he would need someone to show him how.

The children walked from the edge of Mount Hermon to gather the others.

"Come master, we will get their attention soon enough, but first we must set a perimeter and start building. The *Shekinah* is good here," Semjaza urged, as the pair returned to the cave.

Azazel followed in step behind Semjaza but Madina had taken his interest. He looked over his shoulder at her, through the *Shekinah*, still playing with the bull down below.

"Will they like us, Semjaza?" he asked.

"They'll worship us, master," Semjaza said with concern framed on his face. "But first *they'll* try to kill us."

It was then Azazel's turn to feel concerned. He knew Semjaza's cold logic would never entertain mercy, even for little girls playing with bulls. "When they do, Semjaza, please try not to harm them," he said.

Some cycles later but before *'conquest'* had a formal name, peace had been all anyone knew in the land between the rivers. But Sargon of Akkad, once a poor farmer from the Akkadian lands, had suddenly decided that he too could be immortal. To do so, Sargon sought to control something others had not thought of yet, even though it was all around them – land. He discovered that power over people also gives one power over the land they stood on, and something had shown Sargon that the land between the rivers was worth controlling.

His armies had set out, riding over village after village, conquering the land in his name. No-one knew what spawned his conquest but tales of murder and rape would arrive at the ears of villagers long before Sargon's riders ever would. No-one had envisioned that such a lust for power would manifest itself in their time. The very concept was foreign to all, which is why none were prepared when Sargon came for their land.

The young of that time had learned that conquest was human nature, repeating the lie in perpetuity. The old thought Sargon's conquest was foolish. They knew one could control land as easily as asking wind to remember your face – that mankind was like such wind over the face of land; cooling for a time but once gone, never to return.

The strong, however, spoke of another concept to ensure their descendants survival, they called it, *"empire"*. Many rose to oppose Sargon but all were crushed. The clever tried bribery but Sargon's generals had raised their leader to the status of deity, and their loyalty could not be corrupted. The cunning tried ambush but Sargon's armies remained five steps ahead. It was as if each morning, something showed them what tomorrow held. And so village after village fell to Sargon's power. Only one remained free, the little town of Ur where Enoch had made his first home. On one cool desert night, Sargon's riders, led by Marek the Scorpion rode for Ur. Not to pillage, that would come later. That night they came for Enoch.

In Enoch's mud brick home, he had been sleeping soundly next to his wife, their baby between them. In his sleep, a familiar dream played. It would always start the same. He'd be floating in a black expanse with nothing to hold him in place except for his will. He may have been moving or he may have been at rest. It was impossible to tell because there was no edge and no horizon in the dream. Just a blackness that felt as if it might grow a texture at any moment but it never did.

Somewhere, lights would appear, move across a section, then stop and then disappear again. After a while, a tone would sound followed by another, then more changing in pitch and inflection. The tones would settle into a pattern that rose and fell, heralding a golden structure emerging from the darkness.

Lines of golden material would materialize and cross into each other, forming into a shape Enoch had never seen, angles he could never replicate himself. First unclear and undefined but then gaining density. The shape would flash for a moment and then disappear again, never allowing Enoch to see fully what it was.

This night the structure didn't appear because the sound of a hundred hooves beating on the ground had awakened him from sleep.

"Edna, wake up, something is coming," Enoch called to his sleeping wife. Edna awoke from sleep to clay pots shaking from the vibration of the approaching horses. The baby awoke too and filled the air with a cry. Edna moved over and nestled him to her bosom.

"Sargon's riders! They have come for you! You must flee, Enoch!" she said, her voice shaking with a whispered fear as she gathered her robes with the baby in her arms.

"No, they would torture you," Enoch said, hurriedly tying his robes. He went outside to investigate. The thundering horses arrived, an army of them, ridden by soldiers from Akkad, instantly recognizable by their shingled armour and cone-shaped head plates. They were indeed Sargon's men, holding fires to illuminate their path but it was their faces that burned with anger. From the front Marek the Scorpion emerged.

He dismounted his horse and walked over to Enoch. His movements were slow and deliberate but his eyes betrayed a mind that calculated quickly. His sun-tanned and roundish face bore no expression as his tall frame towered over Enoch. When he spoke his voice was soft, barely above a whisper. To anyone who heard but didn't see him, they would have thought they were listening to a gentle man. Marek the Scorpion was not.

"Enoch the Scribe, you are summoned to answer for your crime, come or we shall rid this plain of your family." There wasn't the slightest hint of danger in his voice, as Marek issued his threat.

"What crime? I've committed none," Enoch replied, as he stepped forward putting himself between Marek and the doorway of his home.

"Sargon has learned that you teach of holding the tithe ahead of the harvest, you're to be imprisoned for this crime."

"The frost will be early Marek, the new crops will die in the ground. If the people offer their stores they'll all die by the warming."

"Then so be it! Men, burn his dwelling!" Marek ordered, ignoring Enoch's plea.

"No, I'll come! Do no harm to my family, my son is only newly born."

Edna came outside as Enoch was being led to a waiting horse, his hands already bound. The soldiers ushered him onto the beast, he looked back and saw Edna's eyes speak to him what her voice couldn't convey. He saw that she was scared; behind that he saw she was angry.

"Do not fear, Edna. I'll return to you soon, my love. Warn the others!" Enoch said, not really believing his own words.

"Where are you taking him?" she asked Marek, who was preparing his men to depart. "Enoch is a righteous man, why do you take him and anger *Eloah*?" she continued.

"Fear not," Marek scoffed. "Your Enoch will be safe, he walks with *Eloah* now!" The brigade exploded with laughter as they took Enoch away.

It had been in the days of old when Enoch the Scribe had first counted the days and nights and saw that they signified changes in the moon. From the study, a number had emerged – the number was twenty-eight. Enoch had counted twenty-eight days from when the moon left the sky to return again in full glory. He counted that thirteen of these moons formed one cycle. Studying the path of the sun and moon over the cycles, he learned something about this one; the summer equinox would start with the sun turning black in the sky – a danger waiting for king, commoner and all else who lived between the rivers.

They should have planted the crops one equinox earlier but it had been too late. Enoch had discerned that the eclipse would herald an early winter frost that would see all the crops die in the ground. Tens of thousands of people would starve to death. The only way to survive was to hold the grain tithes to Sargon's stores. Enoch issued an urgent edict to warn the people. Riders had fanned out across the land between the rivers and warned the people in time. For this, no man between the rivers could ever speak ill of Enoch the scribe but when Sargon learned of Enoch's initiative, he ordered his own edict. Marek the Scorpion had just carried it out.

The journey from Ur to Sargon's prison in the Negev desert lasted a moon, stopping at villages to rest, eat and show the other tribes between the rivers what happens when you defy Sargon of Akkad. That even the great Enoch the Scribe was not above his wrath.

Word travelled of Enoch's capture and many came to see the procession of horses leading to Canaan to see if it was true. Some cried at the sight of Enoch when they saw that it was. On the night of the twenty-eighth day of his journey, a new moon appeared in the sky. The procession had crossed the Negev desert to arrive at a prison complex built on a hill.

Enoch saw the Canaanite soldiers in charge of the compound beat and kick at the inmates while other guards stood on towers looking out to the valley for attacking tribes. As they ascended the winding paths to the top, they saw vacant-faced tribes of Edomite slaves carry the dead mangled bodies of the recently released. The procession was followed by wolves behind them and vultures circling above. The sound of bleating goats mixed in with the yells from guards and the grunts of forced labour. The prison was not completed yet. Dozens of inmates smashed at large boulders while other groups carried the broken pieces to the construction around the perimeter. A row of cells lined one edge backing on to a sheer drop behind it but more were being constructed to complete the square.

Marek led Enoch to an old cell where eight men sat tied to the ground. Enoch saw their skin was loose and nearly hanging off their bodies. Their beards and hair were grown and dirty. The cell smelled powerfully of disease and moisture, a rancid smell that hung in the air, lacking direction or source as if whoever built this room had woven it into the layout.

Imprisonment had made it impossible for Enoch to tell if these men were young or old. He saw a thin man etching a vertical line onto the large blank wall using his elongated fingernail. Just above his mark was another grouping of five more. Another man called to him, "Has it been six cycles already?"

"Today marks the first day of the seventh," the thin man replied. "I fear I shall see the remainder of my days in this cell."

Another prisoner, an old bearded man, was telling a tale while the others listened closely. When Marek appeared with Enoch, they all had stopped, regarding him with eyes that were hard, searching for weakness or favour, whichever was closer to achieve. The look told Enoch that in this prison, not all men were created equal. Another man, missing an eye, was the first to notice that it was Enoch.

"Enoch! In the name of *Eloah* and all that is holy! They have captured even Enoch the Scribe. Is no-one safe from Sargon's madness?"

Their hard eyes softened when they realized they were in the company of Enoch the Scribe. In the memory of days outside the walls, they remembered stories of the brilliant man who had first deciphered the stars and used the knowledge to feed all the tribes. Their regard of him changed, it could have been with genuine reverence or maybe with opportunistic hope. Enoch the Scribe might warrant attention from the guards previously destined for them. Enoch would later wish the man hadn't spoken at all. He'd also learn how Marek the Scorpion had earned his name.

Marek's quiet countenance suddenly turned on the outspoken prisoner, as if his rage was a boiling cauldron beneath his demeanor. Without warning, he suddenly kicked the prisoner in the face. The others moved out of the way when he fell. Marek was suddenly upon him with a swiftness that saw his hands grab the rope tied to the man's feet and wrapping it tightly around the man's neck in one deadly motion. The man had never thought death would sweep in from above him today.

"Where is your *Eloah* now? Foolish dog!" Marek spoke through gritted teeth, his face inches away from the dying man's.

The man strained for air but Marek was intent on making an example of him. He squeezed until the man's body went limp with death. Marek released him, the man's body fell to the ground and Marek stood, his chest heaving up and down as the other men diverted their gaze from him.

He motioned to another guard to untie and remove the dead man. They carried his body out of the cell.

Marek then turned to Enoch. "You see, Enoch, *Eloah* will not save you here." He laughed as he led the other guards out of the cell.

The prisoners fell silent but it wasn't long before they slowly returned to what they had been doing, the moment of random violence passing as if it was a natural occurrence. Marek had achieved his goal, for fear now found a home in Enoch's heart.

The old bearded man picked up from where he'd paused, the thin man left his marking on the wall and walked over to a clay jug covered by rock in the far corner. His eyes darted outside to make sure no guards were coming. Enoch watched him closely as he listened to the old man's tale.

"Before any of you were born, many cycles ago, something occurred that no man has been able to explain. All over the land, children – girls only – disappeared never to be seen again. It is said they were taken by *Eloah*, who enjoyed the cries of mothers searching for their children...."

The thin man, Abner, wasn't listening. He was carefully removing a rock from the top of the jug. His neck bent downwards as he smelled the contents of the jug. His face grimaced and turned away at the smell before he whispered to his mate across the cell.

"Baako, bring it, this may be ready."

Baako was a shirtless mute, bearing the scars of countless beatings. He walked over to his own corner and grabbed a cloth that had been made from his shirt, the little bundle moving with the life of something small and alive inside. He brought it to the thin man and carefully unwrapped the cloth to show a little mouse stirring inside. The pair's movements became surgical, whatever they were doing was of the utmost importance, at least to them, at least here. Outside the prison walls they could have been learned men of wisdom but here, confinement had made madness seem perfectly normal.

"Hold the mouth open," Abner instructed him. Baako obliged. Abner dipped his fingernail into the clay jug and scooped up a portion of the brown liquid inside. He brought it carefully to the mouth of the mouse and poured it inside. Baako let the mouse go.

The mouse scurried about the cell frantically in search of freedom, stopping at the feet of each man as the old man's tale of missing children droned on. At Enoch's feet, the mouse stopped and fell to its side. The mouse's stomach heaved up and down and became erratic. Convulsions took hold of the mouse's feet. Baako and Abner smiled.

"It is working, by the glory of *Eloah*, it is working!" Abner said.

"You have fashioned a poison?" Enoch asked. "Do you believe Marek the Scorpion is foolish enough to drink your offering?"

The other men laughed at Enoch's words. Abner approached the dead mouse and scooped it up.

"Wise Enoch, this poison isn't for Marek. There's no escape from here but for when Sargon deems it so. This, wise Enoch the Scribe, is an escape of our own choosing." Abner accompanied his words with a version of the mad man's smile that Enoch had never encountered before – not that of an actual mad-man, but a man driven to madness.

"Do you not have hope? Do you not long for the day when Sargon comes to his senses and releases you?" Enoch asked. "...Releases all of us?"

"Hope doesn't reside within these walls, Enoch the Scribe. I pray you will learn it sooner than the man who just left," Abner said, returning to the jug and covering it again.

He raised his head to address the others. "It isn't ready, my brothers, when the mouse dies instantly, the poison will be ready for us."

The other men shuffled passively with the development. They truly cared little for hope, even the hope that death could be of their choosing, Enoch thought. The old bearded man paused his story and turned to Enoch. Age and poor light had made the man's eyes look like spheres of grey in his sagging face. His words though, saw through to what was in Enoch's heart.

"If I were Sargon of Akkad, raptured by his madness, I'd take the greatest scribe in the land and make an example of him. I fear for your days here, Enoch the Scribe, more so than ours," he cackled.

The days passed and routine took hold. The morning would start with the sound of guards praising the return of the sun. Their voices would travel through the granite walls of the complex as other guards threw stale bread and old vegetables into the cells.

The early morning would see the prisoners gathered in the courtyard and divided into three groups. One group was led to a quarry and in the evening would return with tales of giant men moving boulders with sounds emanating from their hands. Another group was led to a mine. They would return with accounts of a golden substance; soft, yet heavy and wrought from the ground to be taken to Sargon. The third group were kept apart from everyone.

That group remained in the courtyard where they waited under the sun or rain, passing the day aimlessly in the square. Some stayed silent, some formed groups to speculate if one would be chosen that day. Most days they would all return to their cells at day's end, but on other days a man would be chosen from the third group and led to the top of the mountain at dusk. A procession of elect people would follow them up but would return without him. The hands and attire of guards would be stained with his blood, sending a terror at being chosen for the third group permeating out to every man in the prison.

The moons passed and thoughts of Edna kept Enoch sane. Holding an image of her tightly in his mind so he'd not soon forget it. At night while the men slept, Enoch would whisper letters to her.

My Dearest Edna,

It seems I've grown accustomed to life here because the days have become shorter. I've counted 1,072 days here and I still long for your sight. I pray this feeling never wavers from my thoughts. Though I try to resist the ways of men here, I've still eaten all manner of vile animal, for if I don't my stomach will be empty. But I don't want to fill you with worry about my state. It is yours I worry about. I have a fear growing inside me that the land outside is changing, that something evil has taken hold of the elect and I cannot decipher it. Guard yourself my love.

My Dearest Edna,

Imprisoning the body does not count for much but imprisoning the mind is a most terrible thing indeed. I fear I have become dulled by the cycles. I assure you Sargon will never imprison my mind because I still long for the days of pondering over the mysteries, but here mysteries do not stay so. I still dream in the tones consumed in blackness as before, do you remember? What I've come to notice is that some of the tones repeat in a pattern but I do not know what they mean. Recently I've heard UR-RI-EL, but the pattern I hear most is A-ZA-ZEL. It is strange how what used to haunt my sleep now becomes my only form of study and I cling to its bosom as our child clung to yours. I remember those moments fondly, just thinking of our son now fills me with a wish to see what he has gained in appearance. I've so many questions and I long for the day when I can see you again and have you answer them. Does he walk now? He must. Was his first utterance, "Ima"? I'm certain it would be, since you're his world now. Just as surely as I know his first question will be where his, "Aba" is. He dances daily in my mind now but his face fades from my memory, everything is fading Edna, pray for me.

The cycles passed but Enoch had stopped counting them. He didn't need to. Abner's lines had grown by six more. The knowledge only reminded him of the time he'd already lost from his wife and son. One morning, Enoch's cell awoke to find that the old bearded man had died. The guards came to collect his body. They also collected Enoch.

They delivered him to a room where a hooded man, tall and with skin an unnatural shade of green, stood over a table of tools, the manner of which Enoch had never seen. Wood fashioned into spiked branches and metals made into rings that connected with each other. Enoch was placed in front of the table on a stump of wood. The man moved about making final preparations for whatever he was about to do. His hand tapped at the table anxiously. His breathing growled forth from his nostrils. He was waiting to begin something. *"But what? And on whose orders?"* Enoch thought.

The guards left, bowing their heads as Enoch's answer entered. Sargon of Akkad entered with two armed sentinels walking in step behind him. His robes and jewelry designated his status as supreme ruler, but his clipped stride, focused eyes and sullen expression signified he had a general's heart. His face was long, made more so by a dark beard that hung down obscuring his neck. The blue and crimson robes draped on him were adorned with golden ingots. When Sargon adjusted the sword at his side, the fragrant smell of lavender wafted into Enoch's nostrils. To Enoch, the presence of such clean clothes felt obscene in the septic prison. Hygiene was foreign to him now. He had been here too long.

"Enoch the scribe, does your time bode well?" Sargon asked.

"You know it does not. Six cycles have passed. My family waits without joy, *my King*. The injustice you do, is not only to me."

"You can earn your freedom," Sargon offered.

"How?" Enoch asked.

"You're to scribe an edict that all must tithe to me or face imprisonment, no matter the condition of the land, the position of the sun nor the face of the moon."

"You're king, I'm but a humble imprisoned scribe, who am I whose words have such great account now?"

"Do you know what they say of you in the land? They say, *'Enoch the scribe was taken by Eloah and now walks with him in the heavens'*. When they see that you scribe for me, they will call me *Eloah.*"

"This is blasphemous, I will not."

Sargon had expected this. He looked over to the hooded man and nodded. The hooded man walked over to Enoch, his steps heavy under his muscled body. The armed sentinels joined and together, held Enoch's arms and legs down, making his protests futile. The hooded man struck Enoch's head then reached down and grabbed one of Enoch's hands. He brought it up to his face and removed his mask. Enoch gasped at the sight.

The hooded man had one eye on his forehead and teeth like a dog's. His nose was no more than two viscous slits on his face. *"What monster created you?"* Enoch thought. When the hooded man snarled, the smell that escaped his mouth was of rotting meat. He brought Enoch's finger to his mouth and bit down on the elongated nail. The hooded man tore his head away removing the nail in one swift motion. Enoch's scream carried through the halls, terrifying even the men waiting to be sacrificed.

"What say you now, Enoch?" Sargon asked.

Enoch's breath had quickened and his heart was beating wildly. The pain was sending the sensation of a serpent running along his arm to his body and down his leg. "You are not *Eloah*, I will not, Sargon!"

"Then, wise Enoch the Scribe, the mysteries of the *Shekinah* shall continue to elude you. The Shekinah makes all things possible. All one needs is enough souls to believe it true. You will scribe the edict and I will be immortal!" Sargon said. Then, "Punish him!" he said to the torturer.

Enoch's scream again carried through the complex. It would be the first of many. At first Enoch's screams become a daily occurrence but when his injuries needed more time to heal the screams became weekly. When the injuries became graver, the screams turned to monthly. Over time, a scar where his right eye used to be, healed and took over his once kind face. Even when the only teeth remaining in his mouth were the ones he used to chew with and his nose had become a blackened lump on his face, he didn't scribe the edict. Even when his bones had been broken, healed, and then broken again– so that when he walked now, the joints in his arms and legs protruded at uncomfortable angles, through it all Enoch held fast. As the cycles passed and Enoch became an ugly shadow of his former self, Sargon was no closer to his edict.

My Dearest Edna,

I've not spoken to you in a stretch of time, in fact I've not spoken, thinking of what manner Sargon's beast will torture me in next. The new mouse Baako and Abner captured told me that I will lose one of my arms before I leave this realm. Such a wondrous little creature the mouse is otherwise. Though he often smells most foul. It robs me of appetite but the other men still save their food for me. 'You will need this so that your strength does not waver,' they say. I sometimes offer some to the mouse. I fear he needs it more than me, he grows rather thin. He is but bones now and his skin is gone. The mouse says Sargon will never let me die and that I should do it myself. I told him the thought of you keeps me from leaving this realm. He then told me most distressing news, 'Your wife is dead now, Enoch,' he said to me– is this true, Edna? Are you dead? I need to know so that I may join you if so. I await your answer my love but I must go now for the mouse calls to me to eat.

Abner had been etching his twenty-seventh mark on the wall when a new man was brought to the cell. The others had long died. Enoch and Abner were the only ones left now. The new prisoner – a soldier – had been taken from a village near Mount Hermon. Abner asked him of the world outside, while Enoch held the bones of the dead mouse, rocking back and forth on his own old bones.

"There's all manner of wickedness in the land, other soldiers have heard tales of men the shape of beasts that wander the forests. Winged serpents in the night sky that can carry off a man as easily as a wren does a blade of grass," the soldier said, his brown hair marked with a scar running along his scalp.

"Where has Sargon's wickedness come from?" asked Abner, still mixing his poison.

"From the *Bene Ha Elohim (children of Elohim)*," the soldier said with fear in his voice.

"He and the elect are counselled by them and it is true, they have brought many gifts to the people but their ways and customs are..." The soldier paused. "...strange." The man spoke in a scared tone.

Abner looked on with curiosity as he continued. "Who are they?" he asked

"It is said they descended from the stars, but no-one knows. My old sabba used to tell us, some cycles ago, a tribe of children suddenly appeared at the top of Mount Hermon. Gatherers had stumbled upon them and found there were no adults to exercise care over them, only children, mere babes, no more than the height of shrubs. He was sent to see himself. He approached their village and saw a boy, a mere boy with feet of a cheetah's swiftness. He saw the boy chase down a bear in the forest and bring it down with one blow to the head. Says he saw him carry it back to his village as easy as you would carry a bundle of cloth. They're not of this realm – of this I'm certain."

"Impossible, either your sabba was a drinker or you're telling tales. Children must be born of a woman, do you take us for fools?" Abner rebutted him. But the man's face didn't move. He believed the words he was saying.

"If you don't believe me, when you get out, go ask what happened to the Ammonite and Hittite mercenaries who went after them. They had heard that the *Bene-ha-Elohim* had fashioned a substance from the ground and wrought it into thin sheets that could be thrust into their enemies, killing them instantly. They gathered a force, three hundred of their strongest, to attack and steal the weapons, no doubt to also make vile slaves of them. They left for the battle but none ever returned, none have been seen since."

"But worshipping children? Who can believe such a tale? Who is their leader?" Abner asked sarcastically, the fantastic tale being the most entertainment he'd had in a long time. The revelry was clear from his incredulous grin. He peered over at Enoch to join in but Enoch was still looking upward towards nothing in particular. His mouth moved in a conversation Abner thought he was having with himself. Enoch's hand scratching at the knotted mess his hair had become. *"Poor Enoch wouldn't know what revelry felt like anymore,"* Abner thought before peering back to the soldier.

"They say *he's Eloah* and they call him Azazel," the soldier added. The word caught Enoch's attention. He interrupted his conversation with the dead mouse to suddenly glare at the soldier.

"No!" Enoch corrected with an unhinged tension lining his voice. "It is Ah-ZAH-zel! Your inflection must be on the middle tone! Say it correctly? You fool!"

The man regarded Enoch with an anger that changed quickly to pity once he saw the crippled old man Enoch had become, bitter now with age and disconnected from all reality.

"Who is the mad man?" the soldier asked Abner.

"If I told you, it is me who you would think mad, leave him be," Abner said, not wanting to crush the man's hope with the story of what had become of Enoch the Scribe. The prison's aim was to do that soon enough, Abner saw no need to help it.

The next day the soldier had been chosen for the third group, then chosen again in the early evening.The guards later descended the mountain with his blood on their hands. *"How lucky he was,"* Abner had thought, *"His sentence here to last only a day."*

My Dearest Edna,
I no longer fear that madness comes for me. I used to feel it creeping closer, day by day, cycle by cycle, but now that the mouse no longer whispers in my ear, I feel that I've avoided it. It never even told me its name, how rude of it I know, but I fear it grew silent at me because of a jealousy growing in it. You see, the guards have now taken to leaving me outside in the sun where it beats down on me but I sense no heat, in fact it helps me decipher the tones. The tones in my dreams, do you remember, my love? It seems the mouse does not approve of what I've deciphered from them. None here know the truth but I've found that the tones in my dreams are in fact words! They're words, my love. I suspect the mouse became consumed by jealousy for it knew that once I've deciphered the tones, the first thing I'll do is fashion them into a tale that tells of your beauty. To decipher them will be my greatest achievement yet because Sargon has now died and his son does not concern himself with me. They're words my love, they will be words for you!

My Dearest Edna,
Only numbness consumes me and the days pass by so quickly now. Pray for me my love, I gaze upon the thought of you but I no longer see your face, all I see is a void, waiting for me. Forgive me, I fear there is no other way to be with you. I will see you soon, my love, but wait for the words, wait for me."

On Enoch's last night in the prison he'd tried to sleep, but Abner had kept him awake with incessant coughing for the whole night. He had been fighting for the stale air of the cell, but it seemed that working in the mines had blackened his lungs, and that night, he coughed until the breath left his body. Abner had left this realm but not of his poison as he'd always hoped, it laid now in the corner of the cell next to his still body. Enoch rocked back and forth in anger at the dead man.

Enoch looked at his hands, now lined with age and brittle from non-use. His fingers had elongated and his body felt tired, his soul even more so. His eyes, unblinking, bored into Abner laying dead in the cell under the twenty-seven markings of the far wall. Every waking second of the night had felt like an eternity. *"How can I decipher the tones unless I can sleep?"* Enoch had thought when an idea came to him.

"Of course!" Enoch thought. *"The poison! It helps the mice to sleep, perhaps it shall help me too! Then the tones will be deciphered!"*

The sun was set to rise in moments. The guards had yet to discover Abner. Soon they would appear and also find Enoch, but they would surely not let him sleep. Enoch drank the foul liquid quickly, he stood back while he waited for sleep. When it came, it was not what he expected. He didn't expect to decipher the tones in the instant it took for his heart to stop. Knowing instantly that it was actually the language of *Eloah*. He didn't expect to use this language and he certainly didn't expect to meet Uriel for the first time.

As Abner's poisonous concoction careened through Enoch's body, his breath tightened and expelled itself in one last powerful exhale, forced from his lungs. His mind exploded with light as a dream took form. A dream he saw while his eyes were still open.

Enoch had been taken back to the expansive black of his old dreams. This time it whisked him upward. In the distance, if such a thing could exist in this realm, a tiny point of light grew into a sphere that pulsated with raw energy. Enoch felt his face warming from its heat.

Behind the sphere, a womanly figure appeared walking forward with her hands held in front of her, stopping just behind the sphere as would a dutiful servant. Her face downward, her hair of black held neatly in place by a golden band around her forehead. Her white robe dancing around her, as if affected by wind but there wasn't any there. Enoch thought it was changing shape reacting to her will.

His mind cleared, his senses returned and he understood why she stood subservient to the sphere with a deference that was palpable. The sphere was a powerful being but so was she.

The sphere could only be *Eloah* and she could only be one of his *Archs* spoken of by the men of the Shinar.

The sphere spoke into Enoch's mind but the words weren't the common Aramaic spoken throughout the land between the rivers. It was the tones that Enoch had heard in his dreams all his adult life, coming to him now as easily as the leaves of spring to an acacia tree, as if they had been with him the whole time. If there had been any doubt that it was the language of *Eloah*, it ended when the volume of *Eloah's* voice rattled the black expanse.

> **"You have come before me with defeated eyes,**
> **"Sullen, trodden but bearing no disguise.**
> **"Your once strong spirit, now burned to ashes,**
> **"As you reject a realm constructed of lies."**

There were no more mysteries for Enoch the Scribe. The sphere of light's billowing statements were projected at him with the force of an angry volcano. He saw the hand of judgment finally invade his shattered soul. The mask of madness was evaporating in the surety that where he stood now marked the beginning of his own long-awaited end. But words had escaped him, Enoch was silent. He opened his heart and looked up to *Eloah*, replying only with.

"Fragments of a dream."

The silence that ensued pierced Enoch's eardrums. A hollow yet acute sound that resonated all around him. Unbridled knowledge careened through his veins, the knowledge that had always been his ultimate quest. It was a knowledge he now felt bursting from him. He looked up at the sphere and in a voice that had the serenity of a lake on a windless day continued to explain why he drank Abner's poison.

"Fragments of a dream, that I once knew,
"Sparkling, shimmering, shining, blinding,
"Like the refraction of sunrays off the morning dew.
"Fragments of a dream,
"That lingered vicariously in my mind,
"Of what I used to be and know now,
"Shall never again be able to find."

"Is it that you have shared the company of hatred's vacuum?
"More so than you have love's glare?
"Or is it that you merely lack the valor to persevere?
"While heavily burdened with such despair?"

"No! It is neither my sense of injustice,
"Nor the fortitude of my will that condemns me to this misery and grief.
"But it is the pace at which time passed me by,
"And the fate chosen for me, by you, that I have a grievance with.

"But as you glare at me now with eyes bitter cold,
"Your past – behind you, yet your decision – bold.
"Your flawed reasoning allowing you to think what is tangible –
"A pillar upon which to support your reality,
"And what is merely in front of you- the concept of which to base your clarity.
"I see it isn't the longing of time forgotten that brings you now to my face,
"But the fear of continuing your existence being just a complex set of numbers,
"That is merely taking up space.
"Should you choose to accept your action,
        "Then I shall hinder you no more.
        "The direction of your fate -
        "As destiny awaits,
        "Is yours, I implore.
        "What say you?"

"I'm haunted by fragmented nightmares, Eloah,
"I'm at wit's end with carrying its guilt,
"I would be committing the most heinous atrocity,
"Should I decide to compromise,
"If only for the sake of continuing to live."

"Then this is what I shall give," replied the sphere of light.

The last syllable pulsated in all that was Enoch. All traces of anger, failure, frustration and fear dissipated from his being. Unencumbered by his aspirations and unconfined by his longing for Edna, he was finally free. Pain impeded his path no more as he was liberated from himself. The thoughts that lingered vicariously in his mind dispersed and faded as the windows to his soul slowly drew their curtains.

As Enoch awaited death, silence overwhelmed his senses again. He stared glaringly at the sphere of light but softened when he gazed on the beautiful figure next to it. She walked forth and leaned into Enoch's face. He saw her nose was round on her homely face and her lips and cheeks were full. An aura of astral fire raged around her taking shape as wings for a brief moment.

Enoch knew he was dying but he couldn't wrest his gaze from her eyes as they came so close to his now. Powerful and large, the colour of her pupils flashing from blue to green to black. They radiated and regarded Enoch with an expression impossible to decipher. It could have been admiration or it could have been pity. It would be lifetimes before Enoch would gain the wisdom to know, but he knew her name. In Enoch's mind a voice said, "*Uriel watches you.*"

Her lips came close and touched his. As she did a mist travelled from her lips into Enoch's mouth. Enoch's eyes widened as the mist shuttered through him like a bolt of lightning. Her face was disappearing, the expanse was evaporating. "*No,*" he thought, "*please stay.*"

Enoch's eyes opened and he found himself back on the cold floor of his cell where he felt something was different. He looked around and saw that, in fact, everything was. The air was now silent and as he sat up, he instantly felt a strange tingling sensation in his body. Something was wrong, he was not the man he was before and an image formed in his mind. An image he couldn't hold on to and couldn't clarify. He looked at his hands and saw his skin was smooth again and his fingers were full and strong.

Around him the cell was empty except for dust that floated around in the air as if with a purpose claimed long ago. In the distance the sound of calling birds carried to the cell. The noise had come from above. When Enoch looked up he was stunned to see a cloud move away from a giant hole in the ceiling that hadn't been there moments ago.

His eyes wandered over to the entrance to see the cell door had also eroded away. It seemed nature had long since started the process of reclaiming this prison. The walls were stained now with the shadow of moss that had long died when moisture had ceased to find its way to the prison in the form of human residents.

He clenched his fist and felt the power of a younger man tensing from his forearm again. Out of the corner of his eye, he caught the scurrying of a mouse. *"Odd,"* he thought. He should not have been able to, because that eye had long been taken by Sargon's torturer. How had his vision returned to normal now? How could he see out of both eyes again? A headache suddenly exploded in his mind from the returned vision. *"How am I not dead?"* he thought.

Sunlight drove a streak of light through the room landing on a spider's web in the corner just under the wall where Abner had marked his cycles. To Enoch's shock, the wall was now covered in marks from corner to corner. Varying hues of lines no doubt made by varying tenants of this room after him. *"This is impossible,"* Enoch thought.

Enoch hurried over to the empty corner where Abner had died just moments ago, *"Have I gone mad?"* he wondered. *"Is this death?"* The image of Uriel flashed in his mind again followed by another wave of the headache, he doubled over in pain. *"No",* he thought, *"I'm surely alive but how can this be?"* He looked at the wall again, Abner's marks had ended at twenty-seven, he was sure of it. Enoch had seen them only a moment ago, but when he finished counting the new lines, there were now over six hundred of them.

Apprehensively, he ventured outside, settling into the truth that this must be madness. What he saw there was shocking, the silence was all he heard. The air was still and vapid, telling Enoch that noise had not been heard here in centuries. The wind whistled through holes in new cells that had been completed in the square and around the courtyard. A thin sickly wolf saw him and became fearful, running away through the empty courtyard now tattered with the old bones of battles lost by all. Guard Rooms, previously inhabited, now contained no-one to remark the wind's or anyone's intrusion. The front gate and ramparts had been reduced to mounds of rubble. Enoch simply walked out of the prison as if there had never been one.

When he was clear of the gate, his stride become a powerful run."*If this was death, then Edna should be here too,*" he thought. "*If this was madness, seeing her would surely prove it real or not.*" Terror suddenly gripped Enoch because his thoughts were clear and alive with memories. His powerful strides beat against the desert sands as he ran to Edna with all the power he could muster. His head, still ringing with vertigo as he did so.

CHAPTER FOUR
Village of the Gods

Visibly shaken by Enoch's story, Holly said, "Edna must have been gone." Enoch didn't reply at first, instead adjusting the pocket square in his jacket.

"Time had indeed taken her, taken my family, taken anyone who had known them or knew me. When I made it back to *Ur,* my whole village was different and I was alone in a world that I no longer understood."

"How did you get back home?" Holly asked.

"It was true what the soldier had said, I met a...urrm...a man. I hesitate because he had the body of a man from head to waist but everything below was like a horse. He took me back to Sumer on his back."

"A *Centaur?*" Holly asked incredulous, "like in the Greek myths?"

"Stories have a way of changing the further they are told from their source but yes, the Greeks and Romans were taken to exaggeration but many of their tales talked of strange beings that once walked this realm. In fact their *Titans* are the *Bene Ha Elohim*. The one they call Apollo is in fact Azazel, but there were others too."

"What others?"

Enoch told Holly of magical creatures, many in fact. Some that could even talk as humans. He explained those were the wisest and best natured, trying simply to make sense of how they were to fit into the realm. That the only ones to be wary of were the ones born of mixing with humans. Dog headed men and human headed wolves who resided in the forests along with insects the size of lions.

"Even Fairies," Enoch said, "mischievous little creatures the size of a human foot and known for infecting the dreams of husbands."

"How?"

"They would kiss one, then fly away as the unlucky man would chase them. Sometimes the men never returned, chasing them all their lives."

Enoch told Holly of Nymphs too, harlots of such immense passion that they would pleasure a man until he died. That many of the young men of his age were killed this way.

"Dragons though, were the most formidable," he said. "Awesome hunters, they could mimic the sound of any animal or human they hunted."

"Where did they all come from?"

"Azazel made them."

"Why?"

"He fancied himself an artist and everything to him was a muse. His mistake was in thinking that *Eloah* would let him."

"What did you do in Ur?"

"Nothing. I felt like you do now. I wanted to know what was happening to me. If the legends of the *Bene Ha Elohim* were true, then I thought they might know. So I went to Mount Hermon. When I got there I didn't want to bring attention to myself so I sought work from a miner who gave me work in his iron mine. At night I slept in his shed."

"But wait, those other creatures aren't here now, where did they go?"

"The Bible tells that the great flood was due to the iniquity of man, that man had sinned against *Eloah* but this was not true. Humans hadn't known how to deal with these extra creations but they adapted as best they could. The flood had been *Eloah*'s way to rid the realm of all the creatures that Azazel had created, mainly the giants."

"Giants?"

"Indeed, the flood was to erase Azazel's experiment. I never counted on the knowledge surviving beyond the flood, in fact the giants had changed everything."

***

Azazel and *The Bene Ha Elohim* grew into tall, beautiful beings with slender yet powerful bodies, like young trees made of granite. Their dark, adult eyes gazed forth in menacing perfection while hundreds of human sensations and emotions careened through them. Radiant, white hair framed their faces with each a squared-jawed countenance perfectly even on each side.

At Azazel's side, Semjaza had offered his counsel and sword and together they defeated the first attacking tribes with a simple strategy. Semjaza and his captains first defeating the strength so Azazel could seduce the hearts after. In the end, Semjaza's predication had come true.

Stories of the *Bene Ha Elohim* spread out to the Indus Valley and onto the far eastern lands, all people came to know the tales of Azazel – the bringer of light and God-King of all of creation. But his kingdom grew too fast, his influence weakened the further it spread. Semjaza's solution was simple. Together, they showed humans like Sargon of Akkad that certain materials, wrought from the ground, could be used for making weapons, tools and jewelry. Teaching those who had gathered the most how to be kings and queens.

In hindsight, Azazel never saw that while the new kings and queens; raptured by the technology of jewels, weapons and the thought of abject power – willingly did his bidding, the *Bene ha Elohim* had become raptured by the beauty of royal daughters.

As the monarchies and fiefdoms grew and fought for supremacy, the *Bene Ha Elohim* would travel freely over the land and be treated like Gods by the elect and élite they had created. The daughters of the new kings and queens, enchanted by their words and displays of magic, formed their own notions to describe their enamourment for the *Bene ha Elohim*. They described being in their presence as like falling, but with feet on the ground. *Falling into love* they had called it.

Semjaza had watched all of this unfold with great worry but he understood the sense of enamourment growing in the hearts of the *Bene Ha Elohim*. He felt the same whenever he and Azazel were alone. He always had, though before, back above the firmament, there was no outlet for his love of Azazel. All expression there was sterile and devoid of desire. Now, with an earthly body, subject to human emotions, they were unlocked and came forth like a song previously trapped in the mind of a composer with no instrument to play it.

Unlike Azazel and the others though, Semjaza wore no unneeded adornments and didn't grow hair on his face. He never darkened his eyes and kept his white hair close to his head in perpetual preparation for battle, his face remaining as hard as his armour.

Still, in his quiet moments he would count the lazy days he had spent with his head rested in Azazel's lap as they watched humans revel in the new technology. While Semjaza would secretly revel in the sensation humans called 'touch'. Sun filled days with no pressing cares to invade their thoughts, they would be together at the edge of the *Village of the Gods* on Mount Hermon. Azazel, emitting a creation tone, vibrating through the *Shekinah*, creating an invisible nest of ether that would suspend them in the air from sunrise to sunset. The day passing under them quietly as Semjaza rejoiced that, for those moments Azazel was his and his alone.

Azazel's fingers would run gently through Semjaza's hair. Semjaza could have sat there for eternity listening to Azazel's tales from the far reaches of the societies they had created. He remembered the last time they had spent such a day together. It had also been the last day Semjaza would ever think of Azazel as being his and his alone.

"You know..."Azazel had started. "...In *Sumeria* they call me *Enki*, it means *Lord of the Earth*. In idols there, they have even given me wings, Semjaza," Azazel remarked. "They call us the *Announaki* – what a pleasant sounding word, do you not agree?"

Semjaza hadn't replied, instead enjoying the moment for what it was – a chance to be close to Azazel, *"There were so few chances now"*, he thought. It seemed Azazel had also developed a sense of enamourment. One that had grown too big to be focused solely on Semjaza anymore. It had started wandering long before, but unlike the others, his enamourment had been wandering closer and closer to one special, human woman.

Azazel's fingers had stopped their play in Semjaza's hair and Semjaza sensed why. *"It was happening again"*, he thought. Semjaza felt Azazel's gaze turn from him to the edge of Mount Hermon. Over it, through the *Shekinah*, and down to the village below. Landing at the little girl who played with bulls. Azazel had long watched her become a beautiful woman.

Azazel would often gaze at Madina through the Shekinah, while a different emotion would spike through

Semjaza's heart. Spurned by a simple question he could never answer. *"Why would he love her – a simple girl with no more intellect than a bull?"* He'd asked himself.

"Does he not know that I love him so?" Semjaza had wondered. *"He must have seen."*

It was true, Azazel knew the genesis of every human emotion as if they were the strands of hair that fell before his eyes. He used Eloah's creation tones as if they were extensions of his own fingers. Using them to create in anyone, any emotion he desired. He must have long noticed Semjaza's gaze holding his for longer than was needed.

But by then, Azazel had long noticed something else. He'd seen how the kings between the rivers carefully chose wives to bear them sons, he wanted the same. He needed the same. Semjaza knew then that Azazel would never be his.

"Why do you not revel, brother?" Azazel had asked instead, "Do you feel you're so above the humans that the touch of one of their women doesn't entice you?"

"I am above the humans," Semjaza replied coldly, "So are you, master."

"Is this why you do you not take a wife as the others do? Can you not see that we've created a society where justice reigns alongside pleasure and the people here are filled with knowledge? Do you not long for the joy the others sense when they lay with a woman, thrusting their phallus into them until they're raptured with ecstasy? The others tell me the human women scream with such pleasure at this, some men too, demanding more and more."

Semjaza sighed, Azazel's idealisms Semjaza could have done without but to take them away would mean taking away what made Azazel so beautiful.

"In my thoughts," Azazel started, "I ponder over what the humans will create when they know what we know, when we teach them what we know."

But Semjaza was uninterested, his ideals were never as lofty.

"In my thoughts, master, we build an army of the humans. Arm them with power beyond anything they could imagine, and attack the higher realms to reclaim your glory once and for all."

It was Azazel's turn to sigh, he knew Semjaza's concern was only for their safety, but to Azazel, the higher realms held little now. On this realm, they could create beautiful things, eat delicious meals and revel in the pleasure they give, and that was given to them. Storming the higher realms was the last thing he wanted.

"Why must you live in the past my dear, Semjaza?" Azazel asked, reaching out and placing his hand on Semjaza's face and running his fingers along the powerful jawline of his truest follower. Semjaza's eyes closed in the comfort of Azazel's touch, leaning into it unconsciously as a gentle breath left his nose.

"I know you feel *Eloah* wronged me, wronged us, but I don't want to bicker. *He* can rule the heavens! I'll rule here and I'll do so justly, much unlike *He* ever could."

Semjaza felt himself raptured by Azazel's words again. The moment ended when he slowly opened his eyes, remembering that to show weakness in the open was to invite danger. "Peace reigns now, master, but we will have to fight again. One day more armies will raise to challenge us, we must be ready," Semjaza said.

Azazel smiled at him, the smile of a dreamer facing the logic of the one charged with making his dream possible. "With you in charge of our security, oh wise Semjaza, I'm certain no human army will ever match us in battle."

Azazel returned his gaze to the town below, returning to Madina. "But until that day comes, *wise one*, try to enjoy this for you are a God in your own right!"

Azazel got up and left the invisible pocket of air, leaving Semjaza alone. Semjaza watched as Azazel glided down to the edge of Mount Hermon where he stopped and bent down to the soft, brown earth. He kneeled and made a perfect circle in the dirt with his finger. He then found its perfect centre and touched it. A purple flower sprouted from the point, its stem twirling upward until the bud opened to hang thirteen petals in the air. Azazel picked it from the ground and brought the flower close to his face. He closed his eyes and blew a breath onto the petals. The bud suddenly died, its stem withered and became a brittle puzzle, waiting for the slightest breeze to crumble and scatter it. After a second, the colour returned to its petals and the stem came to life again.

Semjaza had looked on with the face of a hardened general led by a gentle soul. Like the flower, a pain in his heart grew, then died, only to grow again.

"It isn't the human armies I fear most," Semjaza spoke softly to himself, as he watched Azazel disappear down Mount Hermon. His master had changed that flower for a special person, Semjaza knew. Semjaza shut his eyes tight, trying to banish the sense of loss rising in him.

***

Madina's black locks of hair fell in tight curls around an oval-shaped face dominated by large, kind eyes. That afternoon, her robes had been flowing gently about her while she collected corn for the coming harvest. It had been late in the day and the sun had started to descend behind Mount Hermon in front of her. Soon the daylight would give way to the encroaching darkness and the cool of night. Madina was looking forward to rest as the basket she held gained more and more weight from the fresh stalks she picked.

She paused to wipe sweat from her brow. When she reached for another stalk, her hand, now slippery, lost grip and an ear had fallen. She bent to pick it up but when she stood up, Azazel was suddenly behind her, having appeared from nowhere she could discern.

She jumped in fright, dropping the basket. Spilling the contents around her feet. When she fell to her knees again, it was not to retrieve the corn stalks but to worship her *God*.

"Do not bow to me, I'm sorry, I didn't mean to startle you." Azazel said, reaching down and softly helping her rise, placing his hand at her waist.

"My name is….."

"I know who you are," she had said, instantly embarrassed that she would interrupt him. Her cheeks swelling with red when she looked into Azazel's shimmering black eyes, her heart quickening in his presence.

Sharp at the chin and wide at the top with hair growing wildly back from his hairline, as if seeking to escape his head at full speed, each individual feature on Azazel's face was quintessentially human, Madina thought. He had wide, square shoulders, high cheekbones, powerful hands and smooth skin of an almost golden hue. But together, their perfection made it clear to her that Azazel was something else, not of this realm. Her gaze couldn't hold his, though her heart longed to do so. *"He was so beautiful..."* she had thought, *"...so powerful, even as I'm sure he tries to mask it in front of me."*

"Why do you visit me, great *God-King*? In Sargon's courts there are many women who would love the company of Azazel, I'm just a simple girl gathering stalks of corn. I fear the harvest is more interesting than I, *my lord*." Madina had rambled, her head held low.

Azazel reached for her chin, guiding her eyes to his. "Which is more beautiful?" he asked, "a queen's hand taught grace since birth, or the hands of a simple girl whom grace has found naturally?" Azazel reached for her hand and brought it forward to his. He opened it and placed the purple flower in her palm.

Madina gasped. The flower was cold to the touch. The day was still warm but the flower was colder than water in the dead of night. Madina's hand flinched from the sudden sensation. Azazel reassured her by bringing her hand back to his. She ran her fingers over the petals and down the stem.

"Surely the queen's, my lord." Madina replied, her chest tightening with abated breath, her fingers twirling the purple flower. She had never seen any other like it near Mount Hermon, she never would again.

Azazel reached for her chin, again raising her gaze to his. "I disagree," he said. "To me, true beauty only resides in the simple and in my thoughts I have willed that you should one day have my eyes, so that you may see how beautiful you are."

She couldn't help the smile that grew across her face. Love had planted a seed in her heart. A seed Azazel nourished as he visited her every day after that. A seed that blossomed into love when he finally approached her parents and asked for her hand in marriage.

Her parents thought they were harvesting a blessing from the Gods. They couldn't have known that it would be a curse. No-one could have known that the curse would, in fact, be on all of them.

***

Many cycles later, Madina would become the favoured mother of the land between the rivers. Her marriage to Azazel bringing to her worship from all – worship she tried her best to live up to though by then, it had become harder and harder to do so. The daily rumbling thuds coming from beyond Mount Hermon made sure that she never would. Her round eyes, once tinted with kindness and full of attention, were now tired and sunken. Her skin had gained the yellowish tint of jaundice and the veins in her hands now protruded visibly.

In the centre of her village, she stood one day wondering where it had all gone wrong, wondering if she could ever return to that simpler time long ago. But by then she had come too far from the little girl who played with bulls to ever go back.

THUD

A resounding 'thud' suddenly erupted from the distance, shaking the ground under her feet. That morning, as most others now when the sun was nearing mid-day, she held a ladle. Next to her sat a cauldron, from where she poured portions of soup made from corn husks, into bowls carried by the villagers who were lined up in front of her. The cauldron shook slightly from the thud but didn't fall over. She heard the noise of the ladle scraping the bottom. *"There will not be enough,"* she thought. *"There was never enough."*

Still, tucked into her now greying locks of hair, in the space above her left ear, was the purple flower Azazel had made just for her cycles before. Here it had sat since the days of Enoch first whispering letters to Edna in Sargon's prison.

At first, the thought of an immortal flower, made just for her, was a warm one that had filled her with ever more love for Azazel as the cycles had passed. But by that day, the day Kokabel would be banished, its cold petals only reminded her of what she'd done, that what they all had done was more than just wrong, it was unnatural and the punishment was more than she was willing to take.

THUD

Another thud shook the ground. Madina then poured another bowl and another stomach fought back starvation for another day. To Madina, the fall of the *Village of the Gods* had started this day. She'd soon learn that the rules the Gods played by were more complicated than a simple girl like her had ever imagined.

First, it had been the bees disappearing, leaving the honey-combs empty. When the flowers didn't bloom, many had thought that another instance of early frost was descending on the land between the rivers. But when the fruits and vegetables didn't pollenate, fear had set in. The blight that came next saw only the corn continue to grow. The first to starve and die had been the farm animals, it was not long until people began to follow.

Corn husk soup became all that remained for sustenance, the taste of meat having long become a forgotten one. In despair, the people turned to their *Eloah*, they turned to Azazel but he couldn't help them. Madina though, tried her best to help.

THUD

Another crashing thud rumbled over the land, like a thunder roll coming from deep in the ground. The suddenness of this one made her flinch, reminding her that she must never stop trying. She couldn't let her people starve. She looked out at them, the famine having robbed them of attention, as they walked forward to her with the dull eyes of mal-nourishment.

Around everyone the murmur of massive voices, distant but loud, had stunned them all into silence. Daily, the loud bursts of revelry would carry to them from the source of the thuds, as if mocking at their shuffled steps. The voices often followed by the rasping noises of distant moving earth, shaking the people's steps as they waited for their daily ration of soup.

THUD

This one was louder and heavier than the others. Kokabel's unmistakable footfalls, Madina knew. The people in line tried to keep balance by holding onto each other. Some folks lost balance under their own weakness.

THUD...THUD...THUD-THUD

A series of thuds suddenly shook the cauldron next to Madina again. She heard loosened boulders rumble down the slopes in the distance. She attempted to ignore the noises as if they were nature's own breath but the sound had been like hundreds of trees crashing down at once. She couldn't help but flinch. The sudden jolt of her head as she tried to balance herself loosened the purple flower from her hair. It fell, landing in the mud by her feet. She bent down to pick it up but paused just before her fingers wrapped around the stem. She couldn't do it, feeling the action would be obscene.

"How does my vanity help my people now?" she asked herself. She thought, "it doesn't", and left the flower where it had fallen, where it would remain for six hundred cycles until the first great *Council of Archs*. Madina instead looked up to Mount Hermon where she knew Azazel watched, hoping he would understand.

***

High above, Azazel and Semjaza had indeed been watching, the clouds moving under them while Azazel pondered over the villages below, focusing on his wife's village and his queen's choice. Semjaza peered over at the look of loss in Azazel's eyes; the look telling Semjaza that while Azazel did understand, the pain was just as at present.

From their vantage point, they saw all the villages near Mount Hermon and beyond, watching a death march over them all. The villagers, remaining powerless to stop its approach. Distant fires burned as people moved around with hunger slowing their steps. In the land between the rivers, people had become like jackals, scarcity having caused lecherous instincts to come forward in them, with crime and violence awaiting all from the shadows. This hadn't been what Azazel intended.

"Why does *Eloah* do this to us, Semjaza?" Azazel had asked. "Does he not bless our unions with the earth women?"

"It isn't the unions that angers *Him*, master," Semjaza had replied, "It is Kokabel and the others."

"Will they always be so large?" Azazel asked as he watched Madina try to feed her people below. Their pleas for deliverance had long turned from Azazel to her, their worship soon would follow too.

"When they further breed, they'll become smaller but they'll always be superior to humans, master. The *Shekinah* to them is just another sense – as common to them as humans know honey by its smell." Semjaza said, "They are perfect."

Azazel turned to the source of the rumbling thuds. He gazed beyond the mountain to a plain of dry, red earth where his son, Kokabel, was holding an oak tree and drawing shapes in the earth for his cousins to see. Two hundred of them, men and women, larger than hills stood side by side listening attentively to Kokabel, who was the largest of all. All with hair the colour of fire except for Kokabel, who had the black locks of his mother Madina.

Kokabel held the oak tree as if it were the oar to a child's boat. He taught what he'd discovered about the world to his cousins, showing them how to use the *Shekinah* to build monuments that humans could never mimic.

It had been the people who had come up with a name for them, *Nephilim – children of the fallen*. The children of the *Bene Ha Elohim* and human women had all been born as normal babies but within days grew to be larger than the tallest trees. They all had six fingers and toes and their voices would echo for miles, scaring birds and beasts from the land, with some never returning.

Azazel, watching, remembered how, as children, their games would rumble the ground like a rolling storm of earthquakes. How as teenagers their massive eyes had peered forth with instant knowledge of all they gazed upon, every mystery revealed to them through the *Shekinah*. But he never considered that, as adults, it would take entire herds of sheep to fashion robes for them. entire generations of cows to feed them.

In the land between the rivers, the question on everyone's mind, that no one dared to ask was, *"What will happen to us when the Nephilim start to have children themselves?"*

Azazel knew then that the land between the rivers would not survive long enough to warn the rest of humanity. "What are we to do with them, Semjaza?" Azazel asked.

"I fear we've only two choices, master," Semjaza started. "Either we let them stay here and all the humans starve to death or we banish them elsewhere. I'll follow your order, master."

"How am I to choose?" Azazel thought. Kokabel was everything Azazel could never be. When the crops still grew,

Azazel and Madina had spent many days watching Kokabel draw his figures in the sand, mathematical symbols displaying ratios, sequences, perfect triangles and shapes, all manner of shapes.

To Madina, the symbols were just pictures but Azazel's eyes beamed with joy when he'd first seen them, finally seeing Eloah's colours of creation that he had fallen in love with above the firmament, now explained and given life from the hands of his Kokabel. As if his child's mind was one with the *Shekinah* itself, allowing all of creation's mystery to flow through from his fingers. Azazel had never felt so proud. Azazel knew in truth, he was left with only one bittersweet option. He too hoped Madina would understand.

"We banish them," he told Semjaza. "I'll tell him myself."

It had been the first humbling of the gods the *Bene Ha Elohim* would have to suffer but it would not be the last.

Azazel went and told his son what he had decided. In the centre of town, Kokabel's sudden wail filled the sky and rumbled the village houses. The villagers dropped their bowls, wanting to be out of sight of Kokabel's wrath. They were still hungry but hunger was useless to those crushed by giant feet, they also thought.

Madina dropped the ladle into the cauldron. The noise hadn't frightened her at all. Wails of children rarely frighten their mothers who quickly learn that each one seeks to relay an emotion. A sudden intake of breath before a prolonged wail signals sudden physical pain. A single loud burst signals anger and an elongated bray is the signal of hunger. The one Madina just heard in the voice of her child signaled that Kokabel was in emotional pain. She ran to her son without a second thought.

The noise of Kokabel's rage was heard beyond the land between the rivers. The other *Nephilim* kept their distance from him while hills were flattened with Kokabel's fists; streams emptied from his steps and dragons were torn to shreds by his wrath. It was only when Madina – unwilling to see their land destroyed any more than it had been – went to stand in his path, that Kokabel saw what had caused his mother's eyes to grow so tired, hungry and weak.

When she came upon him, the wind battered her from his movements. His leg, like a giant redwood tree, nearly rammed into her, its wake leaving a vacuum that pulled her forward. But he had stopped. When she looked up, his shoulders still heaved with exertion but he reached down and slowly gathered her into his palm, then carefully lifted her four hundred feet up to his eyes. She held on to his index finger during the ascent, her arms barely able to wrap around it for security.

When she reached his face, she could hear his breathing. It was like a battering wind. She apologized for bringing him into such a cruel world. Kokabel's face softened when he looked into her eyes, looking past her gentle pleas for him to stop destroying the land, for his own reflection in them. As Kokabel listened to his mother, he kept scanning for his image in her eyes but he still couldn't see himself, he was far too large.

The bitter choice he was left with planted a toxic seed of anger in his own heart. One that wouldn't bloom until much later. But on that day, he instead blew a gentle breath on his mother's forehead, then dutifully gathered the other *Nephilim* and their children and left the surrounding plain of Mount Hermon to search out new lands, never to return.

The steps of their procession carved a river when it later rained. In front of them, birds and animals fled the forests, signaling their arrival. Back at the *Village of Gods*, the other human wives wept for their banished sons and daughters but Madina took it the worst. Her mind, unprepared for the sudden sense of loss, shattered completely.

"How could you let *Eloah* make them like so? My child, Azazel! Our Kokabel! He did not choose this!" Madina later asked of her husband. Azazel had tried to explain, but Madina didn't have Azazel's sight for the higher realms. All she saw was Azazel capitulating to Eloah's will; making him take away her only child, her first-born child. For this Madina would never forgive Eloah.

At the *Village of the Gods,* she wept for many moons. Moons that became cycles, demanding that *Eloah* bring back her Kokabel but he never did. Madina had discovered the limit to Azazel's power, learning that he was no God at all. Her transformation would begin soon after. It would take fifty more cycles but by the end of it, she would no longer be "Madina" By the time of the first great *Council of Archs*, she would become "Moloch".

***

Human sensations had been what first called the Bene Ha Elohim to their first Earthly lives. First "fear" at the tribes of humans attacking them. Then "power" when all attempts had failed. Followed by "love" at the prospect of family. The last one they would know would be "loss" when their wives started to die. On Semjaza's orders, they were told not to try and re-animate them. They all listened except Azazel.

When Madina died the first time, Azazel had not been ready to part with her. Each time he reanimated her, she grew in size. Each time losing more and more of who she had been but eventually she would start to die again. Despite Semjaza's protests, Azazel never stopped trying. No matter how many times Semjaza told him that what he was attempting was akin to painting beyond the edge of a canvas. It would simply never work.

But Azazel still heard Madina's voice in the monster he had made. He even tried fusing the head of her favourite animal, the bull, onto her body in the hopes she would return, but this only made Azazel's canvas smaller and smaller. In the guttural grunts the monster came to utter, Azazel could still hear her last wish, *"Eloah's….First……born……children!"* For 550 cycles, the monster the people came to call Moloch, demanded the first-born of all children born in *Eloah's* realm. For 550 cycles Azazel complied. He would only stop at the first great *Council of Archs*.

***

To an insect, whose life cycle is a day, life is marked with a period of darkness followed by light. Only to end at the start of darkness again. To a tree living a thousand years, the seasons pass like long days of death, cold, rebirth and sun. To eternal beings like the *Bene Ha Elohim,* the concept of time doesn't exist. Events could have lasted a minute or a millennia, all that mattered was the outcome. Patience, for them was more than an abstract virtue, it was as common to them as humans know that day will follow night and that winter precedes the spring. For 550 cycles, Semjaza had been more than patient with Azazel. That would end now.

On the day of the first great Council of Archs, Semjaza walked with angry purpose toward the centre of the *Village of the Gods*, to stop the madness Azazel had started. He made his way through a procession of people extending from the villages below leading to the ten concentric circles of their home. Around him, the air was alive with the sound of thousands of crying babies and thousands of wailing mothers, so loud that the soothing coos of their fathers was barely heard in between. Semjaza peered around the plateau, *"Village of the Gods" the people had called it once, it was now a village of death,"* he thought.

In the time before time was counted, on top of Mount Hermon, the eternal spring time created by Azazel had vanished. What remained there now was a barren plain where the grass had stopped growing. Semjaza's eyes focused in on the innermost circle where Azazel now wept in front of the giant figure of *Moloch* next to him.

Moloch towered above him. Nearly double his size, it sat on a golden throne, looking out to the procession of worshippers bringing their first-born children to its hands of elongated and powerful fingers. Its hairless body; scaled in scattered, discoloured parts, looking as if the monster had been throttled by a herd of wild animals. But in truth the blood of its body had settled, never to flow again through its hardened veins. Azazel's last creation was dying, his attempts to save Madina had been in vain, no matter how many babies *it* now demanded as food.

Among the procession of town's people undulating around the bridges connecting the circles of their plateau, the fairies scurried about gathering bones spewed out by Moloch. Semjaza saw the looks on their little faces; once delighted, but now fearful and robbed of joy, knowing only the duty commanded by their creator.

Semjaza's chest and hip plates of golden armour, clinked together with each step over the thousands of little bones scattered around the outer circles of the plateau. They had come from the innermost circle where the procession of people, carrying their first-born children, ended. Semjaza had decided that enough was enough. *"Azazel needed to realize the error of his ways,"* Semjaza thought. He hoped to be the one to show him. In truth, only he could.

"Gather these bones faster! The sight is fearful to the humans, we're not savages!" Semjaza heard Azazel order, the fairies following dutifully.

"Poor creatures," Semjaza thought. When Azazel had created them long ago, they had been the happiest little creatures; multi-coloured and moving in groups as if guided by a single mind. They had spent their days giggling with each other as the human men chased them across the plains and forests, following their laughter into madness. Now their little hands couldn't gather the bones of dead children fast enough.

Azazel's vision had evolved from beauty to an atmosphere of casual death and misery on the plateau, but yet he still cared that it looked beautiful. Making it obvious to Semjaza that Azazel had lost more than the woman he loved, he'd lost the objectivity to lead, maybe he'd never had it. Still, he was their master but in Semjaza's heart, he'd always been more.

Semjaza shoved his way through the crowds of people to the front and came upon the innermost circle, guarded by the *Archs*, Jamoriel and Balotel. Their tall armoured frames standing on either side of the entrance at the front of the procession where the next couple had just come forth. Jamoriel stopped the mother, his large hand reached down for the baby and taking it from her while her eyes quietly protested. Jamoriel examined the baby for defects and nodded approval to Balotel who made a mental notation.

"55,597", Balotel counted out the total before Jamoriel allowed the woman to enter.

Semjaza continued past the bald husband holding his wife while she tried to soothe their crying infant. The man looked up at the tall figure of Semjaza suddenly walking past them, looking to him for help.

"Please, my lord! Why does God-King Azazel require this from us?" the man asked; but Semjaza ignored him, stepping past Jamoriel and Balotel, who let him pass when they saw the anger in Semjaza's eyes and the purpose in his rocking shoulders.

"*A-ZA-ZEL!*" Semjaza bellowed. His voice echoing for miles.

"This cannot continue! You must stop this now!" Semjaza yelled at Azazel.

Semjaza's words echoed throughout the land in the language of *Eloah*. To the humans, Semjaza's words sounded like broken syllables spoken in crashing metallic tones ripping through the air at a volume louder than lightning.

"OI......ADA....GI.....TA....BO..LA..PE!" is what the humans heard, punctuated by pauses, rising and falling in an angry melody that sounded like brass being sheared by lightning. It was a language the *Bena Ha Elohim* had left behind long ago but had never forgotten. *"Though Azazel had forgotten everything else,"* Semjaza had long come to notice.

Still, Semjaza didn't want the people to know what he was saying. He didn't want to show them that Azazel could be questioned. Still, even now, Semjaza's first consideration was of damage to Azazel's respect from Semjaza's own protest.

Azazel lifted his head from the feet of Moloch. He'd heard Semjaza, but the voice was distant. His thoughts were elsewhere, looking deep into Moloch's mind, hoping to find Madina somewhere beneath the mass of muscle and terror that he'd turned her into. *"You're here!"* he thought. *"Show me you're here, my love,"* he pleaded in his heart.

Behind Azazel, the couple approached, he turned to them and took the crying child. The mother's hands tried to protest but she didn't want to tussle for the little baby. *"Another foolish human instinct,"* Semjaza thought, watching the woman vainly try not to harm her child before she delivered it to Azazel, ultimately to be sacrificed to Moloch.

"Our society has followed these human instincts for too long," Semjaza thought, having long seen that it would be their downfall.

"No! Please no! Don't," the woman pleaded but to Azazel, her plea meant nothing. He could barely hear her as his eyes focused softly on the baby, on the food for his Moloch. He took it and looked to the woman.

"My child, tell *Jamoriel the Wise* your wish. By my word it shall be granted."

Azazel turned and held out the baby to Moloch. The monster reached down and took the little crying child. Moloch looked to the sky and shrieked, the sound echoing through the plateau and down to the town.

When the monster spoke again, Azazel felt hope but to his dismay, it was not Madina's voice. *"Until you bring back my first-born child, Eloah! I'll take all of yours!"* Moloch said.

As the monster devoured the baby, the mother broke down. The father couldn't watch and carried her to Jamoriel to make his wish.

Azazel again looked to Moloch. "Yes my love, he'll come back, I'll bring our Kokabel back to us, I swear it."

Semjaza couldn't believe his eyes. He had long come to know loss. The now childless woman's pain; in gut-wrenching agony at her child being murdered with such cruelty, was to Azazel nothing more than a by-product of his insanity. Ignoring the depth of her grief, Azazel's eyes held no empathy for her loss, offering not even the hint of an apology for her sacrifice, seeing it as nothing more than the means to his own ends.

Semjaza felt the pit of his stomach stir with discomfort, finally realizing that Azazel cared for no one but himself, but it was too late now. Semjaza learned suddenly that some come to find they have loved the wrong person, when it is far too late to change it.

Azazel placed his hand on Moloch's knee but the monster's large, bloody hand slapped Azazel away, knocking him to the ground, sliding him along with a force that stopped at the feet of Semjaza, nearly knocking him over. *"For how long can we pretend to be something we're not,"* Semjaza thought, as he bent down to pick up his master.

On his feet, Azazel's posture was of a broken man, Semjaza watched the tears that now ran down his master's face. What Semjaza had known, and what Azazel was just learning, was that the woman he'd loved was gone and no magic he could bring forth would ever bring her back. *"It is not Madina any longer, Master!"* Semjaza pleaded with Azazel. *"You must destroy this creature before it is too late."* But he knew that it was already too late. Releasing this many innocent souls, quickly meant the higher *Archs* would soon take notice.

"No! She's in there, Semjaza! She'll return to me!" Azazel replied as he walked back to the monster, blood and bones falling around him. *"Bring forth another!"* Azazel ordered angrily, blind now with desire.

"*Master, this is not wi...*", Semjaza started but Azazel had also had enough of Semjaza's protests, not to mention the insult in calling Moloch a '*creature*'. Azazel suddenly turned and approached Semjaza in one swift motion. To the humans watching, it was as if Azazel had disappeared from Moloch's feet to reappear in Semjaza's face, interrupting his protest mid-sentence. In front of Semjaza now, Azazel's earthly countenance settled into one of powerful rage. A rumbling sound of moving earth erupted around the plateau. Boulders defied gravity and floated into the sky as the air vibrated with Azazel's fury.

"*Bring forth another!*" Azazel commanded, heard for hundreds of miles away. Semjaza, at first stunned, reached out to Azazel's angry scowl, hoping to soften his master's anger; but just as Moloch had rejected Azazel's touch, Azazel slapped his hand away, leaving Semjaza to watch bitterly as Azazel returned to Moloch, addressing Semjaza obliquely over his shoulder, "*Whatever they desire Semjaza! We shall grant them whatever they desire! This is my command!*" he said. Semjaza's face trembled; his own eyes started to water.

Jamoriel and Balotel, taken aback by the interaction, turned their gaze away from him back to the procession. The *Bene Ha Elohim* were a family of brothers, but now their home was crumbling before their eyes as a crisis of leadership ensued. They shared a look that questioned how many orders they should continue to follow, as Semjaza cried for the first and only time in his eternal life.

"*More humanisms,*" Semjaza angrily thought of himself as he fought the well of emotions boiling inside him. "*When will I be rid of these useless human emotions?*" It would be sooner than he knew, but in his heart, another question burned. It had been burning since they all first descended to this realm. "*What of my desire, Azazel?*"

Semjaza peered downward, and there his eyes caught sight of a lone purple flower lying in a footprint in the grey earth, bones scattered around it. Alone in the expansive grey of the plateau, the flower's presence was like an act of defiance to the reality they had created here. "*It must have been carried here on the sole of someone in the procession,*" Semjaza thought. But as he looked closer, there was something different about this one. The journey to the top of Mountain Hermon was hundreds of thousands of steps from the villages below, yet the purple petals of this flower looked as if it had just been picked. *"No,"* he thought. He remembered this flower, he would know it anywhere. It had been Madina's.

He reached down and gathered it from the earth. It was still cold to the touch. He felt his heart sink as he remembered a different Azazel, such a long time ago, six hundred cycles by his count, whom he called master now. An Azazel who was gone forever like the green grass of their mountain-top plateau.

Still watching Azazel, Semjaza brought the purple flower to his lips, blowing a breath on it that finally saw it die and turn to a brittle shell of its former beauty. Semjaza crushed it, unlocking the pieces that blew in the wind, landing now at Azazel's feet. Azazel never even noticed.

A sharp tone suddenly pierced through the air. Semjaza covered his ears and grimaced from the pain. He looked around and saw the other BHE do the same. The humans looked on at them, stunned but they didn't cover their ears, as if they didn't hear the piercing tone. Something was happening.

The sky above turned grey, followed by the low whistle of a winding wind. The temperature on the plateau dropped and for a second, there was total silence. It was pierced again suddenly by the sound of a thousand lightning bolts erupting at once. The lightning bolts streaked across the sky but didn't disappear as normal lightning does. Instead, the bolts remained suspended, like glowing rods, scaring the procession of town's people into a mad dispersal.

A melee of voices ensued among them, followed by a mass exodus back down the mountain to the towns below. Semjaza peered up and saw the sky looked like it had been lowered from its perch, as if it now waited for the humans to leave the plateau so it could open up and swallow everything.

More lightning bolts streaked across the sky, the *Bene Ha Elohim* wandered outside from their golden jeweled dwellings. Their faces were worried because the *Shekinah* was silent. Semjaza moved quickly to Azazel, hoping to pull him to safety. *"Azazel must have known this would happen someday,"* Semjaza thought.

He pulled at him but Azazel wouldn't leave Moloch's feet. The monster shrieked into the storm, while from a distance another tone sounded, followed by a loud crash of moving earth, then another lightning bolt, striking Moloch with a deafening blast.

The shock-wave knocked Azazel and Semjaza clear across the plateau. They crashed into a rocky wall, shattering it with their force. The lightning bolt left Moloch covered in thick white smoke. When it cleared, Azazel saw that Moloch had been turned into a solid gold statue, its hands now outstretched forever, waiting for the next infant to appease its appetite.

Azazel fell to the ground, his mouth aghast, his lungs looking for the breath to power his wail but none came. Instead, the sky opened up and the higher *Arch*s, followed by a battalion of white spectras, finally descended on the *Bene ha Elohim*.

***

In the faraway desert land where the giants had gone, Kokabel held a sack of wine while the noise of giants making camp murmured around him. He drank from the sack as he did every day now. His old face set with a quiet anger, his eyebrows tensed into a menacing bitter arc. Above him, the sky suddenly rumbled. The sound lasted longer than it should. *"This is not the season of rain,"* he thought. He looked up to the sky, as it shifted from grey to black, flashing sudden darkness across the desert.

A blue latticework of diamond shapes formed in the sky and extended across the entirety of it. Gasps erupted from the others as the ground shook with the sudden far away echo of Azazel's words, carrying to them through the Shekinah. Kokabel heard his father's voice warning him of a coming danger but not revealing what that danger was. Kokabel closed his eyes and rose, it was time to prepare.

CHAPTER FIVE
Council of the Archs

Guided by a dream on the morning of the first great council of *Archs* on Mount Hermon, Enoch saw clouds rushing by as visions flashed before him. In the way dreams have of filling in the truth, this one showed him moving images. One of them was Azazel.

The ten concentric circles of the *Village of the Gods* came into view. Enoch knew instantly what they were though he had never seen them before. In the innermost circle, Enoch saw Azazel kneeling at a golden statue, powerful winds battering at him from every direction. Something was happening but the dream didn't tell Enoch what it was.

The time-space in front of Enoch's face transformed into an image of Azazel's face, the entire spectre leaning in close to him. The sensation frightened Enoch but he didn't wake up. He felt instead like a man trapped in his own dream. Azazel's face transformed again, showing Enoch an image of Madina long before she had become Moloch.

"Bring back my child! Bring back my Kokabel!" Enoch heard her chant, as she rocked back and forth. Azazel's voice then spoke over it. *"We would only learn what her loss felt like when our own wives were banished by the cruel fate of mortality, Enoch. We all learned to weep when our wives began to die. They died no matter how many creation tones we chanted into the Shekinah, hoping to save them."* This was what Azazel's loud voice said as the image returned to his face again.

"Who are you?" Enoch asked.

"I am the ruler of earth and why Eloah allows you to still walk the realm, Enoch! But we are more alike than you know," Azazel's spectre replied.

A question had burned in Enoch's mind since his days in Sargon's prison, "What is the *Shekinah*?"

"Long ago, when I helped Eloah evolve this realm, we created the Shekinah, Enoch. It is an invisible force binding together all created beings with a perpetual energy harnessed from the magnetic ends of the realm and the salt water in between."

Then Azazel's spectre told Enoch that everything *Eloah* had created vibrated with a sound that echoed into the *Shekinah* – echoes that humans would not be able to hear for millennia yet to come. Nevertheless, they could affect any of Eloah's creations if the right creation tone was played.

Enoch saw the tones make a dead animal rise and work the land once more. He saw a tree become fluid like water. He saw limbs growing where before there had been none and boulders floating as if they were feathers. Enoch learned that the tones could stop a human body from dying but not its soul.

The dream started to crumble in front of Enoch. Azazel's voice erupted into a wail that was nearly as loud as *Eloah's* had been in Sargon's prison. The dream faded away.

He awoke with a start, jolting up from his bedding of hay tied with lamb skin. His young eyes opened as a sound filled the air, followed by the crackling ripple of thunder. Enoch thought he'd heard the sound of Azazel's voice echoing from his dream back into the earthen hut where Enoch had made his home after Sargon's prison. Each passing minute now erasing what he had just seen.

Enoch's new life had felt like another prison without Edna, but the thought of who had freed him was clearer in his mind. After today, there would be no more doubt as to why.

He ran to the door and opened it to see what was happening. The early morning light came in followed by the noise of goats and animals bleating with something more than their wait for breakfast. For a moment, Enoch was uncertain if his dream had been a dream at all. The next thunderclap told him he may have been right. Something was happening outside. Enoch's robes hung on the door just above his tools, he grabbed them and went to see.

Outside, he found that the miner, his wife and the rest of the village had come out to listen to the noises coming from Mount Hermon. To his left, at the stables, the horses stirred with fear as giant boulders tumbled down the slopes of the mountain, shaking the ground and landing in the valley with a crash, scaring everyone around.

A massive dark cloud had enveloped the entire sky above, undulating above Mount Hermon like waves of an ocean storm. Around the village, the wind howled ferociously. Residents had scattered to secure their belongings. Enoch saw some of them kneel down and slice the throats of their throats in an attempt to appease the angry Gods. But it didn't work, probably because the gods weren't angry at them.

In the distance, he saw caravans of the forest creatures heading south away from Mount Hermon, carrying their own belongings. Centaurs and Minotaurs – the men and women with bodies like horses or bulls – the wolf-headed men and all the fairies of the forest were now leaving the land of the *Bene ha Elohim* in droves. It seemed they knew something the people didn't. Enoch would later learn that even if they had, the knowledge would not have saved them.

Above the snowy mountain top dragons circled. Their beating wings slapping air aside and echoing across the peaks. Then Enoch heard the call. A series of tones in the language of Eloah erupting from the sky itself, it seemed. What future sages would call the great council of *Archs* had started. The villagers covered their ears at its volume. To them, they were alien noises, barely syllables and not matching any language they had known. It rang in their ears like, "**IOL-CAM...MA-NA-DA...!**"

The tone was metallic, vibrating through the air with its own life and it was not alone. A chorus of them chimed in together, as if fighting for dominance.

The villagers were people who had long grown accustomed to sharing the land with all manner of beasts and monsters, but whatever was happening now was frightening them beyond anything they had ever known.

A lightning bolt struck the ground in front of Enoch, knocking him to the ground as smoke danced around the scorched earth. To Enoch, who knew the language of *Eloah*, the tones weren't random sounds, they were an order and he knew what they meant... *"Bring forth another!"*

Enoch felt his bones tremble from the cacophony. He now knew his dream had been real and the answers he sought were at the top of Mount Hermon. Then, while he was gathering supplies and food for the journey up Mount Hermon, another tone in another voice made him pause. This one wasn't a crashing metallic tear through the sky. *"No more iniquity will exist after today,"* Enoch understood it to say. The ringing words rose and descended to end in a vibration.

"AG......MADA-RIDA.....GAHA-LANA......BASA-GIME!"

The sound was like a flower growing in a forest where monsters lived. As thousands of people descended from Mount Hermon, Enoch went against the current to the top.

On the way, a group of fairies buzzed by Enoch, the beating of their tiny wings creating little gusts that bellowed out Enoch's robes. The aroma of mint leaves wafted around Enoch's nose as he watched them buzz away, their eyes now filled with terror.

Beyond them, Enoch saw a family of Minotaurs walking eastward, carrying all heir belongings. When they approached he stopped one to ask what was happening. "Why do you all flee?"

"The children of the mountain have angered Eloah! The Shekinah proclaims it! Eloah will soon turn his attention to us. The land is not safe for us anymore, it is not safe for anyone, flee to high ground or you will all perish."

When Enoch arrived at the mountain top, he found a village gripped by a siege and surrounded by an army of white spectras of light, circling the entire village like an invading force. In each circle of the plateau, the *Bene Ha Elohim* had left their homes and were now kneeling in prayer facing the innermost circle where Semjaza, Jamoriel and Balotel stood trying to protect Azazel from four other figures who weren't BHE, Enoch saw. One of them was Uriel.

The other three with her, he didn't know, but they all wore flowing robes of light that billowed around them. They had a similarity to the *Bene Ha Elohim*. They were tall and beautiful and radiating with a quiet light that had no discernable source. Their hair was a shimmering black. It was only in their presence that Enoch saw that Azazel and the others were of a darkness; a darkness that came from their hearts and was only visible in the presence of light that came from the other figures, that came from Uriel herself.

Enoch saw the blood-soaked land around Moloch and that none there were fazed by the gruesome sight. Uriel, Raphael, Michael and Gabriel stood across from Semajza, who had taken a defensive posture, trying to protect Azazel. Uriel was speaking to Azazel.

He heard her speak to them in the language of *Eloah*. Her voice ringing like a chorus of bells, loud and rich with presence, as if it were coming from inside Enoch's head, wrapping him in its warmth. Hers had been the beautiful sound he'd heard before, *the flower in the forest of monsters*, hearing it again as she pleaded with Azazel next to the statue.

"You will release no more souls, Azazel," Uriel said.

"Why have you done this to Madina? What has she done to deserve this cruel fate?" Azazel asked, still kneeling at Moloch's large golden feet. Azazel's angry reply was the metallic ripping tone that had awoken Enoch and the villagers. Each word saw more lightning arch across the sky as his voice lifted boulders, dropping them back down when he'd finished talking.

Semjaza stepped forward and placed himself in between Azazel and Uriel, his chin lowered and his chest heaving in quickened breath. Semjaza's eyes tightened on Uriel, his fingers dancing with nervous energy, waiting for the perfect moment to draw his sword.

"Jamoriel, Balotel, take Azazel to safety!"

But Azazel was not going to move. His head bowed in anguish while Balotel and Jamoriel tried vainly to lift him away to safety.

"You may admire the quiet elegance of a swan, Semjaza but should you try to live life as one, you would surely be disappointed, have you not learned this yet?" Uriel asked.

"It is not me, whom you need to convince, Uriel, It never has been," Semjaza replied.

They all stopped and looked at Enoch when he entered the innermost circle. Even Azazel stood and turned.

"Who is this man?" asked Semjaza in the common Aramaic, the others following.

Uriel was surprised but didn't show it. "His name is Enoch," replied Uriel,

"Why is he here?" Semjaza questioned.

"I called him here," said Azazel softly. "His dream this morning will say it is true."

"Why?" asked Semjaza, regarding Enoch apprasingly.

"Because he's also lost his love. But for his loss *Eloah* granted him a gift, a gift that also gives him *Eloah*'s ear. He'll speak for us and plead for *Eloah* to allow us peace. His heart knows of my pain, our pain."

Semjaza was offended,

"We will not subject ourselves to *Eloah*'s whim again, Azazel! We cannot! Have you forgotten who you are?"

"What choice do we have, *O Wise One,* what choice remains?"

"We storm the heavens! Take his throne for yours!" Semjaza bellowed.

Azazel knew that that would be Semjaza's reply. His head looked up towards the closed metallic eyelids of his dead wife, willing them to come to life. But he knew they would not.

Azazel stood and approached Enoch. To Enoch, Azazel's steps landed heavily on the ground as if every muscle and bone in his body were made of dense iron. From afar, Azazel had been a beautiful man. Up close, he was like a beast in human skin, Enoch thought. His hot breaths escaped powerfully from his nose, blowing Enoch's hair aside when he approached.

"Is it not so, *Enoch the Scribe?*" he asked, looking Enoch up and down. "Have you also not lost a love through the cruel fate of *Eloah?*"

Enoch should have been afraid, any other man would have been, but Enoch had given up the idea that he was a normal man. *"What use was the fear of death if you were only to return from it a young man again?"* he had thought.

"Who are you people?" Enoch asked. Azazel's face softened but he didn't answer. Instead he placed his hand on Enoch's shoulder and led him to the statue of Moloch.

"She was beautiful once, just as your Edna was." Enoch felt his heart crash with the unhealed memory.

"Please stay and hear our council," Azazel said. Enoch turned and listened to their hopes in the language of *Eloah*.

That morning, Enoch learned Eloah's language was not merely constructed of words. Each ringing tone had an extra dimension to it that contained within it the sacred intention behind the idea being conveyed. It was a rich language needing very few words to convey large and complex meanings. In the instant when Enoch had died in Sargon's prison, he'd learned the vocabulary and structure, and today he learned the perfection it sought to express. Learning that the tone of "**Kh**" meant"*love*". That "**oo**" meant"*growth*" and that "**Mhm**" meant "*another*".

So that when Enoch heard Azazel put them together to form the tone, "**KHOOM**", he understood Azazel's love for Madina was a love that wanted her to grow. To Enoch, it was a more complete meaning of the word. The danger, he saw, was in the tones for which no human word equivalent existed. Those tones could reach into the Shekinah and affect the physical world in a way that would have scared a man who could still be scared. To the casual observer, it would have looked like magic.

As he listened, rocks and dirt shifted around them. Objects lost mass and shifted in and out of view, some disappearing into the ground never to be seen again. Large broken boulders started spinning, gaining speed until the friction became so great that the boulder glowed white and then melted where it stood.

Enoch thought what he'd seen that morning would never be believed by any human. He wouldn't have believed it himself, had he not seen it with his own eyes, learning that humans had been the greatest creation of *Eloah*, the greatest creation since Azazel and the others, including Uriel.

He learned that Azazel's desire to create had been born from the elegant figures and symbols locked into the mechanics of humans. As Enoch listened, he stole glances at Uriel, wondering if she was made the same.

Enoch had long ago counted the cycles and fed the tribes with what he'd learned, but he'd never seen numbers like this. He learned of mathematical operations impossible to describe but ever-present, like a mystery hidden in plain sight for all who knew where to look; numbers so perfectly aligned within every part of man that they created a balance, knocked it asunder and then balanced it again. The process created an enamourment that today would be similar to love, binding all into one. This was the sensation Enoch caught himself feeling for Uriel when she spoke, the thought fighting the love he still felt for Edna.

"All over the land, far and wide, your children – the giants – are eating more than the land can provide. When they have no food, they eat the people, when the people have no food they eat each other. Can you not see what you have done, Azazel?" Uriel asked

"I've brought humans knowledge, and all I ask in return is to love and be loved, I do not wish to usurp Eloah, but he wishes to rob me of joy, why?"

"This realm isn't for you Azazel, you know this well, you have always known this."

"Why not? Am I not also a creation of Eloah? Like you? Like all that we see? Why is it that only humans have a choice when they do not even know how to make one?"

"You are eternal, the humans are not. When the humans pass from this realm, their spirits return to the higher realms. Your giants, however, their spirits become trapped between this realm and the others for all eternity, Azazel. There, they suffer in anger that humans pass, but they do not. Eloah cannot allow this to continue any longer."

Semjaza's interest had been piqued. He knew what followed when *Eloah* didn't allow something. The time had come to draw his flaming sword. It materialized in his hand as if it had always been there, hiding in a dimension humans couldn't perceive. "What does he intend to do?"

"I'm sorry Semjaza," said Uriel. "You're to be punished. Seize them!" Uriel ordered.

The spectras around the village at once descended down and grabbed each of the kneeling *BHE*. Their movements were incredibly fast, instantly forming into bindings of glowing light that held each of them. Just as quickly, the spectras disappeared, taking all of the *Bene Ha Elohim* with them, leaving ten of the senior leaders remaining, stunned and now looking around at the empty village.

"Where have our brothers gone?" asked Semjaza.

"They have been returned to *Eloah*."

"What of us?" asked Jamoriel, who had been spared.

Uriel's eyes glowed and an invisible buzzing noise filled the air. Semjaza's confrontational face was suddenly gripped with pain as spikes formed on his back and his skin turned green. The muscles in his body grew and formed scales. He fell to his knees, the others following when the same happened to them, except Azazel who now stood watching, powerless. They screamed as their faces changed to that of deformed snakes; a wide mouth, two slits for a nose and eyes that were yellow and now squinted into their faces. Enoch nearly retched with the smell that came from their new forms. In future times it would be called *sulfuric acid*, before that, *Brimstone*; but this day, no word existed for the odour that had hit Enoch's nose.

Azazel watched in horror as his brothers morphed into reptilian-like creatures. Their bodies grew in size and expanded beyond what their armour could contain. The golden plates that had protected them fell to the ground with a *clank*. Azazel remained the same as he'd been while the others now hissed in anger trying to find their new voices.

"*Eloah* has decreed that your leaders are to walk the earth as serpents so that you may never enrapture the hearts of people again, and for you Azazel, he's created a realm where you're to be bound for seventy generations until the humans have attained the knowledge to properly judge you for your crimes."

Uriel's tones again filled the sky. The ground at Azazel's feet shifted and lost density. He was suddenly swallowed by the earth, screaming as he was being pulled down. He called to Semjaza for help but Semjaza was frozen in his new form.

Semjaza shrieked. More dragons flew away in fright.

Azazel's shoulders had descended into the earth and only one arm remained free. He looked towards Semjaza as he clawed at the ground trying to escape, as if he were nothing but a breath choking the Earth. He gave his final instruction to Semjaza. "Semjaza, prepare my return! We shall storm the heavens!"

"Yes master!" Semjaza shrieked. "Glory will be ours again!"

The hole closed and Azazel was gone. The clouds spread and sunlight began to streak down. The rays hitting the backs of the reptilian fallen, forming smoke as the light of the sun cooked their new skin.

The force holding Semjaza and the others released them. Semjaza ran to the ground where Azazel had just been standing. He called to the earth, clawing it away, crying for his master, crying for his love. He turned to Uriel with fury burning in his reptilian eyes. "You will pay for this Uriel, I swear by the light of Azazel that you will pay for what you have done today!"

"This is the will of *Eloah*, not my doing Semjaza. Show him repentance and *he'll* allow you to serve your time in human form, *he'll* have you back."

"The insolence, he wants repentance yet binds Azazel?" the others hissed in agreement.

"*He'll* remove it if you show repentance, that goes for any of you here today. What say you?"

The group of nine ghastly reptilian creatures stirred and looked to each other. "Do not waver brothers, Azazel commands it!" Semjaza ordered them.

Jamoriel was not convinced. For him it was time to stop following orders. He stepped forward. "I repent," Jamoriel said.

"Wise choice, Jamoriel," replied Uriel. "As penance, keep the wisdom of creation tones, and with time you shall again earn the favour of *Eloah*."

"How much time?" Jamoriel asked.

"Time itself will show you," she responded.

Jamoriel turned to his companion, "Balotel, please come! I will need you!"

Balotel weighed his choices and stepped forward also. "I shall help him," Balotel spoke.

Uriel nodded. Her eyes glowed again, turning the pair to human form. They were now like Enoch and had become eternal humans, with hair the colour of silver.

"Any others?"

Semjaza shrieked as the dark clouds cleared and the sun grew stronger. The other seven fallen fell to the ground in pain as the sunlight burned them too.

"We will work against you until the ends of the earth, Uriel," Semjaza said. "Where you seek to create love we will create hate, where you seek faith we will create knowledge, where you seek virtue we will only seek sin. We will become legion in the final day when we will storm the higher realm and take it for the glory of our fallen Azazel."

"Then so *Eloah* now waits," Uriel said. "Remove yourselves!"

Another tone from Uriel sped up the passage of time, a high pitched grinding noise following. The sun rose faster to stop at mid-day. Under the heat of the sunlight cooking their skin and with pounding animal steps, the fallen *Archs* scattered back to the cave where they had been born. The light from outside careened inside and still burned at their skin. They dug into the ground seeking to escape the light. Gabriel, Michael and Raphael descended down to where Uriel stood. *Eloah*'s will had been fulfilled, it was now time to cleanse history of Azazel's fall.

"There are still great preparations to be made, Michael and I must go, come Raphael!" Gabriel said to Uriel. Gabriel then turned to Enoch and regarded him with a look that Enoch didn't understand. It asked a question that Enoch himself had wondered for a long time. "*Why me indeed?*" Enoch thought. They ascended with the speed a thousand times faster than a falling stone, disappearing into a point in the sky. Enoch watched, amazed. Uriel then turned to him, her face softening.

"Are you frightened by what you have seen here this day, Enoch?"

"I'm not frightened by many things these days but what has happened to me? Why am I still here?"

"I know you have questions and many more from the answers, but have faith. Come, I want to show you something."

"Wait!" Enoch said. "Who are you?"

"You know my name, Enoch."

"But *what* are you?"

"I'm an *Arch,* there are four of us now – Michael, Gabriel, Raphael and myself."

"I still don't understand."

"I know, you will soon, come."

Uriel took Enoch's hand, the air transformed around them. The outlines of the Earth became a shapeless form. They were transported to a realm of all white where there was no up or down. Just space for eternity.

"Am I dead?"

"No."

"The realm you and the humans live in is made of measures. Three of them to be exact. In your realm, everything has shape; it is long, it is wide, it has depth. When the *Archs* and

I see humans, we see them in *four* measures. The extra one is time."

Enoch saw a long undulating form materialize in front of them. It grew into a tunnel encompassing all the space they were in, extending infinitely. He and Uriel were then whisked inside and saw that it was populated by images along the entire form, a life made up of images of time. The life was Edna's.

Enoch was flying through Edna's life as seen by Uriel. The images flashed by as sharp angles. In them, they saw a baby born, grow into a child, play and learn and feel. They saw Edna become a young woman and fall in love with a young scribe. He saw their marriage and watched through Edna's eyes as he was captured and led away long ago. He saw her brave a strong face during the days after, but weeping in solitude during the nights that came.

He saw her find joy in caring for their son yet a space remaining in her heart, still hoping for Enoch's return. Her face told him that a void had formed in her that knew no bottom, but growing deeper as it fed on what was left of her perseverance. Enoch saw her one day reach for a knife with the thought to plunge it into her own belly.

"No, Edna!" Enoch said, as he reached for the moment in the undulating tunnel. His hand passed through the image, impotent to change its history. He saw her take pause only when the baby called to her from the other room. Her hand returned the knife to the table before she left to go check on their child.

He saw her put the idea aside in her mind but not her heart. He saw the idea lose power only when a hunter sought lodging on their farm after a deer had broken his arm. Enoch saw the good man enter her life. He saw Edna open their home to him while he healed. He saw her thoughts turn to the hunter at odd moments, leaving little room for the thought to end her life. It was bittersweet for Enoch to watch, at once wishing she'd go to the hunter because it would save her, yet, watching the woman he loved fall in love with another man. Tears formed in his eyes.

He saw his wish come true as Edna formed a new life with the hunter. He saw that it didn't erase the pain in her but instead gave her a reason to persevere. He saw the longing for Enoch's return subside to a distant memory, a memory that grew smaller as the cycles passed. He saw her become a grandmother, then finally come to rest in a grave next to the hunter who had saved her with his presence, at the right moment in time. Enoch saw all the moments of her life in that one shining instant.

He couldn't stop the tears that now flowed from his eyes like a river carving a path through a mountain. Uriel watched, with sorrow for Enoch in her own. She wanted to place a hand on his shoulder, but did not. It was not her place; instead she spoke.

"She died a happy woman," Uriel said. "I know her happiness was all you ever wanted."

"What is this *place*?" asked Enoch, through tears that now dripped into his mouth.

"It is called a *tesseract* and it is how we see all humans, it is difficult for you to fathom because humans can only experience the fourth measure. Here, we see it in its entirety. We see humans as babies being born into the realm and then on their death bed when their life spirit has ended. We see all of that as one singular image. No past, no future, but all of it just the same."

Enoch watched in amazement as a form appeared and became the translucent figure of a woman next to the tesseract. It was Edna. She took form. When she noticed Enoch, she turned away but Enoch ran to her. He reached her and the joy of seeing his wife again was clear on his face. She turned and regarded him with the polite smile of a stranger, the smile of someone she had loved once, but couldn't anymore. She put her hands on Enoch's face. Looking at him with a question she had wondered a lifetime ago.

"Why did you drink the poison, my love, why?" Enoch couldn't answer. In that moment he saw his wife's love for him wither and die as another form appeared. It was the hunter she had met during Enoch's imprisonment. The two smiled and embraced each other as they turned to watch the images.

Enoch stepped back in agony, his heart was crushed by the sight. He watched as she stuck out her hand and chose an image from the tesseract frozen in front of her. It was a moment of her younger self eating a root that had made her ill. Edna couldn't help but yell to herself.

"Don't eat that, you silly girl, don't eat that." Edna and the hunter giggled as only those in love ever could, their love finding a home built by the sum of their experiences. Enoch felt his presence to them suddenly become foreign.

Enoch watched as the girl in the image was about to bite down on the root but stopped suddenly and looked out to space as if she could hear her own soul yelling to her in the past from a realm far in the future. The girl in the image paused but bit the root anyway. Edna and the hunter smiled.

"Can she hear herself?" Enoch asked, failing to hold back tears.

"No, here their paths have been set already."

"Is this where the souls of people go after they die?"

"Yes, other places too, this is one of them. When humans pass, many like to visit here and watch the entirety of their lives as she's doing now," Uriel said. "When her spirit came here, she saw yours too."

"Did she weep?" asked Enoch.

"Here no-one weeps, Enoch. Seeing you take the poison healed her choice. She'd fallen in love with the hunter but her love was always tainted with the thought that you were imprisoned and longing for her."

"I did, I do, but I'd become a mad-man. If I could change my choice I'd do so in an instant."

"She's happy, Enoch. When she saw what you did, her soul truly rested," Uriel said, as Edna and the hunter reminisced over their moments together.

Enoch turned away.

"Come," said Uriel, "there are higher realms for you to know."

"Higher realms?"

Uriel touched Enoch's chest again. The outlines all around them shifted and pulsed away. They came to a new place. Another elongated tunnel formed in front of them but was then joined by others growing forth from it, turning it into a bulbous circular mound encompassing all the space around them as Enoch saw Edna's life branching out from different choices.

"This is the fifth realm. Here we see every human's life but with an extra measure that humans have yet to fathom."

"What measure?"

"Possibility."

"Here I see a human life through all that is possible. I see them born and live to be a hundred years old. And I see them die newborn in their mother's arms. I see them become paupers through choice and rich men through luck. I see them live their lives praising the word of the *Eloah* for all their days and I see them turn to evil and lost forever. We see their thoughts and dreams and wishes, their pain, their angst, their joy – it is all here."

Enoch saw them too. He now understood the paths and choices of lives but another question formed in his mind.

"Why are you showing me this?"

"Your mind held on to the memory of Edna, it stopped your growth, you needed to see, I wanted to show you."

"But why?"

"Your realm has now changed, iniquity will now spread to all and many lies are coming. You needed to see the truth, to know the truth."

"But if you can see all iniquity before it happens? Then why not then just stop it before it even starts?"

"Our job is only watch and know, not to intervene."

"But you just bound Azazel. Was that not intervening?"

"Evil doesn't spread at the moment a hand is committing it. It is often born of a singular moment in time where a thought is first born and nurtured, long before it ever knows it is evil. It is only in those moments that we can work, it is only in those moments that we need you."

"To do what?"

"To intervene."

Enoch saw the undulating sphere glow red, blue and yellow as they were pulled inside and travelled through all the possibilities of Edna's life. He felt the wind blow on their faces as they jumped from moment to moment. To Edna, Enoch's movement had been like the times when she had heard the rustle of leaves but no-one had stirred them, or a jug that had fallen but no-one had pushed it. It was like a ghost that had followed her all her life trying to make its presence known.

"With Azazel, *Eloah* had no choice," Uriel said as they returned to somewhere outside the possibilities. Enoch felt his stomach turn from the sudden stop. "Azazel gave him no choice.

This is why *Eloah* has decreed that a ministry be brought forth. This is why he's chosen you to do what we cannot."

"Wait, so you saw my timeline too?" Enoch asked, steadying himself. "And all my possible timelines, what did they look like?"

"It was most interesting. Your path started as a tesseract but with one difference. When it stretched to become a sphere of all possibility, the sphere turned into another tesseract and that one stretched out of all the possibilities into the realm above this one."

"There's still a higher realm?"

"Yes, it is the sixth realm, it is where I and the other watchers watch over all of creation. Your tesseract of possibility stretched out of this realm and wound through all of creation. Through the timelines of all humans now and forever.

"Can you show me?"

Uriel touched Enoch's chest. They were brought to a swirling mass of shades and hues, solidifying into structures and then reverting to colours, repeating over and over. Spheres of colourful light were undulating into each other creating outlines of people, places and even great epochs of time. Enoch felt his body became one with this realm.

He felt the entirety of human consciousness become as one here. In the lower realms Enoch had seen one human life and all the possibilities, but here he saw the further connections of people, how their possibilities would meet and create or meet and die. How a thought might permeate through the minds of many, and then evolve into truth and history or just as easily never see the light of day.

He saw all the possibilities form into paths that took shape and become all that could ever be and all that never was. Paths that led to destruction for either one or for many and ideas creating enemies, morphing into violence or providence, for enemy or loved one alike. Enoch saw lies repeated so often that they became a false truth, forming in the heart of one, then spread to two, four, eight and then a million.

He saw thoughts wither and die never knowing creation. And people with common souls who would meet, fall in love and celebrate their love with acts that benefitted all humanity. He saw the same people meet and revel in the magic of their union.

And people whose love would complete each other, destined never to meet. Or worse yet, meet and separate, never to meet again.

He found himself. His path was a black line that swirled through every possibility, glowing red and black and lost in the sea of colours, yet impossible to ignore. Had he not looked he surely would not have seen it.

"This is everything," Enoch said,

"No, there's one more realm, *the seventh* but you would not be able even to grasp its complexity. Even we *Archs* are barely able to. It is where *Eloah* does his work and it is reserved for Him alone. But in this realm, we *Archs* find moments where ideas are born, then we look backward and see where and when it almost was not."

"Which ideas?"

"Any of them, all of them, but now we concern ourselves only with ones that seek to draw worship toward Azazel or away from *Eloah*."

"What do you do then?"

"Before we did nothing, now we cannot ignore them," Uriel said. "Now, we need you to make sure they do or do not."

"So I'm to be your agent in the human realm? Is this a punishment for me?"

"*Eloah*'s will is like the water that finds its way all through your realm – it always finds a path, Enoch. Nothing stops it, the only variable is time – you have been given time now, your life now cannot be extinguished by earthly means. *Eloah* wants you to use this gift."

"I cannot. I've no reason to stay on this realm for all eternity. How can I without my family?"

"Not for eternity, Enoch, I see your heart is shattered by the news of your wife, but she's the hunter's wife now."

Enoch looked into the swirling mass of colours and found his wife. He looked for her possible paths after his imprisonment. He saw Edna choose not to be with the hunter and die an old woman filled with bitterness and regret. He saw her abandon their son and become a harlot. He saw her try to avenge his capture and be executed for it, leaving their son just as alone. He saw his wife's heart healed by the hunter who came to her after his imprisonment. How she grew and died a happy woman in his arms. In all the possible paths, the one where she walked with the hunter was the only one where she had found happiness again. There was nothing Enoch could say, time had said all. Again, Uriel fought the desire to touch Enoch's face when she saw the sadness again rise in him. Enoch wanted the same, though he didn't know it yet.

"*Eloah* just wishes one mission from you. After that you may return here as all the tales of you have told. If you agree, you would be doing a service to your realm, a service to me." She said this with a sadness in her voice that Enoch didn't notice.

"One mission?" Enoch clarified, as his chest tightened with the knowledge that the woman he loved now loved another. He thought of Uriel saying how no-one weeps in this place, longing for the day when he too could also rid himself of Earthly pain.

"What is this mission?" he asked.

"The giants....Find them and lead them to the ice gates. You must find them and connect them with their divinity for they're like babes now," Uriel continued.

"How?"

"The giants are heavenly creatures bound by the earthly shackle of their own mortality. They don't know they're divine and they too have a choice. You must find them and settle their spirits so that when they pass, their spirits can come here. If you do not, Semjaza will command their spirits to harm humans through a magic most vile. You must not allow their spirits to die in this realm without knowing they're loved by *Eloah*."

"How can I show them that?"

"*Eloah* has created a realm for them, beyond the lands of ice. Find and lead them there, the gate is there for them to cross."

"How will I find the lands of ice?"

" Observe the star in the north, follow any path away from it and you will find it."

Uriel parted the mass of colours and revealed a frozen land ringed with mountains. On top of the mountains, a glassy fixture was attached and extended across the peaks, climbing to the sky and disappearing into the clouds. Beyond it, on the other side, the mountains descended down to an ocean that extended forth to further lands.

"I'm to find all the giants? There are so many? How am I to do that?"

"You do not have to find all of them, only the ones who survive."

Enoch was puzzled. "Survive what?" he replied.

But Uriel had already vanished, and with her, the realms they'd just visited. He was now in a raging storm on a vast ocean. Enoch could have been far from Mount Hermon or right on top of it. He'd no way of knowing because there was no land in sight now. Instead, all around him water ravaged with angry waves under a sky that was black. Heavy rain fell on the vast ocean while lightning lit up the sky in a storm.

The waves carried and jostled him violently, sending him below the surface where debris of homes and dead people washed him further. He returned to the surface gasping for air but another wave sent him sinking again. This time further down, each time further down. Undercurrents pushed him deeper and deeper and terror struck inside him. It was one thing to have Uriel tell him that he'd been filled with a life that couldn't be exterminated by earthy means, but it was quite another to die of drowning a thousand times in a storm that raged for forty days and nights. Powerless, Enoch bid his former life a painful adieu.

CHAPTER SIX
A Walk with Giants

Incredulous, Holly stared into Enoch's eyes. She sensed no deception. This man believed what he was saying. "The great flood? God? The Devil? Heaven? You saw heaven?" Holly asked.

"Names, mere words really, words and names created by organizations, which, for the most part, pervert the word of *Eloah*, though some truly revel in his glory. I avoid them whenever possible. But yes, you could call them that."

"You don't follow the scriptures?" Holly asked.

"If you knew their history, you wouldn't either."

"Why?"

"It comes down to the hearts of people and not the doctrines of their institution. Let me ask you this. How many times has the church said they're rising up to fight evil and instead ended up fighting another church, another system of belief?" Enoch asked.

"Catholics murdering Christians before becoming like them, Muslims fighting Christians, Hebrew tribes fighting each other. No, Holly, I've found that love for *Eloah* rarely resides in any of these institutions. Most of them mean well but I keep my distance, it's best if you do as well."

Holly fondled Uriel's charm necklace, Enoch noticed, wondering if Holly would take on her role as he had long ago. He remembered how he'd accepted it only when circumstance had driven him to the precise moment where it couldn't be avoided any longer, as if the moment itself had been pre-ordained in the seventh realm.

"God – *Eloah* – doesn't seem any better, Enoch. I mean you loved your wife, it seems rather cruel of *Him* to keep you away from her for all eternity."

Enoch pulled in a deep breath.

"The seventh realm, Holly, it is true what Uriel said, humans can never understand how it works – it is so perfect that every mistake we've ever made was already pre-set to happen long ago. Take this fair – had the mayor not chosen the theme of *Rome and White City*, it would not have needed special lighting to display it. No special lighting and the people of the world would not have been as compelled to come and visit. Tesla would have still lit it but the fair would have been a failure. And all of that; coming from me with a slip of the tongue to the mayor in Jackson Park two years ago. You see, in the seventh realm, an innocent answer to a question can change the course of history and even going to the wrong place turns out to be the correct path."

"That makes my brain hurt," Holly said.

"Mine too, Holly, mine too," Enoch replied. "But when I understood there were things I couldn't understand – I learned that losing Edna was something I could never have controlled anyway. I wouldn't learn why until later but it's true what they say; time does heal all, it's just no-one ever mentions how much time it will take. Besides, Edna had moved on, how could I not allow her the joy of being healed?"

"So why was I chosen to do what you did? To *intervene*?"

"Because I cannot do this anymore, the world is changing at too fast a pace now for me to keep up, they need someone new to do what I've done. This person is you."

"So you're here to train me?"

"Fill you in perhaps, after all you have to know where you came from to know where you're going?"

"But what if I don't want to?"

"Then that is your choice, all creations have a choice."

"What did you choose?"

"I chose to find the giants. It turns out it wasn't that hard."

"Why?"

"The giants were half human, half *Arch*. Azazel had wanted to be a *creator* but fallen *Archs* can only mimic and pervert. The giants though, everything they made was beautiful. Their fingerprints were everywhere. After the waters receded, I landed in South America at the foot of the Andes. It took me a few years to get settled again. I built a shelter and got a lay of the land first. The forests had survived too but it was a strange time, nothing stirred, not a sound of anything living. The only noise was from the sea."

"Weren't you lonely?"

"Dreadfully so, it was like another imprisonment, just this time my cage had become bigger."

"How did you find the giants?"

"It was only finding the first ones that was difficult, finding the others was not so hard."

***

The vultures had returned first. *"Perhaps they had never even left,"* Enoch thought. Still, with no more natural enemies and food in abundance now, their numbers had grown after the flood. He watched them circle the sky day after day in small flocks of five or six. When their numbers grew to twenty and thirty, Enoch knew they had found something large. When the circling started moving north toward Nazca, he followed.

At first he was slow but soon his feet gained a sense of flight over the terrain, making good pace over the rocky path into Nazca. His oak-guide stick found the crevices on the path with ease now, the colour telling him which patches of rock were safe to step on. Light grey meant hard granite and firm leverage, dark grey was brittle shelf rock and a swift fall. *"Just a few more steps to the ridge, then I can get a better view,"* he thought.

His clothes were a patchwork of hides. The wind battered him from the left but couldn't bite through the layers he wore, made mostly from scraps he'd gathered along the way. All over the land there was no shortage of them but Enoch only took those that weren't attached to bones, thinking the dead deserved a proper burial, and if not that, then at least the clothes they had worn in the last moments of their lives.

The sky was undecided whether it wanted to be grey or blue. The vultures had gathered high above a ridge ahead, they circled, gaining speed and purpose as if on the verge of frenzy. Enoch watched one suddenly dive down but couldn't see where it went. A few seconds later, it rose back up and rejoined the circling. Then, suddenly, the vultures dispersed and flew off back toward the south, clumsily into each other as if their wings had forgotten how to flap or the air had forgotten how to flow over them, or perhaps something had scared them.

Enoch climbed the ridge and came to an opening where a flat plain of grey earth, surrounded by distant mountains, came into view below. The Nazca plain was a desolate grey expanse but tucked into a valley remained a small patch of green land where food still grew. Around it, in the grey earth, Enoch saw designs carved into the ground. When he looked closer he saw they were pictures; monkeys, birds and spiders separated by long angular lines that extended for dozens of miles across the plain. Their size and perfection told him they were pictures not meant for human eyes. *"They must be here,"* he thought.

When the smell of sweat hit his nose, he knew this was the place. Sweat meant life. He'd left the jungle a week ago and his own sweat had just dried. This new smell was not his. *"This must be the place."* When he saw the smoke, he was certain it was.

He saw a group of four giants next to an immense fire – two men and two women. The larger man and a woman were both the size of several whales if the animals could stand, while the smaller man and women stood half their size. The men wore giant swathes of brown woolen fur over their lower halves and the women wore the same but with an extra one covering their breasts. No doubt made from hundreds of animals, Enoch thought.

Their bodies contained not an ounce of fat on them with muscles set into perfect proportion, not large but far from weak and tensing repeatedly as they moved. Their skin was the colour of milk mixed with honey, but Enoch would later learn that greens and blues were just as common. They stood around the prone body of one much larger than they, making them look like young children next to the unmoving figure lying motionless before them.

The bigger man, with hair the colour of fire, stood holding the bigger woman. His large hand rubbing against the small of her back, his other – rubbing at her hair. The smaller two must have been their children, Enoch thought. They all stood with solemn faces around the large dead figure before them. Enoch had found the beacon calling the vultures, the family was mourning the passing of someone dear to them.

The larger woman detached herself from her husband and found a space for herself. Her eyes on the verge of tears, but like a mother, knowing that it was time for strength, she shed none. Instead, she bent her finger, and started tracing a new figure into the ground. Her husband turned and watched her finger move slowly but with quiet purpose. A picture of a flying bird came into view.

Enoch saw in the husband's face how he watched her, imagining he thought of her grief now giving way to healing. *"Turning her pain into a work of creation,"* Enoch thought. The husband's large green eyes; protective and softening at her, saying he would protect her from whatever danger still awaited them in this new world.

Enoch watched their interaction. He thought it best to make camp and wait until they had finished mourning. He didn't want to intrude. What he had to tell them was going to be jarring, best they heard it in the right state of mind – if that even existed for people whose entire life had just been erased. But certainly not now.

The next morning Enoch descended. He approached and found them preparing to leave for the little patch of fertile land. The husband had his arms stretched out while the wife tied a large swath of leather around his waist to hold his bottom garment in place. The wife motioned with her head and the husband turned. She secured the swathe at the small of his back. She motioned again and the husband turned back around. *"How had he seen her move?"* Enoch asked in his mind.

As Enoch approached their camp, it was the wife who saw him first. She tapped her husband on the shoulder. He looked out to the little approaching figure of Enoch. The husband's face was puzzled by the sight, puzzled by the thought that humans had survived what had decimated nearly all of their people.

The children came and joined their parents watching Enoch arrive at their giant feet. Even the light steps of their shuffling feet rattled the ground under Enoch as he stopped in front of them. They looked fearful, Enoch thought. Maybe he should tell them he doesn't mean them harm. He didn't, when he realized that he couldn't, even if he wanted to. The smaller man broke the silence.

"Who are you?"

"My name is Enoch the Scribe and I come with a message from *Eloah*."

"How did you survive the flood?" the son asked. "All the humans perished."

"In a way I didn't and maybe I'm not," Enoch said. The young giant squinted and pondered over Enoch's reply. To Enoch, the giant's guess as to how he'd survived would have been as good as any, maybe better than his own. Enoch tried to show the young giant that he wasn't being flippant but all he could muster was a shrug and he said. "We live in strange times."

That day they didn't go to work the field. They instead sat around the simmering embers of last night's fire. The mother, Beba, left to prepare a meal from the meat of their fallen. In the silence Enoch was searching for the best time to tell them what Uriel had told. He couldn't find one so he listened first.

He asked their history and learned they were all born after the exile of the giants from the land between the rivers. They had survived the flood by riding the storm on the back of their fallen.

"He was my grandfather," started Lingdar, the fire-headed father. "Do you see his great stature? He was the son of the *Arch,* Jamoriel."

"How did he perish?"

"The *Archs* like to say water always finds a way and his body took in much of it. When we found land, he became ill, it seems that water had found a path all the way into his bones." Lingdar looked away as a tear rolled down his face and settled on his beard. The tear-drop ran down the hairs and formed a bulb before it detached and fell to the ground next to Enoch. To Enoch, it sounded like someone had thrown out a handful of water.

No better time to tell them was forthcoming, Enoch thought. Enoch took in a breath and told them what *Eloah* had decreed for them. The news came to them like bittersweet fruit to a hungry man, nourishing with the prospect of learning they were divine beings, but leaving a foul after-taste at how their divinity was not wanted on this realm.

"Why does *Eloah* forsake us? First the flood and now this!" he asked, an anger rising in him. "We didn't choose to be brought forth! Why should we be punished for something we cannot control?"

"You're right, Lingdar," Enoch replied. "But *Eloah* intended this land for humans, it isn't that he doesn't love you, it is that the humans do not have your power. They would find it too hard to bear if you shared the land with them."

"But there are no humans now, they all perished in the flood," protested Lingdar.

"They'll return," Enoch stated. The rest of the words stuck in Enoch's throat. He saw that Lingdar understood but was also hurt with the knowledge. Lingdar scratched his beard, his giant finger tracing a circular pattern in the ground making a rustic sound. He looked up to the sky and then back at Enoch. His eyes suddenly squinting with a turned emotion.

"So what are we to do, Enoch the Scribe? Just die because it is convenient for *Eloah*?" asked Lingdar, his voice gaining volume, shaking Enoch's bones. The giant then stood and walked purposefully toward Enoch. His son quickly saw the anger in his father and rose to stop him. The young giant, who had the look of his mother, must have stood twenty feet above Enoch's head but his powerful arms weren't strong enough to hold Lingdar back. The father's anger was unconstrained and it was now aimed at Enoch.

There was nowhere for Enoch to run, the blocked sun behind the rushing giant had created a shadow so large, he'd never escape it had he tried. Lingdar grabbed him, lifting him quickly to his face. Enoch felt his stomach flip with the speed. His shoulders pinned by the giant's grip and the force of the swift ascension, left him frozen in place. In his large hand, Enoch gasped for breath.

"What if I were to do away with you now?" the giant's voice threatened with a loud rush of air that slapped at Enoch's face. "I could just squeeze the life out of you, then I'd not have to follow any decree from *Eloah*." Lingdar's eyes glared at him and seemed to be the size of Enoch's head, his hand squeezing tighter. Enoch felt his bones start to cave from the pressure.

Beba appeared and placed her hand on Lingdar's shoulder. Lingdar paused and looked back, sensing her presence.

She brought her hand to the hand that held Enoch. Softly, she lowered it until it was safe for Lingdar to let go. Enoch fell to ground with a few coughs, shaken but unharmed.

Beba took Lingdar's face with both her hands and brought it close to hers. She closed her eyes, he did the same. She blew a gentle breath onto the bridge of his nose. The lines on his face relaxed and a breath escaped his nose as the tension left his body. Their foreheads touched and anger erased itself from Lingdar's body. Enoch got the impression they had done this a lot after the storm.

"Since the flood, we've been running, Lingdar. We've lost so much," Beba told her husband.

"I swore to protect you, Beba. This man asks us to commit suicide in the name of *Eloah*."

Lingdar pleaded with his wife as he nestled his head on his wife's shoulder. To Beba's enemies, Lingdar was no doubt fury personified, but in her arms now his spirit was laid bare, his eyes closing in the comfort.

Enoch had been let into a tender moment, catching a glimpse of their love. He saw it was not any different from his for Edna, when Edna was still his.

"Look around you Lingdar, this land is asking us to do the same. If you tell us to stay, would you not be asking the same of us?" asked his wife. "Maybe it is for the best," she said with the heavy heart of a mother's judgment and a wife's love.

"No!" insisted Enoch. "There's another way."

Beba opened her eyes and looked towards Enoch. Her tone warmed. "What way, Enoch the Scribe?" she asked.

"There's a place for you. *Eloah*'s *Arch* tells me it is beyond the gates of ice, that if you go there he'll bless the land for you. You will find peace there and humans will find peace here, you have a place Lingdar, it is just not here."

The giants looked from one to the other, weighing the thought among themselves. But Lingdar had made his decision. For Beba he would do anything. He stood up and walked over to a pointed hill as tall as he. He leaned in and sniffed at the slope of rocky earth. Satisfied, he then took in a breath and swung his hand into the hill cleaving the top off with one mighty blow. The sound was a rumbling crash that followed Lingdar's hand as it drove across the top, sending shockwaves that exploded through the air. The crumbled hill-top fell to the ground with a crash. Tumbling into dozens of broken pieces of grey mixed with black ore. When the dust-cloud cleared, Lingdar's blow had left a perfect flat plain on the hill where the peak had previously been. As Lingdar shifted the broken pieces, looking for iron, he called to his son. "Come! We must fashion weapons, the other tribes may not take this news as lightly as we."

"Do you think they'll fight us, father?" asked his son, approaching and gathering the boulders. "Giants only respect strength and intelligence," Lingdar said to his son, turning disdainfully to Enoch. "This man seems to have neither, they'll certainly not respect him." He spoke sternly. "And neither will I, but for the sake of my wife I'll listen and take us to the ice gates."

Lingdar looked towards his wife, then back at Enoch, before getting to work smashing more boulders. Watching their strength, Enoch felt smaller than ever.

"Other tribes?" Enoch asked. "How many others?"

"Before the flood we numbered in the hundreds of thousands, but now we do not know. But fear not, the Shekinah will lead us to who remains," Lingdar said. Enoch was interested. It was the second time he'd heard someone speak of the Shekinah.

Lingdar told Enoch that there were points on the Earth where the Shekinah lines intersected and greater energy could be harnessed from these points using the vibration of creation tones. He told him that all giants could find the Shekinah, but that some were better at it than others.

"Giants always build where the Shekinah intersects, there's more power there," said Lingdar. He looked at his daughter. The young woman had been rolling a boulder towards her brother. Her locks were red curls that framed her round face, and her eyes were the blue of the mid-day sky.

"What can you see?" Lingdar asked her.

The daughter paused and found a quiet patch next to the fire. She held her hands out and placed them as if she were sitting inside an invisible box. She closed her eyes and her mouth moved as the chime of a low hum shook the air with warmth. Enoch saw a blue light flash to life in the sky. It was a pattern of diamond shapes worked into a latticed frame extending far into the horizon. The lines pulsated with her tones and then slowly faded as she lowered her hands and opened her eyes again.

"There are giants to the north, and across the water there are more and further across the water again," she said.

"How many can you sense?" asked Lingdar.

"Ten thousand, father," she said, her face suddenly taken by a question in her mind. "And I sense something else, something...large. I sense Kokabel."

"Kokabel lives?" asked Lingdar, incredulous.

The girl nodded her head.

"Who is Kokabel?" asked Enoch.

Lingdar told him.

"There's something else, too," the daughter added, "Something even larger than Kokabel!"

Beba took pause at the daughter's worry but Lingdar and the son continued crushing boulders. Enoch surmised that the thought they would have to face someone like Kokabel meant they had to be prepared.

"Ten thousand giants?" Enoch remarked. "Do you have a leader?"

"You wish to be *Giza* of Giants?" scoffed Lingdar. He laughed, his son doing the same.

"What is a *Giza*?" asked Enoch.

"Giza is our word for *'King'*," replied Beba.

"Of course not, Lingdar, but that many *giants* will not follow of their own accord," Enoch stated. "If you're to build a new society beyond the ice gates, you will need to have a *Giza* to lead them."

"My grandfather told me that at the first exile of giants on Mount Hermon, Kokabel became the Giza. If he lives, then he still is. Come now, we've much work to do. Do you wish to help or will you spend the days dreaming of your future kingship?" Lingdar chuckled.

***

"Other tribes?" asked Holly, back in 1893.

"Not really tribes, I'd learn, but families like theirs. It took some months, but we fashioned swords and set off north. Lingdar's daughter had nimble fingers and fashioned a sword for me made of iron mixed with silver. We left the Nazca plain and it was just as Lingdar had said. Along the Shekinah lines we found other giants traumatized by the flood. Families who had lived peacefully before the flood were now erased from the earth as if they had never existed. From what we found, it seemed all they wanted was to be remembered."

Enoch told Holly they had left Nazca and gone to Ollamtaytambo, where another family had attempted to build steps to reach the heavens. At first, the family laughed that Lingdar would be following the orders of a human like Enoch, but once they learned of *Eloah*'s decree, of a land just for them, they changed their minds.

The caravan then travelled to Cuszco and Sacsayhuaman where another enclave had been built high in the mountains but all they found there were bones. The remains of a family who had died huddled together in each other's arms, while all around them, the land was barren with a consuming emptiness. Their only legacy was the precisely constructed walls and monuments which they had started constructing but never finished, dying of starvation before they could. As Enoch and the others travelled, he came to see that this was the giant's signature – great societies on the verge of flourishing but interrupted and hidden forever into history.

Enoch had never seen such craftsmanship. They would take giant stones and fashion them together with such precision that not even a thin leaf could get between them, the large pieces fitting together as if nature had created them for that one purpose.

"To this day their monuments still stand, and to this day, humans don't know how they were made."

"Do you know how they were made?" asked Holly.

"Strength, some mathematics and a lot of what we would call magic. To the giants though, magic was just another element of their world," Enoch replied. Holly looked on curiously. "What we would call *ghosts*, to them was just family."

"Ghosts?" asked Holly.

"Sort of, more like spirits. To any sane human, the thought of disembodied spirits would be frightening, but the giants had a different relationship with their dead. They would call on the spirits of their dead to help with shaping stones for building. The spirits would manifest in our world as a great whirlwind of powerful spinning wind. Imagine if you condensed the strength of a fierce typhoon into a spool the size of a human. It's focused power would be strong enough to grind the hardest stone into any shape desired or push water aside as if it were blades of grass."

Enoch told Holly that by the time they reached the eastern coast of South America, they had gathered a caravan of five hundred giants and were followed by an army of wind spirits who stayed invisible until called upon by incantations; words in the language of *Eloah* the giants knew as if they were nursery rhymes.

"How did you cross the ocean?" Holly asked.

"We walked across the ocean floor with walls of pulsating water at our sides, held there by the wind spirits. Along the path we found more bones along with cities that would never be gazed upon again. It took the better part of a year to cross. I called it 'The Sleepless Year'."

"Why?"

"If you ever try to sleep between two walls of water, a thousand feet high, you'll know why."

***

Enoch and the giants were greeted in the Dogon lands of Africa by a tribe of giants led by Dogon, a black-haired stocky giant the size of Lingdar and with eyes that shone blue like a still sky. His tribe of four thousand giants made their home along an angry coast battered by storms. At first, when Dogon had seen the waters recede from the coast, he thought it might have been a Tsunami but the Shekinah told him it was something else. When five hundred giants emerged from the ocean, he saw it was Lingdar with what looked like a human sleeping on his shoulder.

When the initial shock subsided, Dogon led them to a cavernous mountain where they could stay, rest and hold council. The first council was held that night and lasted until morning. Enoch awoke to find it in full swing.

"You follow this human. How do you know what he says is true?" Dogon asked Lingdar.

"This land will not harbour us any longer, this is a truth we cannot deny," Lingdar said, looking at his wife, who nodded her head in agreement. "The land beyond the ice gates may be our only chance, Dogon."

"It matters not," replied Dogon. "Your journey ends here. Kokabel commands the lands to the north at the mouth of the great river. He is building a beacon calling all the giants who remain."

"He seduces with the illusion of choice, Lingdar," another giant chimed in. "Follow him or leave, but all who go either become his slaves, or die."

"Not content to be Giza, he now wishes to be *Eloah* of all. Those beyond his lands are terrified of him," continued Dogon, his eyes telling Lingdar that maybe he was too. "Kokabel will never let us pass to get to them."

"You have so many men here, surely you could attack and slay him!" questioned Lingdar.

"Easier said than done," Dogon said, his eyes widening with remembered fear. It shook Enoch's peace to see a giant tremble with fear.

"How big is Kokabel?" asked Enoch.

"What did he say?" asked Dogon, shifting his ear closer to hear the little human. Enoch repeated the question, this time yelling at the top of his lungs.

"A drop of sweat from his brow would be more water than you drink in a day, little human. His thumb is taller than you but it isn't he whom we must worry about. Kokabel commands a great beast," Dogon said, "A leviathan that emerges from the sea at the call of his horn. When it emerges from the sea, the coasts flood and its mere breath carries even as far as here. The beast makes Kokabel look like a child. It is most grave indeed, Lingdar." The giants in the council stirred with the shared memory.

Lingdar pondered this revelation as Dogon bit from a tree he'd been eating. Lingdar sensed a fear in Dogon. "*A fear that there was no more time for,*" he thought.

"Here is what I see, Dogon," Lingdar began. "Either we perish here or we perish in battle. We've an army, is it not worth the chance to make a home for our people?"

"A fool's errand, Lingdar, even if we could separate Kokabel from his horn, long enough to attack. His six thousand slaves would run over whatever force we attack with, holding us just long enough for him to find his horn and summon the Leviathan to demolish us from the rear."

"And so we do nothing?" asked Lingdar. "Is this what you suggest?"

"I do not know," replied Dogon. "I suppose we wait until it is our time to fight, until he comes for us."

"His beast?" asked Enoch. "Does it follow whoever has the horn?"

"Yes," replied Dogon.

"Then it is simple," stated Enoch. "We steal his horn and take control of the beast." Enoch looked at Lingdar. They shared a look that said Enoch's plan contained a shared danger for each other but their eyes accepting it in the silence of the council.

"And what of Kokabel's slaves?" asked Dogon. "*They'll* not turn on the hand that feeds them."

"A slave may fight for his master, Dogon, but his heart always desires freedom. If they know we will give them freedom, they may fight for us," Enoch stated.

"What is your plan, Enoch?" asked Lingdar.

"Fool! I'll not follow the plan of a human," Dogon suddenly bellowed. Lingdar drew in a breath and rubbed at his eyes. He had expected this, knowing the first battle would be for the hearts and minds of the other giants in this council. He knew the only way they would respect Enoch's plan was if Lingdar had respect for Enoch himself. Lingdar said a quiet prayer in his heart to his old spirits and then stood, his presence suddenly taking command of the council, drawing the eyes of the others still sitting. The time for passively waiting the coming of your enemies had passed, Lingdar thought.

"Dogon, I urge you, before we dismiss his plan, let us hear its merit!" said Lingdar.

"Lingdar, what sort of plan can come from the intellect of a human?" Dogon scoffed. "I will certainly not entertain it."

"A human that survived the flood with no sea vessel deserves our ears."

Lingdar looked around to the other giants in the council. Some shuffled with boredom, some were curious. Most were resigned to the idea that there was nothing they could do anymore. Lingdar needed to show them that this was not true. *"Die slowly or die quickly?"* he thought. *"What is the difference if death waits just the same?"*

These giants had survived the greatest calamity the realm had ever known, Lingdar thought. What they must have done to survive meant that bravery resided in them. They only needed to know that it was there. Lingdar drew his sword, pointing it at Dogon in challenge.

"You may not, brother, but do you speak for the hearts of ten thousand giants waiting to be shown a path?" Lingdar spoke with an authority Dogon hadn't thought would be imposed on him. Dogon didn't take it well. Lingdar turned to the others.

"Which of you wants to form a land for our people? A society for our children? Who would rather die here knowing they never at least tried? Who? Raise your hand now and show your ancestors how cowardice has taken hold of you," Lingdar said. His voice, gravelly and full of bass, now fuming with anger.

The group stirred. A few faces turned to Lingdar with their own rising anger. Lingdar's plan was working. He needed to channel their anger towards the barrier that held them back from salvation. He needed to channel their energy toward Kokabel himself.

Dogon stood and drew his sword at Lingdar. This had been enough. *"How dare Lingdar enter his land and show him such disrespect?"* His hard eyes said as much as he moved toward the offending giant. Lingdar steadied himself for the battle to come. The other giants suddenly shifted to give them space. In the commotion, Enoch lost his footing. The shuffling steps of the council rumbled the ground under him. As Enoch scurried to safety, he saw a shadow form above him. A giant foot was stepping down onto him. Enoch froze. The giant hadn't seen him standing there. Enoch tensed, waiting for another death.

Instead, he felt a sudden sweep of air by his head as Beba had scooped him up and carried him away from the impending danger. The soft skin of her palm felt like a bundle of cashmere wool, he thought. Within her gentle grip, Enoch watched as Dogon raised his sword, but Lingdar's face was calm with knowledge. *"What are you thinking Lingdar, he'll surely kill you,"* Enoch thought.

Beba held Enoch close to her bosom, while her other hand rose to reach out for Lingdar to stop him. Lingdar saw her action and turned to his wife, raising his own hand at her but with a softened face that lasted for an instant. Just long enough for the look to tell her that it would be okay.

"No, Lingdar!" Beba protested. In response Lingdar winked at Beba, then turned quickly toward Dogon.

Lingdar's eyes were on the fast-approaching giant, but instead of tensing for battle, Lingdar suddenly shifted his head and dropped his sword. He then let his weight fall onto his knees, creating craters in the rock. Lingdar closed his eyes and held out his arms, offering himself as a sacrifice to Dogon's wrath. Dogon stopped his rush, his face stunned by Lingdar's sudden subjugation.

"Rise! You offend my honour! Fight me, you coward!" Dogon said but Lingdar stayed where he was.

"Dogon, you offend the honour of ten thousand by asking us to await death at the hands of Kokabel's leviathan. If we're not to forge a path for ourselves, then I do not want to see another day on this realm, I only ask that you make no request of my spirit once I am gone." Lingdar closed his eyes again. Beba watched with anxiety, Enoch could hear her massive heart-beat thumping inside her, slowing down when Lingdar offered his life.

"What is he doing?" asked Enoch. Beba spoke downward but kept her eyes on her husband.

"Giants cannot kill an unarmed giant. It is our law," she said, while Dogon paced, his face locked with frustration.

"No! Dogon," a voice from the crowd said.

"Do not do it! Your spirit will be cursed!" another said.

"Listen to the scribe first, what harm can it do?" yet another called out.

The pleas became a cacophony. Dogan dropped his sword and turned his back on the council. His complete frustration was a nauseating wave of fear that tried to hide behind anger, an anger he felt towards himself for not being brave enough to face the monster waiting to enslave them all.

Dogon walked over to the ridge and looked out to the tribes Lingdar and the human had gathered. Over the green and rocky expanse of their valley and down to the coast, he saw thousands of giants who didn't know they had choice. If he held them back now, how was he different from Kokabel?

Lingdar rose slowly, he turned to Beba and winked again. Despite herself she smiled nervously at him. His gambit had worked. Enoch could see a little rose form in her cheeks, he heard her heart gain a sudden extra beat. Lingdar gathered Dogon's sword, leaving his own, and walked over to him. Dogon felt the movement of Lingdar stirring behind him but didn't look back.

"You will need this, brother," Lingdar said, handing Dogon his sword. When Dogon turned and accepted, Lingdar placed his hand on Dogon's shoulder and lowered his tone.

"I'll not only need your strength, but the wisdom of knowing when to use it, which, as you have just shown me, you possess. Please listen for our sakes Dogon," he pleaded. "For mine too." Lingdar turned to Enoch. "Tell us your plan, Enoch."

Beba handed Enoch to Lingdar. He brought Enoch to his shoulder and listened. As he did, Lingdar grabbed a tree and started to trace the plan into the mud as Enoch spoke it into Lingdar's ear. The others watched. The plan was ambitious but no other option existed now. After Lingdar had outlined the plan, the only thing left to do was to prepare more weapons. The task took several months as they wrought more iron from the hills and wood for the kilns to forge more swords, shields and armour. When they finally left the Dogon lands, never to return again, Lingdar saw that they had left a barren wasteland of Earth and crumbled rock. His heart broke at the sight. Enoch was right, this realm couldn't support them.

They found more recruits in the *Tassili* valley of *Niger*. Their caravan then travelled to the *Siwa oasis* in *Algeria* where they gathered the last of the giants.

***

At the mouth of the Nile, Kokabel walked across a plateau holding a sack of wine made from the skin of 300 bulls. His great beacon was now capped with a golden tip at the top. Its brilliance reflected into Kokabel's watery eyes. As he gazed at the pyramid, his craggy, swollen face released a smile. His fingers ran along the smooth sides, fueling his drunken joy. Behind him a large statue had been carved into the body of a lion, but with the head of Azazel adorned with a headdress. A homage to his father.

A group of smaller giants holding tools, led by Akanel, the first son of Kokabel, stood a few paces away, waiting for Kokabel's next order. Behind them a whirlwind sprit awaited an incantation to get to work. It spun in on itself blowing sand away from them, but Kokabel didn't need it anymore. The great construction had finally been completed and now vibrated with perfection.

The pyramid's four sides aligned perfectly with the four directions and in perfect proportion to the golden number of all creation – *Phi*. The lone Pyramid now towered above anything in the desert. Its every dimension and figure were set perfectly in harmony, as if Kokabel's hands had been guided by the sun and moon itself when he'd envisioned it. The sun caught the gold, the reflection emanating outward in all directions, a blinding beacon for all.

"We shall build the others here and here," Kokabel ordered, pointing to two other locations near the great Pyramid. "Draw up the plans Akanel, when you're *Giza*, these will be your crown jewels!" The dutiful yet sickly looking son agreed and ran off to start work, his elongated and lanky frame a contrast to his father's imposing presence. As he left, another giant approached. Out of breath, the smaller giant carried a message for Kokabel.

"Great Kokabel! A caravan approaches, the largest number we've seen!" The messenger pointed south. Kokabel peered toward it. In the distance, he saw the faint outline of a long undulating procession led by Lingdar and Dogon. Kokabel saw all the giants east of the Nile now snaking across the desert toward his plateau. His beacon had worked better than he thought, he turned to the sickly messenger.

"What do you feel in the Shekinah?"

"It vibrates with deception, great Kokabel, be wary of their words."

Kokabel's face didn't move. He took another swill from his sack of wine, the last of it, and dropped it to the ground. "Assemble the men and prepare a force," Kokabel ordered as he left to get his armour.

He stumbled into his chamber, an open air expanse with a black and white tiled floor the size of a lake. Two pillars stood aside a raised platform where he slept and drank under the stars.

From a cave he gathered his golden armour with fumbling hands. Not really reaching but throwing himself into the movements, his eyes barely staying open, he sat down to wait for the caravan. His knuckles dragged across the rocky ground, looking for the sack of wine as slaves were being led into the chamber.

"Wine!" his graveled voice bellowed to no-one in particular, yet expecting it to be delivered soon.

Lingdar and Dogon had left the procession at a sand dune just below the plateau and entered Kokabel's chamber with a small contingent of their own guards. One guard carried a sack on his back that was laden with supplies. The most important of these was Enoch, who peered out from a hole, making mental notations of where everything was.

More slaves were ushered into the chamber and gathered into a ragged formation in front of Kokabel. They were a mix of giants, ranging in size, but none as big as Kokabel. Enoch looked at their faces and saw that they stared forth with the look of dull minds. He'd known that look well at Sargon's prison long ago. Many were thin under Kokabel's rule now. It seemed Kokabel's subjugation did not bode well for them.

As Lingdar arrived, Enoch could smell the odour of fermented wine escaping from Kokabel's skin. The giant sat back down and took a seat at the altar, splaying his body out at rest, his eyes scanning forth in drunken boredom.

"Where is my wine?" Kokabel bellowed again. Two slaves entered holding another large brown sack. Kokabel took it and drank of the contents, throwing the sack aside where it landed on the head of a slave who hadn't been paying attention. The slave didn't feel the blow, Enoch saw the giant's dull eyes say as much.

"By what manner do you arrive unannounced?" Kokabel asked.

Lingdar stepped forward, even as Kokabel sat, he was still double the size of Lingdar. "Mighty Kokabel, we come with a message from *Eloah*."

"What message?" he asked through a yawn.

Lingdar told him of a land beyond the ice gates. Kokabel listened but with only half attention, his mind wandering over the thought of the great constructions still to be built. This realm was now his and no decree from *Eloah* could tell him otherwise. When Lingdar finished Kokabel responded.

"*Eloah* now attempts to claim dominion over me?" Kokabel scoffed. "He banishes me from my family, binds my father for seventy generations and then expects me to submit to his dominion now. Such insolence!"

"It is the only hope for our people, Kokabel, please consider for their sakes," pleaded Lingdar.

"My subjects are content to serve their *Giza* here. I've heard your plea, I'll not follow you and neither will my people," Kokabel said. Lingdar had expected this answer, in fact he'd hoped for it.

Kokabel's followers and slaves shifted with fear and longing but stayed silent. Enoch saw their eyes shift downward and then timidly look towards Kokabel, as if hoping their Giza would see their wish to be heard, their wish to be free. Enoch saw that Kokabel was uninterested in their opinion, not fearing any decree from *Eloah*. "*How sad that his followers were not as brave, so they could stand up against Kokabel, as he was doing now against Eloah,*" Enoch thought.

"You may stay here for the night and in the morning, you will decide if you want to join my *army*," Kokabel said.

"And if we do not?" asked Lingdar. "You will let us pass to warn the others?"

"Your angst will be the death of you, all of you. If you choose not to follow me, my leviathan will rid you of your angst." Kokabel waved them away. Guards approached and led them out. As they were escorted out, one guard peered at the hole in the sack where Enoch hid. His eyes made contact with Enoch and held his gaze for a second too long. Enoch thought they would be found out and slain instantly but the guard looked around, then brought his finger to his lips. Motioning for Enoch to stay quiet. In the distance, Kokabel's voice echoed.

"More wine!"

Enoch and the others retreated to camp. They waited until nightfall and held the final council before the assault. Enoch told them of the guard.

"It is as you say, Enoch. His people wish to flee with us, the Shekinah tells me so," said Dogon as he ate.

"Kokabel has a fondness for wine. Those that do often have a fondness for sleep. We will wait until he sleeps. Gather your forces just beyond the dunes, Lingdar, and attack when you hear his second scream," Enoch said.

In the higher realm Uriel watched. Gabriel, Michael and Raphael stood behind her. Enoch's plan was dangerous, failure would mean the realm would forever be ruled by Kokabel. The thought of intervening crossed her mind but she couldn't. The others would not let her.

"He's a fool," Gabriel remarked, "*Eloah* wastes the gifts of eternity on a fool."

"Take pause, Gabriel," Uriel replied. "For what would you attempt if you knew you couldn't fail?"

As Kokabel slept a drunkard's sleep, Enoch maneuvered around his great courtyard like a mouse, ducking from alcove to little alcove with the sword at his side. Their plan had hinged on Kokabel not knowing Enoch was there, for if one doesn't know a mouse is in their midst, how could they ever know to set a trap for one. Entering unnoticed was easy, now came the hard part.

He approached Kokabel's body and looked for an entry point. *"His ear would be too small and the other openings even smaller,"* Enoch thought. Deciding that it would have to be his mouth, but first he'd need to get the giant to open it. He quietly advanced waiting for the right moment to climb the torso.

After he made his way up the rungs of his armour, he tip-toed across the heaving chest. Rising and falling as Kokabel breathed in deep sleep. Enoch counted the breaths and only moved when the chest moved to avoid detection. He arrived at Kokabel's beard and thought to hide inside it while he waited for the right moment. But as the giant suddenly stirred, Enoch's leg caught on a coarse hair, trapping his foot like a vine. The giant's hand suddenly rose and slapped at the chin, blowing air at Enoch like a wind-filled sail. He ducked in time to avoid being thrown clear.

He reached the mouth just under the nose, the air from the large nostrils blowing down on him like a heavy sea wind, warm and thick, settling for an instant and then pulling him upward again as the giant breathed in. Enoch counted the pattern and waited for a moment to strike.

"It is now or never," he thought. He removed the sword and waited for the full lull of breath. When the air settled, he plunged the knife deep into Kokabel's upper lip. The sword cleaved through the skin but became stuck when it landed in the gum tissue. Enoch pulled back but the sword would not move. He couldn't leave the sword behind. He pulled again and it came free but the giant's eyes had opened, his mouth forming a scream at the sudden pain on his lip. It was Enoch's only chance to get in the mouth. If the giant fully rose before he could, Enoch would plunge to the ground.

Enoch jumped into the giant's mouth just as Kokabel's scream erupted into the chamber, his head stirring the rest of his body into an awareness of something untoward happening. Inside, Enoch's ears rang from the scream. At the sand dune, across from the plateau, Lingdar looked at Dogon. He counted, "That's one."

Enoch had landed on the wet tongue of the giant's mouth, narrowly avoiding teeth that came down hard on each other with a loud crack, ringing his ears again. Enoch rolled into the gag reflex and the giant coughed. The air blew a foul stench of alcohol at Enoch's face but with it came hope as the abyss of the throat opened. Enoch wasted no time and jumped down into the darkness.

He elbow-crawled down the wet canal and landed in a heap of foul yellow food that had yet to be digested. The smell was atrocious and the acid was starting to burn at his skin. Bones of animals and other giants were strewn about the area, as if a battle had taken place here that no-one survived. He had to move quickly, he took out his sword and began hacking at the stomach walls.

Kokabel screamed again as sharp pains suddenly exploded inside him, blood was dripping from the wound at his mouth. The pain in his stomach causing him to double over and slow his steps. He fell to his knees. He looked over to the cave where the horn was kept, trying to move toward it through the pain. Outside the plateau, beyond the sand dunes, Lingdar and the other giants heard the signal.

"That's two, the time comes! We go!" Lingdar commanded. The battle cry stirred through the giants as they stormed the plateau. The ground shook under their steps while the desert sand danced around in wafts at their feet. The Shekinah vibrated with their resolve, their faces showing the same. They rushed into the altar chamber and surrounding platforms where the slaves and guards slept, too fast for the sleeping guards to have grabbed their weapons on hearing Kokabel's scream. Each soldier awoke to a sword at their necks, held there by Lingdar and the others. This was followed by one simple question.

"A choice awakens you! Freedom or death, *brother*?" It was as Enoch had said, these giants wanted to be free. All chose freedom.

Inside Kokabel, Enoch had escaped the stomach. He gasped for air and was still covered in bile that stung at his eyes. *"That injury will not kill Kokabel, I need to find the heart,"* he thought. He looked up and saw the ballooning lungs swell with air. High above that he saw the beating heart. Dark purple and beating wildly, it was the size of an elephant. Enoch needed to get there fast. Any moment now Kokabel would reach the horn. Enoch thrust the sword into the lungs to climb it, each thrust drawing more blood that filled Kokabel's mouth, dripping out and staining the black and white tiled floor.

Enoch made it to the heart where it pulsated at a faster pace, its walls pounding, fighting to pump more blood for Kokabel's battle, and not knowing that Enoch had brought that battle directly to it. Enoch grabbed at a thick slippery section that looked like an anaconda. He began to saw through it with his sword, releasing the giant's warm blood into the cavity in a gushing torrent that knocked Enoch aside.

Outside, Kokobel slowed down, his hand gripped at his chest, clawing at the pain inside. His eyes rolled up into his head as the strength was leaving his body. The giant fell to his knees and lost consciousness but for Enoch, the danger was only beginning.

The chest cavity was now filling with blood. Enoch fought to keep his head above the warm metallic liquid. He swam to the top of the chest cavity trying to hack through the giant's breastplate but the bone was like iron. He needed to find softer tissue and he needed to do it quickly. He had to break through the skin soon or he'd be trapped by the blood.

Enoch's vision blurred, he felt his knees buckle and a light-headed wave went through him. The giant's blood was causing a reaction in Enoch that he didn't expect. It was draining the power from his muscles, draining his life.

The words of Uriel came to him. *"Yours is a life that cannot be extinguished by earthly means."*

"Of course," he thought. *"Giants are not earthly and neither is their blood."*

The blood came rushing up to his neck and was about to drown him. As Kokabel was dying so was Enoch. The first thought that flashed in his mind was the hope that Lingdar would find the ice gates alone, the second was Edna, the last image was Uriel, staying with him as he fought.

Above him a downward mound suddenly formed on the skin, it grew downward until a giant metal blade suddenly pierced through. Air filled the cavity and the blood rushed out, carrying Enoch with it. When Enoch settled and caught his breath, he looked into the face of Lingdar leaning down and wiping the blood from Enoch's body. The giant couldn't hide his elation. The corners of his eye crinkling as his joy radiated outward.

"It has worked, Enoch, we have control of the complex," Lingdar said.

Enoch looked around and saw that the other giants had been liberated from Kokabel's hold. They cheered now as Dogon's forces smashed their chains. Lingdar lifted Enoch onto his shoulders and proclaimed above the sound of joy for all to hear.

"Hear me! Enoch the scribe has slain the mighty Kokabel. I declare Enoch the scribe the new *Giza* of Giants!"

The giants cheered at the prospect, even Dogon ignored the fact the Enoch was a human. Proud to know the man who had slain the largest giant of all. When they settled and Enoch had caught his breath, it was time for their new Giza's first address.

"I give you all thanks for this honour! I've but one decree and it will also be last. My first decree as Giza is to relinquish my title. In my stead, I name Lingdar to rule as Giza of all giants!"

The crowd was silent, but from the back Lingdar's son started chanting, "Giza! Giza! Giza!" Slowly, the others took to the chant. "Giza! Giza! Giza!" The chant carried far across the plateau. Past the great pyramid to the shadows of the dunes where a group of twenty-five young giants hurriedly made their way away from the assault, led by their sickly older brother, Akanel, his brothers and sisters having just awoken to find their father murdered, and the society he'd created turned against him. He turned to look over his shoulder when he heard the giants naming a new Giza, a title that should have been his, a title that would be his. Vengeance quietly burned in his heart.

***

Back in 1893 Holly listened with attention and a hint of worry, *"Could this man be trusted? There was no way to verify anything that he said."* The thought was tempered by the idea that she now had all the time in the world to find out. "The Pyramids of Giza," Holly said, "I've heard tales of them, that they were built for the old Egyptian Kings?"

"Kokabel certainly thought he was king but it was Dogon who named the plateau. We didn't know it then but Kokabel had twenty-five children. Two of them would later return and start the line of Pharaohs. Some of the others went north but most scattered to the west. We captured twelve of them but the other thirteen stayed in this realm, we never found them. Their descendants are still out there today."

"Who are they?"

"A long time ago they were all Kings and Queens, from the pagan tribes of Europe to Siam – all carrying the blood of Azazel through their ancestor, Kokabel. Later, when the churches formed and went after them, some gave up their titles but kept the power from the shadows. Power from the shadows is the hardest to fight against, this is the big secret of the secret societies."

"Secret societies? Like the men who chased me in Scotland?"

"Most likely," Enoch nodded. He saw the memory of what had happened in Scotland sit just behind the look of worry in Holly's eyes. The poor girl was still scared, she was not ready to know why they needed her; or to know that long ago in Babylon they had needed Enoch for the same purpose.

Enoch's Muse   144

"We humans are curious creatures Holly. Most people live their lives caring only about surviving in this world, while the people we elect to govern us care mostly about power through names and titles. The descendants of Kokabel however, care only about their blood. This is why they do not mix with commoners. Diluting their blood would dilute their claim to power in this realm. To them, their blood is proof they're descended from *Eloah*, everything else is just *bread and circuses*, as the Romans liked to say."

"Where did you go next?" Holly asked.

"It took us twenty more years to get ready for the final leg of the journey. We needed ships and more weapons in case any of Kokabel's children waited for us in the lands to the west. Humans hadn't returned yet, I thought they could use the great intellect from the giants so I transcribed the account of what I'd learned from the Giants onto emerald tablets, mined from a quarry by Lingdar's daughter. On our last day, Lingdar ordered one of his spirits to re-carve the head on the sphinx to the figure of a human."

***

As Enoch and the giants left the Giza plateau, Lingdar stood on the edge of a wooden barge leaving the coast. He looked back to the land they were leaving, to the great Pyramid, soon to become a memory. – "*A structure no flood could ever destroy*," Lingdar thought.

For all of Kokabel's faults, Lingdar couldn't fault him for wanting to be remembered. "*If one cannot live in happiness, then being remembered is the next best thing*," Lingdar thought.

The barge was joined by hundreds more as they became an armada setting off to find the rest of the giants. They crossed the Mediterranean and headed to *Petra* and Enoch's old home of *Ur*. They went to *Persepolis* in Iran and then *Mohinjo Daro* in Pakistan.

On the way, in the Indus valley, their procession had been traversing through a muddy marsh when the giants suddenly stopped. They were commanded to do so by Lingdar at the front with a sudden wail that came from his massive lungs. Enoch thought some new danger was upon them. Noises came from the distance, followed by a rumbling in the ground from something large. Enoch tensed for battle but Lingdar knelt to the ground and bowed his head, the others followed. Enoch was confused but his confusion ended when their path was suddenly crossed by hundreds of large grey animals, running by the procession with curved white tusks and long trunks for noses.

Enoch had never seen such magnificent beasts, had never heard animals make a noise like they did. Enoch saw that the giants held these animals in great respect. Lingdar glanced toward Enoch as they were passing.

"Kneel and lower your head Enoch, the EL-LA-FANT is our most sacred animal," Lingdar said.

Enoch obliged. When the animals passed Lingdar rose and the tribes, with a now stunned Enoch, continued on. Lingdar later explained that spirits of giants often find resting places in the souls of elephants. That like giants, their intellect was unmatched on this realm.

They later took rest. Enoch took his under the shade of an Acacia tree on the bank of the river but a sudden noise brought him out of sleep. It was the same whelping trumpet Enoch had heard from the elephants but from a much smaller one. He opened his eyes and looked past the bank. The tide had gone out but was coming back now. In the middle of the riverbed, a baby elephant was fighting to free itself from a mud puddle.

Around the struggling infant, Enoch saw streaks of shimmering water running along the riverbed. It was gaining strength, signaling to him that a raging river would soon follow. Enoch stood and walked onto the riverbed.

As Enoch got closer to the infant he saw it was the size of a hyena and that it now no longer struggled. The animal's back foot had become stuck in a puddle made of a sand and water. The baby must have fought to get free for hours and was now waiting either for death or help.

Its wide thin ears flapped, trying to keep itself cool, Enoch thought. Enoch kneeled down and started to work the leg free. As he did, an ear slapped into Enoch's face, stinging his cheeks. He saw the other bank through a hole in the earlobe that was a perfect circle. He wondered how the little elephant had managed to make such a perfect hole through its ear. The leg got free and the little animal ran back across the bank to find the rest of its herd. *"I guess they are only intelligent when they grow up,"* Enoch thought before he returned to the bank.

They travelled to the lands where humans would later name the homes of the Gods. *Kajuraho* in India. *Paya* in Burma. *Sukothai* in Thailand. *Angkor Wat* and *Preah Vihar* in Cambodia. The armada crossed another ocean and ended up on Easter Island.

More than ten thousand giants now waited there as they gathered strength for the final leg of their journey to the ice lands. They made camp and told stories to pass the time. The atmosphere buzzed with excitement as the giants reconnected with each other. Societies that had evolved thousands of miles apart from each other now connected with the realization that they descended from the same sets of ancestors. Each new connection was a meeting of distant cousins. During the days many took to carving giant figures of stone and leaving them in the Earth, a beacon to the future of a past gone, but not forgotten.

Enoch and Lingdar had travelled a distance clear across the realm, farther than any man, human or giant would travel for more than a thousand years. Their journey from Nazca to Easter Island had taken 40 cycles. Enoch now wore the years on his face but when he'd first met Lingdar, he'd been a young man alone in the world. His face was now that of someone knocking on the door of old age, looking for rest and hoping death would be kind when it let him in.

On the curved green plain of Easter Island it was the eve of their departure for the ice lands. Their camp hummed with activity in anticipation. Clothes and supplies were being gathered and stored away for what they knew would face them on the ice – sharpened swords and axes waiting for the unknown and unexpected. All were taking care to not step on Enoch who was sitting at a fire grilling a hare for his dinner.

He turned the sizzling hare over on the flame, he couldn't remember the last time he had eaten. Hunger had become like a forgotten tool that had grown dull but yet couldn't be discarded. Not because it was useful but rather a reminder of a time he wished never to forget, no matter how dull it had made the days to feel. The aroma wafted to his nose, he felt saliva form in his mouth at the thought of the first bite. In that moment, he felt like the old Enoch again.

Night was soon to fall. To his far left he noticed Lingdar walking with Beba, the sun low in the sky in front of them as they drew nearer to a mound. The pair strolled slowly with a giddy expectation in their movements, their fingers dancing with each other. Lingdar leaned and whispered into her ear, she smiled and playfully tried to turn her head away. The sudden blush of her cheeks told Enoch she wasn't going anywhere. They ascended the mound, looked back to see if anyone had noticed them, and then disappeared over it. Curiosity got the better of Enoch, he left his dinner and walked over to see where they were going.

At the edge, the mound gave way to a slope that led to black sand running along a wide beach. The sun had formed an orange reflection on the water directly in front of Lingdar and Beba, making their figures look like shadows. The waves lapped at their feet as they walked in silence down to the dark blue ocean.

Lingdar's arm was around her waist, their faces toward the sun, watching the day slowly give way to night. Enoch saw their heads inching closer together as if drawn by a magnetism stirring inside of them. Enoch had never known Lingdar's or Beba's age, he'd never thought to ask, nor even wondered. Being made immortal had robbed him of the thought of time as anything more than a simple measure. To Enoch, it had become a foreign construct. As he watched Beba and Lingdar, walking along the sand, as if they had fallen in love only yesterday, he thought it might be the same for them too.

Lingdar stopped, his head shifted over to Beba's locks of fire-coloured curls. She leaned into the contact, turned her head, and met his lips for a kiss. They turned toward the water. Lingdar held her hand, drawing it closer, Beba followed. Enoch saw the water rise to their knees as they waded farther out. The sun was starting to disappear in front of them as the water continued up to their waists. When the water was at their necks, Enoch saw their garments suddenly float up to the water's surface, floating there as the sun set behind them and the stars became visible. Enoch had seen so many of their intimate moments, he didn't need to be in this one. He turned and returned to his burning dinner before their bodies locked into love-making under the stars.

When he finished eating, Enoch remained at the fire. He held a stick drawing figures in the dirt. His mind was clear, no single thought drove his hands but the figure he was drawing was of Uriel as she had been after Enoch had taken Abner's poison. Lingdar appeared and joined him, Beba was not in sight.

"Is she the *Arch* who told you of the land beyond the ice gates?" Lingdar asked looking down at what Enoch was making. Enoch caught his own thought at the suggestion. He hadn't realized that he'd been tracing a figure of Uriel, now it was impossible to ignore.

"She showed me everything, Lingdar, but there are times I still feel blind," replied Enoch softly. Lingdar listened but his attention was suddenly taken by Beba emerging from behind the mound and moving over to where she and Lingdar had made their camp. Her hair was wet and was close to her head. Her eyes caught Lingdar's for only a moment, followed quickly by a guilty smile and a flash of rose on her cheeks again. Enoch looked over to Lingdar, who seemed to grow silent as his head followed the motion of his Beba walking away, his eyes relaxing into the hypnotic movement of the garment covering her wide hips below her slim waist. A crooked smile of the often dim-witted formed on the giant's face. Enoch felt his own longing for love, a longing divided by Edna and Uriel. One gone forever, the other one lasting a moment between lifetimes.

"How did you meet her?" he asked Lingdar.

"Other giants had found wives long before me," Lingdar began. "But one day I saw Beba near a rock garden where the red moss grew. I was there gathering boulders. She'd go there to gather the moss for her drawings. I was never a handsome man, my words stepped out of my mouth like a man born with two left feet. We were much younger then but I saw her and it was the way her hands moved, Enoch, not slow or fast but with no wasted movements either, and gentle – her fingers avoiding every mistake or misplacement as she gathered the red moss. She caught me watching her and would you believe it, she gave me a wink!" Lingdar said, turning to Enoch.

"Can you imagine that? Me? As charming as a stone but yet this woman had shown an interest in me?" Lingdar laughed with the memory.

"What did you do?"

"The whole night my mind was awash in what that wink meant, my heart fluttered at the possibilities. I thought the wink must have meant that she wanted me to pursue her. So the next day I did, I returned to the rock garden and asked her to teach me how to draw, to teach my fingers to move as hers did."

"You liked drawing?"

"Not even slightly. A blind man has more talent than me. I just wanted to be near her. She agreed and taught me for many cycles, though I made sure never to learn too much for fear that she'd one day catch on and stop teaching me."

"Are you any good now?"

"Probably better than she is," Lingdar replied. "But promise you'll never tell her."

"Something tells me she knows, Lingdar. It is still very different from humans though," Enoch said. "It is rare for a human woman to make the first move. Is this common for giants?" Lingdar laughed again.

"Not common at all, giant women are very modest."

"But she still winked at you?" Enoch questioned. Lingdar looked at his fingers and traced a perfect figure of Beba's eyes into the ground.

"Love, Enoch, is merely magic trying to reveal itself. You see, as I was pretending to be unteachable, I came to see that Beba had a curious affliction of her eyes. In a normal day her eyes blink 1,253 times, I've looked at them long enough to know. Most times it is with both eyes but for Beba, twice a day, every 520th time to be precise, will see only one eye blink. That day by the rock garden, I'd just happened to catch Beba's 520th blink. From that one moment grew a love that will never end, would you not call that magic?"

"I guess I would," replied Enoch, his heart warmed by the thought of Lingdar's *magic* though his mind knew it was just circumstance, coincidence really. But when it appeared to conspire and make one fall in love, magic might be a better name. Enoch wished a little magic for the love growing inside of him for Uriel. Lingdar looked down at the figure Enoch had drawn on the ground. His nose twitched as he sniffed at the Shekinah around Enoch.

"Your technique, it isn't good but I can tell you think she's beautiful. The Shekinah says you long for her in your dreams. Such dreams your heart will not allow because of your Edna."

"The Shekinah says all that?"

"No, you also talk in your sleep, Enoch," Lingdar confessed.

"Indeed she is beautiful and indeed I do long for her, Lingdar. What am I to do?"

"Nothing, if it is meant to be, you will not need to do anything except follow your heart and follow the magic. By the time I realized that Beba's wink didn't ask me to pursue her, I was already in love. How I got there mattered very little to us."

"I wonder if this *magic* will conspire against me too."

"How unfortunate you are, Enoch the Scribe."

"Why?"

"Uriel doesn't sound like a woman with imperfections to mislead you in the right direction."

"No, she doesn't," Enoch fell silent as he thought of the last time he'd seen her just before the flood. He gazed up to the sky where millions of stars shone down on the sleeping camp. Above him, a shooting star streaked across the sky, disappearing behind the southern horizon; the direction they would travel the next day.

Lingdar looked down to the small human who had earned his respect, the human who had shown him that *Eloah*'s creation included the giants, his mind wondering how it could ever include someone like Enoch or the man's love for an *Arch*.

"What'll you do after we find the ice gates?" he asked.

"I'll have fulfilled *Eloah*'s mission, I'll be free to leave this realm," Enoch replied with a sadness in his voice. Lingdar noticed and offered a solution.

"You may come with us instead. You will be an honoured man for the rest of your days, our history will speak of you with favour."

"You're a great man, Lingdar, to offer me a home, but it is my time to leave this realm."

"Your Edna is gone and Uriel cannot love you. Loving any woman on this realm will only end in further anguish for yourself. Giants live longer, come with me and I'll choose a wife for you," he said. Enoch laughed.

"I'm not sure I could ever bring love to a giant woman, but thank you, I'll consider your offer."

"I know you will not, your Shekinah vibrates with resolve to return to *Eloah*. I just ask that when you speak to him again, you give him a message from me?"

"What is that, Lingdar?"

"Tell him I said thank you."

They travelled south and came to the ice lands where it was cold beyond anything Enoch had ever experienced. No human could survive here, he thought. No human would ever have to. The sun had erased itself from the sky and the journey saw the caravan brave winds that didn't stop or end, battering them incessantly as they tried to avoid crevasses in the ice, waiting to claim the clumsy and weak, the dark and jagged depths, staring up at them like crocodiles waiting at riverbanks for prey to cross.

When they found one, one of their largest would be called forth to act as a land bridge. Enoch, bundled in camel and bear fur, followed at Lingdar's side. The giant peered down every few minutes to make sure Enoch hadn't been lost, swallowed by the consuming whiteness or blown away by the wind. On the final morning, after having spent a month on the ice, Lingdar looked down but Enoch was not there.

The giant spun around quickly, "Stop!" he commanded. Others relayed the message down the procession until the massive line of trekking giants came to a halt. Lingdar narrowed his eyes but the white snow made it nearly impossible to focus on any object. Finally, he found a protrusion on a ridge of snow. Enoch was standing there, facing southwest, not far from where Lingdar had stopped.

Enoch was looking at something approaching from the southwestern sky. He'd found something. When Lingdar joined him, he too saw the second sun. It was rising and daylight was starting to streak in. In the distance another mountain range came into shape, at first blocked by the white haze but then clearing under the light of the new morning. It peaked out from behind a mountain top and was larger than the sun they had known their entire lives. Lingdar looked back in the opposite direction, all he could see was darkness. "Well that is a most strange development," he remarked.

"It is certainly not our sun," Enoch stated. "It can't be, the sun should be rising behind us back to the east." Lingdar sniffed at the Shekinah for confirmation.

"You're right, Enoch, the light vibrates at a different frequency. It isn't of this realm," Lingdar replied. "Where are we?"

"I don't know but we must be close," Enoch said.

Lingdar's puzzled face turned to the procession. They had stopped and watched the new sun rise in the sky. As it got higher, the large mountains in front became clearer. Enoch saw that the mountain range went on further than they had been able to see in the darkness. He saw it wind from their far left to directly in front of them and continued on, until it disappeared far to their right, leaving their visual perspective field.

When the light had filled the morning something else came into view. On the tallest peak, directly in front of them, stood two long, black protrusions set perpendicular to each other. They rose from the peak of the mountain and appeared to be large, maybe the height of Kokabel by Enoch's estimation from that distance. They needed a closer look. Enoch and Lingdar left the procession and went to investigate.

In silence as they climbed, the same thought ran through both their minds as they climbed the path to the double pillars, *"These must be the ice gates to the outer lands."*

When they arrived they saw the pillars had been carved perfectly flat on every side, as thick as a large elephant but as long as three horses lined end to end. Enoch touched one, it felt like metal but its coldness was of stone. They were smooth and devoid of markings, perfectly rectangular and made of a black stone. The pillars dominated the mountain top, an intrusion into the natural world of ice and snow. They were not *natural* Enoch thought, *"At least natural in terms of what man understands."*

Beyond the pillars, he saw the mountain descend on the other side to more snow and then fading to green and a new ocean in the hazy distance, shimmering with warm blue waves lapping at black volcanic rock. When he tried to get a closer look, he became certain that this was the right place. Enoch's face suddenly crashed into something when he tried to step around a pillar to see its backside. His entire body was stopped in mid-motion by some invisible force. Stunned, he nearly fell over.

He ran his hand along the space where his face had just crashed. He pushed harder but his hand still could not push through. To Lingdar, it looked like Enoch's hand was being held back by the air itself. Enoch stepped back.

He looked to the left of the pillars, the mountain tops extended far into the distance, as if they would never give way to flat ground again. To the right was the same thing, he smiled at Lingdar.

"This is more than just a gate, Lingdar," Enoch said, "I think we've found the edge of the entire realm."

The new sun rose higher in front of them. A wavy structure suddenly glinted across the mountain tops as the light of the new sun streaked in from behind the pillars. At first Enoch thought his eyes were playing tricks on him. It was as if whatever had stopped Enoch from passing through, was also affected by the light from beyond the pillars. As the light got stronger though, he saw what looked like a wall in the sky. He looked across the peaks of mountains again and saw there was an opaque barrier running along the peaks and climbing into the sky. It was nearly invisible as if made of water that flowed upward, rising to the clouds. It was clear without any hint of the ocean's blue.

The barrier seemed to travel endlessly across the peaks of mountains to their left and right. Whatever lands the new sun nourished were beyond the pillars and behind this barrier, Enoch thought. Enoch and Lingdar moved to the space between the pillars. The barrier there pulsated from clear to dull white, yet everywhere else it remained clear. Enoch and Lingdar looked to each other, the surprise in their eyes asking who would be first to try.

Enoch looked behind to where they had just come from and saw in the distance the old sun rising. Enoch then looked forward again to the new sun in front of him, climbing, nearly to mid-day it seemed. He hadn't seen the sun move so fast since the first *Council of Archs* on Mount Hermon. He removed a covering from his hand and reached out to the barrier.

The material, almost ethereal, was different from that outside the pillars. This one was dense and gelatinous to the touch. It moved. but as Enoch pushed harder, it solidified, still not letting his hand pass. Enoch picked up a piece of ice and rapped it heavily on the barrier. It clanged with the sound of metal.

Lingdar looked on with a quizzical face. In all his years he'd never seen anything like this structure, "Not even the great intellect of giants could have envisioned such a thing existing," he thought as he placed his hand on it too. The section he touched glowed a luminous green and phased into a liquid. Lingdar's hand pushed right through. He drew his hand back and regarded the structure.

"Seems I was wrong, Enoch. You cannot come with us," he said.

"But I think we've found your home," said Enoch.

"It seems so." The giant's voice was shaking as he turned to look down behind them to his people waiting below. Lingdar drew in a breath, Enoch saw the giant's chest swell with air, and covered his ears. Lingdar let out a guttural wail that only massive vocal chords could have made, as if their size had given them a new range. The sound churned at Enoch's bones, but the caravan heard and made their way to join them at the top.

The section between the pillars turned into a sea of clear water that shone like diamonds in liquid form. Lingdar watched as his people crossed with a new joy in their eyes and the heady expectation of a land made for them – a land where they would find peace. Joy was etched on all of their faces. The last of the giants passed and Lingdar turned to Enoch, his giant eyes glassy with the beginnings of tears. Enoch had never seen Lingdar cry.

"Will you be okay to return on your own? I can travel with you, then return here if you wish, Enoch."

"I'll be fine, Lingdar. Go and lead your people. What is beyond this gate is unknown and they'll need your judgment in the early days."

Lingdar pushed out a breath from his nose and looked into the distance. "I'll summon Kokabel's Leviathan to take you back across the sea once you reach the coast again."

"Thank you, I've a long journey ahead."

Silence descended upon the pair. The time had come for goodbyes, and they didn't come easy for either of them.

"I'll ensure my people never forget what you have done for us." Lingdar knelt at Enoch's feet and drew his head close. He gently placed his forehead on Enoch's in the sign of respect. "I bid you well, Enoch the Scribe."

Enoch broke free and tapped at the giant's shoulder. "Take care of your people, Lingdar because if you do not, I shall find you and slay you while you sleep," Enoch joked, smiling while his own eyes also started to water. Lingdar shook with laughter and smiled back.

"Then the rest of my days, I shall sleep with one eye open. In fact, I'll place an eye at the top of the Pyramid in Giza, so that I'll see you coming. Farewell my friend." Lingdar turned and passed through the gate.

When they had all left, the sudden realization of where Enoch was hit him at once. The biting cold wind, wanting to find every inch of warmth still left in him, whistled around the peak. A sudden profound silence told him he was alone in the world again. Maybe he always had been, maybe he always would be. Enoch watched as Lingdar the *Giza* led his people down the mountain to the other side of their new home. Enoch thought it was time to return from where he had been spawned.

CHAPTER SEVEN
Young Again

Enoch ran his thumb over an itch on the back of his other hand, his head was down and a smile formed at the corner of his mouth at the memory. Holly thought Lingdar may have been the last true friend Enoch had known. "Are they still out there? – the giants, I mean, in the outer lands?" Holly asked.

"They must be.... I often think of Lingdar. There have been times when I could have used his friendship, his strength too."

"So the ones who stayed in our realm are normal-sized now?"

"Yes, in this realm they got smaller with each generation, except for their fingers. Descendants of giants always have six fingers and toes. The 13 families in this realm who descended from them always have their sixth finger and toes removed at birth."

"Are their monuments still here?" Holly asked,

"Yes. In fact, if you trace a line on a map today of all those monuments the giants made, they form a perfect circle around the Earth," Enoch told Holly.

"They built them by following the lines of the Shekinah?" she asked.

Enoch nodded, happy that Holly was starting to ask the right questions. "The Hindus called it *Prana*. In the Orient they call it *Chi*. The western humans will soon call it the *electromagnetic ether*. Today only a handful of men truly understand it but only one man wants to use it for what it was designed for, he calls it *radiant energy*."

"Tesla?" Holly asked.

Enoch nodded again, she was starting to understand. Soon it would be time to tell her who she really was, but not yet.

There was still too much at risk and still much for Holly to know, much more even for her to understand.

"That is why this fair was so important," Enoch began. "Long ago, the sixth realm of all possibility showed the *Archs* that Tesla would soon not only prove the existence of the Shekinah, but he'd show humans how to use it to power any machine they build. The humans will learn that the Shekinah connects them directly to *Eloah*."

Holly peered over to Enoch whose head had veered upward towards the sky as if he were looking for something, perhaps even wishing that something was looking down at him.

He turned to Holly. "Tesla will prove that God exists."

Holly had never questioned whether God existed for no-one did then. Her questions were always deeper. But she'd seen others though, mostly young people, start to do so more and more. Enoch's words made Holly think of Jackson. It had been years since she thought of him, or even remembered her first year in Whitechapel when she'd worked as a maid for the preacher and his family. The preacher, his wife and son – Jackson; all good, God-fearing people who in a past age might have braved a passage overseas, leaving their home to become community pillars of one English colony or another around the world. But in this age they were born a generation too late to avoid the ever-increasing pervasiveness of scientific advancement into their world view, except for Jackson who welcomed the natural sciences looking for what he called *fingerprints of God*.

He'd seen Holly as a simple girl, uninterested in intellectual pursuits, but this was far from the truth. Secretly, Holly wanted everyone to see her this way. Jackson was nineteen and had hoped to become a school teacher one day. He'd spend Saturday nights reading scientific journals until the wee hours by candle light. Saturday evenings would also see Holly scrub the wooden floor of their home because the foot traffic would be light. Occasionally Jackson would remark on something he'd found.

"Holly, listen to this," he'd start, reading from a book, *"A bit of science distances one from God, but much science brings one nearer to Him, the more I study nature the more I stand amazed at the work of the creator,"* Jackson had said.

"Who said that?" she had asked, masking her deep interest with an aloof politeness.

"*Louis Pasteur*. He postulates that there are *organisms* in our bodies, so small that we can can't see them and that they might be behind some of the illnesses we experience." He was proud at his ability to reduce the most complex ideas to a single sentence.

"Do you think he's right?" Holly had asked, turning to Jackson, who hadn't even looked up as he spoke, his eyes remaining on the pages.

"Well, he conducted an experiment where he kept milk from turning sour so quickly. He says that milk grows these...hold on..." searching the pages for the right word... "*bacteria*! And that the foul taste of sour milk is caused by them."

"But what if milk going sour so quickly is what *our Father* above intended? What if God puts the...*bacteria* there because *He* only wants us to drink fresh milk?"

"Not *put* Holly, it *grows* there! That means it has its own life cycle, like everything else. Even the human body goes through all sorts of foul changes at death, so why not these...*organisms* too? No, I think God *grows* the bacteria there for a different reason," Jackson had said.

"What reason?" Holly had asked, planning a late night viewing of the book Jackson was reading. Making a mental note to hide a candle just for that purpose.

"I think so that people like *Louis Pasteur* would find them – so that mankind could then discover people like Louis Pasteur."

Sunday mornings back then would see Jackson's family attend church services. It was mandatory for Holly to go with them where Jackson's father would channel the same spirit of Christian revival that had spread across the American east coast in the early 1800, but in a reserved English tone. At his side, Jackson would sit reciting from a Bible whenever his father called on him for a passage. His brown hair was parted on the left and close to his head. His words would ring with passion throughout the pews, every few sentences unlocking a strand of hair that would fall to his forehead, his hand returning it to its place without missing a single word. Despite her thoughts, Holly had caught herself several times wondering about a life with Jackson. If not him, then perhaps someone like him. Mark would want that, she had thought.

One Sunday after service, Jackson and Holly had been wandering through town, perusing more study books, when they came across a crowd of people gathered around a square in front of a church. At a table sat two men; one was the Cardinal of Whitechapel, the other was none other than the naturalist, Charles Darwin. The crowd clamoured like crabs in a barrel to get within earshot.

The two men were in a heated discussion about something called *"Evolution"*. Holly and Jackson listened but Jackson listened more closely. What Darwin was saying explained so much to him – in the process challenging Jackson's view of the world, even his view of himself. On the way home he was silent. His eyes were held wider than usual, as if he were suddenly more fearful of something, as if something he'd heard shook his core.

The weeks after saw Jackson spend more time reading all he could about evolution. The theory was not elegant, he'd thought, but the evidence was compelling nonetheless. When he looked deeper for the *fingerprint of God* in Darwin's work, Jackson found none. Instead he saw an abyss of time and chance where once a *Genesis* had been. At first his mind rejected the notion, not able to reconcile the idea that he shared an ancestor with the day's common chimp, but as a believer in the scientific method, he couldn't deny the evidence. The idea that he was not created by God's will, grew slowly in him. His thoughts, once pure like fresh milk, began to entertain all sorts of new leanings, turning a sour shade right before Holly's eyes.

Jackson's presence at church diminished as he chose to spend weekends at the zoo. When he did attend, his once passionate voice now merely went through the motions, the verses his father had asked him to recite having taken on an air of fantasy to him. After more time, he stopped going to church altogether. His father, angry and worried, thought that a demon had possessed his boy and others had felt the same.

The theory of evolution was spreading to other young people too. Jackson's father and others petitioned the Bishop to ban Darwin's books under the claim of heresy but they couldn't.

Nowhere in Darwin's books did he say that God didn't exist. Instead, he merely reduced the complexity and perfection of the human body to a happenstance gathering of random parameters. Jackson's father and the other Church-goers thought that under such an idea, the mental leap to atheism would be a short one. For Jackson though, it would be a fall much further – into depravity, but Holly would leave long before the horrors began.

Holly left Whitechapel forever the day Jackson cornered her while she cleared supper. The evening had seen the mother and father go out, leaving them alone to eat a dinner prepared of lamb and vegetables. Something had changed in Jackson. She had noticed that his eyes had started watching the shapes under her dress. On that night his hands finally followed. It was the first time she'd seen the look of blind lust in a man's eyes.

"What does it matter?" he had pleaded as he chased her around the dining table. "Just a little touch, give me just a little touch!" At first his smile was playful but when Holly didn't acquiesce it turned to frustration and then anger.

"What does it matter? We're friends right? Would you rather a brigand from the East End with his dirty fingers and foul breath? We give you lodging and food! We give you good standing in the community! What have you done for us? Do something for me, Holly, it is just a little touch."

His swift steps caught up to her, grabbing her by the shoulders while pushing his pelvic bone into hers. Holly fought but the fear set in when she realized Jackson was not going to stop. His hand found the edge of her dress and reached up to her vagina, clawing at her undergarments, scratching at the skin just above her pubic hairs. She was over-powered and felt helpless, her scream echoed through the house but fell on no-one's ears. As he pushed her into a side table, her hand found a silver candle-holder. Without even thinking she brought it crashing onto his temple. He finally broke free to examine the blood now rushing from his forehead.

Holly wasted no time, she quickly gathered her clothes and belongings. Jackson watched her with a handkerchief held at his head.

"I'm sorry," he pleaded."I don't know what came into me, promise me you will not tell my parents."

Holly had drowned out his words, she wanted to leave as soon as possible, leaving nothing for Jackson's parents except the sight of Jackson himself to answer for why Holly had left. They would figure out why, she had thought. She later wished she'd left a note when she learned that Jackson's father had tried to drown him, hoping to rid the boy of his demons. When the preacher couldn't, he instead kicked his son out to live as a vagabond. It was hard to feel sorry for Jackson but Holly still did, wondering if Jackson's faith would have been as shaken, had he known what Enoch said Tesla knows.

The scar Jackson had left on her was still there but the wound had long healed. Holly looked out to the lights above the fairgrounds. The *John Phillip Sousa* orchestra started the opening chords of Vivaldi's *"Four Seasons"*; it fit into the evening perfectly. It was nearly midnight but couples and families still walked below, oblivious to how late it was getting, as if the fair had changed the passage of time itself, placing every attendee in a time bubble and giving them just enough of it to see every exhibit. The people's steps below, as if conducted by the noise of singing violins, wafted up to Holly and Enoch on the roof, perhaps even guided there by the gently meandering 'cello, Holly thought:

"Does Tesla know how important his work is?"

"Not yet, it is better if he doesn't right now, but he's a very smart man, he'll figure it out, but we have to protect him. Semjaza and the others have worked against him his whole life and they'll never stop, so we must never either." Enoch paused and placed a hand on Holly's shoulder.

Holly's mind was at odds with her instincts. She didn't flinch when Enoch touched her, normally she'd not let anyone get so close to her, let alone touch her, but Enoch was different, his presence seemed to speak to the smallest organisms of her body and say, *"Don't worry,* I'll *not harm you."* Despite what she knew men were capable of, she let herself listen. Besides, if he was going to harm her, he'd have surely done it by now.

Enoch hoped the idea of Tesla's *radiant energy* was turning over in Holly's mind. He hoped she was seeing why she'd been called to the White City. It was only when she saw her purpose that she could see who she really was. Enoch readied himself for her next question. He knew the moment after he answered it that their paths might diverge but he was ready. He'd been ready for the last five hundred years.

She looked into Enoch's eyes and started to form a question, but her mouth suddenly froze. She looked instead to the side of Enoch's face where she thought her eyes were playing tricks on her. Her hand reached out and touched Enoch's beard. Grey hairs had suddenly formed there whereas moments ago there had been only black ones. "Your beard, Enoch!" she gasped, "It's turning grey!"

Enoch's eyes shifted downward, his hand stroked at the section of his beard Holly had touched. *"Could it be true?"* he thought. He looked towards the sky for the shooting star he knew should streak across the sky if Holly was right. When they saw it, his eyes suddenly filled with joy at the news. Enoch stood and spun on his feet. Holly looked on with a quizzical look at his sudden change in mood. The man was rejoicing, Holly thought. He held out his hands for Holly to follow him. She followed him up. The look in her eyes asking, *"What are you doing?"* Her mouth though forming a different question, "Why are you dancing?"

"This is wonderful news! This is wonderful news, Holly!" Enoch said as he tried to click his heels together in tune with the music coming from below.

"What is?" Holly asked, "And what are you doing?" Holly's inquisitive stare turned into a stifled laughter when she saw Enoch's arms flailing about as if trying to free themselves from whatever his legs were doing. She couldn't help but laugh out loud at Enoch. *"Poor man,"* she thought, *"A newborn giraffe has more rhythm."* Her hand modestly tried to cover her smile. The snapping of his fingers, as he tried to spin on one leg did not help in the slightest. She decided to put him out of his misery.

"That isn't how you *Waltz*. If you're going to look stupid at least do it right," she said, showing him where to place his feet and taking his hands to lead. "I cannot believe that you have been alive nearly five thousand years and haven't learned to dance yet?"

"Music didn't exist until after Babylon."

The chorus picked up. Holly showed Enoch how to dance. Enoch spun Holly a few times but she soon thought herself silly. Why was she dancing with this practical stranger on a roof top overlooking the Chicago World's fair? The answer she heard from her heart was that he was not a stranger. It was impossible for her to place her finger on it, but something told her that Enoch was more than a man who had walked forward in time. A part of her knew him. "*But from where or how?*" the back of her mind asked. The answer didn't matter because she knew no-one else in the world could ever understand her journey.

Her hands were nested perfectly into his as their eyes held each other. She felt his callous palms tell her a story, a story that sounded much like hers. In preparatory girl academies everywhere, young ladies were told to never, under any circumstances, go off with strange men – especially those with kind, sad eyes like Enoch's. But the man's joy was infectious, something was making him very happy. The last time she'd seen that kind of joy was with Mark nearly a hundred years ago.

That scar, however, had never fully healed. Holly caught herself feeling happier than she was ready to allow herself. She let Enoch go and walked back to the edge. Enoch watched her, knowing his joy was not hers yet. She sat back down.

"Do you miss being normal? Being with your wife?" she asked,

"I used to, but I feel I may be a different man now. Too much time has passed, too many memories have formed where I once held hers. Perhaps she'd not like the man I've become."

"But what of love then? How can we love anyone if whomever we choose to love is destined to leave us? Why does *Eloah* torture us by making us watch those we love die?"

"I suppose it depends on who we choose to love, Holly," replied Enoch, taking a seat next to Holly again. Without thinking, Holly placed her head on Enoch's shoulder where it nestled perfectly into the mound of muscle and bone. She was happy that she was no longer alone in the world. "Did you choose anyone else after your wife?"

"What I've found is that you rarely choose love, that it nearly always chooses you."

Below them, they saw a group of police constables running after a thief across the pavilion. The nimble footed boy was no more than twenty years old, the constables chasing him were at least twenty years older. Holly and Enoch could hear the boy shout.

"I'm not a serial killer, it was just a bag of popcorn!" the boy said through puffs of air, a look of burden on his face as the stamina was running out of him. Luckily he found a group of circus performers warming up and disappeared into them. The constables arrived at the performers, stopping suddenly to look around for a sign of the boy. Holly saw the look of confusion on their faces, a sudden sense of safety next to Enoch swarming over her.

"Can you tell me now why a grey hair suddenly growing on your beard makes you dance like a fool?" she asked when the frustrated constables walked off.

"I shouldn't."

"Why?"

"Because it may change your mind."

"If you want me to be an *agent of creation* with you, then I need to know what you know."

"It means we've won Holly! We've finally won!" Enoch stated, looking forward. Holly still didn't understand. Her eyes said as much when they peered up to him from his shoulder.

"You see, the greying hairs are like a signal to me from the higher realms. When something I do corrects a path in this one, I'll age more rapidly. It means that in telling you about Tesla, his future has been secured because you will secure it. It means that after this fair, Tesla really will become a household name."

"Grey hairs and a shooting star can mean all that?"

"Yes, it happened before."

"When?"

"In Babylon."

***

Enoch's mission was finally complete but he wasn't ready to die yet. He wanted to look on the home he and Edna had built one last time before Uriel finally took him. The journey back across the realm to *Ur* was harder than the first one to the ice-lands. He was old and weak, the only consolation being that he knew the way now, giving him time to enjoy the different terrains he'd previously encountered. *"But if only I could do so as a young man again*," he thought, envisioning his younger self walking the journey without the fear of danger that now plagued him. How easy it would be now for any beast to grab hold of him and shake him until his old bones broke. Maybe he should have accepted Lingdar's offer of an escort.

As he back-tracked along the path he'd taken with the giants, it was not the animals he was most afraid of. There was now a bigger danger. The people had returned. Along the path of monuments and cities the *Nephilim* had been built. Enoch found that tribes of people had now turned them into places of worship. At first he tried to communicate with them but language was gone again, they only spoke in grunts and noises. The slow climb back to civil society had only just started. Enoch travelled through the realm without uttering a word. Instead, he chose to listen.

In the forests of Burma, when he was hungry, he hunted and ate. In the frozen Afghan steppes when he was tired, he made camp and slept. In India he learned the language of the jungle. The clicking call of tapirs taught him when the mating seasons started. The rustle of leaves increasing in volume taught him the approach of big cats. The low hum of crocodiles digesting a meal told him when it was safe to cross a river. It took ten cycles but he finally made it back to the land between the rivers.

One night Enoch found himself making camp on the bank of a river. Night was soon to fall and he hadn't made a fire yet. No matter how much he tried, he just couldn't work fast enough. As Enoch dragged a large banana leaf in from the marsh, a sudden growl came from the bush. Enoch stopped suddenly, careful not to make any more noise. Another growl sounded, this one behind him. Enoch spun round and looked for the source.

The first tiger came out of the bush to Enoch's side, its snarling face and hunched shoulders ready to pounce. Enoch's legs gave out in fright. He fell to his back. Another tiger came in from in front of him and joined the first. Enoch spun his head hoping to keep them in sight but it was hopeless, the third came out from Enoch's blindside. The tigers circled Enoch waiting for the best moment to take their kill. He thought it was the end, knowing that to die now would be the final death.

The ground suddenly shook with the footfalls of a large beast. The tigers spun their heads round to the source, as from the bush, a large elephant broke through the foliage and rushed forward to Enoch. Its large tusks curled upward in majestic circles and it must have stood at least thirteen feet tall. The tigers, annoyed at the sudden intrusion to their kill, turned their anger toward the elephant.

Before they could attack the elephant, it charged first, lowering its tusks and then raising them under the back of one tiger, sending the animal flying into the air. When it landed, the other tigers joined it and the trio ran off to look for an easier kill.

The elephant returned to Enoch's side. Its trunk sniffed at Enoch and the animal let out a trumpeting call. The elephant then extended its trunk to Enoch's hand. Enoch took it and the animal pulled him to his feet. It lowered its head and flapped at his face with its ear. Enoch was trying to regain his balance, rising slowly on his old bones, but the animal kept slapping at him with his ear. Enoch was getting annoyed, *"What do you want, animal?"* he thought. Then he saw it. The perfect circular hole in the ear. Enoch was shocked. This was the elephant he'd saved from the bank long ago. *"Had it remembered me?"* he thought.

The elephant lowered itself onto its front knees. Its head moved from side to side as if the animal was trying to communicate. The animal then used his trunk and pointed to its back. Enoch understood and climbed onto its back. It stayed with Enoch, carrying him on his back and safe from the jungle floor for the rest of the journey. Enoch understood why the giants held the elephant in such regard – they both had the same spirit.

At the foot of a mountain pass they parted. The goodbye was easier than with Lingdar, but Enoch would not soon forget the animal that saved him just as the animal hadn't forgotten Enoch.

Enoch's hunched frame shuffled over the last mountain pass before the descent into the Ur valley. He was an old man now with white hair down to his mid back. A long white beard now hung under his chin, moving in tandem with his torso. At the ridge overlooking the valley, he stopped to look over the rooftops of his old village. Not much had changed, the flood had erased the old Ur but the new one was still the lone patch of civilization in the wide empty valley. He smiled at the sight, a smile that suddenly vanished as his chest was gripped with a swift, seizing pain. Dizzy from the sudden lack of oxygen, his knees buckled and he fell to the ground. He knew time was running out.

He'd been feeling death creeping into his breaths since he'd left the Mongolian steppes. He'd breathe in with no problem but when he breathed out, his lungs would pause for a moment too long. The pauses had been getting longer and longer. Sometimes he'd only feel that he hadn't breathed when his heart suddenly jolted from the lack of oxygen.

Enoch caught his breath and then slowly rose to continue. *"No way will I survive this night,"* he thought. It was only dusk but he already welcomed the dawn that would see him finally taken to the higher realm. *"You do not wait for me in heaven, Edna,"* he thought to himself. *"But Uriel says no-one weeps there."* Deep in his heart, he also welcomed something else; the brief moment when he could gaze, once again, upon Uriel herself, if only for the last time.

When he tried to walk again, another jolt erupted from his chest. He fell back down and he knew his journey would end on this ridge. The hot Middle Eastern sun wasn't helping his breathing but at least he'd die in its warmth. He lay down and waited. He'd seen more of the realm than any other man alive. As last thoughts go, it was a comforting one.

He suddenly heard a voice approaching from below that then became two more. The first man Enoch saw approach wore new robes and had a dark beard. He couldn't have been more than twenty cycles old. His hair was dark and curly and his skin was the colour of olives. Behind him, two others walked. One had dark skin and wore a turban with a white robe. The other had peach-coloured skin and hair like golden hay. They walked with the laughter and joy of youth but stopped when they noticed the old man lying on the ground.

"I'm fine," Enoch protested as they helped him. "I'm just an old man who lost his breath, do not bother with me, please." Enoch tried to wave them off but the trio helped Enoch to the shade of a tree. The dark one left to find water. The olive-skinned one spoke first.

"I'm Abraham, this is Assyrios," he said, pointing to the peach-skinned one. "And this is Zoraster," he continued as Zoraster returned with water. It was obvious they were from very different tribes but they worked together as if they were of one. Enoch drank and quenched his thirst, feeling a joy at watching the trio. If the trio represented the type of people returning after the flood, then Enoch was going to die a happy man.

Enoch asked them where they were going. The trio spoke of their journey together. They said they were in search of a valley where a tree that produced black, green and red olives grew. They were certain that such a tree existed and they were set on finding it. Enoch smiled at the frivolity of youth, seeing that humanity had returned to an idealistic stage where everything was yet to be discovered.

"I'm Enoch," he said, watching their reactions to see if they knew of him. They didn't, it seemed the flood had truly erased all the knowledge of the past. It had been so many cycles since he'd last spoken to humans that curiosity got the better of him. He had to know how the new humans were faring. Enoch wondered if the tribes still fought each other. Zoraster spoke first but his tone was not what Enoch had expected.

"They do, but our differences mean little," Zoraster said. "*Eloah* has shown us a danger. He's shown us that our enemy is a common one."

"Who is your enemy?" Enoch questioned,

"He has many names; *Marduke, Moloch, Baal* and others," said Assyrios.

"It is our suspicion that *they're* actually the same," Zoraster interjected.

Enoch felt another seizing pain in his chest, but this was not from the lack of oxygen. Hearing Moloch's name killed the notion of a different humanity to that before the flood. They told Enoch that all over the land, tribes had taken to worshiping a multitude of gods. That the most popular was the fertility God, Moloch. Enoch had known her by a different name. He learned that people had constructed giant bull-headed altars where they would still offer their first-born babies as tribute to bless their lands and their unions. Enoch's worry returned. This must have been the work of Semjaza, he thought, "*But how was he still influencing people?*"

"Do you worship this Moloch?" asked Enoch.

"We do not," said Abraham."But we do not say this for fear of being arrested by the elect. We cannot fathom the idea that *Eloah* would require the death of our children."

"I assure you *Eloah* doesn't," Enoch said. "This Moloch is a false god, you're right not to follow him."

"You speak as if you know of *Eloah* personally, old man," said Assyrios.

"The old always speak in this way," added Zoraster, but Abraham was curious.

"What do you know of Moloch, old man?" asked Abraham.

Enoch debated whether to tell them of how Moloch had come to be. Their faces looked quizzically at Enoch but they didn't register his pause. Enoch didn't know if they would ever find a tree that grew three different kinds of olives but that was not what they were actually searching for, he thought. He saw theirs had actually been a quest for knowledge, a quest that had led them now to Enoch. He gathered his breath and told them all he knew.

He told them of the council of *Archs* on Mount Hermon and the decree by *Eloah* to bind Azazel for seventy generations. He told them that Semjaza and the fallen *Archs* still walked this realm in reptilian form and that the worship of Moloch and the other Gods must somehow come from them. He told them of his journey with the giants to the outer lands beyond the ice gates. Enoch's account took hours to retell but the trio listened with attentive ears. When Enoch finished, he saw that Abraham was nodding but Zoraster and Assyrios remained sceptical.

"How easy it is to fool the young with fantastic tales, isn't it, old man?" postured Assyrios.

"What would I gain?" asked Enoch, "What favour do I now seek of you? None, dear boy. A man who seeks no favour has little need to trade in falsehood." Assyrios and Zoarster grew quiet. The account of what had happened before the flood had shocked them into silence, a confirmation of the idea that had brought them together in the first place. Abraham looked carefully at Enoch. He saw Enoch's parched lips and brought the jug of water to them.

"Don't mind them, Enoch. Your knowledge is important but why do you not scribe an account and give it to the people?" asked Abraham.

"Look at my hands, dear boy, these hands would barely hold the quill to do so," replied Enoch. Another pain suddenly seized Enoch's chest, this one was his heart. Abraham's first instinct was to help. He brought his hands to the back of Enoch's head, holding the neck and raising it to give his wind pipe a path for air to flow. Zoraster and Assyrios shifted closer, they also looked on with worry for the old man in obvious pain but, from what Enoch had just told them, they shouldn't have been done.

"Go!" said Enoch softly, "Learn as much as you can and make sure that you always follow the one true *Eloah*."

"Will you be alright Enoch?" asked Zoraster, "If we leave, you will be alone here."

"I'll soon be with *Eloah*, go forth and worry not of me, young man, all of you."

The trio left and Enoch found himself alone again. Night had fallen and the stars had come out. He closed his eyes to accept death and the sight of Uriel once again. A sight he'd been looking forward to for a lifetime. When the blackness came over him, he returned to the expanse and waited as the giant golden structure pulsated again in and out of view. It looked far away but was getting closer. He could now see the shape. It was a cube, larger than the tallest mountains and with angular lines extending from each corner, the extending lines converging together to form triangles just outside the cube.

Enoch was drawn inside the structure and learned its true size. All around he could see other golden structures begin to appear. A mist had gathered into a giant circular track that solidified next to him, followed by a sound emanating from the distance. On the track a giant golden ball rumbled by with the slow grinding noise of metal being churned. The giant sphere glowed with a dull yellow light. Enoch knew it was the sun as it looked behind the veil of reality.

Lights appeared around Enoch and sparkled across the black expanse, slowly marking time on Earth. From them, three spectral figures materialized and approached him. At first Enoch squinted, not recognizing them but as they got closer he saw that it was the *Archs*. Enoch smiled, welcoming them, waiting to gaze upon the sight of Uriel but she was not with them. It was only Gabriel, Michael and Raphael but where was Uriel? When Enoch could make out their faces, he saw they were angry. They stopped in front of him. Gabriel came forward, a scowl firmly on his face. Gabriel opened his mouth and released a sound like that of the shearing metal he had heard on Mount Hermon. The noise of his scream filled the black expanse. Enoch covered his ears but the noise turned to a radiant light, a light that pulsed and Enoch woke up.

When Enoch awoke he was prone on the ground and night had fallen. He sat up quickly and looked at his hands, he was young again. Beside him he heard the noise of a town.

He got up and quickly walked over to the ridge and saw that the empty valley of *Ur* was now a sprawling metropolis taking up the entire valley. Fires, animals, and hundreds of mud-brick homes now surrounded his old village. Enoch hadn't passed to the higher realm but instead had gone forward in time again. His first thought was how much time.

He descended and walked into town, looking as if he'd just come from the stars. To his right, women were washing clothes; while to his left, two men carrying clay pots of water, passed by with the speed walk of the burdened. He came to the village centre where a group of four dark-skinned men stood with frightened faces on a wooden platform. Their clothes were tattered and their faces were dirty from imprisonment. Behind them stood soldiers with stern faces. Next to them, a rabbi was calling the village people to attention.

"Here ye! Here ye! Enemies of *Eloah* have no refuge. Our resolve will find and rid the realm of their blasphemous ways. Our soldiers rode over twenty nights to capture these men from the gates of Assyria. They stand here charged with blasphemy. Gather and hear their renouncement of the teachings of Zoraster!"

Enoch was shocked. *"How far in the future have I gone?"* he wondered, as people ran towards the spectacle to watch, speeding past Enoch and knocking him out of the way to get the best views. Enoch turned to a spectator standing next to him.

"What have these men done? Who are they?" he asked.

"They're *Djinngeers* from Persia," the spectator answered without looking at Enoch.

"What is a *Djinngeer?*" asked Enoch. The spectator turned and looked Enoch up and down curiously. *"The man's robes are a style not seen in many cycles,"* the spectator thought. "A *thugee from Indus no doubt, he must have stolen the robes from some poor old man."* The spectator rudely left Enoch's side. The rabbi continued.

"These men deny that the teaching of Moses – son of Amran – son of Kehath – son of Levi – son of Jacob – son of Isaac – son of the most wise and great **Abraham** himself – is the true word. These men instead command the evil spirits of the Shinar to do the bidding of Ishmael's followers and their Zoroastrian ways." The rabbi turned sharply to one prisoner, "What say thou?"

The prisoner managed a fearful swallow. He paused, steadied his resolve and then said. "There's but one true path to *Allah*, and that is to follow the *Asha*! Moses leads you astray! Do not follow him! His words mock the true commander of the *Djinns*, the great and wise Zoraster!" the man bellowed in defiance. The rabbi's face contorted with anger. He shot a look to one of the soldiers who kicked the man out in front of his friends and told him to kneel.

The other three prisoners watched as their defiant countryman was bent over and told to pray to one of his beloved *Djinns*. The executioner's blade came swiftly down on the base of his neck. The man's head rolled away as the crowd of people let out a cheer. The rabbi moved on to the next man.

"And what do you say? What is your *true* word?"

The next man was not so defiant. His eyes were still fixed on his dead companion. His breaths were laboured as he saw death awaiting the wrong answer. "*Eloah* blesses me, through the wise teaching of his prophet Moses, descendant of the most wise and exalted Abraham."

The rabbi nodded to a soldier. "Take him to the holds so he may have time to repent of his past choices."

Another soldier grabbed the man and led him away through the crowd. The rabbi continued. Enoch thought it would be best to move on himself. It would be centuries before organized faith would emerge but Enoch had seen enough to know that perhaps he should not be around the new holy men.

It seemed the different tribes weren't united anymore, the rabbi had mentioned Abraham and Zoraster as if they had become enemies when Enoch had known them as friends. Something had happened. Enoch hoped to find someone who could fill him in on what he'd missed but first he needed to blend in. That meant finding work.

At the edge of the village, Enoch came to a brook with a house and olive garden next to it. The olives were ripe and should have been picked, he thought. Goats bleated in front of the mud brick dwelling signaling his approach. A tall, balding man with curly black hair stepped out of the housing and looked angrily at Enoch, his mouth full of food.

"By all that is holy, for what do you disturb my *Sabbath*?" asked Jafar. Enoch had to think of something fast. If what he'd seen of rabbis in the town centre was any indication of the new temperament of people, he needed to tread carefully. He also made a note to find out what a *Sabbath* was.

"I'm sorry, kind man, but I became lost as I strolled by the brook here and I couldn't help but notice that the olives you grow will soon wither on the vine, it seems a terrible waste."

"Do you have a proposition other than disturbing my brisket?" Jafar asked. "My wife's hands are guided by *Eloah* when she prepares it."

"That I should help you pick them, I suppose. I've never seen such fine olives. They should fetch a good barter at market and my hands are idle."

The man chewed on the idea. His fingers raised to his mouth to free a piece of brisket still suck in his teeth. He approached Enoch. The idea was pleasing to him.

"Blasted Ramel, he ran off to seek his fortune in the Pyramids of *Khemet*, leaving me a hand short for the harvest, it seems the lord delivers you to me just in time, blessed is he."

"Yes, blessed is he. *Eloah* has a way of being there when you need him most doesn't he, kind sir?"

"What is your name, boy?"

"Enoch."

"Enoch? As in the old tale of Enoch the Scribe who was taken by *Eloah*?" The man laughed. "Ha! How blessed am I indeed that *Eloah* returns Enoch the Scribe to gather my olives!" Jafar joked.

Enoch went along with it. "It seems so, kind sir, it seems so."

"My name is Jafar, you can start tomorrow. If the Rabbis catch you working on the Sabbath, it will be both our necks. Start at first light tomorrow. For now, you can take lodging in the back by the brook. My wife will prepare you a meal that you may take at night, but in the shed only! She cannot stand the sight of an un-bearded man."

"Thank you, Jafar." Enoch left to find the lodging in the back.

Enoch had become an old man twice already. The thought of growing old again filled him with a new appreciation for youth. He worked tirelessly day and night gathering the olives, tending the goats and channeling the brook to deliver water to the tomatoes and potatoes that grew in the front. At night, after he ate, he would look up at the stars, hoping to catch a glimpse of the world beyond the veil of night, to see the higher realms where the souls of men went, where he knew Uriel was watching him, hoping she'd come to him.

Stars would streak across the sky every night, each one with a hope floating in Enoch's heart that it would be Uriel coming to him once again. When his eyes closed for sleep it was an image of her that he kept dancing on his eyelids as he drifted off. An image that was growing weaker and weaker with each passing moon.

In the summer, a woman made camp across the brook. She was young, not older than Enoch, and with brown hair that fell down to the tip of her buttocks. At first it had been the smell of her honey wash that had caught his attention. That morning, Enoch had been washing stones for the wall to be built around Jafar's property when the smell wafted over to his nose. He looked up and caught a sight of her just as she was descending into the water to bathe.

She was not wearing clothes. Enoch saw her breasts descend under the water's surface. He instantly averted his eyes but his clumsy movements saw him also drop a boulder into the water, creating a loud splash that carried over to her. She heard the splash and saw Enoch but didn't cover herself in modesty.

Instead she lifted herself out of the water, giving Enoch the full view of her naked body. Despite his better nature, he watched as long as he could while thoughts of lust ran through his mind. It was only the voice of Jafar's wife calling him that made him stop. As Enoch sauntered away, he stole one more glance and saw the woman smile at him with mischievous joy.

Enoch began to find reasons to spend more time by the brook. Sometimes he'd catch her washing in the brook, other times she'd be tending to her animals. Enoch noticed that she had no husband and yet was surrounded by men who would visit her daily. Every day, men would arrive and Enoch would hear their words.

"I bring you this wood to help with your fire in the evening, my son has cut too much it seems."
"I bring this kid goat as my nanny has birthed too many, we have an abundance of them now."

Enoch could tell that the men were enamoured by her and that she was enamoured by their attention. Every day her kind eyes would thank them. One day she accepted a gift from a man who then asked if he could enter, she refused. She turned him away with a kind smile. Enoch watched the man leave in a rage then saw that she peered across the brook to where Enoch watched her. It seems she also had noticed his watching and had also found reasons to be by the brook.

"*She has seen me,*" Enoch thought. "*But for how long has she known I watch her?*" Enoch looked back at her. She smiled at him. He couldn't help but smile back.

"What are you doing, Enoch?" bellowed Jafar, having silently approached and assessed exactly what the young man was doing – what young men always did. Jafar might have done the same as a younger man. He looked towards the woman over the brook and nodded in disdainful agreement.

"'Tis a fine view, indeed it is, but best advised you steer clear of her young Enoch," Jafar said.

"Why?"

"War creates all manner of evil. Some we can see and some we cannot. All over the land, from *Khemet* to *Babylon*, there are hundreds of women like her. Women who marry the young soldiers before they go off to die in Pharaoh's wars against Babylon, becoming widows because rich men seek more riches. These manless women carry a curse but no godly man dare cast them out of their villages. Even though they fill godly men with envy and lust at the mere thought of their kind gestures, their kind eyes, their kind ways. Gilgamesh in Ur even slew his wife, so enamoured was he with the thought of such a young childless widow. Be wary Enoch, evil now resides where you will least expect it to."

Jafar led Enoch back toward the farm. He turned back and watched the woman again. "But I don't blame thee young Enoch, 'tis a fine a view indeed," he said.

CHAPTER EIGHT
David

"May I ask a question?" Holly asked.

"Of course."

"What is a *Djinn*?" asked Holly.

"If you ever get a chance, read the work of *Antoine Galland*. He was the first to translate *The Arabian Nights* into a western language. When he came across the word, in a story about a man who had found a magic lamp containing a wish-granting spirit inside, he thought it sounded much like the French word *genie* – the translation stuck. What people today call genies are in fact *Djinn*."

"Where did they come from?"

"They're the spirits of giants who have died in this realm, trapped here without their descendants. Someone had taught the *Magis* and *Djinngeers* from Persia how to channel and use them to do their bidding."

"Semjaza?" asked Holly

"It could only have been him. Uriel was right, he taught the people a magic most vile."

"How much time had passed by then?"

"I didn't know, but Jafar was right. I'd felt such temptation watching that woman by the brook. The tribes were at war with each other, which bred thoughts of revenge that grew into more evil actions, which only spurnned more evil thoughts and actions – and so on in a never ending cycle. I never thought that my lust for her was born from the war and death all around us. Semjaza was influencing this new society in a most indirect way. At the time I didn't know how but I soon learned why."

"Why?"

"It was all about energy and the Shekinah. Semjaza drew power from the negative energy people gave into the Shekinah so he'd to first create it in them. He started the wars by feeding the people lies. Zoraster was never master of *Djinns*, in fact he fought against them his whole life but Semjaza had made everyone believe the opposite."

"So what did you do?"

"Nothing, I thought Uriel would descend at any moment and take me as she had promised, but she didn't. At first, I just kept waiting. Every night I waited for a dream to show me where I needed to go but none came. Decades passed and still nothing. Jafar eventually became suspicious when he saw I wasn't aging. The village rabbi became suspicious when Jafar became suspicious."

"Oh no!" said Holly.

***

Enoch had been setting his bed for sleep when angry voices approached and stirred outside his shed. The voices were a low murmur but were suddenly pierced by the shriek of Jafar's wife. Enoch jumped with a start and ran outside.

He was greeted there by a mob of rabbis and villagers holding flames. They all looked at Enoch angrily. Jafar stood with them, also holding a flame but the look in his eyes was not like theirs. Enoch saw that what had been a simple question in Jafar's mind had evolved into an action his heart was now unwilling to accept. But he still had to live with these people, with their thoughts, with their actions. The head rabbi spoke.

"Seize the demon!"

Their movements were terribly fast. Enoch barely knew what was happening before they had grabbed him and led him to a circular wooden stake protruding from the ground. Terror filled Enoch as he saw the stake had been prepared for a fire. He looked towards the sky hoping for a miracle but none was coming. All he saw was millions of stars, millions of *Seraphim* watching down and noting. The voice in the back of his mind told him he didn't need their help but Enoch wished he could avoid the pain to come. Dozens of hands secured Enoch to the stake. Their faces blurred into one angry mass as they called him names.

"Spawn of Moloch!" they yelled. "Burn the blasphemy of creation!"

The ropes tightened around his muscles. Enoch had no choice but to steady his resolve.

"You'll be fine, you'll be fine, you'll be fine," he told himself but it didn't work. His thoughts turned to Uriel, reaching out to her like a scream through the spectral realms.

"Uriel," he muttered. "I need you now Uriel." The wood at the bottom was lit.

***

"She didn't come, did she?" asked Holly, watching Enoch rub one hand over the other as he re-told the tale. There must be so many memories in his mind she thought, but she saw that this one stood out more than others.

"No," replied Enoch.

"Was it painful?" Holly asked.

"The actual pain became just a noise in the blackness. The worst part was afterwards, I was trapped in my dead body. My breathing wasn't working. I was still alive but my body was charred black and burned stiff. I was blind but I could still feel everything. I felt them carry my body to a river and dump me there. The currents then took me, I couldn't manage them so I had to wait until I landed somewhere."

"Where did it take you?"

"To *Qumran* in Canaan. For weeks I lay on the bank as my body healed. My breathing returned and I could see again. My skin had gone from a charred black to a red open wound. The scar tissue would come later and the normal skin even more so but in the meantime, I needed a place to hide."

***

Enoch shuffled through the desert night. He approached a camel but the animal bolted from view when it saw Enoch. The wind blew and his exposed muscles and tissue howled in anger. He needed shelter and he needed it soon. His steps were slow because the muscles in his legs were still compressed from the burning, disturbing his gait. He breathed but with a heavy wheezing that sounded like the demon he'd been called, each breath a lesson in pain.

The cave was on a hill top. Enoch took up dwelling there to escape the wind, the sun and the eyes of people. In the pre-dawn light he'd watch the sun rise and ask the same question over and over again.

"Where are you Uriel?"

Under the cover of darkness just before dawn, he'd descend the mountain and fetch water. Not that he needed to drink but the water helped his wounds to heal. He stole a shroud one day from a caravan of travelers and then returned to the cave where he'd pass the days forcing breaths from his body and willing himself to heal. At times, he'd try to speak but all that would come out would be raspy coughs, words were even further away.

When the scar tissue formed, his movements became easier. The wind bit less and his breathing became easier. His mobility was returning and he wanted to keep his mind sharp. It had been so long since he'd counted his cycles. So long that he was uncertain of how long he'd walked on the realm. He needed to know so he scribed notations on the cave wall, noting when the sun rose and when it set. He needed more data but he was not healed enough to leave the cave for more than a few hours at a time. Luckily for him, a method to collect more data appeared one day.

He awoke one morning to find a tray of dates and berries next to the mouth of the cave. He shuffled over to examine it and saw that, further down the mountain, a boy walked with a herd of goats. The boy was small but Enoch later learned that he was older than he appeared.

In his robe, the boy carried a sling shot. A moment of terror flashed in Enoch's heart as he remembered the mob that had burned him alive. The knowledge that the boy knew that Enoch now lived in the cave was not comforting.

"Did the boy know? Had he seen my execution? Was he sent by the Rabbis?" Enoch wondered. Even if Enoch wanted to, he couldn't eat the food. His stomach hadn't healed, but mostly he didn't want to encourage the boy. He simply wanted to be alone.

That evening the boy returned, trying silently to avoid being noticed as he crouched towards the entrance. He collected the tray keeping his head down and peering into the cave. He stared forth with wide eyes and a calm breath. He saw Enoch and was not startled by his deformity. *"This was no monster,"* the boy thought. He'd seen enough monsters to know.

"Why do you not eat, Uncle?" the boy suddenly asked. Enoch was startled – stirred with hobbled speed. He lost balance and nearly toppled over. When he rose, he grabbed a rock and threw it at the noise coming from the mouth of the cave.

"Go away, you fool!" Enoch ordered.

The rock flew by the boy's head but he ducked with ease.

"The children told me there's a monster who collects water in the mornings. They say he's like a demon of the morning but I see you're a man," remarked the boy, "an ugly man, but still a man."

"Leave me be!" screamed Enoch, but the boy didn't flinch.

"Why do you hide your face? Are you shamed by your deformity? My mother says we should not be shamed by what *Eloah* has granted us."

"I said, go away you. And stop bringing me food!"

Enoch threw another rock at the boy. The boy got the message and turned to leave but he didn't run. He also didn't stop bringing Enoch food.

Every morning the boy came and left food and every evening he'd come and collect the tray. It became simply another notation for Enoch to make. Sometimes Enoch would shoo him away and sometimes he didn't. But the boy never wavered. The boy's resolve was set on helping the monster who lived in a cave. The boy grew into a young man. He came to observe that Enoch was not going to hurt him. One evening he came and found that Enoch had finally eaten the food. He laughed outloud.

"Ha! I'm right, you're no monster! You do eat!"

Enoch's patience had long been eroded by the boy's persistence. His scowl at him was now empty.

"What do you know of monsters, silly boy?" Enoch asked.

"The land is full of monsters, uncle, but they do not act like you, why do you hide here?"

"You would not understand, you're just a weak boy," Enoch scoffed.

"I understand many great things, and I'm not a weak boy," the boy replied.

"What is your name?"

"I'm David."

"Has your mother never told you to avoid befriending strange men who live in caves, David? Do you not worry that I could harm you?" Enoch asked.

"You will not harm me, uncle," David said, stepping forth and gazing at the notations on the walls of the cave, his attention drawn by the figures while his response came naturally. "For I'm strong and I'd throttle you until the breath left your body," he said, his tiny frame filled with a power from his heart.

Enoch was taken aback by the resolve of this smaller than average boy, believing David meant every word of it. "Forgive my remark about your mother. Thank you for the food David, she's taught you well," Enoch said.

"What do you scribe on the walls? What notations are these, uncle?" David asked.

"It is a measure of the days and cycles, I'm counting them."

"Once you count the days what will you do with them?" asked David.

Enoch explained the equinoxes and the changes that happen at each one. David listened attentively and asked more questions. The boy was intelligent. Enoch explained the patterns that lay in plain view. He explained that the sun and moon were most precise time-pieces, the moon counting months and the sun counting days and minutes, and how together they counted cycles, eons and even great epochs.

"So by this calculation," David started, "Some twenty cycles from now, the moon will transition in front of the sun and the day will grow dark as night?"

"Yes," Enoch said. "That's right."

"But how can you be certain this will pass, have you seen it before?" asked David.

Enoch wanted to say that he'd seen it happen before, cycles ago. That in fact it had been the reason for his imprisonment but he chose not to. Better for David to think he was a monster who lived in a cave, than a mad man.

"At that time, just make sure you plant crops onc equinox before you normally would," Enoch said. David listened and found a new purpose in visiting Enoch. David's curiosity was like a vacuum of questions that had met Enoch's knowledge.

Despite Enoch's best efforts to be an unwilling teacher, David learned all he could.

The scar tissue was giving way to normal skin and Enoch felt comfortable venturing further from the cave. The thoughts of Uriel had subsided to a distant memory and David had advanced greatly in his studies. He grew into a young man and would climb the mountain every day to learn and speak to Enoch. He started to bring parchment and scrolls and make his own notations. He never asked Enoch his name, instead calling him only "*Uncle*". One day the curiosity became too much and he asked Enoch the question that had been on his mind for years.

"What happened to you, Uncle?"

Enoch paused, thinking his account might frighten him, but as he'd got to know David, Enoch had long seen that not much would frighten this boy.

"Always be careful what you wish for David, It seems the *Archs* of *Eloah* sometimes like to punish us with that which we most desire."

"Like a *Djinn*?" David said.

"You have seen a *Djinn*?" asked Enoch.

"Yes, many still live on Mount Hermon. My brothers and I once saw them there – they're like sharp nails of wind that can swirl and turn around a rock until it has been shaped into any tool. Sometimes they're big and sometimes small. My father travelled to Indus where he says the *Djingeers* there used them to display magic – A *magi* will hold the end of a rope, toss it into the empty sky but rather than fall back down, the rope will be held by an invisible *Djinn.*"

Enoch gasped and then coughed from the exertion. It was worse than he had thought. Somewhere, Semjaza was in direct contact with people and he was teaching them to use the spirits of dead giants. Somehow this knowledge had spread through the people after the flood.

"Do the people worship these Djinns?" asked Enoch.

"Some do, others just use them. They say Moloch commands an army of them. The stories also say they can be caught and forced to grant a wish. That is why I came to find you when the children told me of you. I hoped you were a Djinn, so that I could catch you and request that you make the King of Babylon bring back my people."

"What happened to your people?"

"The Babylonian King holds them captive. I wish and pray to the stars every night that I may free them one day."

As Enoch listened, he learned the source of David's strength. A strong man builds a circle around himself and protects himself, a great man builds a circle around his family and never lets harm come to them. But only a king builds a circle around his people and chases its enemies to the ends of the earth.

"Are you the first born?" Enoch wondered.

"No, I am the yougest, why?"

"I hear Moloch demands a sacrifice of first-born children."

"Not only the first born. I am the youngest of eight brothers, my family is very poor. My mother says she was going to sacrifice me too but that an *Arch* came to her and told her to defy Moloch. She said the *Arch* was beautiful, with hair like the black stone that comes from mount Edin, so she listened."

Enoch's eyes widened. "Uriel?" he whispered.

"Who is that?" asked David.

"Never mind. What do the people say of *Eloah*?"

"Moloch isn't *Eloah*?"

"Moloch isn't the *Eloah*. He's a creation by one of *Eloah*'s fallen *Arch*s. The real *Eloah* would never ask you to kill your own child."

"How do you know?"

"It is a long story, David."

"I like long stories, uncle," David replied.

"Another time," said Enoch.

David relented and then spoke again. "You're a smart man, Uncle, I've remembered the symbols on your wall and they're correct."

"Yes, your crops will yield better now," said Enoch.

"Then why do you not descend and share this knowledge with the people? If you did, they would follow you. So would I."

"I share it with you, you can share it with them. What I've learned is that sometimes it matters greatly who the messenger is," Enoch advised. "Besides, it isn't my job to lead people."

"You have a job besides being the monster who lives in a cave?" David laughed. "What is this job?"

"Long ago *Eloah* told me that I was to help the giants find their home," Enoch said, remembering the higher realms with Uriel, the radiance of her face, the warmth of her hand as she had touched his heart. Enoch looked towards the sky. "One of *Eloah*'s *Arch*s told me I was to know the truth."

"Then it seems, uncle," David observed, "That you haven't been doing your job. There are so many truths in the land now. So many gods, that people are confused about which one to follow."

Enoch pondered David's observation. It was true. Could this be why Uriel no longer talked to him?

"I must go, Uncle," David said. "I must bring food to my brothers, they work in the field. What do you wish to eat tomorrow?"

"Anything you catch will be fine, David," Enoch replied.

David left and as Enoch pondered further, an idea came to him. He thought of David's words about how an *Arch* had come to the boy's mother. *"Could that be the work of the seventh realm?"* Enoch thought. *"Saving David from the flames of Moloch's fire so the boy could now befriend me?"* A man who hadn't known of the seventh realm might have believed it to be a coincidence. Enoch was not such a man, a fact known only to Uriel, Enoch and the seventh realm itself. Enoch ran to the mouth of the cave and called out to David.

"David, I need scrolls and quills. Can you find and bring them to me tomorrow?"

David nodded his head in agreement and went to find his brothers.

The next day, Enoch had formed a plan to begin scribing his account of the time before the flood. It would be a true account that would unite the teaching of Abraham, Zoraster and Assyrios. He noted the sun rise as a low wind stirred at the mouth of the cave. He hobbled over to the mouth, to meet David when he appeared, but only the shrubbery moved there, leaving a vapid sense of calm. There weren't even any sounds carrying to him from the town.

Mid-day came and David still hadn't appeared. Enoch walked over to the mouth of the cave and looked out again. In the distance he saw a crowd gathering near a hilltop and disappearing over the edge of the hill. At first Enoch thought they were running away but as he watched more, he realized they were running towards something. Something was happening beyond that hill. Enoch wandered out of the cave, hiked to the hilltop and saw why David had not appeared. His jaw dropped.

The giant stood over nine feet tall. He banged his spear against the golden armour of his chest plate. The muscles in his legs and arms were thick and full. His squared head swung on his wide powerful neck as he swung his spear wildly at David. The boy's nimble feet once again avoided the swing but nearly lost balance when he settled. It seemed he'd been avoiding these swings for some time, the boy was growing tired.

A crowd had gathered and formed a wide circle around the fighting pair. David, in the middle, focused his eyes on the giant in front of him. Enoch couldn't tell from whom this giant had descended but he didn't need to. He could tell the *man* had long since been disconnected from his divinity. Enoch saw sweat dripping from each of their brows. They must have been circling each other like this for some time.

The crowd was mixed with cheers for David to fight and pleas for him to run. Someone sent for his father. David was out of breath and disheveled. A cut had formed on his cheek, no doubt from a moment when he hadn't been fast enough to avoid the giant's ten-foot spear. David now kept his distance as the giant attempted to close the distance and end this battle.

"David," Enoch thought, *"You foolish boy, he'll crush you."*

David crouch-paced, keeping one eye on the ground and the other on Goliath. He was looking for something. He reached down and grabbed a smooth pebble. Enoch saw a little smile appear on his face.

"Go from here Goliath!" David shouted, stopping his pace and standing squared with the giant, "Or I'll throttle you until the breath leaves your body."

The giant stopped and laughed with his own hubris. It would be his undoing. David's eyes sharpened, he'd been waiting for this moment. He quickly pulled out his sling shot and fired the pebble into the giant's mouth.

"Rock of ages, cleft for me like so," David said softly to himself as the pebble flew.

The stone was the perfect size to lodge in Goliath's throat. Goliath gasped for air and stumbled about the ground. He held his throat trying to breathe but he couldn't. David charged and grabbed the giant's spear while Goliath gasped for breath. He used the leverage to swing onto the Giant's back. David climbed onto the giant's neck and brought the spear tip down into the base of Goliath's neck, feeling the long spear push through Goliath's skin and into his chest cavity. Goliath fell with a thud. The people erupted in cheering for David. David saw Enoch and walked over to him.

"He could have crushed you David," Enoch noted.

"Maybe so, but good has come of it uncle, it has made you leave your cave."

"I'll bring you the scrolls later but you must promise me that once you finish you will leave the cave and return to the people. What you know will be of great help to them. If you keep it from them, are you not the same as evil?"

"But my wounds," started Enoch.

"Your wounds are healed now, the people will not be afraid of you anymore, they'll follow you Uncle. I'll follow you."

A crowd had gathered and had scooped David onto their shoulders. They cheered as they set off back toward the town chanting his name.

"They'll not follow me, young David," Enoch thought, *"but they'll follow you."*

Later that day, David brought scrolls and quills for writing. Enoch set to work. By the time Enoch finished, five cycles later, the King and his son had died. The people had chosen David to become the new king. Enoch had also finished writing over three hundred accounts containing all the knowledge he'd been given through Uriel and learned from the time he'd spent alive on the realm. His final account was of the language of *Eloah*. He gave this to David on the day before he was crowned King.

"It seems you have a way of making men into kings Uncle," David said, as he accepted the texts of Enoch's language. Enoch's wounds had healed and he felt such pride for David. The strength in the boy's eyes had given way to wisdom.

"Any king would do well to have your council. Will you return after your sojourn and council me?" David asked.

"Thank you David, but I must fulfill my own purpose," Enoch replied. He looked around the cave that had been his home for so long.

"I shall miss this place though, I shall miss our time together, David."

"As will I Uncle, I shall order this cave sealed in your honour and I'll keep your writings inside."

"Why do you not share them?" Enoch wondered. "This was your wish."

"I've come to see that you're a man who needs encouragement. My wish was that you would leave this cave and share your knowledge. If I made your writings public, you would be less encouraged to share them yourself, and this is your job remember?" David smiled, looking to the sky. Wisdom had also found a home in the boy's words, Enoch thought.

"Where will you go?" asked David.

"I do not know, there's much I do not know in fact, I may have to seek wisdom myself."

"In *Khemet*, my father speaks of a man – a very wise man it is said, who works for the Pharaoh. He may be able to help you," David said.

"What is his name?" asked Enoch.

"*Hermes Trisemegistus.*"

The next day Enoch attended the coronation of King David and watched from the back of the large crowd that had formed to watch. All around, thousands of people cheered their new ruler. The noise carried far off across the desert. David, at the altar, found Enoch in the crowd as he was waving to his people. The new king turned to the mounds of people behind him. When he turned back, Enoch was gone.

The camel that David had prepared was young but accustomed to the journey across the Sinai Peninsula to *Khemet,* long before it would be called Egypt. On the way, Enoch's mind pondered over David. Had it really been Uriel sending David to Enoch at his lowest point or was it rather Enoch that was sent to David to bestow knowledge that would make him king. A perfect congruence of events, yet both born of choices that he and David had made separately. An idea for the tapestry of the seventh realm was forming in Enoch's mind, yet remained elusive just beyond his mental grasp. Even so, Enoch didn't feel blind anymore, he knew it was supposed to be this way.

CHAPTER NINE
Hermes Trisemegistus

Having asked Bedouin tribes along the way, Enoch found out that the Royal lines of the Pharaohs had descended from an incestuous union between two of Kokabel's children twenty-six Dynasties ago. The new Pharaoh was *Khnemibire Amosis* II who ruled from a palace built on Kokabel's former greeting hall just across the Giza Plateau. Having made his journey past the Sinai and into *Khemet,* Enoch saw it was much different now from the society Kokabel had tried to build after the flood, but his knowledge was still here.

There was no denying that the knowledge Azazel revealed was beautiful. It was also clear that whoever designed this society had studied it deeply. The city structures were unlike any that Enoch had ever seen. In the lands east of the Sinai, society hadn't advanced as much as here, Enoch thought. Natural, since *Khemet* was the home of Azazel's first great love, numbers.

Enoch came into the town centre and was instantly knocked over by a disheveled man fleeing from two guards running after him and tackling him to the ground. The two large guards throttled the man, dropping two golden bowls from his robes.

"Thief!" one guard said. "It is the slave-holds for you!"

"No!" said the other guard. "The Pharaoh has decreed that all thieves be sent to Babylon, there's a treaty."

"Khemetian thieves in exchange for more Babylonian favours, do we not need slaves too?"

"What do you expect from a *sister-fucker*?" The first guard said. "The Persian King looks on with covetous lust at Khemet. I suppose our sister-fucker Pharaoh seeks to make friends with the idol-worshippers in case the Persians ever attack." The pair shuffled the thief off to a waiting caravan headed for the other great city across the desert.

Enoch entered the town and the noise of a bustling city came to life. Charmers played songs and the élite were carried in golden chariots led by powerful horses. Enoch didn't know if the rulers here knew of how their great ancestor had died and who his murderer was. He didn't want to take chances. He brought his headscarf up to cover his face.

The great library stood on a hill with wide steps leading up to a row of columns, extending from the marbled floor all the way to a triangular ceiling. Enoch had never seen this type of architecture. Enoch felt the grandness of it meet his eyes. He saw that it was perfect with the same figures and array of numbers that he'd first seen at the council on Mount Hermon.

Enoch tied his camel and entered the library, but a vagabond at the entrance stopped him. The man was blind, his eyes were black and had no pupils. He had sheets of metal strewn about him. His nimble fingers were fashioning circular gears from the sheets of metals with a fantastic speed while his face peered upward, not watching his hands. Other sheets had already been worked into long pieces that were perfectly flat yet the man used no tools. Next to him were two golden figures set to face each other in a future setting. The man was making a box of sorts. The two *Arch* figures should have been a clue for Enoch but he was taken by the man's eyes.

They shimmered in his face like two miniature cut-outs of the night sky. The man had been engrossed by his task but stopped when Enoch walked by. He looked up at Enoch and showed that his face was commanded by a set of nervous ticks. He was square-jawed and beautiful with hair the colour of silver. Enoch thought he'd known the man before but couldn't remember where.

"Give me your hands! I'll tell you your age!"

Enoch had been curious about it himself so he listened to the mad man. He presented his hands. The man took them and the nervous ticks of his face suddenly stopped. He looked up as if he could see Enoch with his shimmering black eyes, as if he remembered Enoch.

"Enoch!" the man said. "It is really you, Enoch. "He'll be most pleased."

"Who? And how do you know my name?" Enoch asked, startled that the man had this information. Had the Pharaoh known all along that he was coming, Enoch wondered. He looked around to see who was in earshot, preparing to silence the vagabond and make a getaway if the need arose.

"Fear not, Enoch. *Hermes* has been waiting for you, he knew you would return," the man said as he released Enoch's hand. A joy suddenly spread across his face. Whatever Enoch's hand had told him had made him happy.

"Finally," the man said, "I've the count I needed." The man's pace and attention returned to his sheets of metal. Enoch relaxed but he didn't know why.

"My hands can tell you my age?" he asked instead.

"Indeed so, the hands tell all if one but knows how to look. I can finally construct the *Ark of the Contract*, thank you Enoch."

"How old am I, I mean how many cycles has it been since I was born?" Enoch wondered. Curiosity had taken hold of him.

"1,993 cycles, 234 sunrises, 13 Horus, 45 mins and 13 counts, 14 counts, 15 counts, 16 counts…"

"Now go! He waits for you no more," the man said. Enoch entered but the man called out to him again.

"And Enoch! Remember the bones! Always remember the bones!" The man quickly returned to his work fashioning the sheets of metal. The entire encounter had been the latest in a long line of strange occurrences for Enoch. It seemed Enoch's life had become defined by them, nothing could surprise him anymore, though much would try. Enoch entered the Library.

Inside, he came to a great hall guarded by two large, dark men who towered above Enoch. They were from the southern dark lands and glared at him when he approached.

"I'm here to see *Hermes Trisemegistus*," Enoch stated, clearing his throat, the presence of these two powerful men requiring an extra measure of assertiveness.

"The thrice great sees no-one unless the Pharaoh commands it!" one guard said in a deep baritone voice that resonated like a granite wheel crunching over gravel.

"Who is it!" a voice asked from inside. The guards parted and a man came into view. He wore a jeweled robe and carried a staff with two snakes coiled into a helix, the staff itself as tall as he. A gold and blue head-dress framed a squared face annoyed at the intrusion. It changed once he saw it was caused by Enoch.

The man also had silver hair and the same square-jawed countenance as the mad vagabond outside. As Hermes drew closer Enoch saw he also had the same dark shimmering eyes. They could have been brothers Enoch thought. In a way they were.

"It's really you!" Hermes said. "Come quick! There isn't much time!"

Hermes ordered the guards aside. He turned and walked ahead with a quickened pace back into his study hall. There was command in his steps. *"This man was respected here,"* Enoch thought. The sound of his steps echoed through the cavernous hall. Enoch followed with a confusion that turned quickly to bewilderment. The internal hall was filled with scrolls stacked higher than the tallest giants that still existed and filled with rows extending far up and down the hall. *"There is much to do now that Enoch has arrived,"* Hermes thought. *"And there's not much time to do it."*

"Please forgive my haste, Enoch, but there isn't much time. Your confusion will soon abate. You do not remember me yet," Hermes said.

"Haste for what? Who are you?" Enoch asked. "How do you know my name?"

Hermes turned and approached Enoch with impatience, "The council, Enoch, the two fallen *Archs* who chose to not follow Semjaza. I'm Jamoriel, now I'm called Hermes Trisemegistus, I found your emerald tablets and I know of your journey with my great-grandson, Lingdar."

The fog cleared from Enoch's mind and he remembered the two *Archs* who renounced Semjaza just after Azazel was bound and Semjaza was transformed. Enoch turned and looked towards the door where the vagabond still sat. The vagabond saw Enoch's gaze and looked at him again. Enoch didn't wonder anymore how he could have known it was Enoch, it was the last moment he would ever think of anything as strange.

"Balotel?" Enoch noticed.

"Yes," Hermes said returning to his pace. "He prefers a form where nothing is expected of him, he sits there day and night spouting numbers and notations. He says he's counting time and marking the procession of Horus, the sun God across the sky, he's not very useful but his time-keeping is most accurate."

"What is an *Ark of the Contract*?" Enoch asked. "He said he's making one,"

Hermes released an annoyed breath. "This society is led by madmen, Enoch. It is to mark the first Pharaoh's contract with Azazel and the other fallen." Hermes rolled his eyes up into his head. "The descendants of Kokabel are big on such ceremony, it is a bore to me. But come, we've much to discuss."

They came to a dark room filled with glass jars containing colourful liquids. This was Hermes's inner sanctum. Scrolls were strewn about the tables and floors as if they had sprang forth from Hermes's mind only to land and stay a fingertip away for when he needed them. On the walls, figures and shapes were drawn explaining the mathematics that architects used to construct this society.

They sat at a table and spoke for hours. To Enoch it was a conversation that could only have been had with someone like Hermes, someone who had shared his experience or at the very least knew the same truth of human existence. For Hermes it might have been the same but it was hard to tell, he spoke to Enoch with a voice that had grown accustomed to authority and a face that didn't know how to smile. Enoch had so many questions and Hermes Trisemegistus had become renowned for having answers.

Hermes told Enoch that the word of *Eloah* was spreading in the land but it was not spreading alone anymore. That a great battle was coming between belief in one God and the belief of many. And that the battle had been created by Enoch himself.

"How? What did I do?"

"When you told Abraham, Zoraster and Assyrios the true word you planted a seed that ended their alliance against Moloch. Your word formed in them differences. These differences made them start their own ministries, their own versions of the beginning of creation. You created an apostasy of faith, Enoch," Hermes explained.

"What does it matter that there are three different versions if all the faiths still lead to the same *Eloah*? It is like a mountain with three roads leading to the top. Do the people not see that even though the stories are different, the paths still end at the same *Eloah*? Is this not logical?" Enoch protested.

"Logical to you, me and the other *watchers* perhaps. But to Semjaza and the other fallen *Archs*, all they see is openings in the differences, openings to the hearts and minds of the people. For if there can be two stories there can be a hundred, and if there are a hundred, then doubt can be raised a hundred times. All Semjaza needs is doubt."

As Hermes spoke, Enoch learned why David had spoken of Hermes Trisemegistus with such reverence. Listening to him, Enoch felt his own consciousness lift just from his presence. He learned that all the new societies that had formed after the flood shared a commonality, a secret knowledge. Hermes explained that the secret knowledge was going to be important for connecting man to his own divinity but not before the right time. He explained that while it would one day become important for the new humans to know of their ancestry; to know of which line they descended; to decipher their own standing through the secret history that had yet to be discovered; it was simply not yet time to do so.

"To a small child," Hermes began, "all that matters is sustenance and protection; knowledge of how to hunt or build a home doesn't matter yet. The humans now are like these children in the eyes of *Eloah*. They are not ready for the knowledge brought forth by Abraham, Zoraster and Assyrios, brought forth by you."

"Are they ready now?"

"No, but it matters not now – when a poisonous serpent has been released into a garden, the danger is to man and child alike, but especially the child."

Hermes told Enoch that the men he'd given the word to were just mortal men who could fall prey to the temptations that existed specifically for them. Temptations created and nurtured by Semjaza were like kindled hay before it became a raging fire. Enoch had told them the word as he'd known it with the hope that they would keep it the way he had. But what Enoch had not considered was that *Eloah* had made him timeless while those men were not. That the confines of mortal time meant that even if they didn't seek recognition for their knowledge, it would eventually seek them.

"Abraham was often taken with fits of rage and his followers too. The Zoraster's followers in Persia still use *Djinn* magic, though he himself attempted his entire life to convince people to abandon the magic of the *Djinns*. The northern men of Assyria and Greece worship the sun thinking it is the *Eloah* spoken of by the Rabbis in Judea. The true word has been splintered," Hermes said.

"And is this why you and Balotel are here? To be the holders of wisdom and time for all men?" Enoch asked.

"Time and Wisdom! You often cannot find one without the other, Enoch," Hermes answered. "He and I were bound by the council on Mount Hermon, this is our penance and we accept it."

"So why then do you keep the wisdom from the people but only give it to the descendants of Azazel?"

"Family, Enoch, there are other ties besides that which *Eloah* requires. When we made the oath with Azazel to fall, we were born onto this realm as brothers, as a family. I'm also bound by Azazel's oath to give this knowledge to all who seek it and are from his bloodline, because it is also my own. The Pharoah is a fool but we do not choose our family, all we can do is arm them with the truth and hope they have the wisdom to use it correctly."

"What of Semjaza? Are they still in reptilian form?" Enoch asked.

"They are but they use light magic to change their appearance. Balotel and I use different vessels. When this body dies, our spirits will travel and find another human vessel; but we will retain our consciousness and memories. The Shekinah turns our hair silver in this realm," Hermes laughed. "I rather like it."

"So what does Semjaza want now? What does he hope to achieve?"

"From the sixth realm, the *Archs* would sometimes tell me of what will pass but they have become silent."

"What does this mean?"

"It can only mean one of two things. Either they have been turned and now help Azazel, which isn't likely, or the sixth realm has been compromised, maybe even destroyed."

"How can that happen? I've seen that realm, it is perfect."

"Yes, but it only works when all four of the *Archs* are together, it is their combined power that makes that realm function. *Eloah* constructed it so. I fear one of them has been captured and so the realm doesn't work."

Enoch remembered Semjaza vowing revenge against Uriel at the council. "Uriel has left my dreams, Hermes, do you think it is she that has been taken?"

Hermes took in a breath. "I'm certain of it. Wait here, I want to show you something."

Hermes returned with a black stone shaped like two pyramids fused together. He placed it in front of Enoch.

"What is this?"

"It is a Merkaba, made of obsidian stone. Persia plans an invasion on Khemet and the Pharoah grows paranoid. He heard that this rock was being mined in Pentak and had guards follow the miners. It turns out they were mining this rock and taking it to a cave in the Sinai, not to the Persians. It seems whoever had instructed them to find this rock, lived underground."

"Semjaza!" Enoch said. "But why is this rock special?"

Hermes told Enoch that, in this realm, the vibrations of any creation could be altered by certain incantations in the language of *Eloah*. More so, if the incantations were focused into certain shapes made of certain materials. He explained how the greatest effects could be achieved if they were done at certain times and irreversible if at certain places. In the future, adepts of the hidden magic schools would come to call it obsidian, *The Seer Stone*. Legends would spread that it had the power to bind demons and keep them in your charge. Enoch was learning from Hermes that it could also bind *Archs*.

"What will Semjaza do?"

"It can only be one thing Enoch. They plan to set Azazel free."

"How?"

"The only way to do that would be to sacrifice Uriel."

"Sacrificing an *Arch*? Is that even possible?" Enoch asked.

Hermes explained that it was the most dangerous sacrificial rite imaginable. The ritual of offerings conducted by worshippers of Moloch, Marduke and Baal opened conduits to the lower realms where Azazel was bound. Whereas a human's natural death meant the conduit opened only large enough for one soul to pass from this realm to one of the others, a sacrifice to Moloch filled the surrounding the Shekinah with an energy that allowed powerful spirits from Azazel's realm to return to this one. But a human sacrifice was not strong enough to sustain any more than that. He explained that the spirit of an *Arch* could open the conduit wide enough for Azazel and all the others to free their chains with enough power to stay on this realm for eternity. Uriel's sacrifice would free Azazel back into this realm.

"It isn't really an offering," Hermes said. "More like the fusing of two powerful *Archs* into one. Semjaza plans to bind Uriel with Azazel. It would increase their power but Uriel would cease to exist as you and I know her and so would Azazel."

"How do you know that is his plan?" Enoch asked with suspicion.

"Because I told him how to do it."

"What?" Enoch questioned in anger. "Do you still serve Azazel and the other fallen? Is that why you do nothing as the realm now stands to be destroyed again? How can you let Azazel return to this realm?"

"I merely keep the wisdom, Enoch. And wisdom remains neutral until it finds a hand to wield it. I'm sorry."

"You have not changed as much as you think you have, Hermes!" Enoch said as he held the Merkaba, his thoughts consumed by rage. His fingers ran along the smooth pointed sections. Its construction was so perfect, Enoch saw that numbers truly held the secrets of *Eloah* but his face dropped with the thought that Uriel was trapped in one of these.

Hermes noticed the change in Enoch's Shekinah. "It matters not Enoch, for *Eloah* is like water. No matter how *He* is obstructed, *He* will always find a way to pass or enter. Whatever *Eloah*'s grand design for this realm is, this is only but a hindrance to him, the only thing *Eloah* loses is time," he said.

"You do not appreciate time. I hope in one of your future vessels you are imprisoned so that you know what it is like to have your freedom robbed from you," Enoch replied. "Your soul would cry out for help, Hermes."

Hermes paused and regarded Enoch closely, seeing something in his body language that Enoch was not ready to admit though it had been forming in his heart for some time. *"Enoch is in love,"* Hermes thought.

"You're enamoured by her, Enoch?" Hermes asked.

"Of course not, it would be a betrayal of her nature." Enoch denied the suggestion, but with too much emotion for his denial to be believed. He turned away, further confirming the truth of what Hermes had said.

"No! You're enamored by Uriel, Enoch! Why do you deny it?"

"I was born a mortal man, made immortal and then promised death for my services to *Eloah*. I'm simply tired, Hermes. The years weigh too heavily, on my soul and on my mind. I wish to return to the higher realm as all the tales have told of me."

"*We're* all blind now, Enoch," Hermes began. "The *Arch*s, myself, Balotel and you, *we're* all like the humans now. We must decipher the path that leads to the *Eloah* on our own. The only difference is that we know such a path exists; the humans are beginning to forget. I fear there isn't much we can do now except prepare for the fight when Azazel returns to this realm."

"What about the other *Archs*, surely they can free her," Enoch protested.

"They cannot, humans do not know this yet but they can influence the Shekinah with their intentions and thought forms. Love and kindness vibrate into the Shekinah at a high resonance creating a path for the *Archs* to flow through. Anger, fear and lust, however, vibrate at too low a resonance even to connect to the Shekinah at all. In fact they disconnect humans from it, giving the *Archs* no path to travel."

"Then I'll go and free her myself!" said Enoch, "I must."

Hermes looked at Enoch. "This isn't wise, Enoch. If you get near Semjaza and the others, *they'll* destroy you. They know how."

"Where is she, *Jamoriel*?" Enoch asked, using Hermes's old name. "You hold the wisdom and I have the hands to wield it."

Hermes stirred with discomfort. Enoch was not of his bloodline but his oath to Uriel could also not be forgotten.

"You will find her where Semjaza has started a mystery school and teaches magic, in a land where iniquity is fed by the breaths of innocents and the Shekinah vibrates with pure evil," Hermes said. "Go east and look for iniquity masked as virtue."

"Where?"

"Today there's no more iniquitous land than Babylon."

Enoch got up to leave. The journey would last at least a month if he made good time. He needed to make preparations, but Hermes stopped him.

"Wait! You will need a cover to get past the *Gates of Ishtar*."

"What do you suggest?" asked Enoch, watching Hermes ponder over an idea that was forming in his mind. Enoch grew impatient as Hermes' head tilted and a sudden frown appeared on his face. The change sent a boulder dropping to the bottom of Enoch's stomach. When Hermes spoke, his words were the farthest thing from reassuring.

"I'm sorry about this, Enoch I fear it is the only way."

Confusion returned to Enoch when Hermes reached for an oval-shaped crystal looking-glass next to him. Hermes threw it to the ground where it shattered to pieces, the sound echoing off the vacuous halls, carrying to the guards outside. Their footsteps came rushing toward Enoch and Hermes now, as realization broke onto Enoch's face. He looked at Hermes.

"You have not changed, Hermes."

"Guards!" Hermes bellowed, "Seize the thief before he steals my formula!"

CHAPTER TEN
Road to Babylon

"Not to interrupt you, but what did Balotel mean about the bones?" Holly asked.

"He meant the bones of giants buried in the realm will prove the history, confirming the account that we hold of creation is the true one. The first bone was discovered in 1676 in England. For a long time it was kept hidden but in 1824, when more had been found, a deception was brought forth to explain them. They were classified as large reptiles that walked the realm long ago but there are too many out there waiting to be discovered, they will never hide them all."

Holly nodded, another question forming in her mind about Uriel. "Had you really fallen in love with her?" she asked.

"I've learned two things about love," Enoch replied. "First is how love has a way of sneaking up on you when you least expect it and from a direction you never imagined. Uriel was there when I learned of my wife. She saw my pain and it was her words that comforted me through it. Who else but Uriel could I speak to of what I'd seen, of what I'd done. She was the only one who knew my soul."

"But if the flood came because the fallen *Archs* had fallen in love with humans, then to love you, she'd be doing the same as them," Holly said. "Could she even do so?"

"The other thing I've learned about love is that it is never easy."

***

Ramod the Slaver had a slender build with short locks of black hair that stuck to his head under the heat of the desert. It ended in a widow's peak just above brown eyes that never stayed still, and a neck that had long learned to stay on a swivel. He'd hailed from Alexandria but now made his living as a jack of all trades in Babylon, spending his days like a coyote long accustomed to passing unseen through dens of wolves guarded by vultures, too ambitious for the élite citizens of Khemet or Babylon to feel comfortable with. He was a man with too many airs ever to be trusted by the working class or slaves.

The slave procession he now led to Babylon would spend a month over the scorching heat of summer to reach the Gates of Ishtar, but Ramod had never made this journey before. He knew the avenues of Babylon inside out but not how to get there from Khemet, only accepting this job from a rich merchant to avoid a debt he owed to another. If the six guards in his command had any idea they were being led by someone who didn't know his way, they would have killed him and left his body for the wolves and vultures.

Forty thieves and vagabonds, ejected from Khemet and destined for the slave-holds of Babylon, now pounded the desert sands. They were bound together by rope and misfortune. Enoch was bound by a longing he had yet to understand but needed to follow.

He was the first in the long procession of human misery walking just behind Ramod's camel. The slaver's headdress was soaked with sweat while his hand rested on the satchel of gold coins jingling at his side, a map he'd yet to consult was tucked into his waistband.

At an oasis Ramod stopped to water the camels. The six guards corralled Enoch and the other slaves into the shade of a tree with whips and yells. Another guard emerged with a wooden ladle and a clay pot filled with water, the guard treated the slaves as if they were camels, each slave bent his head to drink from the ladle when it came to them. Enoch watched Ramod walk out to a ridge and look out over the roads in front of them. Another guard went up to Ramod – facing the two roads, uncertain of which one to follow.

"What is your instruction, Ramod?" the muscled guard asked, with the annoyance common of strong men led by cunning ones. Ramod didn't answer, careful not to appear inept with so many strong men's eyes watching him.

"We wait," Ramod said, mustering an authority he didn't feel to his voice. He needed time. "Tell the men to make camp."

The guard turned and yelled the order to make camp. Enoch and the other slaves were unbound to help raise cloths to block out the sun while they rested before the next leg of the journey. When the sun settled and the cold of night crept into the camp, another guard came and threw large pieces of rancid lamb for groups of four to share for dinner. The other slaves quickly devoured the foul meat. Luckily Enoch wasn't hungry.

The slaves went to sleep and the guards fell into a pattern of sleep patrols, one guard remaining awake to watch the sleeping slaves while the others rested. Ramod's nervous energy wouldn't allow him to sleep, Enoch's study of Ramod doing the same for him. He spent the night watching Ramod pace and make notations in the sand, erasing them and start over again.

"Of all the slavers," Enoch thought, *"I would have to get the one who didn't know the way."*

The thought to escape and fight his way through the Gates of Ishtar had passed through Enoch's mind but he couldn't afford the risk. Enoch waited until the guard left to relieve himself. When his chance to approach Ramod came. He rose and seized it.

"Go back to your place, slave!" Ramod yelled under his breath. He raised his sword when Enoch's steps alerted him, hoping Enoch wouldn't wake the others and draw attention to his ineptness.

"Follow the river, Ramod," Enoch hastily whispered. "It leads to *Ur*, but before you arrive at *Ur* you will reach the gates of Babylon."

"How are you so sure? How do I know you don't deceive me?"

"Only the new roads deceive you, Ramod. Trust me, friend, to me all the roads are old ones. Follow the river."

Enoch heard the shuffling rustle of the returning guard. He turned to go back to his place but Ramod stopped him, the look in his eyes was that of a coyote who had yet again maneuvered his way out of being eaten by wolves.

"Thank you, slave, I'll see you go to a good patron. What is your name?" he asked.

Enoch answered and returned to his place and sat down just before the guard returned. He quickly closed his eyes to feign sleep. Ramod darted around making sure no-one had seen him talking to Enoch. Taking a chance on the advice of a slave was not what he'd wanted but Ramod's options had run out.

Luckily Enoch was right. Ramod's eyes filled with relief when they finally arrived at the path leading to the gate. The path was flanked on either side by walls decorated with patterned blue tiles and adorned with images of lions – one placed after the other, as if hundreds of lions were entering the city with them. The snarling lions were at eye level and served as a tribute to the Babylonian Goddess of war and sexuality, Ishtar.

The path ended at one of the eight Gates of Ishtar. The other seven were placed around the outer walls of Babylon, each extending for eleven miles separating the Mesopotamian metropolis from the desert expanse. This one stood fifteen metres tall and was decorated with gold-painted raised outlays of horses, lions and dragons – glinting off the desert sunlight. The mud-brick construction of the gate had been painted a shining blue, ascending to ramparts where more guards patrolled and observed all who entered from above, turning away many of the unwanted with a swift sword into their bellies.

As Enoch was led through the gates, he looked up and wondered over the blue and gold inlay. *"How long had their construction taken?"* A group of bearded slaves stood on a podium cleaning the shining tiles as a watchmen guarded them. Enoch watched for a moment too long and a whip fell on his back for the transgression. He returned his gaze to the ground as his feet shuffled into Babylon.

Once past the gates, the noise of the city was the first thing Enoch noticed. A cacophony of sounds from all over the city combined into a living hum. The beat and rhythm of construction emanated from the great tower in the hazy distance. To Enoch's left, palm trees lined a river and groups of women carried water and bales of hay to and fro. Men squatted over mounds of wet clay, their hands grabbing at handfuls of the mixture and working them into bricks to be fired in kilns and used for the tower.

To his right, the tall walls of the city buildings loomed above the avenues, offering shade to the people walking below. The people themselves were an eclectic mix of ethnicities and it was the way in which they treated Ramod that told Enoch who was a citizen, an élite or a slave. The slaves never looked up to him for more than an instant, wishing never to be noticed. The citizens and students walked with a nervous purpose that had yet to be defined, but still knew to regard Ramod with nothing but disdain.

The élite sauntered through the avenues at a slow pace, dressed in silks and satins and followed by gaggles of hangers-on, stopping Ramod only to peruse the new slaves and laugh at him under their breath. They were the sons and daughters of the gold and spice merchants who had made fortunes trading with the lands of Persia and the Indus Valley. They had long been shown by their parents that men like Ramod wanted nothing more than to be like them and that it was their duty to remind him that he never could be.

Enoch looked around at the other great society of the ancient age. Like a beautiful painting rendered with foul rubbish, the beauty of Babylon soon gave way to its true face. Whereas Khemet had an underbelly of vice glamourized by a superficial love of form and pageantry, Babylon made no attempt to hide its true nature. The city smelled powerfully of death as rabid groups of dogs ate at the animal remains littering the neatly arranged avenues.

The procession passed a young woman running in horror as three old lecherous men chased after her, her clothes tattered and hanging from her body, fresh from a violent scuffle. Satchels of gold rang from the sides of the men chasing her, a maddening lust glazing their eyes. Her screams turned a corner and faded away. All the while the eyes of the people never rose from their tasks. It was as if the only one to see this crime take place was Enoch.

They came to a market where a man stood with a harem of wives regarding a bull, the seller professing to him that the meat of this bull would be most delicious. The man was not convinced. The seller produced a knife and sliced the bull's neck. The animal knelt on its front hoofs as blood gushed from its wounds and sprayed the people passing by. The man bent down and drank of the blood as if it were a desert fountain. He stood and was satisfied, his face remaining a bloodied mess.

Ramod shuffled the procession past a wedding celebration where an old bearded man sat, cheered on by revelers attending his wedding to a little girl who Enoch guessed was no more than about nine or ten years old. The innocent eyes of the child were bewildered by what was happening around her, a bewilderment that would surely turn to fear once she realized what marriage really meant, banishing her innocence for ever.

Next to the wedding, the procession walked by a great hall where the powerful smell of lust suddenly hit Enoch's nose. He peered inside and saw a naked woman being ravaged by a large, dark man from the dark lands below Khemet. The man was thrusting himself into her on an altar high above fifty or so other people engaged in a massive orgy below them. An undulating mass of skin moved as if conducted by music only they could hear and played by dozens of hands, limbs and bodies. The sound of the combined lust carried far out to the streets in full view of any child that could pass by. Enoch watched but had to turn away when a lecherous man entered from the wedding, prodding a scared little boy to enter with him. The undulating mass inside paused only to cheer their entrance.

All over the city, eyes and whispers had turned to Enoch's procession for as long as it was needed to asses that they were new slaves, forced additions to the underclass of citizens who oiled the gears of the great city. All around the squares and streets of Babylon there was not a smile on the faces of people which reflected genuine happiness. There was no connection that came from love and no intention that was born of an altruistic thought. The only thing that resided here was fear and death, in a land where the *Arch*s had no road to travel.

They continued and the base of the tower of Babel came into view. The stories had said it was circular but in fact Enoch saw that it was square, with each side extending hundreds of metres. It ascended to the clouds and the tip was barely visible from the bottom. A wide ramp wound around the outside of it as slaves pushed freshly-shaped boulders and cured mud bricks to the construction being erected at the top. In a past age, the daunting task might have been left for the tribes of dull giants, but now King Nebuchadnezzar II had found a use for the Judean and Israelite tribes his father had stolen from their land long before. A slave-master whipped at them, forcing the chant, "All hail the Great King Nebuchadnezzar! Long live King Nebuchadnezzar!"

When the first King Nebuchadnezzar died, his son, Nebuchadnezzar II, took over, vowing to finish the tower his father had started, vowing that it would not only touch the firmament, but storm the heavens. It seemed Semjaza was intent on fulfilling Azazel's wish.

In front of the tower, near the base of the ramp, a giant boulder had been placed surrounded by a circular ring of candles. A giant outline of a pentagram was carved on the ground inside the circle, each point touching a section on the circle. The large stone stood 25 metres and was oblong with an alcove carved into the base. Around it the town's élite and elect class had gathered and now stood watching with expectant faces, their murmur telling Enoch that something was about to take place.

As the procession advanced and the front of the giant boulder came into view, Enoch saw that a little girl with hair the colour of golden hay had been tied to a stone altar in front of it. She must have been from the Northern tribes beyond Assyria and was dressed in a white robe that looked as if it would fall away if the ropes were untied. Her face looked around at the élite with glassy eyes. They, in turn, regarded her as if she were a deer, ignorant of a dangerous tiger lurking nearby. Their expectant eyes gleamed knowing of a fate the girl would never see coming, but their smiles masked their knowledge. To the child, their smiles must have appeared reassuring. Enoch knew they were not.

The murmur from the crowd ceased to a sudden silence when, from the left, a group of black-hooded figures entered in slow formation, their steps landing in unison as they took position around the circle. They wore black hoods that covered their faces and were led by a man with a limp. As they took position around the outside of the circle, the limping man came close to the girl tied to the altar. Her eyes looked up at him for only a moment before her breath quickened with terror.

The girl screamed when the limping man produced a crescent shaped knife. He held his hands out to the sky as the girl pleaded for her life. Whatever had been glassing over her eyes ceased to be of comfort to her anymore. The limping man made an incantation that Enoch couldn't hear. He brought the knife down swiftly into the chest of the girl. She gasped with shock before her eyes widened and rolled into the back of her head.

The air settled and suddenly became vapid. The candles all extinguished themselves while a fire suddenly erupted to life in the alcove of the giant boulder, commanded by a force no-one could see. The crowd released a gasp of wonder at the magic on display. As the girl's life-spirit left her body, the sky darkened and the wind picked up, at first soft, but then blowing powerfully and billowing the black robes of the hooded figures. The limping man held his hands out to the sky as the watching crowds held onto their robes and shielded their eyes from the blowing sand.

High above the giant stone, a black whirlwind took form like a dragon eating its own tail in a perfect circle. The violent whirlwind spun faster, funneling itself into an immense conical shape. Moving slowly at first but getting faster and faster and shrinking until it was the thickness of a young tree, it whipped through the air around with a buzzing noise like a raging storm concentrated into one spot. The angry wind spirit circulated downward. It touched the top of the stone and began to carve into the hard granite, causing pieces of the stone to grind off as dust fell down like rain.

"The Djinn magic," Enoch thought.

The crowd cheered as the wind spirit ground away bits of the stone. The shape of a head was emerging but it wasn't clear what the final form would be. The limping man removed his hood and Enoch saw his countenance. His hair was also silver but his face was pock-marked with disease and had an unhealthy yellowish tint. It was the eyes that told Enoch who it was; they were shimmering and menacing like he'd seen on Mount Hermon long ago. *"This must be the mystery school,"* Enoch thought. The limping man could only be Semjaza himself.

Semjaza undid the ropes binding the dying child and carefully wrapped them around the girl. He picked up her limp body, carried her to the fire and threw her into it with a labored thrust. Her last shriek left the fire and her darkening shape stopped moving inside, the last futile attempt at escape before the dead child fell still. Semjaza returned his dark hood to his head and turned to leave. The other hooded figures also turned and started leaving.

The crowd cheered the display but didn't move, staying anxiously to learn into what shape the wind spirit would carve the boulder. *"Would it be another tall obelisk? Or a king- headed lion?"* Enoch heard from the crowd. The fact that a child was murdered to make it so, was of little import to them. *"No,"*

Enoch thought, *"Babylon was not a place where one could mention any angel of Eloah."*

Enoch's procession was edged along to keep moving but Enoch was fascinated by the whirlwind moving along the giant boulder, cutting into it as easily as a child shaped wet sand. He too was curious to see what the final image would be.

"Move, Enoch!" Ramod ordered softly.

Semjaza had been the last to leave when he suddenly stopped. The name, even though spoken so softly, hit his ear as if it had been his own that was called. He looked back to the lone slave standing in awe of the wind spirit. Semjaza looked at Enoch, instantly remembering who he was. Semjaza had found Enoch.

"Stop!" he called out to Ramod. "Come here, slaver!"

"Yes *rector*," Ramod said, approaching Semjaza. The two spoke in whispers, looking over to Enoch between their hushed tones. Semjaza walked away slowly and Ramod returned to Enoch.

"It seems the *Council of the Wise* wish to see you," Ramod said, with eyes that now avoided Enoch's, knowing that his promise that Enoch would go to a good master was not going to be kept.

Enoch was led to a square temple with no windows on the outside and with two obelisks set into the archway on the way in. Inside, he was taken to a great hall where at a curved bench sat six old men wearing robes of gold and blue, adorned with the image of the lion of Babylon, each with silver hair and the same black shimmering eyes.

Enoch didn't wonder how it was possible that sunlight streaked through seven tall windows around the room, windows he had not seen from outside. He had come to accept that magic was everywhere, creating with it a fear that he felt in the hands that led him to a chair, trembling fingers that told Enoch the *Council of the Wise* had to be the fallen *Archs*. Coughs and murmurs filled the council hall as the six old men looked forward at Enoch, some gasping in wonder.

Semjaza entered from an ante-room and took his place in the central seat. A wave of his hands saw the windows suddenly blacken and turn to granite walls. The guards' pace quickened with nervous energy. They took his entrance as a hasty signal to finish quickly and leave through the great doors, slamming them shut with an echoing crash. Semjaza then spoke in the language of *Eloah*.

"Let the light be brought forth for all to see."

A terrible smell of brimstone suddenly filled the room. Enoch shook his head to avoid the smell but he couldn't. Semjaza's body transformed back into the reptilian form that he and the others had been given on Mount Hermon. The smell intensified when the other six also transformed, their cheek bones extending out while rows of horns formed on their brows.

Semjaza paced the room, his large reptilian head hanging over his body like a man with bad posture. The others looked down at Enoch. It was impossible now to tell if they were angry or not, so vile their faces were. Semjaza wasted no more time.

"Do you see *their* nature now, Enoch?" asked Semjaza. "They turned you into an immortal man in a world of mortal men. They gave you great power and yet no versing in how to wield it. Do you see how they now turn against you because you wield it incorrectly? Is this the act of a just creator?"

His voice was deep, incredibly loud and unnatural, though Enoch could tell the monster was trying to speak normally, his words coming out measured and slowly. Enoch didn't answer.

"Why do you help Uriel and the others when we're the true friends of humanity, Enoch?" Semjaza continued.

"You're not the friend of humanity. What you have created here is misery! I know you feed off its misery," Enoch shouted.

"We're freeing them from the misery of darkness. Knowledge is the true and only freedom," Semjaza replied.

"Freeing someone from a misery you create isn't true freedom," Enoch responded.

Semjaza paused his pace. He narrowed his yellow eyes at Enoch, his head leaning closer.

"Then why do you come here unless you seek to join me?" Semjaza asked.

An image of black hair laid against the nape of a pale neck flashed in Enoch's mind. A hand that had touched his chest long ago showing him the seven measures of creation.

It was the gift of time enough to find whom his heart had always sought, and the knowledge now that she'd been with him the whole time.

"I'm here for Uriel!" Enoch said.

The fallen Archs chuckled at Enoch's audacity.

"He's enamoured with her, Semjaza, do you see his Shekinah?" chimed in one of the other fallen archs.

"Fool!" screamed Semjaza. "The power you have been given corrupts your thoughts, Enoch. Do you think she'll ever love you? But who am I to question love? If your heart truly longs for the sight of Uriel, I can give you a thousand Uriels for a thousand years. Is this what you desire, Enoch?"

Enoch again didn't respond.

"Ponder it, Enoch. I can make you a king if you just accept us and help us spread our knowledge. Our descendants in *Khemet* already accept our council as do the line of King Nebuchadnezzar. If you do, I can make you like an eternal *Eloah* of all, here, on the face of the earth, worshipped from now until the end of time."

"Semjaza, I'm wary of your promises. Whatever you promise the adepts of your mystery school or the lines of kings, I know all that awaits them are the chains of Azazel in the lower realms. Free Uriel now! She's but a servant of *Eloah*. It was not her will that bound Azazel, so why do you punish her?"

"*Eloah* took our children! He bound our brothers! They changed our countenances to this vile form! No! We will have revenge by bringing the angry spirits of our children to this realm once and for all," Semjaza exclaimed.

"Babylon will never prosper," Enoch argued. "Let her go!"

The fallen *Archs* laughed again.

"*Eloah*'s gift has made him delusional, Semjaza, We should end his misery!" another arch advised.

"We must make an example of him," added another.

Semjaza nodded. Smiling with an idea born of this new circumstance, he turned to Enoch.

"You wish to be with Uriel, Enoch? Then I'll grant you this wish," he hissed.

Enoch was confused. Semjaza turned to the other fallen, explaining his devilish plan.

"Enoch the Scribe has eternal life granted from *Eloah*. An eternal life is the perfect vessel for Azazel in this realm, once we open the conduit. After Uriel's spirit has been combined with Azazel's, we will transfer the new *Arch* to Enoch's body and our master shall have an eternal vessel for this realm!"

The other fallen cheered in agreement.

"Have the adepts prepare the altar and send a dragon for another virgin from the northern tribes," Semjaza ordered. "Take Enoch and hold him in the cell of the condemned."

Then he turned to the fallen arch who had suggested they make an example of Enoch.

"But you're right too, Raguel, we must also make an example of him to the slaves."

The seven fallen returned to human form. The windows un-blackened and the doors flew open, guards entered and shuttled Enoch off to the Hebrew quarter. Enoch's plan had backfired.

CHAPTER ELEVEN
The Fall

Sages would later tell that the rivers of Babylon would not flow had it not been for the slaves who made it, having long become like the lubricating oil of the machine of Babylon. All the slaves and workers of the city lived in the Hebrew quarter. It was where the women who spent daylight in the brothels, pleasuring merchants and travelers, returned to their children and husbands at night. It was where the market men returned with scraps of unsold meat for their families to share. Every whisper and sentence contained information on where to find the best of anything in the city. And signals of unsaid gestures had long developed to warn the Hebrews of impending danger, having long learned that, in Babylon, danger could come from any direction.

It was a city within a city built of a displaced community strengthened by a shared past. A community disrupted but not destroyed, which wanted only to follow the teaching of their Torah. The seventy rabbis leading this community, whom King Nebuchadnezzar had uprooted from Judea, may once have also wanted the same, but had now developed other ideas.

Enoch was placed in a granite structure with an opening at eye level large enough to see outside. The cell was large enough for him to stand but small enough that sitting was uncomfortable. He was being made an example of to any slave who might dream of freedom. The Hebrews ignored him as if their hearts had grown as hardened to human suffering as the king who had taken them. Enoch would soon learn that his assessment was wrong.

Across the avenue, a little child's eyes wandered over to him. The boy ate dinner with his parents and their friends while discussing the day, their attention consumed by the conversation. They didn't notice the child leaving the table to walk over to Enoch's cell.

Enoch watched the child approach with a piece of bread taken from the table.

"*Little child,*" Enoch thought warmly. "*Your hands will never reach up here.*"

They wouldn't have to. The boy's father noticed and quickly ran over to stop the child, just as the kind little boy reached the cell.

"Do not go near the condemned, Joshua," the father said. "*Eloah* has forsaken them."

The father never once looked at Enoch inside the cell as he spoke, as if Enoch didn't even exist. To Enoch's surprise, the piece of bread the boy carried fell from the hole and landed at his feet. He looked at the father but the man had turned his back to avoid eye contact with Enoch. He spoke obliquely, feigning the action with the gesture of a cough.

"The king and the council of the wise wish to belittle our hearts by placing you here. We do not shun you, brother, but we will not help them, I hope you understand and can be strong."

The father turned to usher the child back to the care of the table. Enoch smiled and ate the bread. It seemed the Hebrew quarter had long figured out that the sense of despair created by placing a prisoner in the middle of the town square – for all to see and feel helpless at their predicament – ceased to have effect if it was ignored.

Night fell and a group of young slaves took a post near the cell. Enoch listened as they started telling a story that Enoch knew well. The story-teller was speaking of a time before the flood when a great council of *Arch*s had been held on Mount Hermon. The man was explaining that the legends told of fabulous tones that had filled the skies that day.

"It was like, '*A...MADA-RIDA...GAHA-LANA...BASA-GIME,*' the man brayed melodically, mimicking the rise and fall of Uriel's tones, Enoch thought. The man's voice resonated perfectly at the end of each note. The sound was like a cool bed-sheet on a hot night, landing on Enoch's ears and making the hairs on his arm stand with a vibration he felt emanate from his heart.

Another man then tried to copy the first but couldn't quite match the tone, the first corrected him.

"No! No! Like this! '*AG...MADA-RIDA...GAHA-LANA...BASA-GIME.*'"

The other man then changed his breathing, and the tone flowed out as if it were an extension of the wind itself. The group smiled at the matching harmony and others copied him, falling into a wider harmony. The harmony made them smile and caught the attention of the townspeople who emerged from their windows and doorways to listen to the joyful noise. Enoch saw a shooting star streak across the sky.

"Again!" said another man from a window. "Such a joyful noise unto *Eloah*! Can you do it again, Shem?" It had been the first time Enoch had ever heard singing.

The quartet were about to oblige when their smiles evaporated under the murmur of the townspeople suddenly stirring with nervous energy. Something was coming. People retreated into doors, and windows suddenly closed as a group of hooded men approached from down the avenue. Their decorated robes said that they were Rabbis from Judea. Four of them, with beards that hung down to their bellies, walked purposely through the square where Enoch was held. Those that couldn't escape their gaze fast enough bowed their heads, one rabbi scanning angrily as if to make sure they did.

They approached the group of slaves, stopping at the man with the beautiful voice.

"Where is your tithe, Shem? Do you think the Synagogue does not need your tithe?" the chief rabbi asked.

Shem shuffled under the gaze of imposed authority. The others slowly retreated, leaving him alone with the rabbis.

"I'm sorry Rabbi, but my patron in the city pays me late, I'll make my tithe as soon as possible."

The rabbi waved away his answer, dismissive of the offer. The rabbi then ran his fingers along his lips.

"Your daughter," the rabbi began. "She hasn't bled yet? Correct?"

Shem's face sank with an anger that he couldn't display. To lie would only incur violence that would find his daughter long before it ever found him.

"Yes, rabbi," Shem said.

"Good, I know you're a good man, Shem. Good men are always prepared to sacrifice all for *Eloah*. Bring her to the temple tomorrow after the ceremony. She'll not be harmed but we will find a way to appease *Eloah* for your transgression." The wicked rabbi tapped Shem on the cheek in a display of corrupted power long unchallenged.

The rabbis continued on their way. Shem turned and watched them as his mouth curled into a snarl, killing any joyful noises that would come from his lips this night. He spat on the ground where the rabbi had just stood. Just as Enoch had heard Uriel's voice during the storm on Mount Hermon long ago, *"Here was another beautiful flower growing in a forest filled with monsters,"* he thought. Only here it seemed the monsters wanted nothing more than to crush every last beautiful flower.

The rabbis were about to round a corner, when another young man appeared in front of them. He was of medium height with black hair and a black beard. His robe matched that of the rabbis. The young man held their gaze as they regarded him with scowling faces. One spat on the younger man's robe, the others following.

"Traitor!" the angry one said, shoving the younger man away and walking off, the others following.

"Each of you is an abomination to the Torah!" the younger man yelled at them in response. As the group continued, the fearful bows of the people ahead greeted them like a wave. Shem ran to the younger man and offered his cleaning cloth. Enoch could hear their exchange.

"Rabbi Daniel, when will we be rid of their oppression?" Shem asked.

"Forgive them, Shem," Daniel said. "They have been here a long time, they have taken the evil of this land to be truth. Their hearts are angry, we must find it in ours to forgive them."

Shem left and Daniel continued on his way. He came by Enoch's cell where Enoch had been watching the exchange with the curiosity of a tourist, a curiosity Daniel had also noticed.

"Time passes quickly in the company of this Shem's joyful noises? Most soothing, are they not?"

"Indeed," replied Enoch.

"It is said Shem's grandfather and his brothers used to weep for Zion in this very square. I suspect Shem's noise is more joyful," Daniel remarked. "But they get better and better as the days pass. It sounds better than weeping, no? – I'm Daniel," he said to Enoch.

"I'm Enoch, are your Pharisees always so...encouraging?"

"What can we do? Our connection to *Eloah* requires them but they only serve the council of the wise."

"Yes, I've met them too. In fact I'm to be sacrificed in the morning," Enoch said proudly.

Daniel regarded the comment strangely. "You do not seem as disturbed by this as the other men who have lived in this cell before you," Daniel observed. "May I ask why? So that I may tell the future residents."

"I do not know, I guess I'm just at peace," Enoch replied.

Daniel smiled with pity in his eyes and adjusted his steps to leave. "I'll pray for you, Enoch, but please excuse me now, a secret message has come from King David."

"What message?" asked Enoch.

Daniel regarded him with suspicion but saw no harm in telling a condemned man. "While the rest of Babylon will plant crops at the next equinox, King David asks that we plant the crops one equinox earlier this cycle. I don't know why, it is quite foolish really, the late harvest will see the ground too hard to render the lentils free."

Enoch listened closely, learning that David still followed his teaching. His heart smiled. "King David is correct. It will not, Rabbi Daniel. Winter will be late this year. You will have ample time."

Daniel looked at Enoch again with another suspicion. "How do you kno...?" Daniel started to ask, but the young rabbi suddenly paused and looked at the side of Enoch's head. Daniel blinked his eyes several times in rapid succession. *"Do my eyes deceive me?"* he thought. Enoch now had a patch of grey hair just behind his left ear, where a moment ago, it had been black.

"Your hair, Enoch!" he exclaimed. "It has turned the colour of ash! By what magic?"

Enoch saw Daniel's amazement. Enoch wished he could see for himself, but the puzzled look on Daniel's face had given him an idea. If he was right, Enoch had just found a path for the *Archs* to travel.

"Do you wish to free your people from captivity, Rabbi Daniel?" Enoch asked instead.

"It is the wish of every song, sung by these rivers, Enoch."

"Then it is *Eloah*'s will that I meet you now. I have an idea, but you must help me at a very precise moment," Enoch told Daniel.

"How do I know you're not the work of the malevolent one? The change in your hair shows there is magic about you, Enoch, and magic is evil," Daniel protested.

"If I were of evil, then why would I now await sacrifice in this cell? Why would I not be exalted by the Council of the Wise?" Enoch replied.

Daniel pondered over the sudden choice given to him by Enoch. He darted his eyes around to see who was in earshot. To see if a sign would tell him whether to agree or not, but there was none. The stars were silent, Daniel had no choice but to look to his heart.

"A condemned man makes a request of me. If it is in my power, I'll grant it," Daniel said.

Enoch explained his plan, but when he had finished Daniel was not convinced.

"Our prayers have never been answered, Enoch," he replied.

"Prayer without faith rarely is, but have faith in me, Rabbi Daniel! Have faith in me now!" Enoch pleaded.

Daniel's mind churned over the suggestion. He looked at the man's eyes and couldn't explain the passion in them. "*He is inspired by something,*" Daniel thought. "*But death has a way of bringing forth this sort of passion.*"

But there was something else in Enoch, something older. It was clear the condemned man had nothing to lose. It was also true that long ago the slaves of Babylon had lost everything.

In the morning Daniel set off to spread David's message to all the citizens of the quarter before they left for work in the city centre. He also told them of Enoch's plan. The workers headed for the tower agreed, as did the sellers in the market and cloth-washers in the quarry. He found Shem, a metal smith, preparing to leave for the foundry. Shem agreed too. What he could lose was too great not to follow.

CHAPTER TWELVE
The Seventh Realm

Secrecy of the ritual was paramount. The next day the guards gathered Enoch from his cell and delivered him to the giant boulder after snaking their way through the avenues to avoid eyes and whispers of pity. The wind spirit had finished and had vanished to whatever realm it had come from. As they tied him down, Enoch saw that the giant stone had been carved into the shape of an ornate owl. The pentagram and circle had been re-set again for another sacrifice. If Enoch was right it would be the last one.

Enoch had seen the crowd grow and gather slowly. First only one or two citizens arrived; but soon, droves walked down the avenues as the time drew closer. A great crowd was now gathered for the return of Azazel. The elect and élite stood dressed in their finest jewels and silken robes waiting for the start of the greatest event Babylon had ever seen.

Beyond them, the slaves and workers of Babylon had gathered behind droves of the élite and now waited to see what was set to happen. Daniel stood alongside them, hoping that Enoch was right – that simple faith would be enough this time. A part of him was more curious to see how Enoch was to avoid the rector's blade.

Silence descended to a hushed murmur among the crowd as the hooded adepts emerged from behind the giant owl again. With them was another little girl with golden hair. She was from the northern tribes. This time the child's eyes weren't glassy. It seemed this time the adepts needed her terror to be present and all consuming.

She saw Enoch bound to the owl just above the blackened alcove. The little girl's eyes tracked down from Enoch to the alcove where the girl's charred bones from the previous day still remained. The awareness of what was happening became clear on her face. Her shriek was met with a low cheer from the elect. Far in the crowd, Daniel looked at the sky and said a little prayer for all of them, saying an extra one for Enoch.

The hooded figures took position but none looked at Enoch. Semjaza emerged holding the Merkaba in one hand as if delivering a tray. Enoch could see that it was different from the one Hermes had shown him. The one Semjaza now held pulsated white with something inside. The crowed cooed as they gazed on it. The ritual was set to begin and complete silence descended on the crowd. It was the moment Enoch had waited for, the sun had climbed to mid-day. No other chance existed beyond this one moment in time. He suddenly spoke forth in the loudest voice he could muster, hoping it would be enough.

"Hear me, gathered masters of Babylon!" he yelled.

Hundreds of eyes turned to him, including Semjaza's.

"I'm Enoch, taken by *Eloah* to walk with him and the other watchers of this realm." His voice carried to the elect and shocked them with its audacity. "I've a display of magic for you, the wondrous citizens of Babylon! Do you wish to see it?" Enoch shouted.

The elect smiled. Normally a sacrifice would just scream in terror or be so drugged as not to know what was happening to him. One that spoke to them was new and exciting.

"Yes!" one voice said from the crowd. "Show us your magic!"

Semjaza watched tensely. He smiled with uncertainty, trying to project a notion that this was of his choosing even though he knew it wasn't.

"The Mystery schools teach *Djinn* magic and falsely claim it is the will of Marduke. They teach that *Eloah* is a myth! Do you wish to see a magic that will prove the existence of the great *Eloah* above?" Enoch asked. "Do you wish to see it now?"

The crowd hissed at the mention of *Eloah*. They booed Enoch's words. Semjaza had been about to silence Enoch but allowed him to continue as his words now angered the crowd further. Semjaza couldn't resist their negative energy feeding the Shekinah.

"You have been deceived!" Enoch continued. "You stand here now about to watch a child die because you think your *Eloah* requires it. I tell you now that the true *Eloah* does not! I tell you now that you're all following a false god! You're all following a false king. In the name of the one true creator of all that is holy and good, I say to you that as the fires are lit for this child to burn, the sun will turn black. Kneel, then and pray to *Eloah*!"

The people laughed and booed further but Semjaza saw Enoch's plan. His smile evaporated, he turned to one of his adepts and hurriedly ordered the man to start the ritual.

"Sacrifice him!" a voice from the crowd said. Activity from the adepts hurried to secure the little girl to the altar in front of Enoch. His eyes tried to tell her to be calm and not feed the Shekinah with her fear but her screams had blocked out any other thoughts.

"The sun will turn black and you will see that my words are true," Enoch screamed. "Pray for forgiveness from *Eloah* and *he'll* forgive you. *Eloah* will free you from the iniquity of this city!"

The elect laughed at Enoch. Semjaza had trained them well. So brainwashed were they, that their minds couldn't fathom that truth could come from the mouth of a condemned man. Their laughter continued but voices from the back of the crowd suddenly made them stop.

"The sun! Look! It is true, the sun turns black!"

"The words of this man are true!"

"*Eloah* is angered by our mockery!" someone else said.

The laughter subsided and turned to gasps when the people looked up to the sky. There, for all to see, was a massive black circular figure transitioning across the sun in a solar eclipse, blocking its rays and darkening the sky. Some bent down as their eyes started to burn. Enoch had told David long ago that this day would see the sun turn black. Semjaza must also have known but had kept this information hidden from the people.

Fear erupted through the elect as a combined thought that *Eloah* had finally come to punish their iniquity spread among them. It was a thought that many of them had felt but which Babylon's Shekinah would never nurture. The elect's frantic eyes were now telling Enoch that they sought to repent but years of following Semjaza and the council of the wise meant that they didn't know how.

It was time for Daniel to show them. The moment had come.

Enoch opened his mouth and sang in the tones of *Eloah*, "*AG...MADA-RIDA...GAHA-LANA...BASA-GIME!*" (*No more iniquity will exist after today.*)

"No! No! No!" bellowed Semjaza.

Far in the crowd Daniel watched the sun blacken in the sky, almost not hearing the signal from Enoch on the altar. When he did, he turned to those behind him and started singing in a loud voice. His voice carried to men tending horses in a stable. He and the other workers closed their eyes and sang out to *Eloah* in Shem's tones when they heard Daniel's distant voice carry to them. Their combined harmony gained a volume that carried further out to a woman who worked in a brothel. The barely clothed woman looked out of a window to the field where the noise was coming from. She closed her eyes and started singing, the other women in the brothel joined her.

The streets of Babylon suddenly rang with a joyful noise that flowed out into the streets and became its own Shekinah. The slaves working on the tower of Babylon stopped working to listen to the combined noise coming from the streets of Babylon. The city had become alive with love. The slaves building the tower closed their eyes in prayer and joined in the song. The Shekinah had opened and love now flowed into Babylon.

Enoch opened his eyes when he heard the singing return from thousands of voices all over Babylon. He saw people in front of him kneeling with their hands in prayer and joining in the song, their faith returning to *Eloah*. Enoch could feel the vibrations of the people turn to a higher resonance. He looked up to the sky. There, beyond the clouds and behind the blackened sun, Enoch saw the *Archs* descending with an army of spectras.

From the sky Gabriel, Raphael and Michael stormed into Babylon. They fired lightning bolts at the great hall where the six fallen had held councils, crumbling its foundations in a moment of explosive fury. Michael and a battalion of other spectras descended on the six other fallen who stood around the giant owl. The spectras grabbed at the six and brought them forth to the altar where Enoch was bound.

In the city, guard captains attempted to mobilize a defense against the spectras but their swords were no match for them.

When the slaves of Babylon saw that the guard's swords were impotent against the spectras, they attacked the soldiers. The shackles of Babylon had been broken. The people saw freedom call to them from a distant horizon. But to get there they knew they had to fight. The people who had been the oil in the gears of Babylon decided now to rage against the machine.

In the rich enclaves of Babylon, the sound of tools clashing against armour sounded from the tower as battles erupted all over the centre of the city. The elect and the ruling class saw the workers of Babylon rise in open revolt.

Ramod, preparing a meal in his home on the outskirts of the enclave of the rich, saw a lightning bolt strike at the tower, knocking pieces of rubble far down below. The shock-wave carried to him, rumbling his modest mud-brick home and stirring his family awake. He saw a giant boulder fall onto a procession of soldiers from the King's court. The tower was being destroyed by a force no-one could name. Ramod's wife emerged from the bed-chamber with their young son's head resting on her shoulder, the rumbling sounds having scared the boy.

"Babylon falls, Malika! Gather what you can! We must flee! The others are doing the same," Ramod said to his wife.

Personal guards of the élite now had to suddenly fight off the droves of slaves and poor citizens who now came to demand the respect they had never been shown. Some of the elect fell in prayer while others simply fled the onslaught. At the owl, Semjaza attempted to gather and stop the people from prayer. A spectra touched the ropes that bound Enoch and they fell away turning to dust. Enoch saw his chance. Freed now, he first leapt to the golden-haired girl tied to the altar, his swift hands undoing the ropes that bound her.

"Run! Find somewhere to hide! Go!"

The girl ran and disappeared into the dispersing crowd.

Semjaza had been facing the crowd pleading with them to stay. Enoch jumped at him, knocking his tall frame to the ground. The Merkaba dropped from Semjaza's hand and rolled into the alcove of the giant owl stopping at the charred bones. As they fought, the battle for Babylon raged on.

Semjaza's countenance switched from human to reptile. Enoch could feel the skin harden under him and take on the strength of heavy hardening clay. The weak old limping man had turned into a beast with a strength Enoch had never faced, his powerful hands suddenly clasping at Enoch's throat and squeezing with pressure. Enoch's vision blurred.

Light peaked out from behind the darkened sun as sunlight was returning. The rays fell on Semjaza's exposed skin and a foul-smelling smoke began to lift and dance off his reptilian skin. The grip on Enoch's throat weakened. Enoch fumbled with the robes, looking for Semjaza's crescent blade underneath. He grabbed it, raised it and brought it down finally into Semjaza's chest. A giant voice shrieked from the giant stone behind them, a noise that had no origin but was everywhere at the same time.

Enoch saw a red whirlwind form in the air above Semjaza's body. He watched as it rose into the air, turning into a sharp sliver of translucent wind that flew off north at a speed faster than light could travel. The body lay limp then disappeared leaving only the flaccid robes. Enoch stood and watched as all over the streets of Babylon the walls started crumbling.

The Pharisees had emerged and now ran through the crowd pleading with the slaves to put down their weapons, to return to their masters. They were like mice on a sinking boat now, scurrying to save the system that had fed them. They knew that when the boat was gone, there would be no more places to hide and in the waters of freedom they would have to fend for themselves.

The magic-school teachers and adepts were being chased from their temples and hacked to pieces by angry slaves wielding tools, bricks and their bare angry hands. Enoch saw Daniel far in the crowd, a smile on his face as the freedom he wanted for his people now came into view. David's wish had come true.

Enoch turned and dived into the fire to retrieve the Merkaba holding Uriel. The flames stung his skin but he knew what to expect. In the Merkaba he could see Uriel's face flash and pulsate, her eyes warm with the sight of him. He smashed it against the giant boulder and Uriel was free. Her spirit force nearly blinded Enoch as it rose to join the other *Archs* in the destruction of Babylon.

In the distance, the tower of Babel burned in an orange crackling rage as pieces fell onto the streets. Large processions of the previous ruling class were leaving with their belongings. Some would go west to the shores of Alexandria and others north to Assyria, Persia and the druidic tribes across the great sea. Around them, slaves danced in the streets. Babylon had crumbled.

Semjaza's spirit had escaped but the other fallen had been trapped by the spectras and now awaited judgment. Raphael and Michael brought forth seven more Merkaba. As they stood around the altar of the giant owl, Gabriel incanted a tone that vibrated the air with a low hum. The six remaining fallen shrieked as their bodies turned to light that funneled into each separate Merkaba, one for each of them.

The Merkabas now pulsated with the red glow of an evil spirit trapped inside. The one for Semjaza was the only vacant one. Uriel then placed a bar of gold on top of each Merkaba. She released a tone that melted the gold, covering each one perfectly.

The four *Archs* then stood in silent council holding hands in a circle, leaving Enoch watching from the ground with the Merkabas at his feet, their figures floating in the air above the owl. Their eyes closed as they watched the realm of possibility return to their sight. They opened their eyes and returned to the ground where Enoch stood. It was the first time Enoch saw the look of worry on Uriel's face. It could have been Uriel's first human emotion, he thought, but soon found out that it wasn't. She'd seen something that troubled her, troubled them.

Gabriel left first and descended to Enoch, his tall figure gliding towards him. Enoch finally got a good look at his face, it was large and still with eyes set in an angry arch of the eyebrows, but this time he felt no fear in his presence. He thought Gabriel could have been like Semjaza, another pure creation of *Eloah* devoid of emotions or human considerations, a being merely following the orders of a higher power. The difference was that Enoch now felt Gabriel had softened his regard for him, with the kind of human consideration Semjaza or the other fallen archs would never address to anyone. As Enoch watched Gabriel's brilliant white aura approach him, he felt that the times they lived in were strange indeed, with every indication saying that they would only become stranger. To Enoch, it seemed the *Archs* needed friends.

Gabriel placed his hands on Enoch's shoulders. "I was wrong about you Enoch, you do a great service to the realm. You shall forever have my respect." His hands fell away from Enoch's shoulders, they fell to his side before he disappeared.

Raphael and Michael, from their floating perch above, then looked at Enoch and nodded their heads in approval before they also disappeared. Only Uriel was left now under the giant owl, her figure pulsating between transparent and opaque as droves of freed slaves ran past with the song of freedom ringing from their throats. The groups passed through her as if she didn't exist, as if they couldn't even see her. Enoch knew she was soon to leave too. He approached her. As he did her eyes watched him, then shifted downward.

"You will leave again soon, right?" Enoch asked.

"I must, Enoch. We've seen much calamity awaiting creation, awaiting you. I'll show..." Uriel began, her face dropping down in worry. Enoch had found his moment, he'd been waiting a lifetime for it. He leaned in. His lips made contact with her lips while his hands descended to hers. His fingers interweaving themselves into hands that didn't resist the touch.

When they parted, he spoke. "I don't care what calamity awaits me, Uriel, I love you and I couldn't stand to have you bound."

Uriel turned away.

"You risked too much, Semjaza could have destroyed you."

"I'd risk it all again in a moment, Uriel."

Uriel's cheeks flushed with a rose tint. Her chest warmed with a sensation she'd heard the other *Archs* speak of in the days before the council – the heady feeling of being connected to one being through the millions that flowed through the Shekinah. Enoch reached for her hands and pulled her close. Her head rested on his shoulders where it nestled perfectly as if it had been designed so to do.

The ambient light of the afternoon began to vibrate. The outlines of the mountains and of Babylon itself were transforming into a different realm. The sky flashed blue, and day became night, then became day again. The new day dawned with a mountain now standing in the distance, above a valley of empty green grass extending for miles and miles. It was Babylon, long before any human ever walked the earth. The desert had vanished.

Enoch looked around to where they were. The air was a cool breeze blowing gently. Enoch saw that Uriel's glow had changed to a natural radiance from her pale skin, her red lips having come to life with a thousand beautiful possibilities. She looked human.

"Where is this place?" Enoch asked.

"We're inside your mind. This is a dream," she said.

"But where is my body?"

"It is safe, surrounded by a special Shekinah that makes you invisible to your realm while you're here with me." She turned, her motion leading Enoch to follow.

They strolled along the mountain-top with hands interlocked, alone now in a world created just for them by Uriel's will. The pair walked silently as their hearts quietly soared with a connection they had sought for so long.

"I like it here," Enoch said,

"But we cannot stay long, your passage of time is linear, a minute here is cycles in your realm, so the longer you stay here, the more strange you will find it once you return."

"Why did you bring me here?" Enoch asked.

"I wanted to be alone with you."

Enoch felt his heart quicken.

"I cannot hide my love for you, Uriel, what am I to do?"

"It is I who should be asking, for I've also become enamoured with you, *Enoch the Scribe*. The only difference is that you have no-one to answer to," Uriel replied. "For me, this isn't so."

They came to a giant tree extending high into the clouds. The trunk was wide and strong and its bark felt hard and cool like granite. Enoch sat down first, he cleared a place in the grass for Uriel. When she sat his arms wrapped around her. Enoch nestled his face into her hair and breathed in its smell. He never wanted to leave this place, never wanted to leave Uriel's side.

"I often wonder if it is from Azazel's bidding that I feel this way for you," said Enoch. "For if I love you and convince you to leave your estate, to be with me as a human, *Eloah*'s creation would all be for nought."

"I've often thought the same," Uriel began. "All Azazel wanted was to create beauty and fill this realm with it. To love and be loved. I've seen that all over the land, this is what all the people want."

"But do you think he knew that in trying to create beauty, he'd also create evil?" Enoch asked.

"It matters not. When he realized that he had, he certainly didn't stop it," Uriel responded.

"And now humans need his evil to know there's good?" Enoch asked. "What if that had been *Eloah*'s plan from the beginning?"

Uriel smiled, her head moved back to nestle under his chin. "You're beginning to understand how the seventh realm works. In that realm, there are no choices and everything is as one. Even Azazel, as powerful as he is, could never fathom that all of his free will is contained within *Eloah*'s mercy."

"Do you think our love is also contained there? Do you think *Eloah* knew this would happen to us?"

"He must have," Uriel replied. "But I fear our love can never exist outside this realm. If he didn't allow it for Azazel, why would he allow it for us?"

"Would the same as happened to Azazel happen to you? Bound in a lower realm for seventy generations as punishment for loving me?"

"Probably worse, Enoch. That is why I must say something that fills me with a pain that I cannot describe. I'm sure you will not like it," Uriel said.

Enoch had an idea of what it was going to be.

"You must abandon your love for me, Enoch. If you do not, I fear a great danger will come to all creation as a result."

Enoch had known it would be so. "And what of your love for me?" he asked. "Can you cast your love for me aside too?"

"I must, Enoch, my duty calls for it. If, for humans, Azazel's temptation is a test, then the love we feel for each other now must also be one. After all, how can *Eloah* allow human spirits to enter the higher realm, unless they have lived a life free of Azazel's temptations?"

"I refuse to believe you're merely one of Azazel's temptations for me," Enoch replied.

"Maybe not Azazel's, Enoch, but perhaps *Eloah* wishes to see if you're worthy of the gift he's given you? So he fills me with this love for you to see if you will choose earthy desires rather than serving his word."

"I chose a long time ago, Uriel. Nearly two thousand cycles I've served His word. Is he not convinced?"

"For *Eloah* that isn't a long time. I suspect he's only getting to know you."

"Do you think, once he knows me, *He'll* let me love you, and you me?"

"You and I know that his choice has no bearing on your love for me, but mine is a different story, Enoch. My choice could have a terrible consequence for the realm."

"'*Could?*' – but how would we know unless we tried?" Enoch asked.

Uriel smiled again. "Slaying a giant has made you brave, Enoch. You seem to have grown an appetite for risk."

"It isn't that I crave risk, Uriel, but I'd move heaven and Earth to be with you here forever."

Her face blushed under Enoch's words, knowing his wish to say them was born a millennium ago.

"If *Eloah* doesn't bless us, Uriel, then why did he choose me for this?"

Uriel broke away and turned her head to face him. Behind them the sun was setting. Time was moving faster. Uriel blew a light breath on Enoch's head. She closed her eyes and brought her head to touch his.

"It was not *Eloah* who decided to give you eternal life Enoch. It was me," Uriel said. "You see, Azazel was not the only *Arch* who had become enamoured by humans," she confessed. Her hand reached down to his. "Many others had also, myself included, but my love was for you, *Enoch*. It still is." Uriel turned away. "I fear it always will be."

Enoch felt his heart flutter with the first bittersweet joy. More was to come. "But why me?"

"It was in Sargon's prison, the way you held fast and refused to scribe the edict for Sargon, even through your torture. I saw how your desire to follow the true word surpassed even your desire to return to Edna. You had caught my attention. Gabriel and the others noticed too. They worried that I'd fall into love for you and become like Azazel."

"Would you ever? Fall to earth, for me?" Enoch asked, half of him hoping she'd say *'yes'*, the other half knowing she couldn't.

She didn't answer, instead her gaze turned away as a scattered gaggle of leaves fell from the branches.

"I couldn't, not then. So instead I petitioned *Eloah* to give you eternal life. My intention was only to see you for a *little* longer, to know you a little better. I just couldn't bear the thought of never seeing someone like you again. That is why I did something I'm not proud of."

"What?"

"You know, as *Archs*, we often see that the deep love one human holds for another is misplaced – an innocent maiden loving the safety she feels sharing the bed of a murderer, or a king loving a queen whose heart secretly wishes for the touch of the knight. It isn't often that we see a man so deserving of the love his wife had for him, as you. Edna's heart ached and was breaking under the weight of loneliness after your imprisonment. Mine broke from watching her. I felt her pain as my own. I could see you – the perfect man she loved, start to disappear as your mind was bending from your imprisonment. I felt I had to do something, I thought it was the only way."

"What did you do?"

"The animals are already connected to the Shekinah, it is easier for us to communicate with them. The injured hunter who had called at your house had been hunting in the forest. His water was low so he stopped by a brook to replenish it. So consumed was he with thirst that he didn't see the deer across the bank, when I frightened it and it ran into him, breaking his arm. Your house was just the nearest place he could call on for help. Your wife's kind heart did the rest," Uriel confessed. "I'm sorry, Enoch."

Enoch was not angry but the thought was another cycle of emotions with no start or end, punishing with the same emotion with which it sought to reward. Had Uriel not done this, Enoch knew his wife would have died lonely and bitter.

"But I thought you said the *Archs* couldn't interfere."

"You say I'm worth the risk. Perhaps, for me, you are too, Enoch."

"But you're a timeless being, you could just have waited until I died and passed into the higher realm and you would have seen me, been with me." Uriel shook her head.

"No, I couldn't. There are hierarchies in the higher realms. You and I would never occupy the same area. In fact if you had passed as a normal human, we would never have seen each other again. I couldn't bear that, Enoch."

"Then what can we do now?" asked Enoch. "Is there no way we can be together?"

"There is one, but it will take time, much of it and unfortunately, only yours. It isn't what *we* do, but what *you* do," Uriel replied. "You have a choice, Enoch."

"What choice?" Enoch asked. Uriel looked towards the sky.

"If you want, you can pass into the higher realm now and rest. I know your soul is tired and that your heart desires this. For what you did in Babylon, you have earned the respect of all the archs, they see in you what I saw. But if you are willing, you can stay in the human realm, walking forward in time, helping *Eloah* combat the evil that will pass. The archs will always help you, so will I."

Enoch paused as he thought of the possibilities, knowing that the only choice for him was the one where he could stay in this oasis of time with Uriel. He closed his eyes having chosen his answer long ago.

"But If I passed into the higher realm, I'd never see you again would I?"

"No, you would not."

"Then you're telling falsehoods, I do not have two choices," Enoch began. "For there's only one option – the one where I can love you."

Uriel smiled.

"But I do not want to travel blind again. Show me how the Shekinah works, so that I can always find you," Enoch asked.

Uriel sat up and folded her legs in front of her. Her face gazed down to the grass in front of her where she cleared an area. Enoch watched her hair as it followed her movements.

Enoch sat up to see what she was preparing. He gazed over, resting his chin on her shoulder.

"First, Enoch, you must know that everything vibrates," Uriel began. "Nothing is ever truly at rest."

She reached down to the ground and traced a perfect circle in the grass. A blue light followed her finger, glowing on top of the blades. She traced another circle and another until the seven circles formed a pattern. She explained that the figure was the *seed of all creation* – what humans will, one day, far from now, call an *atom*, that the circles forming the seeds are the smallest measure of all creation and that all matter is made of these singular elements. She explained that different materials in the human realm are created by the different vibrating speeds of the circles themselves, some slower and others quicker.

She said that, in them, Enoch could find the same golden number that had been woven into the pyramids as well as into the rest of all creation. That *the seed of all creation* was held in place by the hidden dimension of the Shekinah. The mountains, the air, humans, the emotions and even the thought-forms holding the special dream space they were in then, were made of these seeds.

"You see the points where the circles meet are the points where the Shekinah enters and holds them together."

Then Uriel traced more circles, expanding outward. As she did, she explained that humans also are like the points where the circles meet, connected to each other as one singular entity made of millions of vibrating consciousnesses. She explained that what people think are their own individual souls and thoughts and wishes, are actually a part of one giant collective, bound together by the Shekinah. That when human thoughts focus on the pleasures of earthly desires, their vibrations weaken and disconnect them from the Shekinah. Semjaza then harvests these lower vibrations for power as he'd done in Babylon.

"But if humans focus on higher intentions like love, the vibrations strengthen and humans will be filled with an eternal energy direct from *Eloah*. When this energy flows through all, the time and chance of this realm will bend to fulfill every wish born of love."

The round lattice figure of interlocking circles rose from the ground. It lifted off and expanded out in front of them, rising and expanding further until it spread into the entirety of the sky, set in the same form that Lingdar's daughter had shown Enoch on the plains of Nazca.

"At the smallest level as well as the largest, the Shekinah functions in the same way. The lines of the Shekinah flow all over the realm and where the lines intersect are points of great energy as you learned from the giants. The humans haven't found the Shekinah yet, but once they do *they'll* use it to build a great society. But first they must learn it has been left for them. That will take much time."

On the ground Uriel drew and connected more circles. When she finished, the circles had taken the form of a hexagon. She showed Enoch that various shapes were hidden amongst the interlocking circles. Shapes made by connecting the points where the circles connected. Starting with a star tetrahedron and ending finally with the cube. As she outlined the cube, its outline glowed and another image formed inside it but this image moved with the outlines of people.

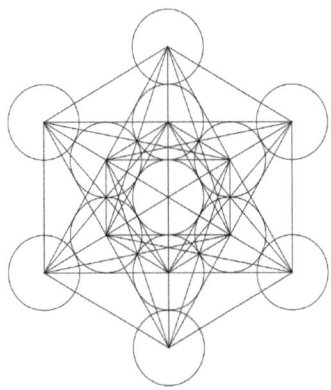

In the moving image Enoch a saw a man with light brown hair and eyes the colour of blue, standing on a daïs as he delivered a lecture to a group of seven younger men. The group of students wore white tunics fastened over their right shoulders. They were from a tribe Enoch had never seen living between the rivers. They were in a large white structure with long white columns rising high above them, ending in a vaulted roof towering above a marble tiled floor.

Outside their meeting hall, a garden flowed over a rolling plain descending to a village below. Enoch had never seen such architecture. It was an alien land that he'd soon come to know well but which now filled his eyes with astonishment. The brown-haired man held a glass figure of a *dodecahedron* – a twelve-sided structure made of ten perfect *pentagons* on each side. The figure required both his hands to hold while the outline of other shapes shone through from inside the glass sides. Something was inside it, Enoch would learn that it was not just one thing.

The man opened it to reveal a smaller figure – a *hexahedron cube* made of blue glass nestled inside. He removed it. That cube then opened to reveal an even smaller yellow pyramid-shaped *Tetrahedron* inside of it. The pyramid opened to give birth to an *octahedron* – a diamond shaped figure that looked as if two pyramids had been placed with their bases touching each other, each face an exact triangular copy of the other. The man opened that and revealed the last shape. An *icosahedron* – a twenty-sided figure with each side a perfect triangle. The man's students looked on with awe and wonder at the shapes. The man repeated the process in reverse putting the shapes back into each other.

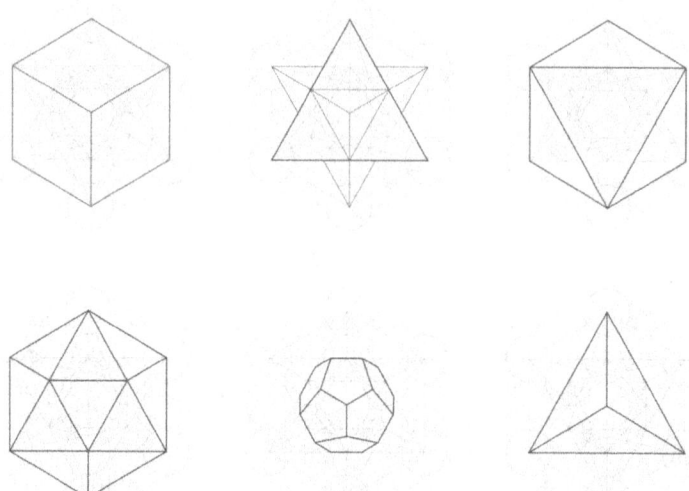

"Where is this land? Who are these people?" Enoch asked.

"Their land is to the north, across the sea. It is where the brightest learned men of Babylon and Khemet have gone. There, the humans have started to realize that the numbers hidden in the pyramids are in fact the song of all creation. It is the first step to finding the Shekinah. *They'll* even have a name for it soon, *mathematics*."

"Who is that man?"

"His name is *Plato*, he doesn't know it, but what he's starting will eventually prove the existence of *Eloah*, but not before practitioners spend epochs trying to disprove His existence."

"The story of Babylon will never be forgotten. How can they ever disprove what happened there?"

"Semjaza will take a human invention and turn it against them."

"What invention?"

"The art of observation, *they'll* one day call it *science*."

Enoch watched the image in the grass in front of Uriel transform back to the interlocking circles of the *seed of all creation* she'd drawn before. The outlines glowed blue again, forming a flower that then sprouted from the ground. A bee appeared and buzzed toward it before it landed on one of the petals. The light blue petal shook under the new weight and settled as the bee explored the flower.

"You see, to this flower this bee brings the promise of a new life, yet to a worm, the bee offers nothing but death. Which one is its true nature?"

"Both are true, it is just a matter of perception," replied Enoch.

"And this is what Semjaza is master of – the Art of Perception. Semjaza will make the people believe that what they observe isn't what they see. That he's a bee to their flower when he actually sees them as worms. Azazel knows this too, he knows it is why *he'll* never win, but not before Semjaza has bent human minds away from the knowledge of the Shekinah to a perception that there is no Shekinah."

A low thunder suddenly rumbled in the distance. The sound felt like dull bells ringing in the sky. Uriel looked up and released a breath, her hand tightened around Enoch's. She didn't want to leave.

"It is time to go, Enoch," she said.

She stood, Enoch followed.

"I do not want to leave. I've walked the realm for so long; I should be the holder of all answers, yet my questions only increase with each passing day," Enoch said. "Can you promise that you will not leave my dreams again, that we can return to this realm and be with each other as *we are* now?"

Uriel turned to him and looked into his eyes. "I'd have it no other way, Enoch. I'll always be with you." Their lips met again and a wind blew around them. The petals on the flower at their feet separated and carried themselves into the wind like dozens of forgotten wishes. Wishes of a past that couldn't be changed and of a future yet to be set.

When Enoch and Uriel separated, night had fallen in Enoch's dream.

"How can I find my way if I cannot call to you?"

"I'll leave you signs."

"What signs?"

"What animal do you love most?"

"The elephant, I suppose."

"Then if you're lost, an elephant will point you in the right direction."

"There are a lot of elephants down below."

"Perhaps, but follow the ones whose trunks are facing upward."

Enoch agreed.

"Where am I to go next?" Enoch asked, his hands on Uriel's hips not wanting to let go.

"First, you must find a suitable place on the realm for the *Merkabas* holding the fallen *Arch*s. King David will have told his son, Solomon, about you. His son will now be King of the Israelites, seek him. *He'll* know who you are."

"And what of Semjaza? What waits for him?"

"His spirit has taken a vessel across the sea from Khemet. Go north from there to a land where all the knowledge from Babylon and Khemet will have been given names," Uriel said. "The land will be called *Greece*."

"And you? Will I need to wait another lifetime before I can see you again?" Enoch asked.

Uriel leaned in close to Enoch's face. "You will never have to, for now *we are* one," she said.

A white light suddenly flashed, erasing the dream. Enoch returned to the realm to walk with the light of Uriel's love guiding his steps.

CHAPTER THIRTEEN
Walk Forward in Time

"In spite of that, Babylon wasn't the end of all the world's evil. What about the Crusades? What the Romans did to Christians, What the Catholics did to the Gnostics. The plagues of Europe. Slavery. There were so many evil things that happened after the fall of Babylon," Holly said.

"Echoes, Holly! All the evils that came after Babylon were just the echoes from an evil allowed to spread there for too long. So long that many of those same evil customs and knowledge have now become tradition and history. It is why Semjaza is so dangerous. Not because he corrupts souls but that he does it without the soul ever knowing it is being corrupted. These days you find the most evil in the only estate actively seeking to destroy any good the church has done."

"Science?"

"And the worst part is that most scientists don't even know they're helping Semjaza, though these days he's called *Satan*."

"But you said you avoided the church because they perverted the word of *Eloah*. So you also avoid scientists? But don't they wish only to explain the mysteries of creation?"

"Some do and some don't. The scientists don't know it, but *they're* secretly being guided, not by any living men but by an eternal idea started by Azazel and carried out by Semjaza. They spent thousands of years preparing humanity for Azazel's return. That is why you always have to look at the hearts of people and not the institutions they represent. All that matters is the heart, Holly; everything else is just noise."

"When did Azazel's sentence end?"

"In 1643. I'll tell you about that battle someday but there was another council of *Arch*s about it. It was decided that Azazel was to stay bound in his realm but Semjaza, ever the trickster, had succeeded in convincing humans to allow Azazel one more lifetime in this one. That was a huge mistake. Azazel lived only eighty years in this realm but the human vessel he used is going to affect humanity for millennia to come."

"Who was his vessel?"

"A very special man. Azazel's spirit found the womb of a woman whose husband had just died. His spirit was so violent that the baby was born severely premature. It was said he could fit into a mug, he was so small. No one thought the baby would even survive but he did and the mother named him *Isaac* – after the departed father. Newton was the family name," said Enoch.

Holly gasped. "*Isaac Newton* was Azazel's human vessel?"

"If you ever study his life, it will be easy to see. A brilliant man, with little interest in forming any human bonds, born with nothing less than a profound thirst for knowledge. His parents were simple farmers, no-one could explain where his superior intellect came from. But to me it made sense. Azazel had been gone so long that he needed to learn as much of what he'd missed as he could. All of Newton's time was spent mastering mathematics, alchemy, astrology and all the sciences born of the knowledge Azazel had first brought to humanity."

"How were you sure?"

"He never married, was never even with a woman, even after becoming the most famous man in the world. No-one could ever understand why, but it told me everything. I could understand the wish."

"Madina?" asked Holly. "Azazel's heart never recovered from losing Madina?"

"Sometimes, I actually feel sorry for him – Azazel, that is. He and Semjaza have often been at odds over what happened with Newton; their followers too."

"So what did Newton do that was so bad?" asked Holly. "I mean the man discovered *gravity*. So you mean that gravity and *Newtonian Physics* are the work of Azazel?"

"Parts of it, yes. Gravity itself is a theory that can never be proven. But it isn't what Newton did but what he created trying to prove gravity."

"What did he create?"

"*Calculus* – Azazel had found the perfect vehicle for the numbers he'd loved so much. Calculus was not that important to Newton's own timeline, but more so to the ones before his, and now to ours – the future – too."

"How?"

"Have you ever heard of *Nicholas Copernicus*?" Enoch asked.

"The astrologer who first proposed the heliocentric model; that Earth and the other planets orbited the sun and not the other way around?" Holly replied.

"A tragic man, actually. But the theory of Gravity was needed for the *Copernican* model of the solar system to work. Without it, the heliocentrists had nothing but a fantastic hypothesis. Newton's gravity, backed up by calculus, fixed his theory."

"But why was that so bad?"

"It is the most important truth. If *we're* at the centre of the universe, then that must be the work of an intelligent designer. If *we're* instead a miniscule speck, made from a series of random accidents, on one of eight random *globes,* circling one of a billion suns in a never-ending void, then the thought that our world was created by an *Eloah* starts to lose credence. It isn't that gravity seeks to explain our world; but, in fact, seeks to replace the idea of an *Eloah*."

"Like Darwin's theory," Holly realized. "Replacing a genesis of creation with a random happenstance of cosmic accidents, I see it now."

"Darwin, *the scoundrel*, I called him, but yes. It used to be that scientific theories had to be proven by observation – a scientist had to be able to *show* what they thought was true to prove their theory. Calculus had now given them another method for establishing proof, *equations* – mere numbers and operations. And the problem with numbers is that beyond certain parameters they can make deceptions appear to be true. The Muslims were wary of this. They had been on the verge of discovering calculus in around 800 AD but stopped. They halted their mathematical advancement after they discovered *Algebra*. Having seen that, beyond it, the mechanics of mathematics left this realm and moved into magic."

"The bee, the flower and the worm," said Holly. "Perception?"

"Exactly, sometimes the only difference between good and evil is the perception of it. The difference is so subtle that no-one ever notices. Agents of Azazel and Semjaza never say anything outright, but let the minds of people make the leap to a creation-less creation all on their own. The old battle for souls is no longer spiritual, it is now scientific."

"So what happens now?"

"Now it is just a matter of keeping Semjaza's echoes from spreading out further. He's been putting together another great deception and it has to do with Tesla's notion of radiant energy."

"The Shekinah?"

Enoch smiled. "It has other names now. The church calls it the *Holy Spirit*, other scientists call it the *ether. They're* actually the same. One connects spiritually, the other physically and it doesn't require gravity to work. Semjaza hadn't wanted humans ever to discover this but he's failed. Tesla will bring this knowledge to the whole world. Hopefully it will be enough to drown out the echoes of Semjaza's deception."

"So that's why you had to make sure Tesla lit this fair with his technology?"

"Precisely! Before you can tell the world of something so great, you have first to make sure the world is listening. The world is ready to listen now."

"But the Shekinah is invisible to humans. How can we ever see it?"

"That will come later. First we had to detect it. In fact, we already have. Six years ago two scientists at *Case Western Reserve University* in Cleveland – Albert Michelson and Edward Morley – conducted an experiment to find the speed at which the Earth rotates. They shot a beam of light through two pathways, one in the direction of the earth's motion and the other at a right-angle to it. The light traveling with the rotation should have taken longer to return than the light traveling at right angles to it. The light bounced across two mirrors placed at 90 degrees to each other and returned to the source – the differential in the returning times should have been the speed at which the Earth turns, the hypothesis being that, as one light beam bounced back and was in the *ether*, the Earth should have shifted over, even if by a miniscule amount. The result, though, was very surprising."

"What happened?"

"The two beams of light returned at the same time; the experiment was a failure. They repeated it several times in different locations but each time it was the same result."

"What does that mean?"

"Only one of two things: either there was no ether, no radiant energy, no singular binding element for all – or that the Earth didn't rotate as previously agreed. We have to follow this closely because this is where the next battle will be."

A sudden baritone voice pierced the darkness behind them. "What are you two doing here?"

Enoch and Holly spun round to see two constables advancing towards the edge of the observation tower, guns drawn and pointed at them. They stood to face the uniformed constables, instinctively raising their hands.

"Ma'am, is this man harming you?" the first constable asked. "There's a nutcase luring women from the fair to kill them."

"No, he's my friend," replied Holly, hoping to allay the constable's fears. Whether it did or not, Holly couldn't tell because they kept advancing.

"I don't like his look, *Smith*," the other constable said.

"I'm thinking the same thing," said the first. "I'll watch them. You go down and get back-up. We may have found the serial killer."

"What?" screamed Holly, "NO! He's not a serial killer!"

The other constable holstered his gun and ran back through the staircase they had used to reach the roof. Holly dove in front of Enoch to protect him.

"I need you to step towards me, ma'am!" the remaining constable said, stopping but keeping his firearm trained on Enoch. "You may be in danger," the constable continued, his eyes staying on Enoch, waiting for any sudden movements. "Serial killers can often be very persuasive."

Enoch and Holly were trapped between the suspicious constable and a 200 foot fall. There was no escaping this, there was never supposed to be. Enoch knew that only one of them would escape this roof top and he knew it had to be Holly.

"Don't be frightened, Holly," Enoch began, stepping forward to face the constable. "Everything will be fine," he said calmly.

Holly didn't understand at first.

"Know that I'm with you, Holly. I always have been. Uriel too," he continued. Then he turned to the constable.

"I'm the serial killer," Enoch said to the constable. Holly was dumbstruck.

"I intend to harm this woman, you must stop me!"

"No Enoch, What are you doing? *They'll* take you away! I need you, no-one else can..." she began.

Enoch turned to Holly suddenly, his kind eyes asking her not to protest.

"They won't take me away, Holly; this has to happen. The seventh realm isn't only for *Eloah* to understand."

"What do you mean?" Holly reached out for Enoch.

In the darkness just before dawn, it wasn't clear to the constable if the woman had reached for the man, or if he'd reached for her. The constable had his orders and he wasn't taking chances. He fired three rounds, two of which struck the chest of the old bearded man.

The first shot hit one of the search lights. The glass shattered and fell down to the pavilion. Gasps erupted from the crowds below who tried to avoid the dozens of little falling shards. The constable saw blood splatter onto Holly's clothes and then onto her face. The little spatters caused her to flinch just before the old man's eyes widened at the sudden pains in his chest. Holly held onto Enoch as he slumped down, streaks of black sheen forming on the lapel of his dark suit.

Holly wailed, "Enoch!"

She bent down to hold his head, now shivering in shock. His skin was turning pale right before her eyes, his hands came up to hold her face. He rubbed her cheek gently as tears ran down her face.

"You will be fine, right, Enoch? Tell me the bullets won't harm you!" she pleaded through sobs.

"No, this is to be my final death, Holly. This night, meeting you, helping Tesla, was all one event seen long ago in the realm of possibility. Uriel and I decided to love each other but she couldn't descend. We needed a way, you were the way."

"You mean that I..." Holly began. "...I'm a vessel for Uriel? Is that why I felt so close to you tonight? Why you left this locket for me? So I could come here to meet you, so we could be together in this realm? I understand it now! Please, Enoch! Tell me you will not die now, please! Enoch!"

Enoch's eyes were shutting, he was straining to stay awake. His shaking hand reached out to Holly's crying face, her lips had pursed and were frozen in place as she tried to hold back the sobs. He smiled and ran his fingers along her cheeks.

"Your cheeks, *they're* just like hers," Enoch managed. "You're not a vessel for Uriel my dear, but you're more like her than you will ever know. She's your mother." Enoch's eyes closed. His body went limp, he was gone.

"Enoch! Enoch!" she screamed.

She could hear the tapping footsteps of the advancing constable behind her, knowing they would soon be upon her to take her away from Enoch for ever.

But a sudden pulse shook in the air all around them. The first change Holly noticed was the sudden silence. In the vacuous emptiness, her ears started ringing. Holly gazed at the people below in the pavilion, who all of a sudden had stopped moving, frozen in time as if reality had become a three-dimensional photograph. She looked behind her to see the advancing constable also frozen in mid-motion toward her, his face set in the frightened realization that he'd killed his first man.

The anger rose in Holly, focused on the constable who had shot Enoch. Her body followed and turned with a furious resolve towards him. She was set on taking the gun out of his hand and shooting him dead with the remaining bullets. As she moved towards him, she saw in the staircase frozen shadows of the other constables coming to save her from Enoch. She was about to take the gun when a voice stopped her.

"It isn't his fault Holly, the constable was only trying to protect you."

Uriel's voice was the most beautiful thing Holly had ever heard. It stopped her in her tracks. She turned to see Uriel floating just above Enoch's body. Holly looked into her mother's eyes for the first time; big and round with a menacing perfection, and thought she could have stared into them for a lifetime. It was just as Enoch had said.

Uriel's billowing robes were made of a soft white light and moved as if guided by an invisible wind. A golden band held Uriel's shimmering black hair in place around a face made of soft curves. Her full lips sat on her face as if they could smile at any moment, or just as easily frown.

"Uriel!"

Uriel smiled and tilted her head at the words. "I was hoping the first time you saw me, you would call me *mother*," Uriel said. "But *'Uriel'* will do for now."

Uriel glided towards Holly and looked into the woman's bewildered face. The *Arch* embraced Holly and held her tightly. Holly instinctively returned the hug, feeling as if she'd known Uriel her entire life. Holly's shoulders relaxed, dissipating the tension and replacing it with an intangible sense of providence.

"Why did this happen to me?" Holly asked, her face buried in her mother's shoulders.

"I'm sorry, Holly," said Uriel, her hand placed on the back of Holly's hair.

The pair rocked back and forth, filling the crevices of Holly's soul, just as Enoch's soup had done to her stomach.

"Making you was the only way Enoch and I could be together without destroying all of *Eloah*'s creation, but we had to place you in the realm without that knowledge or else Semjaza would have found you through the Shekinah. It was only when you started to realize that you were special that he sent the secret societies after you. *We're* sorry, but not telling you was the only way to protect you."

"I needed you, I needed you both so much..." Holly said, pausing a moment before uttering the next word, "...*mother.*"

Her pain was giving way to something building up from her stomach. Everything she'd gone through to get here – all the pain she'd seen; all the lonely nights filled with questions about herself – became the effect a pin-prick has on a mountain made of stone. A new knowledge had found a home in her heart. A knowledge that her existence was the result of a love that had spanned five thousand years, that her purpose would now see that love last forever.

Uriel broke away from the embrace but still held on to Holly's hands. "There isn't much time now, Holly. It takes great energy to hold back the passage of time in this realm, but fear not, you will see me again – rather I should say, "*us*", again."

Holly pondered over the statement with a quizzical expression. Uriel turned and gazed back towards Enoch's body which was now behind them. A directionless tone sounded, emanating from Uriel but her mouth didn't move. The light of the surrounding time-space rippled as if it were made of liquid and the tone had been a drop of water falling into it. When the ripple settled, Enoch's clothes had turned white.

The colour had returned to his face, the blood had disappeared.

Enoch came and stood next to Uriel, his hand held hers as he planted a kiss on her cheek. Holly thought it was the greeting of a long-married couple. Uriel's eyes, closing slowly in acceptance, telling Holly that every expression of their love had long become as natural as breathing. Holly beamed.

"*We're* your parents, Holly," Enoch said. The news didn't stop Holly's tears but changed them to ones that were soon to become joy, but which now still wandered somewhere between pain and loss. She reached out and embraced her parents, hoping they would never leave, knowing they would have to soon.

Holly dried the rest of her tears with her sleeve. She had so many more questions. But now, at least, she knew that answers existed. Like a good daughter, her first thought was the fate of her parents.

"What happens to you two now?"

"Not us *two*, us *three*. In the language of *Eloah*, the word is '*KHOOM-METATRON*' – *It means the joining of three spirits through love*. Enoch will finally walk with me and together we will walk with you," Uriel said.

The frozen time-space around them suddenly rippled again. Holly saw the shape of people and buildings wave as if whatever held them together was made of a gel turning soon to liquid. Uriel scanned the area. She turned back to Holly with a sudden sorrow in her eyes.

"We must go now, Holly, but Jamoriel will have the answers you seek. Find him!" Uriel said.

"Where?" Holly asked.

"He has a bookstore in Germany," Enoch interjected. "You will know it by the vagabond who resides in front of it wearing many watches. Jamoriel will know you by the name we gave you."

"What name?" Holly asked.

"Call yourself, Holly Esse," replied Uriel. "It is the name of what you are, what Enoch used to be."

Uriel and Enoch began to fade from view. They rose and combined to form a singular sphere of light. Holly followed the sphere with her eyes as it climbed slowly into the night sky and became one of the stars, where it sat there shimmering brightly in the sea of others. Holly quickly looked around for the constellations she knew. She got her bearings from *Sirius* in *Orion's belt*, she knew now that she would never lose sight of the star again.

The noise came back as if it were dropped onto them from the moon. Holly knelt to the figure of Enoch on the ground in front of her, his beard having become a sea of white hairs and his skin now like aged leather. The sound of the constable's footsteps were directly behind her now. When his fingers found her shoulders, she could feel the man's fright from the timid pressure of his hands.

"Ma'am," he spoke softly, "are you alright?"

"I'm fine," Holly replied, knowing that she would be. She turned and rose to face the constable, ready for whatever may lie ahead of her, ready to walk forward in time. Knowing she walked with more than just luck.

Major Characters (appearing throughout the story)
in order of appearance

Enoch	A scribe from biblical times
Uriel	An angel who guides Enoch
Holly	Lost woman at fair
Azael	An evil angel
Semjaza	An evil angel
Jamoriel / Hermes Trisemegistus	A repentant angel
Balotel-	A repentant angel
David	Actual historical figure King David
Madina / Moloch	Azazel's wife
Lingdar-	A giant who become king of giants
Beba	Lingdar's wife
Dogon	A giant who helps Lingdar
Kokabel	Azazel's evil son

Minor Characters (appearing in limited chapters)
in order of appearance

Josef	A man trying to save his sick daughter
Irina	Josef's wife
Mischa	Josef's daughter
Dr Jones	Mischa's on-call doctor
Mayor Carter Harrison Sr	Actual historical figure, (Mayor of Chicago)
Steven Johnson	The mayor's chief of staff
L. Frank Baum (author of *The Wizard of Oz*)	Actual historical figure
Maud Gage	Frank Baum's wife
Edna	(Enoch's Wife)
Marek the Scorpion	Soldier who imprisons Enoch
Abner	Enoch's cell-mate
Sargon of Akkad (First Semitic Ruler)	Actual historical figure

Gabriel	Archangel
Michael	Archangel
Raphael	Archangel
Akanel	Kokabel's son
Lingdar's son	
Lingdar's daughter	
Jackson	Holly's flat-mate who tries to rape her
Abraham	Biblical figure
Assyrios	Friend of Abraham
Zoraster	Actual historical figure
Jafar	Offers lodging to Enoch
Ramod	slave catcher
Shem	Babylonian metal worker
Daniel	Biblical figure

THE INTERNATIONAL PROVERSE PRIZE

The International Proverse Prize, an annual competition for an unpublished single-author book-length work of fiction, non-fiction, or poetry, the original work of the entrant, submitted in English (translations are welcome) was established in January 2008. It is open to all who are at least eighteen on the date they sign the entry form and without restriction of nationality, residence or citizenship.

The objectives of the prize are: to encourage excellence and / or excellence and usefulness in publishable written work in the English Language, which can, in varying degrees, "delight and instruct". Entries are invited from anywhere in the world.

The Prize
1) Publication by Proverse Hong Kong, with
2) Cash prize of HKD10,000 (HKD7.80 = approx. USD1.00)

Annual Entry Deadlines
(subject to confirmation and/or change)

Entry forms available from	No later than 14 April
Closing date for entry forms, fees and entered work	30 June
Judging	July-September
Semi-finalists announced	No later than November

THE INTERNATIONAL PROVERSE POETRY PRIZE (SINGLE POEMS)

Entry forms, entry fees, and entered work received from	7 May
Closing date for entry forms, fees and entered work	30 June
Judging	July-September
Winners announced	No later than November

More information, updated from time to time, is available on the Proverse website: proversepublishing.com

PREVIOUS WINNERS OF THE PROVERSE PRIZE

Rebecca Tomasis, "Mishpacha – Family"

Laura Solomon, "Instant Messages"

Gillian Jones, "A Misted Mirror"

David Diskin, "The Village in the Mountains"

Peter Gregoire, "Article 109"

Sophronia Liu, "A Shimmering Sea"

Birgit Linder, "Shadows in Deferment"

James McCarthy, "The Diplomat of Kashgar"

Philip Chatting, "The Snow Bridge and Other Stories"

Celia Claase, "The Layers Between"

Lawrence Gray, "Adam's Franchise"

Gustav Preller, "Curveball: Life never comes at you straight"

Ivy Ngeow, "Cry of the Flying Rhino".

FICTION PUBLISHED BY PROVERSE

Those who enjoy **Enoch's Muse** may also enjoy the following novels, novellas and short story collections.

Novels and novellas

A Misted Mirror, by Gillian Jones. 2011.

A Painted Moment, by Jennifer Ching. 2010.

Adam's Franchise, by Lawrence Gray. 2016.

An Imitation of Life. 2nd ed, by Laura Solomon. 2013.

Article 109, by Peter Gregoire. 2012.

Bao Bao's odyssey: from Mao's Shanghai to capitalist Hong Kong, by Paul Ting. 2012.

Black Tortoise Winter, by Jan Pearson. 2016.

Bright Lights and White Nights, by Andrew Carter. 2015.

cemetery – miss you, by Jason S Polley. 2011.

Cop Show Heaven, by Lawrence Gray. 2015.

Cry of the Flying Rhino, by Ivy Ngeow, 2017.

Curveball, by Gustav Preller, 2016.

Death Has a Thousand Doors, by Patricia W. Grey. 2011.

Hilary and David, by Laura Solomon. 2011.

Hong Kong Hollow, by Dragoş Ilca. 2017.

Instant messages, by Laura Solomon. 2010.

Man's Last Song, by James Tam. 2013.

Mila the Magician, by Zhang Jian (Catherine Chin). 2014.
    (English/Chinese bilingual edition).

Mishpacha – family, by Rebecca Tomasis. 2010.

Paranoia (the walk and talk with Angela),
    by Caleb Kavon. 2012.

Red Bird Summer, by Jan Pearson. 2014.

Revenge From Beyond, by Dennis Wong. 2011.

The Day They Came, by Gérard Louis Breissan. 2012.

The Devil You Know, by Peter Gregoire. 2014.

The Handover Murders, by Damon Rose.
    Scheduled, November 2019.

**The Monkey in Me: Confusion, Love and Hope
    Under a Chinese Sky**, by Caleb Kavon. 2009.

The Perilous Passage of Princess Petunia Peasant,
    by Victor E. Apps. 2014. (Young adult fiction.)

The Reluctant Terrorist: in Search of the Jizo,
    by Caleb Kavon. 2011.

The Village in the Mountains, by David Diskin. 2012.

Three Wishes in Bardo, by C. S. Feng.
    Scheduled, November 2018.

Tiger Autumn, by Jan Pearson. 2015.

Tightrope! A Bohemian tale, by Olga Walló.
Translated from Czech by Johanna Pokorny, Veronika Revická
& others. Edited by Gillian Bickley & Olga Walló,
with Verner Bickley. 2010.

University Days, by Laura Solomon. 2014.

Vera Magpie, by Laura Solomon. 2013.

Short Story Collections

Beyond Brightness, by Sanja Särman.
November 2016.

Odds and Sods, by Lawrence Gray. 2013.

The Shingle Bar Sea Monster and other stories,
by Laura Solomon. 2012.

The Snow Bridge and other Stories, by Philip Chatting. 2015.

Under the Shade of the Feijoa Trees and other stories,
by Hayley Ann Solomon. Scheduled, April 2019.

Fiction – Chinese Language

The Monkey in Me, by Caleb Kavon.
Translated by Chapman Chen. 2010.

Tightrope! A Bohemian Tale, by Olga Walló.
Translated by Chapman Chen. 2011.
Chinese translation supported by the Ministry of Culture
of the Czech Republic.

FIND OUT MORE ABOUT PROVERSE AUTHORS BOOKS, PRIZES AND EVENTS

Visit our website:
http://www.proversepublishing.com

Visit our distributor's website: <www.chineseupress.com>

Follow us on Twitter
Follow news and conversation: <twitter.com/Proversebooks>
OR
Copy and paste the following to your browser window and follow the instructions:
https://twitter.com/#!/ProverseBooks
"Like" us on www.facebook.com/ProversePress

Request our free E-Newsletter
Send your request to info@proversepublishing.com.

Availability
Most books are available in Hong Kong and world-wide from our Hong Kong based Distributor,
The Chinese University Press of Hong Kong,
The Chinese University of Hong Kong, Shatin, NT,
Hong Kong SAR, China.
Email: cup-bus@cuhk.edu.hk
Website: <www.chineseupress.com>.
All titles are available from Proverse Hong Kong
http://www.proversepublishing.com
and the Proverse Hong Kong UK-based Distributor.

We have **stock-holding retailers** in Hong Kong,
Canada (Elizabeth Campbell Books),
Andorra (Llibreria La Puça, La Llibreria).
Orders can be made from bookshops
in the UK and elsewhere.

Ebooks
Most of our titles are available also as Ebooks.